"Psi is not tightly bound to now in either space or time."
—Dean Radin, PhD

Star Trails Tetralogy: Volume IV

REFRACTIONS OF FROZEN TIME

Marcha Fox

Kalliope Rising Press
Burnet, Texas

Kalliope Rising Press
P.O. Box 23
Burnet, Texas 78611

Copyright © 2014 by Marcha Fox
First Printing: December 2014
Cover design by Steven James Catizone

ISBN 978-0-9883335-4-3

Publisher's Cataloging-In-Publication Data
(Prepared by The Donohue Group, Inc.)

Names: Fox, Marcha, author, illustrator.
Title: Refractions of frozen time / Marcha Fox.
Description: Burnet, Texas : Kalliope Rising Press, [2014] | Series: Star trails tetralogy ; Volume IV | "Illustrations and book interior design by the author." | Interest age level: 13 and up. | Summary: "The discovery of yet another unique crystal in the caverns has the ability to link two dimensions of time as well as amplify psi waves for telepathic communication across space and time. Creena Brightstar believes these crystals can bring her family back together at last. But before she can finish unlocking their secrets, Integrator forces discover their underground hideout, forcing a harrowing escape loaded with unexpected consequences. The dark and lonely days that follow change Dirck forever as fate plays out a hand dealt on Earth years before."-- Provided by publisher.
Identifiers: ISBN 978-0-9883335-4-3 | ISBN 0-9883335-4-6 | ISBN 978-0-9980789-3-9 (ebook) | ISBN 0-9980789-3-X (ebook)
Subjects: LCSH: Families--Juvenile fiction. | Telepathy--Juvenile fiction. | Crystals--Juvenile fiction. | Escapes--Juvenile fiction. | Outer space--Juvenile fiction. | CYAC: Families--Fiction. | Telepathy--Fiction. | Crystals--Fiction. | Escapes--Fiction. | Outer space--Fiction. | LCGFT: Science fiction.
Classification: LCC PZ7.1.F69 Re 2014 (print) | LCC PZ7.1.F69 (ebook) | DDC [Fic]--dc23

Cyrarian Territories
Epsilon Regional Map

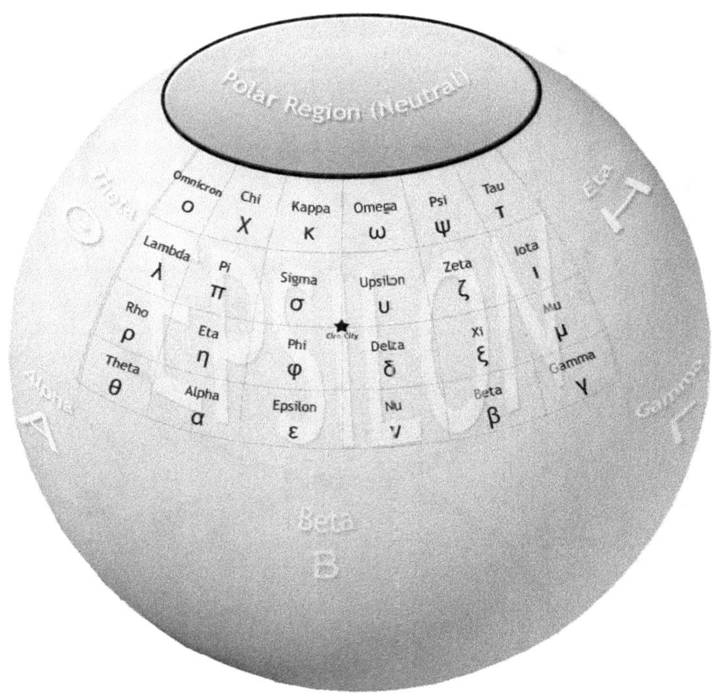

Find more information on Cyraria at
www.StarTrailsSaga.com

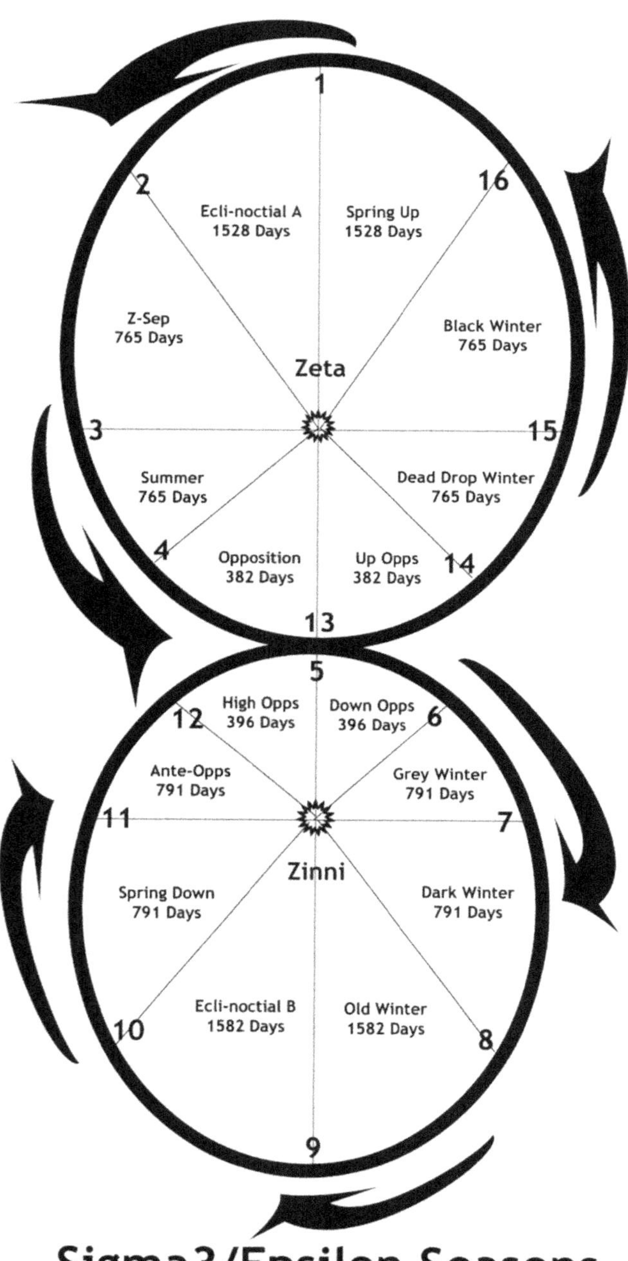

Sigma3/Epsilon Seasons
45 Degrees North Latitude

PROLOGUE

Integrator Central
Cira City

Examining an S3 data dump wasn't something that Augustus Troy enjoyed. Nonetheless, he glared at the results with dark, narrowed eyes, determined to figure out what had happened, once and for all. His dark brown hair had increasing slashes of grey at the temples and was starting to thin, his large physique spreading and getting soft around the middle from sitting behind a workdeck too long, but his lust for power remained. This was a battle he would win, no matter the cost. He set his square jaw and glared at the information spread out before him. The answers were there. Had to be.

At least the holographic output hovering above his workdeck was in the visual spectrum, not raw infrared, enhancement a command away. As expected, there were gaps when every satellite was out of range of the target, but fortunately integrating the sweeps into a nearly contiguous timeline was easily accomplished. The system had been initially designed for weather and climatic data, which could deal with gaps but required sequencing. Mineral exploration and surveillance capabilities were added later and it was this that allowed him to view the past as if he were observing from a few hundred meters altitude. While he'd viewed this time and place before, it had been at lower resolution. This time it was the military enhanced version, sufficient to observe individuals to the point of facial recognition. Of course there was no audio, but action would reveal everything he needed to know.

Tedium notwithstanding, he was driven by more than idle curiosity. He'd obtained the technical data for the pertinent period just before its purge date and now, as he found more and more information he could have used earlier, he wondered what had taken him so long to give it the scrutiny it deserved. What good were surveillance data if it wasn't utilized to achieve his objectives?

After compressing a few hundred days' worth of observation for a remote sector of Sigma/Epsilon into less than an hours' viewing time, he'd watched a primitive ballome unfit for human habitation become an unattractive, yet functional abode. The sense of loss it evoked had been unexpected, likewise the demeaning sense of failure that he'd never been able to apply those same engineering talents he was witnessing directly to his own advancement.

In spite of what many believed, especially Bryl Woeyel, Delta's insidious Regional Governor, Troy was not ecstatic that Brightstar was on his way to Bezarna. Admitting their relationship had been of the classic love/hate variety would have required more emotional maturity than he possessed, but a profound sense of misfortune wasn't. While necessary, losing such a valuable asset was still a horrible waste.

Visual data flickered by, nothing of interest apparent, so he tripled the speed. The image was three dimensional when at least two satellites were in view allowing parallax, flattened with only one. A constant data flow of calmanac data, which included date, time, and temperature, chattered along the top.

He straightened as an armored transport appeared, a boxy splash of gleaming metal, in the upper right. The seat's padding adjusted, followed by the subtle massage of nanobots as tension gripped his shoulders. He immediately slowed to real-time playback and backed up to its arrival, a dark smile forming as seven commandos exited, four surrounding the perimeter while the others jumped the lock and entered. It wasn't long before they exited with their quarry, three family members following in futile pursuit. He zoomed in to watch the emotional scene of those left behind through cold, dark eyes, but satisfaction evolved quickly to renewed futility.

If only Brightstar had listened to reason, caught the vision of what they could have accomplished. What would it have taken to win him over? Troy cringed inwardly at the answer, a resounding slam that the man would have turned at nothing, fresh anger flickering in its wake. He should have expected as much from the man who'd convinced the HIO to expand their ethics requirements to include all races and worlds, even during exploration, when members of the Hostii Intergalactic Organization were involved.

He fast-forwarded again, eyes fixed on calmanac data until it approached the time he was interested in. Again, he slowed the advancement, eyes fixed on the projection. The familiar streak of the settlement transport occurred three times, the last without a matching return. Odd. All was still, so he upped the speed again, alert for movement. Shadows darkened the rear of the ballome as Zeta and Zinni languished near their respective horizons before activity occurred. A 'cruiser arrived, a short time later melting into the terrain.

Cloaking on a 'cruiser? Impossible.

He backtracked and zoomed in, detecting two darting figures somehow disguising the vehicle such that it dissolved into oblivion. He made a mental note to go back later under enhanced resolution to find out how, then sped up again until two male figures appeared, substantial activity taking place on the domed roof. He zoomed in, slowed it by another ten percent and watched, fascinated, as what was apparently a crude heat exchanger came together, the ballome's infrared signature changing at its completion. He leaned back, pensive, knowing that Brightstar had been detained in Territorial prison at the time. Who did the work? His kid? But who was that other person? And how did they know what to do?

After that, the primary movement was boxcarts of dirt being removed from inside, no doubt the family digging a safe. He sat up straighter, thoughts escalating. A good safe would have protected them from that gigantic PV, the usual reference to a violent weather phenomenon known as pressure vortices as Cyrarian tornadoes were called.

Suddenly, a poof of vapor blurred the domed image. He backed up and slowed it to half actual speed, enhancement maxed, watching an explosion blow the rooftop device apart, leaving a misshapen array of twisted metal. Shortly thereafter, an adult and a child who, judging by the heat signatures were protected by oppsuits, exited the structure.

He leaned closer, fascinated, as the pair left, their steady, deliberate pace indicating they were following a familiar trail. When they suddenly disappeared, he replayed it again at half speed, zooming in until the resolution fogged, then called up other bands, from infrared to ultraviolet. All he could figure was it had to be a cave of some sort, no other manmade structures apparent. A short time later, the adult figure appeared again, alone, and returned to the ballome, then promptly left again with two more adults and disappeared in the same mysterious place a kilometer or so away.

So where did they go and who was that other adult? Probably the owner of the 'cruiser, which would be easy enough to trace, given there simply weren't that many. But the main point was that they'd undoubtedly survived. Just to make sure, he watched to see if they'd returned, which they hadn't, then witnessed the structure entirely destroyed two days later by that huge PV.

So as he'd suspected, Brightstar's family was still alive. *Alive!* Only when his vision tunneled from hyperventilation did Troy sit back and close his gaping jaw.

Now it made sense. The geology in that region was ideal for caves of every kind. But that still didn't explain the prison break. He zoomed back out to capture a square kilometer surrounding where they'd disappeared, motion detection maxed for the relevant time period. Nothing. He surfed through the spectrum, IR to visible to UV.

And the data ended. What the—?

He checked for malfunctions, the persistent message *End of Data* the only response. Sensing he was on to something, he sat back thoughtfully, then queried the system for other S3 data repositories.

Of course! Cyraria's moon, Nifeir. Where Brightstar ran the research outpost until his final arrest.

His jaw hardened, even as he berated himself. How could he have been so stupid? He turned to the comcon, called up the Nifeir data steward, and within less than an hour had the remaining data processing. His heart raced, fueled by an adrenaline rush he hadn't felt for a long time. It took much longer than expected to crack the encryption.

The results were not disappointing.

Answers

Dununda
Psi / Epsilon

Even before the tunnel ended in Dununda's transport bay, Dirck Brightstar could tell something was different. While he hadn't noticed anything audible during his previous excursions, there had been a certain feel, perhaps off-scale acoustic vibrations or electromagnetic fields, something that had granted silent witness to activity in the domed city above. This time it felt as if they were entering a sepulcher.

"Something's wrong," Dirck commented, parking the boxcart, which wouldn't fit through the final section anyway, as he stopped to listen more closely; still nothing. He and his friend, Win, had almost reached the section where the ceiling dropped near the exit. Once they left the dirt-walled confines, they'd be out in the open where being seen could have lethal consequences.

After a few more steps he stopped again, holding his breath as he tried to scope out the difference between now and his last visit. He wiped the sweat from his brow and pushed his sandy hair out of his face with a single deft motion. Stillness persisted, unabated, a death-like pall that penetrated everything from the soles of his feet to the depths of his gut. The latest intelligence paraded through memory, but none extrapolated to anything that would affect Dununda.

"What do you think?" Win whispered.

Dirck's gaze remained on the exit, still several meters away. "It's too quiet."

"That's usually not good."

"Right."

Dununda was in Phi/Epsilon, a sparsely populated region amongst the first to be INTEGRATED, yet largely unaffected by the planet's political turmoil. The five thousand-some-odd residents were largely employed in iridium mining operations which had originally spawned the settlement's existence. Residents were allowed to travel freely within the region and to Cira City without restriction. Colossal transports, ten times the size of the one they'd hijacked after bringing Creena back, left several times a day, loaded with ore deliveries to Cira City and numerous other destinations within INTEGRATED territories. In fact, it was one of those very transports that they'd originally hoped to procure for their eventual move to Apoca Canyon.

Unable to identify anything specific that could jeopardize their mission, Dirck shrugged and crept toward the exit, finally dropping to his hands and knees, as the clearance lowered. From that point on their covert passage contracted to a mere half meter, which extended far enough to necessitate a clumsy and claustrophobic belly crawl. The narrow egress point still loomed several meters ahead, marked by a pale circle where it opened into the transport storage yard.

An arm's length from the opening, Dirck paused to listen again. Nothing. All senses on full alert, he reminded himself that the bnolar, the indigenous creatures who'd performed the excavation on their behalf, never would have placed the exit there in the first place if it had been a high traffic area. Somewhat assured, he eased halfway through the opening, taking one last quick and wary look around before easing outside, where he scrambled awkwardly to his feet. He listened again. No sound or movement anywhere, other than the whir of an air handler in the ductwork high above. He stooped over, peered back inside the darkness and signaled Win to follow.

The sprawling storage yard was dark, as expected for the season, except for the pale glow of green security lighting. While the yard was below ground level, it nonetheless opened to a sliver of the settlement's dome overhead, dust accumulated during the heat season obscuring any stars in the darkened sky, the planet's moon, Nifeir, a lopsided orange smear overhead. More transports than usual reposed in the dim light, hanging from support cradles like restrained beasts. He paused behind one, waiting while Win examined the vehicle's underside. Moments later, he joined him, the hint of a conspiratorial smile gleaming from his blue eyes.

Dirck crouched down and continued to dodge from one vehicle to the next until he'd stealthily crossed the bay, Win on his heels. When he reached one of the vehicle tunnels on the far side he hunkered down, again listening. Transports were relativity silent, but their size displaced enough air to emit a whooshing sound that the tunnel's confinement amplified. Everything remained still and lifeless.

They crept a few meters to their right, reaching a flight of narrow, waffled-metal steps which led from the storage yard up to a ramp connecting the terminal with the ground-level concourse above. Passengers were usually in evidence, regardless of the hour. It was mid-afternoon according to standard time, when the first string of commuters would be leaving, particularly mine management personnel who chose to live in Cira City. Yet, when they reached the top, a cautious look revealed the sprawling ramp was bare. Not a single intelligent creature from jendak to human shadowed its gentle incline in either direction.

They exchanged mystified shrugs, then crept to the inside wall and followed it up the ramp to ground level, Dirck leading with Win a few steps behind. Just short of where the ramp yawned open on the expansive concourse they paused again, Dirck holding his breath in another attempt to perceive any possible sound. He froze momentarily at the barely audible murmur of distant voices, then jumped, heart racing, when a recorded announcement blared around them, echoing from the domed enclosure's naked walls

The Dununda Transportation Terminal is temporarily closed. All passengers should secure themselves inside the nearest heatlock with air handlers deactivated until further notice. . .

While Dirck's first instinct was to assume a gas leak or other catastrophe and get back to the Caverns posthaste, something stopped him. The temperature was cool, but within normal range, the air handlers were working, and there were no unusual odors. Win's eyes sparked with unmistakable curiosity, indicating his partner's choice was no different, and thus they tiptoed the remaining distance, still hugging the wall. Senses still on full alert, Dirck signaled *stop* when he detected the muted din of activity.

He dropped to his belly and scooted forward until he could peek around the wall. The first thing he saw, dead-center in the concourse's central area, was INTEGRATION's standard, an imposing, holographic, column-like *I* about six meters tall, the figurative meaning of its recently added blackened border all too clear. Dirck winced at its implications, the remainder of the scene no less troubling.

"What do you see?" Win prompted lowly.

He replied with a groan as he inched back out of sight and rested his head on his arms.

"Well?" Win insisted. "What's going on?"

His response was another groan as he recalled how useful their bogus commando uniforms had been for other missions, yet stood out in most locales like tracer lights in Dead Drop Winter. Thus, when anonymous movement was required, their normal, nondescript attire served best. Such they wore now, dusted generously with dirt from their graceless exit from the tunnel. The personnel swarming the main concourse in clusters of random points of activity, however, were without exception in yellow armor.

He looked up finally, expression saturated with disgust. "Commandos," he replied, shaking his head at the irony. "Lots of them. Everywhere."

Win's facial expression reflected his own as they ducked back a few meters and crept back to the bottom of the ramp to confer.

"What do you think's going on?" Win whispered, expression intent with speculation.

"I don't know. Those troopers aren't exactly falling all over themselves to get to a heatlock. Their life support helmets aren't even on."

"Something's funny, all right. What next?"

Inclined to err on the side of conservatism, Dirck gave the safest answer. "Let's go home and see if any new data's come in that'll give us a clue, then take it from there."

Win nodded, the pair cautiously descending the metal stairs, then weaving a path amongst and between the dangling transports. Halfway back to the tunnel, Win waved Dirck to a halt.

"Hold on," he said in a hoarse whisper. "I wanna get a closer look at one of these things."

With that, he dropped to the ground, portalume in hand, and edged beneath the nearest one while Dirck stood a wary and mystified guard. When Win wriggled back out a short time later, his satisfied look stretched from the cleft in his chin to his devious blue eyes

"What's going on?" Dirck asked as they resumed walking, knowing Win's optimism could be a bit overstated.

"It's just been torquing me how they power these things through Dead Drop Winter, when zetarrays are useless," he answered. "Turns out my theory's correct."

"Which is?" Dirck asked, pausing as they arrived at the tunnel.

"Fuel cells. When it's dark, they use fuel cells."

"Regular fuel cells, like in vekes?"

"Exactly."

Fuel cells were an incredibly efficient, even elegant method of generating electricity which were used whenever solar power was unavailable and more exotic methods impractical. By combining hydrogen and oxygen, numerous useful by-products were produced, such as water, heat, and best of all, orphaned electrons for electricity. All were useful in space, and all were useful on Cyraria during Dead Drop Winter.

"How much time would that buy us?" Dirck asked.

"That depends on how much is left in the tanks of the one we have. Best case, probably a week. But by the looks of things, we have a ready source of re-supply." He grinned wider. "If you catch my meaning."

Dirck allowed himself the luxury of smiling back, an action that felt oddly foreign. Win was right. For all intents and purposes, they'd found a quick fix for the power problems, which had been their reason for coming there in the first place. If nothing else, it was at least enough to bring the comm systems and datalogs back online, thus buying some time.

The long walk back was broken by their stop at the interred transport they'd hijacked following their arrival with Creena. Win examined the control panel, eventually finding the relay under the console that made the switch from zetarray to fuel cell power buses. Immediately, displays came to life, indicating each tank had a full load.

"Do we have enough cable to run the line directly, or do we have to move it?" Win asked. "They're probably too heavy for that," he added, nodding toward the cart.

"Should be enough," Dirck answered. "We have that big spool in stores."

"Insulated?"

"Yeah. Certified for interior volumes."

"Guess what, buddy?" Win said, raising his hands to invite a celebratory Miran grip. "We're back in business."

* * *

Creena sat on the stone floor with Thyron beside her, his array of multi-faceted leaves not quite fully spread, yet better than he'd been in days. Thanks to the small light panel they'd set up since running the power line, the vegemal's photosynthesis was active again, his stature gradually reaching his normal one-meter height after being dormant since shortly after their arrival. At this rate, the *flora peda telepathis,* or telepathic walking plant, would be ambulatory again soon. On the other side of the chamber, their cylindrically shaped 'troid, Aggie, was also showing the benefits of increased power, her steady green photoreceptors strong with a fresh charge.

The day's intelligence briefing had barely begun, the group gathered in their new location, a small niche formed by a huge cluster of stalagmites that separated the far corner of the greatroom from the main living section. The move had been part of their recent attempt to avoid any further confrontations in their former briefing chamber, which tended to trigger Dirck's usually nascent temper. The action had come at Win's insistence after Aggie had called Dirck a reverse-biased junction diode when he'd once more encountered his negative node and lambasted the 'troid for using so much power on unnecessary chatter. The resulting argument had not been a pretty sight.

Currently, Dirck was giving his portion of the briefing, reiterating that they'd still found nothing to explain the situation in Dununda, neither an increase in tactical activity nor confirmation of a gas leak. Her brother was rambling, speculating on whether the situation they found there had anything to do with the sudden lull in intelligence traffic.

No matter how hard she tried to listen, her mind refused to cooperate, wandering instead amid crystalline lattices of complex molecules. Notelog balanced on her knees, her determined dark eyes were continually drawn downward to scan screen after screen of crystal data, some fact, most speculation.

Identifying the exact constituents of cristobalite was necessary, not only to explain why the Think Tank worked for psicomm and teleportation, but to understand its application to other technologies. Her father had relayed everything he'd discovered so far and she'd thought of little else since he'd been ambushed on Nifeir and sentenced to Bezarna, praying that some new capability lurking in the crystalline depths could expand the Tank's capabilities to beyond Cyraria and bring him back home.

If only they had his c-com, a device that not only held the majority of his knowledge, but links to related material. Unfortunately, he'd had it with him at the time of his arrest so it had either been confiscated or was likewise on its way to the ultimate security prison, a blackhole, from which 'Merapa couldn't be rescued by Dirck and Win like when he'd been incarcerated in Epsilon's Territorial Prison. Clearly, his enemies were making sure that didn't recur.

But according to her calculations, he wasn't there yet, leaving the tiniest shred of hope.

She'd never quite vocalized her intention, yet could tell that 'Merama suspected her plan and shared her aspirations. Dirck, on the other hand, ignored her research as before, so whether he had a foggy clue regarding her ambitions, much less commitment, was unknown; which was fine, if it meant he'd leave her alone.

While she was genuinely grateful that he and Win had at least temporarily solved some of their power problems, it hadn't done her any good, whatsoever. After a few immediate essentials, such as recharging Aggie and providing Thyron's light panel, all electricity was being directed toward catching up on intelligence work.

She couldn't argue its importance, especially in light of losing 'Merapa only a few days before coupled with concerns over the impending move to Apoca Canyon, but she couldn't progress in her research without some of the bounty. Her suspicions that she'd been deliberately slighted had little evidence and she hesitated to bring it up for fear of another explosion, meeting in the area near the greatroom notwithstanding. What she really needed was substantiation that she was on the right track, particularly toward those projects that Dirck thought were important. Such as cloaking their radio frequency, or RF, signals. Fortunately, the solution fit nicely with her ultimate objective.

As with any scientific application, the most difficult achievement evolved from simple principles. 'Merapa's first assumption, which had proven correct, was that the Think Tank contained silicon dioxide, but in an ultrapure form. That alone gave it semiconductor properties, which meant it didn't conduct as well as a conductor, such as copper, but didn't insulate, either, so when manipulated properly could function as both.

Furthermore, it was subject to large increases in electrical conductivity when exposed to light in either infrared, visible, or ultraviolet wavelengths, but decreased with cold, the opposite of conductors. Whether it made a difference or not that it was birefringent, meaning it split light into two separate beams, they didn't know. Yet, semiconductor and optical properties, which were well known and documented, couldn't account for the strange psi and teleportation phenomena they were trying to explain. Unless its elemental components were cooperating in some strange and wonderful chemical way.

The last thing her father had been working on prior to his self-imposed exile in the Territorial Tower in Cira City had been to define cristobalite's molecular structure as a complex hexagonal molecule with an iridium ion in the center. Other elements were present as well, such as europium and selenium, which yielded magnetic semiconductor properties. That information prompted him to seek out and eventually discover the magnetometer blooms recorded by the S3s, Cyraria's surveillance satellite network, which could betray their location and thus stopped them from using the Tank for teleportation or anything else. Selenium was light sensitive like silicon, yet rarely found in isolated form, except when generated as a byproduct from electronic ore extraction processes.

The elements were bonded in a way that was not only unique, but partially explained how they interacted to produce such unusual effects. Actually, they weren't bonded at all, but rather arranged as an intercalation compound, where the atoms, ions or molecules of one element were trapped between the layers of a crystal lattice. Whatever the actual scheme happened to be, nature had composed a remarkable symphony of synergistic effects that presented a mystery they were well-advised to decipher.

So far, they'd used their properties as manifested by the Tank for teleportation and, more recently, psi-directed remote viewing, which provided a holographic view of 'Merapa's horrific fate on Nifeir. Thus, she knew it could reveal something occurring in another location, even if the teleportation abilities were strictly limited to Cyraria. Perhaps they could even allow access to another time or different dimension, depending on how the collapsed time tensor Aggie had identified actually operated. Typically, warping time and space required the manipulation of gravity waves using rapidly rotating electromagnetic fields, but so far it appeared cristobalite had the capability to do so naturally when stimulated by psi, otherwise known as thought waves.

Gradually, her musings meandered back to the present and focused on Dirck's briefing. From what he'd said so far, there'd been few changes in INTEGRATOR activity since their power crisis. That seemed strange in light of what they'd found in Dununda as well as 'Merapa's arrest, both of which should have appeared in open, non-encrypted data. Aggie had been scanning as fast as her data rate permitted, but so far there was no evidence in any new comm traffic or transmission pattern to account for the seemingly missing information. If anything, it was almost as if they were receiving old data, its similarity to past transmissions unexplainable. In an atsna shell, it was too quiet.

She avoided eye contact as Dirck finished up, brown eyes fixed on the projectron while she wondered why there was enough power for that, but not her lab. Here she was, charged with figuring out why the Tank only worked on-world; how to design the cloaking system for their transmissions; and how the cristoviatic, or matter transfer via teleportation functioned, any of which was a formidable task, yet she was trying to conquer them all single-handed, with no power at that, while he and Win gloated over their success with the fuel cells. In reality, they were no better off, only back where they started. Maybe.

"It's really great you and Win got us some power," Creena said, coyly slipping a strand of dark hair behind her ear. She smiled, wanting to preface her request such that he wouldn't get reeked, first thing. He'd been trying lately not to be so combative, but the friction remained, worsening since their father's arrest, which he undoubtedly blamed on her. As planned, Dirck nodded beneath the *kudos,* his satisfied smile lasting only until her next statement.

"But I really could use some in the lab," she added cautiously, bracing for his humility to do a one-hundred-eighty degree reversal.

"We need to catch up with the comm work first," he said, a little too quickly.

Creena's voice, though seemingly calm, was no less determined. "I know, Dirck, but I need more power in the lab. There must be someplace we can cut back."

"Why?" He paced as he always did when he was uncomfortable, a strange emotion clouding his green eyes.

"Because I need to find out whether or not the cristobalite has photon acceleration properties."

"Why?" Dirck asked again. "Does that have anything to do with cloaking our RF?"

"Plenty," she replied, fighting to hold back anger, which was struggling to emerge in an explosive display of will. "There's no better way to cloak RF than take transmissions out of RF." And left unsaid was the hope that contacting 'Merapa could be accomplished with the same technology.

Before Dirck could respond, Win stepped in. "How much power do you need?"

"Enough for a small transmitter and receiver, plus generate electromagnetic radiation in a limited, coherent band."

"A small laser?" Win asked.

"Exactly."

"What ever happened to that pocket laser I gave you, back on Mira III?" Dirck interjected.

She sighed wistfully, remembering. "I gave it to someone who really helped me out when I was stuck on Terra," she said quietly. "Don't worry, Dirck, it's in good hands. It's the greatest thing you ever gave me and it really came in handy, lots of times. But unfortunately, it's gone."

Dirck was giving her a funny look, as if he was really hurt she'd given it away, but before she could say anything further Win jumped back into the conversation.

"Why don't you just borrow Aggie for a few hours?" he suggested.

"Hey, wait a minute!" Dirck protested. "I need her, especially now, when we're trying to re-establish our knowledge base of INTEGRATOR activities."

"How many of you think cristobalite is worth a few hours' of processing time?" Win asked abruptly, ignoring Dirck's protest.

'Merama and even Aggie voted in the affirmative, Creena pleasantly surprised by the sudden turn to democratic rule.

"Okay, that settles it," Win stated. "Aggie, determine when the best time would be to go off-line."

Dirck's initial protests clearly rejected, he sighed heavily. "Okay. Why don't you make a list of what you need? Then we can work out some sort of power budget and schedule. I suppose if cristobalite research was important enough for 'Merapa to spend so much time on, we shouldn't give up now."

Agreement was unanimous, but instead of pondering Dirck's unexpected attitude change, Creena's thoughts shifted forward to relative time en route to Bezarna, wondering if she really wanted to know when it would be too late.

* * *

Integrator Central
Sublevel 9
Cira City

"We've found some interesting data among Brightstar's research records on Nifeir."

Troy smiled inwardly as Rohtik Spoigan's steel-colored eyes darkened with interest from the other side of his sprawling workdeck. Spoigan was not only Epsilon's Territorial General, but second in command of the Quadrumvirate formed when two-thirds of Cyraria's territories chose INTEGRATION as their means of government. *Chose*, of course, was beyond subjective, yet as far as the Hostii Intragalactic Organization was concerned, that was the case.

Since Troy's own promotion to his position as Spoigan's Deputy Territorial General, he had often imagined himself in an expansive suite of similar luxury, lined with shiny, black marble illuminated by a rare crystal chandelier. Located at sub-level nine of the Territorial Tower in Cira City, it was no accident that the chamber's dark sense of security from planetary threats, whether natural or man-made, represented INTEGRATION so well.

"Go on," the Territorial General prompted, his stocky frame straightening with interest.

Troy's smile leaked to the surface, knowing he had his TG's undivided attention. "At first, we thought it was only standard magnetometer data," he continued, "but it was stored differently and secured with an exceptionally high level of encryption. Once we cracked the code, we found the timestamps dated back to Peak Opps."

"So?" Spoigan commented, eyes starting to glaze over.

"Sooooo, they matched the timeframe just prior to Brightstar's escape from territorial prison."

"I don't follow you, Troy," Spoigan said, an increasing cloud of impatient skepticism shrouding his eyes. "What exactly did you find?"

"A series of unexplained magnetometer blooms. The signature appears similar to a rare isotope sometimes imbedded in cristobalite."

Spoigan's harsh features were still non-reactive, mind apparently not processing the implications, not surprising considering he lacked Troy's technical savvy. "Interesting. So where exactly were these emissions located?"

"The resolution is poor, but in the general vicinity and not too far from where Brightstar's ballome used to be."

"Are the blooms constant?"

"No. Short, random bursts. There was some activity after his first arrest, right after his family left the ballome two days before it was destroyed. After that, a few times a week following his escape, then it abruptly stopped with nothing since. After which these data were suddenly tightly secured."

Spoigan folded his arms and scowled pensively. "The blooms could have been generated by our exploration efforts outside Dununda. Play the data against their activity logs and see if there's a correlation."

"There isn't," Troy replied smugly.

Ever so slightly, the TG's eyebrows raised and interest appeared in his eyes. He didn't say anything further, however, so Troy turned to leave. He was just short of the alloyed steel door when Spoigan finally spoke.

"If this works out, I suppose I owe you one," he said.

Troy froze in mid-step, then looked back, the TG's gaze fixed on his in what was half promise, half threat, while his own unsuccessful attempt not to gloat reflected back from the opposing wall.

"Yeah," Troy replied, not even trying to stifle the smirk tugging at the corners of his mouth. "I know."

Transitions

The floor was hard and cold, likewise the bulging limestone behind his back, as Dirck sat, arms resting on elevated knees, staring at a luma branch in the passage a few meters away. No matter how hard he tried, he still couldn't sustain a breath of optimism. He knew some of it was the natural consequences of grief, yet it was more than that, almost tangible, and everyone felt it. It wasn't quite contention, but a dull and lifeless gloom. It permeated the Caverns with an atmosphere impossible to eradicate, its influence even reaching this particular niche not far from the Think Tank, where he went to be alone or simply recharge.

Not that there was anything to be happy or optimistic about. He knew they still needed to relocate given they were deep in enemy territory, but they were just as stuck as before regarding how. They still hadn't heard a thing from Clique HQ about moving or anything else. He wondered if Igni had made it to their base at Apoca Canyon, still remembering the sting of his father's criticism for letting the insectoid leave. For the past few weeks it had been as if all comm traffic had ceased. It was becoming more difficult by the day to ignore the implications, that maybe the Clique no longer existed, following the fate of his father, yet something no one dared voice aloud. If it had been dissolved or defeated, there was little if any point to their activities at all. Yet, if that were the case, it seemed such a decisive INTEGRATOR victory would have been all over the net. No, they were probably still out there, just quiet, perhaps reorganizing now that 'Merapa was gone, a thought that added to the weight in his heart.

His thoughts turned to Creena, who seemed to be working hard in the lab, yet still hadn't come up with anything promising. At least using Aggie for decryption wasn't that crucial with nothing much coming in, yet tension persisted between them.

Which was why he'd never gotten around to talking to her about his suspicions about Bryl Woeyel, a fellow Clique operative who was also Delta's Regional Governor, who'd given their father asylum following the prison break.

The more he thought about it, the less likely it seemed she'd set up 'Merapa in such a vicious way. He'd been around both of them, a lot, and couldn't quite imagine her doing anything devious, even though claiming 'Merapa as her bondling, as he and Creena had witnessed in a shared veridical dream, carried implications which would turn their family upside-down. Having him eliminated if he refused, however, was too much. Knowing Creena already didn't trust her, she'd probably go off like spikes from a spickle tree if she thought he was defending the woman, which wouldn't help a thing.

Maybe at some point he'd run it past Win, but that would mean he'd also have to tell him about the dream. Under the circumstances things were bad enough, so it hardly seemed worth discussing at this point. As Win always said, what is, *is*. There was enough to deal with without indulging in speculation. Distractions could mean trouble, as the entire situation had already proven. He and Creena had been so upset by Bryl's intention to claim their father as her bondling that they'd missed the vision's true message, that the Eta Territorial General was already in tight with INTEGRATION and meeting with him about joining the Clique needed to be averted. It hadn't, the end result his father being accused of high treason, condemned, and exiled on the spot.

On the other hand, there was 'Merapa's question during his arrest regarding whether or not Bryl knew. Why would he ask such a thing? Clearly there was plenty they didn't know. Nonetheless, it had little bearing on their current situation.

Which brought him back to the move. It was still a necessity, in spite of the reprieve the fuel cells had garnered, but without knowing what the situation really was in Dununda, or the Clique Base at Apoca Canyon for that matter, the odds of making a sound decision had gone to zero like some sordid probability figure. His father certainly hadn't anticipated being on his way to Bezarna when he'd promised that Dirck would know when it was time to leave the Caverns.

Convinced doom was no farther away than the calcite winking at him from the opposing wall, he folded his arms across his knees and rested his head on them wearily. He'd nearly dozed off when he heard footsteps. He listened, trying to identify who it was by the gait. It was more than one person, maybe Win and Deven. Or 'Merama and Deven.

He stood up quickly and tried to shake his dismal mien, not wanting to let on how badly he felt, knowing his mother undoubtedly felt a lot worse. She was doing better than expected, another cause for concern since that could mean she was in denial or harboring false hopes, which would abandon her in short order.

The footfalls drew closer, yet still defied identification. The fact someone was coming to find him probably meant something had changed. The surge of hope was short-lived, dropping off the cliff of gloom and doom when he quickly realized it could just as easily be bad news.

There were definitely more than two sets of feet, yet their cadence was lighter than boots, almost like the drip of condensation.   He left his retreat and turned down the passageway which led back to the Caverns, driven by curiosity. By the time familiarity congealed in remembrance, Igni was before him, antennae waving in greeting.

"You're back!" Dirck exclaimed, enthusiasm sincere while waning nonetheless under the weight of multiple sorrows.

The Arcturian returned his proffered Miran grip and nodded his huge insectoid head. "Concede," he replied, translator crackling. "Arrival expected?"

"No, not really. We'd just about given up, especially after...after what happened to 'Merapa, since we didn't know how to contact anyone."

"Worry not. Your location and status known, always. Ready to be gone to new site?"

"Yes!" he replied, surprising even himself with the sudden will to action. "I've had about all I can take of this isolation. We were going to try and come to you, but couldn't get transportation. Our intelligence lately has been useless and Dununda's all but closed down, but I haven't been able to figure out why."

"Some data, not conclusive," Igni responded. "Appears as mineral hit or similar discovery. Valuable. Residents removed, alleged ionizing radiation leak, likely sham. Not logical, with movement of officials and equipment into area." A trickle of static followed, reflecting his discomfort with unresolved data.

"When Win and I went there a while bac, there were commandos all over, but they didn't act as if there was any kind of danger. The public address system was broadcasting advisories to take cover in unventilated heatlocks, but they weren't using any form of protection, much less life support."

"Will find truth in time. What preparations need for departure?"

"Break down the comm equipment and gather our stuff, then close the exit to Dununda. That's about it."

"Win working equipment stow. When complete, all work tunnel closure. Should be gone by tomorrow, latest. Transport vehicle at risk in open." Igni hesitated, translator buzzing like it did when he encountered conflicting thoughts. "Creena not to leave."

"*What?*" Dirck gasped, not sure he'd understood correctly.

"Not to leave, insists to stay. Research not moveable, not enough samples. Wants stay. Mother yours, Deven stay with."

Dirck groaned with renewed discouragement coupled with exasperation. It wasn't surprising. He thought back to when he'd brought his mother there for the first time, how it meant their very survival after the heat exchanger blew at the height of Peak Opps.

That had been one of the lowest times of their very existence, when 'Merapa was in territorial prison and Creena still missing. Their new home had not only redeemed them from life-threatening heat, but ultimately offered the means to rescue 'Merapa via the Tank's logistical magic.

'Merama loved it here. From the very first day she'd adapted to the Caverns as if they'd been prepared as her abode for the eons they'd taken to form. Of course she wouldn't want to abandon them now, in spite of more recent happenings, probably hoping that once more the Caverns and the Tank would see them through. And in good conscience, Dirck couldn't bring himself to tell her otherwise, except their location within enemy territory was serious business and the primary reason they needed to leave.

"All right," Dirck sighed. "I'll talk to them and see what I can do."

'Merama was sitting in her favorite spot in their grotto, looking pensive as they entered the greatroom. She looked up with a weak smile, and then back at the floor, avoiding Dirk's eyes until Igni excused himself to go assist Win.

"'Merama—" he started, but before he could say anything further, she looked up and pinched her fingers together in the Esheronian silencing gesture.

"No, Dirck," she said, voice quiet but firm. "And I'm not just being stubborn or emotional like you think. I've known this was coming as well as you. I've seen all the data you have and agree we can't stay indefinitely. But the time isn't right for us yet. I hate to see you and Win go. It scares me to see us separated again. But I understand why you have to leave, and I feel as if your father would agree. But Creena is starting to make some progress with the crystals and we both feel it's important enough for us to stay a little longer."

Any relief he'd originally felt at leaving collapsed under an internal burst of negative pressure. It wasn't the Caverns he wanted to get away from so much as their miserable circumstances; not knowing; feeling isolated; the inability to act on anything, save data reduction and encryption codes. And as much as he and Creena had fought, he knew leaving wasn't the solution to that, either.

"Oh, 'Merama," he moaned, voice breaking as the flux of emotions he'd kept inside the past few days reached uncontainable amplitude.

She got up and put her arms around him and for the first time since witnessing the events on Nifeir he broke down, at the same time ashamed for not being able to provide strength for her. Here he was, so much taller now that it was more as if he were holding her, yet, once again, he was on the receiving end of comfort.

"We'll be just fine," she whispered, patting his back. "And so will you. I'm really proud of all you've done. Go on ahead. The Clique needs you and Win at Apoca Canyon. We'll be fine."

"I can't just leave you here," he responded. "It's too dangerous. You won't know what's going on or have a way to escape if they find you."

"Of course we do," she said reassuringly. "What are you thinking, Dirck? If all else fails, we have the Tank! If it comes down to that kind of a crisis, we'll use it, that's all. If they find us, it won't matter if it shows up on the magnetometer readings, will it? So don't worry. When it's time to leave, we'll either use it to summon you or, if necessary, for teleportation. Okay?"

"I don't know, 'Merama," he replied. "I don't like the idea of you being here, entirely defenseless. It just doesn't seem right. Besides, there's the power issue. It's not unlimited, you know."

"Win said if we watch our usage it should last a month or more. That's probably enough. Think about what your father would want, Dirck. You know he'd want you and Win to help with the Clique, yet he encouraged Creena to pursue the crystal research, too. Don't you think he'd want all of us to be as useful as possible to the cause he helped establish, regardless of where we had to be to do so?"

"All right," he sighed, reluctant to agree, yet unable to come up with a viable argument. "But be careful. Don't take any unnecessary chances." He paused, wanting to add not to maintain any false hopes, either, but decided against it. Sometimes false hopes were better than none.

"We won't," she agreed. "But, just in case, I want you to do me one last favor before you leave. Okay?"

He knew without asking what that favor would be.

* * *

The Bezarna Express

As soon as the wrist wrings securing him to his seat released, Laren Brightstar used every possible method known to intelligent lifeforms to compromise the spacecraft, hoping to alter its destination. If he could get to the controls before warp drive kicked in, he had a chance. It didn't take long, however, to discover that his intentions were vain.

He glared at the instrumention panel dangling lifelessly below a gaping hole in the opposing wall in angry defeat, wondering if its readings had been accurate or fabrications in the first place. His original plan had been to use its assumed electronic connections to hack into the ship's avionics, but it had turned out to be no more than a cluster of wireless slaves embedded in a fake bulkhead. Now it didn't even provide data, digital read-outs blank, having succumbed to his intrusion. It was almost as if the display were there simply to taunt them, expecting it would be ripped apart occasionally by those who knew anything about spacecraft electronic systems.

Still fuming with outrage, he pondered what else he might be able to do. The ship was much larger than it appeared from inside. The flightdeck was somewhere above, although trips such as this would be fully automated and lack an onboard crew. Reaching the flightdeck was impossible, their quarters a virtual prison enclosed by steel bulkheads impossible to breach. The interior had been drastically refitted to suit its macabre mission, the area he and his fellow prisoners occupied the original cargo hold, supplies and replacement parts kept in a similar compartment on the starboard side. The only exit was the airlock, through which he'd entered and now led directly to the inhospitable vacuum of space.

At first he was surprised that the *Bezarna Express* was more than some surplus craft ready for retirement. In a practical sense sending such a high quality vehicle on a one-way, irretrievable mission appeared a dreadful waste. In the political sense, however, it was obvious that his captors had taken every possible precaution to assure it reached its destination. Ironically, they were being exiled in the fastest, safest, and most reliable spacecraft of its size ever built.

He was reasonably familiar with RA-681s like this one, coincidentally the same model as Igni's which remained in an oblique parking orbit above Cyraria. The spacecraft were originally designed for HIO exploration, not warfare, and therefore lacked weapon systems. It was amazing that being defenseless and therefore vulnerable to attack didn't result in numerous hijackings, yet he'd never heard of such occurring. On the other hand, threatening an official HIO spacecraft would make the perpetrator the target of the most powerful organization in the galaxy, which was backed up by numerous fleets of warships, undoubtedly an adequate deterrent to such a foolish move.

Anger spent and the uselessness of intervention decided, he withdrew to contemplation once more, only now beginning to toy with reality. He slumped back in his seat and perused the others assigned to this oneway trip to hell with narrowed dark eyes. The spectrum of emotions displayed was vast with some still furious, others bitter, a few despondent, and one still in sulky denial. He wasn't sure where he fit in, as it varied moment to moment. He had to admit that the ambush had been aggravating to say the least, but far from unexpected.

That was the risk of sedition. Sometimes you got caught.

Playing dangerous games was nothing new, not by choice as much as circumstance. After his tour with the Space Command, he'd completed his education in terralogy, the most peaceful and productive career he could imagine. What could be more constructive than making planets habitable? Little did he ever imagine that his first job with the HIO would lead to where he was now, on his way to the galaxy's premier prison outpost.

Of course the most important information to a terralogist dealt with planetary resources. Remote satellite surveys generally were limited to surface areas and took valuable time. And thus the birth of planetary tomography.

Tomography was done by reflecting radio waves from the atmosphere's ionized shell. Numerous effects that ranged from weather manipulation to a detailed map of what lay below the surface could be gained, depending on frequency and power input. Unfortunately, while weather manipulation and control held great promise as a terralogist's greatest tool, it was likewise the military's most powerful weapon. Atmospheres stored tremendous amounts of energy in often unstable ways that a small, well-placed trigger could direct and release. Why not defeat your opponent by wiping him off the face of the planet with a monstrous storm? Violent cyclonic disturbances commonly known as pressure vortices or PVs wielded an incredibly destructive force.

Other options included creating devastating tectonic disturbances like earthquakes, or even volcanic eruptions to bring the enemy to his knees. Using tomography to survey vast regions for resources also played right into military areas of interest, such as logistics depots and weapons monitoring. Communications disruption and network design potential were in there, too, but, all that aside, no one was more surprised than the Space Command when evidence surfaced that the side band emissions were causing interesting side effects on the ground.

As their testing program progressed, confusion, disorientation, vertigo and dizziness, even a few rare instances of psi reception enhancement which constituted an increase in telepathic abilities, were not only reported but documented. While such effects were a tremendous disadvantage to a terralogist pursuing peaceful exploration and development activities, the military immediately saw strategic applications. If they could control human minds, they could affect combat readiness and even the attitude of their enemies and captives.

About the time he was preparing his resignation packet, his commission in the Space Command was reactivated and he was granted a Zeta5/NR clearance, which allowed him full access to any and all research documentation and data. Quitting was no longer an option as his employer switched his priority from identifying global mineral resources to weapons development.

His tenure with the project had been short, terminated by an HIO treaty which forbade such weapons or their development. He'd seen to it personally that all data were destroyed before he left, hoping to leave it all behind. But it appeared Project Spectra had come back to haunt him, thanks to a politically well-connected, but mediocre research engineer named Augustus Troy, who'd been less than pleased with the project's demise.

He wondered, if he had it to do all again, what he'd do differently and came up blank. That he'd done tremendous good as a terralogist went without saying. But nonetheless, he didn't miss the irony that Project Spectra would follow him, quite literally, to the end of his life.

Departing

The Caverns
Sigma/Epsilon

The boxcart was big enough for receivers and smaller electronics, but rack-sized equipment had to be carried, sometimes by two. The loading phase was taking far longer than Dirck expected, even after leaving several items behind that the main base was sure to have, such as projectrons, workdecks, workbenches and basic supplies such as electrical cable, though at the last minute they decided to bring that along, too. Furthermore, if the INTEGRATOR found the Caverns, they didn't want to leave any bounty. In what was hopefully an expansive operation, you could never have too much, and the huge spool rolled, which allowed Aggie to push it relatively easily.

The equipment was there when Dirck, Win, and Creena had returned from Mira III, having been brought in by his father with the assistance of Clique troops, any S3 data documenting the transport's arrival conveniently destroyed. Having not been there at the time, however, Dirck had no idea how much there really was or what a hassle it would be to move.

Fortunately, there was a fairly large alcove a short distance from the caverns' main entrance, which served as a staging area where they could move everything first, before having to deal with the additional weight and bulk of suiting up, which they'd have to do soon enough to load the transport.

Nonetheless, the walk between there and the lab was long and convoluted, winding through passages ridden by obstructions as well as inclines and declines, the path barely wide enough in some areas to get through. The 'troid disliked the uneven surfaces, which required her to switch between her rolopeds and claw-like climbing apparatus as she plodded along, photoreceptors blinking red and emitting electronic bleeps of protest as she assisted with the transfer, albeit reluctantly.

Yet for Dirck, the exertion had served as a much-needed physical outlet for his roiling emotions, which found a new sense of purpose. All in all, the effort was less exhausting than expected and even invigorating, adrenaline surging at the prospect of a new beginning of sorts, a final look-see at what the Clique was, or wasn't, as the case might be. He still wasn't comfortable with leaving his mother, Creena, and Deven behind, yet forced himself to accept it. There was enough to worry about without adding that.

The hoped-for one day to prepare for departure turned out to be too optimistic, ultimately taking more than two. As a precaution against the transport's blocky signature being detected by S3s, Igni had moved it to the arch bedecked cave about a kilometer away, where Win had stashed his 'cruiser when he'd first joined them during Peak Opps. After the final load was deposited in the staging area, Igni left to retrieve the transport while Dirck surveyed the huge array of equipment they'd collected with a hint of nostalgia, remembering how little they'd started with along with the major challenge it had been to set everything up. Now, in some respects, they were back to square one, but at least they wouldn't be alone. That thought alone provided a sense of relief he could barely contain, in spite of the guilt it evoked that he was somehow shirking his duty and letting his father down.

The ambivalence accelerated when he noticed Creena, 'Merama, and Deven shivering just outside the tunnel, having followed this last trip to bid them goodbye, something he didn't look forward to. Once again he reminded himself that it was their decision to remain and there was nothing he could do about it.

"All right," he said, stifling a sigh as he grabbed his oppsuit from the boxcart and tossed the other one to Win. "Thank the *Benefics* we didn't have to move all that stuff in these."

"Let me give you a hug before you put that thing on," 'Merama said, coming toward him with her arms outstretched.

He dropped the oppsuit and turned toward her, eyes immediately tearing up, much to his chagrin. He blinked them back the best he could and gathered her into a heartfelt embrace, playfully lifting her off the ground as he'd done since growing enough to tower over her. Her arms were cold to the touch and he could feel her trembling, whether from chill or emotion he couldn't tell.

"Take care," she said softly, hugging him firmly. "He would be very proud of you."

He grunted in reply, remembering that the last time he'd seen his father he'd felt more like an idiot than anything deserving of parental pride.

"I wish you were coming with us," he said. "And remember, go easy on the power."

"We will. It's okay. We'll be fine." Then she folded her arms tightly against the chill and gave him a look along with a nod toward his sister, reminding him to make peace with her before leaving, something he'd procrastinated, then never found time to do.

Conveniently, Deven rushed over to him first, hugging him hard around the waist. "I'll miss you, Dirck," his brother said.

"Me, too, Dev. You be good, okay? No exploring alone, understand?" The admonishment's irony didn't escape him, however; if it weren't for the youngster's exploits they probably would have all been dead a long time ago.

"Yeah, yeah," Deven replied with a grin, clearly reading his thoughts. The boy had grown a lot since their arrival, also, and been a mainstay in so many ways.

Dirck sighed for numerous reasons as he rumpled the boy's dark, shaggy hair, then cautiously met his sister's gaze. Her eyes were sad and somewhat pleading, but the barrier was still there. She was such an enigma and usually an annoying one at that.

His thoughts raced back to when Dead Drop Winter's dark, bitter cold had come upon them, solar collectors suddenly useless. At least survival power had been assured, thanks to Creena's idea to put their limited supply of zetarrays in the Think Tank, where they accumulated some charge from cristobalite's ever-present glow. It wasn't much, but it was better than nothing, and he had to admit it was both ingenious and intuitively obvious, something he or Win should have thought of long before. The chamber's crystal walls emanated constant yet gentle energy, covering the entire spectrum of visible light and perhaps beyond. Of course the arrays could absorb and store it! He was annoyed by his own oversight and admonished himself with a vain dose of team spirit. It shouldn't matter whose idea it was.

But it did. A lot.

Back on Mira III, he and Creena never got along, and lately the reason was manifesting itself as an unwelcome encore—she was too smart. Her crazy, unorthodox ideas were, more often than not, exactly what they needed, making him feel like a dolt.

He'd always thought the problem in their relationship had been all those noncompliance reports she'd gotten at the Academy and his embarrassment when her name would appear in lights on the NCR Board. But it wasn't. It was the fact she was usually right, her reasoning sound, while his was based solely on what he'd been instructed, not his own, inherent, logic-based, conscious decision. Original thought simply didn't come as easily for him; his memory was sharp and recall precise, which made it easier to simply regurgitate information already stored.

Not that he couldn't synthesize data. He not only could, but could do it well, but it usually took practice and conscious effort. Even 'Merapa had told him that, many times, emphasizing how in many respects he was more effective at digesting data than he was. So what was it then? He wasn't stupid, just...just what? Limited, perhaps. The originality, the ability to see something that wasn't there, the illusive big picture, that's where he came up short.

But did he really? Creena made mistakes. Big ones. Real big ones, like getting herself jettisoned in an escape pod. Or that hangup she had about Bryl. If she hadn't made such a fuss over that, maybe they wouldn't have missed the entire point of the dream, that the Eta Territorial General or TG couldn't be trusted, an oversight which ultimately resulted in 'Merapa being found guilty of treason and sent to Bezarna.

Yes, that mistake had cost them dearly. So much so he still couldn't bear the thought without his heart dropping into a well of grief. Yet Creena had actually been right about that, too, sensing Bryl's intent long before the dream occurred.

He came back to the present, discomfort amplified by 'Merama's pleading look piercing his peripheral vision.

"Hey," he said, gesturing awkwardly for her to come over. She approached somewhat hesitantly, almost as if she were afraid. Their embrace was stiff, short, and definitely uncomfortable, which apparently was obvious enough that it didn't fool their mother, whose expression was unreadably Miran, yet certainly not one of approval.

"Uh, yeah. Good luck. With the, uh, crystals," he muttered

"Thanks," she replied, nodding, while avoiding his eyes.

He stifled another sigh, glanced at his mother one more time, then sat down on one of the transmitter relay boxes to work his way into his oppsuit. He'd forgotten how restrictive they were, something that rapidly became apparent as he struggled to don the clumsy, uncooperative garment. A fortuitous gift from his father's brother, Jen, they'd literally saved their lives when they'd had to evacuate the ballome for the Caverns. After Peak Opps had passed, the temperature gradually dropped to a more livable range, at least for a while, until it quickly dove far beyond survivable temperatures again, this time in the opposite direction, necessitating their use again.

"Human flesh not well with Dead Drop Winter," Igni commented with good-natured smugness as the insectoid watched the various contortions required to get situated into the suit's protective folds. Everyone laughed, at least a little, breaking some of the tension.

Dirck had grown just enough in height and breadth in the nearly two standard galactic years since Peak Opps to make it snug and somewhat restrictive, even with the built-in adjustments maximized. Outgrowing anything was a new experience since leaving Mira III, between the ability of Academy uniforms to expand with growth, and the family's previous affluence, which precluded lack of any kind.

"You been sneaking genour in the logistics room again?" Win teased with a wicked smile. Fortunately for him, the one he wore, which was originally intended for Dirck's father, still fit perfectly, and he was all suited up and ready to go except for the helmet.

"Shut down, Win," Dirck growled. "You'll be lucky to get your helmet sealed with all the hair flopping around." Win laughed, their diverse hair length preferences a long-standing dig between them.

Dirck grunted, partly at Win's amusement and partly with effort, as he hefted the top half over his shoulders. He shoved his arms through stiff sleeves, adjusted the wristbands and gloves, then finally secured the front flaps and set the switch to heat instead of cool.

"How cold is it out there?" he asked, stretching his arms and rotating his shoulders in another futile effort to get comfortable.

"Seventy-nine below freezing, not with wind factor," Igni replied.

"Wonderful. Nice planet we have here."

"Concede. Conditions ideal," Igni answered, either ignoring or missing the sarcasm.

"Yeah, yeah," Dirck muttered, sitting down to pull on the boots. "Perfect."

"It's easier to generate heat than run a heat exchanger," Win put in.

"Yeah, right," he replied dryly, rising somewhat awkwardly to his feet, ready at last.

He looked back at his mother and siblings one more time, nodded a final farewell, then grabbed the boxcart and headed for the entrance, grateful the helmet hid the fact his eyes were tearing up again. He stopped dead a few steps from the cave's entrance when his visor iced up from the frigid air. He fumbled with the defog switch with his gloved hand, waiting for it to clear, Win doing the same.

He'd never felt this way leaving before, and he wasn't sure whether it was the lingering grief of losing 'Merapa or something more. No matter, at this point, there was nothing he could do about it, one way or the other. By the time the visor defrosted, his tears had cleared as well. Setting his jaw, he ventured into the cold, forcing himself to focus solely on the task at hand.

The fan-shaped vehicle had about six times the interior volume of commuter transports, like the one they'd hijacked when they brought Creena back. It had two straight bulkheads behind either side of the piloting chamber, the remainder of the cargo bay curved, which worked well for troops, but wasn't the optimum setup to move equipment. It took some creative stowage to secure the load, but by the time they finished everything was jammed together tightly enough there was no room for shifting, thus requiring minimal strapping to hold it down.

At last the three of them settled into the cockpit prepared to leave, Igni and Win up front, Dirck just behind them. The interior was as cold as outside, a purposeful ploy to avoid infrared detection as much as possible. The vehicle had a slightly different heat signature than the terrain, but was more likely to look like static or noise with a similar ambient temperature. This time any S3 data wouldn't be deleted.

It took a while for the fuel cells to stabilize, storage batteries losing their charge quickly in the hyper-chilled air. Dirck peered through the wrap-around window into the darkness beyond, searching for anything familiar. His eyes had largely adjusted in the dimly lit tunnels so the terrain was discernible as a conglomeration of shadow, dark upon dark, dusted with an eerie coating of white which had precipitated from the atmosphere.

Unlike the view inside Dununda, the sky was ablaze with a multitude of stars, nearly as bright and profuse as they were when viewed from space. The cold had stabilized the atmosphere, the frozen ground no longer contributing the usual payload of dust, which precluded such a view during warmer seasons. Dirck stared at them in amazement, something stirring inside he could almost call hope in spite of the swarm of S3 satellites visible as well. He glanced at his companions to see if they were similarly taken, finding Igni concentrating on displays and bringing up the wave generator, Win's gaze fixed straight ahead as the pair engaged in conversation directed primarily toward lidar settings for the final phase of their excursion to Apoca Canyon, over two thousand kilometers away.

Dirck leaned back in his seat and stared once more at the stars, besieged with memories of the time he'd spent with 'Merapa learning to pilot the TL-87, a time that had somehow elevated itself to among his happiest moments, regardless of the consequences generated by their futile jaunt.

The transport hummed to full power, gradually lifted, and moved forward. Igni kept their altitude to less than fifty meters, forward speed little more than a hover, as they dodged geological formations and deep-frozen vegetation which presented formidable obstacles as rigid as stone. Using the vehicle's sensors to avoid such things increased the probability of detection, making manual piloting their best option, even though it presented other risks. The vehicle was hardened for space travel, which made it more likely to survive a minor collision or, if necessary, last long enough for help to arrive, especially with oppsuits, but it was a matter of who actually arrived, first, friend or foe.

The configuration of arches and pillars cast still and steadfast silhouettes against the backdrop of stars, familiar in shape, yet somehow foreign in the changed environment. It was as if the planet had evolved into another world as it pursued its unusual figure-eight-shaped orbit around Zeta and Zinni.

Dirck scowled, his first, miserable impression of Cyraria reaffirmed as the ground swept by beneath. Cold or hot, it was an inhospitable wasteland which humans were ill-advised to inhabit. No matter how remarkable 'Merapa was as a terralogist, this place was beyond impossible, more so now than ever before.

Once they were beyond Epsilon's border an hour or so later, Igni quickly elevated to the free fly zone and covered the rest of the distance in less than an hour. He slowed the craft once more and dropped closer to the surface. Up ahead, the landscape grew suddenly dark, no reflection or highlight from Nifeir's slivered remains escaping to illuminate their path. Dirck strained to see something—anything—even the slightest interruption in the flat terrain, but the effort was vain.

Forward motion eased to a stop, then lowered slowly toward the ground. To Dirck's surprise, after several hundred meters they were still descending. He leaned forward to see and realized they were only a meter or so away from a vast and abrupt precipice, the sheer sides a trickle of motion beside them. Unlike the canyon he'd navigated with Win, these walls were separated by several hundred meters, the bottom obstructed by darkness, but undoubtedly a kilometer or more below.

Vector disks hummed, rotational speed relaxed in submission to gravity. Their frequency dropped again as the craft decelerated, then once again moved forward. What remained of the stars above was occulted, nothing but blackness surrounding them, as they proceeded at what Dirck felt was an incredibly reckless speed. Their trace on the display indicated a winding path about twice as wide as their vehicle, the end of which remained off-screen.

After what he guessed to have been about ten kilometers, a dim light appeared, an artificial red glow that resolved to individual points of light as they drew closer. The craft eased to the left, running lights on as they followed crimson tracers a few meters away from either side, then once again descended.

Gradually, a glimmer illuminated the surrounding walls, revealing the rugged texture of naturally shorn stone set with stratified minerals. He squinted against the gathering light, startled when the walls disappeared. The vast space beyond extended for close to a kilometer and was filled with numerous vekes, transport vehicles similar to theirs, and a host of uniformed personnel. Dozens of 'troids dodged organic lifeforms, all busily maintaining a veritable fleet of both ground and spacecraft, a few large enough to move hundreds of troops. For all appearances, they were within the confines of a well-established and powerful military base.

Igni eased their craft to a nearby nest with an attached loading platform, then shut it down, Dirck's meager expectations evolving to apoplectic shock.

"This is Apoca Canyon?" he asked, eyes wide, doffing his oppsuit helmet with the realization that was one of the stupidest things he'd ever said in his life. Of course it was. Where else would they be?

"Concede," Igni replied, exiting the vehicle to give the egress 'troids instructions. After that, the Arcturian directed them toward a massive door. He palmed, or rather clawed, the latch, then let Dirck and Win precede him within. A short passage, another door, likewise secured with a palmlatch. The obstacle heaved forward on mighty hinges, the ensuing light bold and blinding.

Communication equipment and processing terminals attended by more people than he'd seen in one place since leaving Mira III stretched for as far as he could see. He stopped, speechless, Win's expression implying a similar reaction.

"Did my father ever see this place?" he asked.

"Concede. As commander, designed and supervised Clique excavations," Igni answered, folding two sets of arms. "After, until defense secure, a few, mission-specific short times only. Not take chance to reveal location. Or involvement, by absence from Cira City."

Still astounded by the mammoth citadel, much less his father's extensive involvement, Dirck thought back to their pitiful efforts at the Caverns and wondered why they'd bothered. No wonder his father hadn't taken his input seriously.

"What was the point of what we did, compared to this?" he asked.

"To train," Igni said. "Practice. Without preparation, not would be ready to assume command."

"Command? What are you talking about?"

Igni's translator crackled in response to Dirck's lack of confidence. "Not worry, will achieve. Few here met father yours. Will find in you him."

Responsibility closed around him like unwieldy armor. "I can't possibly take his place," he replied, intimidated by what would undoubtedly be stellar expectations. "Never. Not even in the smallest way."

"Concede. Primary task to demonstrate Clique motto."

"What motto?"

"Victoro de Unitus. Victory through United Strength."

Something inside Dirck wrenched as he wondered what he could possibly contribute. Each of those before him, men and women, Erebusites, Zinaanians and jendaks alike, bore determined, competent expressions, as if any of them could be the one to defeat the INTEGRATOR singlehanded. All were clothed in burgundy uniforms, trousers bearing a navy stripe accented with gold braid. A different color, but certainly similar to the uniforms he'd worn most his life. At the Academy, however, there was no pride, unity or significance other than the wearer's age. Yet, for some reason, the sight of hundreds thus attired stirred something deep inside him.

Unsettled by his reaction, his gaze shifted upward to the over-sized chamber's zenith where a steady flow of information occupied the projectron while real-time mission status reports chattered along data strips embedded in stone walls.

Higher still, a holographic image presided, an ensign far removed in spirit from the one in Dununda's contaminated depths. A multi-dimensional star comprised of innumerable facets, each defined by a unique color, yielded the impression of a finely cut diamond, nature's ultimate achievement in the transformation of simple carbon, the basis of human life, to its most durable substance. Within shone every territory and every individual, serving as a beacon of sorts for the collective hope that freedom would yet prevail, even as it subtly commemorated the name of one of its founders and most significant members.

Something about it struck him to the core, heart swelling with pride. As much as he'd admired his father, he'd never imagined such a formidable group doing the same. To Dirck he'd simply been 'Merapa, a man he loved even as he'd matured enough to see his flaws. A new level of respect arose from the realization that he'd been far more important than he'd ever imagined.

His eyes misted again, this time with conviction, marveling to be even a small part of an operation of such magnitude and determined to represent his namesake well. And for the first time in a long, long time, he believed success might actually be possible.

** * **

Integrator Central
TBA
Technical Breakthrough Advisory

TEAM: Communications	PROJECT: Encephalographic Access
Date: DDW-84	Clearance: TOP SECRET
Breakthrough/Milestone: Cristobalite Properties	
Schedule Impact: Y/N? Y	Days: Unknown - Favorable

SUMMARY: A large deposit of the crystalline substance known as cristobalite was located SSW of Dununda a fortnight previous. So far investigation indicates that birefringent reflective properties show considerable promise for psi instrusion, manipulation and communications applications. Discovery of this natural substance eliminates the need to develop a synthetic version which results in a positive schedule impact, dependent on whether impurities can be removed without destroying carrier properties.

Apoca Canyon

Dirck leaned back in his chair, satiated appetite entirely unfamiliar after the meager fare at the Caverns. The bnolar stockpiled large quantities of bowlbush roots and various other rations which they freely shared, but it did little other than sustain life. By comparison, what he'd just consumed was a veritable feast.

Regular food deliveries came courtesy of Chi/Alpha, a sympathetic Neutral in the trailing mid-lats. The harvest had been completed shortly before Opposition, the bounty distributed in a spacious messhall, now empty except for Dirck, Win and Igni.

Upon arriving on Cyraria, he'd concluded the planet had no more redeeming value than a bushbird, the local equivalent of a cockroach. After the tangible and delicious evidence of planetary development he'd just devoured, however, his thoughts wandered paths that might have been.

One of the things that made 'Merapa valuable as a terralogist was his ability to identify what would grow, given a certain set of climatic conditions. His immediate plans when he'd been sworn in as Delta's Minister of Regional Development had been to cultivate the spickle tree, expecting to exploit its extensive medicinal properties that rivaled Lemitini. It was less palatable than the exotic cocoa to say the least, but nonetheless an effective healing agent, the primary drawback its spike hurling defense system. They identified a potential location and even worked out preliminary planting and harvesting techniques while they genetically altered its defense system.

Doing so, however, compromised its healing ability, so they finally decided to design harvesting equipment to deal with it. Nature clearly had wisdom humans lacked and outsmarting it was always difficult and often impossible. Nonetheless, Bryl was enthusiastic, knowing the economic boost would help launch her own aspirations.

Until Krai Laitselec's assassination had redirected their primary focus to the Clique.

Turning deliberately from further thoughts of Bryl, Dirck considered how everything since had only confirmed the second law of thermodynamics; truly disorder in a closed system did increase with time.

With the possible exception of Apoca Canyon.

Igni had spent the better part of the day showing him and Win around, explaining their capabilities, fitting them with uniforms, and introducing them to numerous key personnel. He'd met the leads, or in some cases their backups, for numerous divisions including Surveillance; Intelligence Processing and Synthesis; Logistics; Tactical and Strategic Planning; and Recruiting.

He'd sincerely hoped to shed some of the responsibility he'd carried at the Caverns and thus found the implied expectations that he'd eventually replace his father more than troubling. He felt at best pretentious, at worst a fraud, mingling like an equal with so many better-trained and experienced Cliquers. The uniform didn't help, either, especially holding the rank of captain, even though Igni had explained that his experience warranted such a level and that both he and his superiors would have been uncomfortable with anything less. It startled him every time someone saluted, those of higher rank nodding without ire whenever he'd forget to do so. Conversely, Win looked comfortable and competent and entirely unfazed by the transition, in spite of his unruly shoulder length hair, which he grumpily agreed to contain during duty hours, but refused to cut.

There was no question in Dirck's mind that 'Merapa couldn't be replaced, by him or anyone else, inspiring one unanswered question that skulked in the recesses of his mind. It increased his discomfort, defied asking, yet he'd have no peace until he did. His gaze shifted to Igni's, whose huge eyes searched his as if reading his thoughts. He wondered if the insectoid's telepathic powers had improved, but failed to ask, not sure he wanted to know. He squirmed uncomfortably at the prospect, suspecting the Arcturian's expectations of him were among the highest there.

He stalled another moment by picking the last prozi off his plate, a small, crunchy vegetable they'd had on Mira III, then dragging it through the remaining sauce a few times before popping it in his mouth. A sudden shot of bitterness blasted his senses and he winced, Igni's antennae striking a whimsical angle as he watched, apparently amused. Dirck took a deep breath and let it out, the words with it.

"So," he asked, "Who's in charge?"

"To what?" Igni answered.

"Everything."

Win's attention returned from some distant focus as the insectoid leaned back in his chair, clicking two of his claws together pensively before responding, translator crackling with the usual static as his thoughts organized in linear fashion. Dirck was accustomed to the halting, fragmented syntax typical of normal communications and hardly noticed it anymore.

"Two things Commander Brightstar did to be true leader," Igni said. "First, had way to get most and best of all, deputies to bay techs. He set task foundation, then those with responsibility for work define remainder. Commitment strong, staff learned to cooperate and decide with loyalty fierce. His respect and care for them brought much care and respect to him."

Dirck nodded, intimately familiar with the methods described, even though it felt strange to hear it explained.

"Second," Igni went on, "he not believe in single-point failure. Assassination always threat. Organization built strong, whether or not he be here. Good for Clique and him to stay alive."

"So who's in charge now?" Dirck asked again. "No one?"

"Officially, your father, until Council appoints other."

"Who's on the Council?" Win asked, taking note of Dirck's wide-eyed reaction.

"Representatives of Cyrarian Liberation Quango territories," Igni continued. "They are CLQ ruling body. Not come much here, most because of security, and comm network not secure for online meet. If one in charge, at least of here, that be Director of Site Operations. Zinaanian with name Prnir Vronis. Did call PV until mistaken for pressure vortex, which brought unfortunate false panic. Then changed to Storm."

Dirck scowled at his empty plate, studying the swirls and tracks as if they could provide answers. "Is he here, at the base?" he asked.

The insectoid nodded. "Never leave. Probable location at site with exploration crew."

"Why's that?" Dirck asked, still contemplating the artistic value lurking within the remains of his meal. "What are they looking for?"

"Locate main aquifer. Excavate caves for raw materials. Need reliable power source."

"Power?" Win asked, feet dropping heavily to the floor from an unoccupied chair. "Seriously? This place has power problems?"

"Dead Winter ops difficult," Igni said. "Many fuel cells, but electrolysis unit breakdown of water to oxygen and hydrogen not meet demand due to loss of zetarrays. Aquifer active. Many small tributaries and springs. But primary source not found."

"Isn't that rather primitive?" Win commented. "Why can't you use geothermal energy? Or harness the usual world energy grid inherent through nodes in the magnetic field?"

"Worldgrid nearest vortex too far. Would need massive structure to convey, then direct beneath ground. To transmit requires towers, but would reveal location. For geothermal, many problems. Orbital position with Zeta and Zinni unstable," Igni explained. "Heat extremes on planet combined with much gravity in opposing direction. Infrastructure required could trigger groundquakes. Lack detailed tomographic data of ground faults. Risk not good for underground base."

Win laughed humorlessly. "Right. So how does he plan to use the aquifer?"

"Hydroelectric power. Primitive, simple, reliable."

"How?" Dirck asked frowning, the concept entirely foreign.

"Mechanical energy transfer. Water turns turbines that contain magnets. Moving magnetic field create electricity."

Win's skepticism clung to his face like a mask. "Sounds too easy."

"Not easy, but feasible. But power not yours to worry of. Must take assignments tomorrow. Settle in quarters and tomorrow begin."

* * *

The next day after breakfast Dirck and Win followed Igni through a labyrinth of passageways. Their beauty was undeniable, yet totally different than the intricacies of precipitated limestone found in the Caverns. The walls were smooth and solid, worn by waters long receded, the ebb and flow of erosion evident. Domes accented with concentric rings in shades ranging from golden tan to bluish black illustrated Cyraria's stratified crust and rose high above their heads where roaring whirlpools once swirled angrily, protesting confinement. Rugged and austere versus delicate and ornate, Apoca Canyon witnessed nature's destructive power while the Caverns whispered creative patience.

"Apoca Canyon fine fortress, but with weaknesses," Igni explained, dropping easily to all six as the ceiling lowered briefly, then towered above them once more in the next passage. "Now good," he went on. "Hard to access, easy to defend. Evacuees from INTEGRATION housed and organized. But cannot remain passive for all time."

"What kind of weapons do you have in mind?" Win asked.

"Selective. INTEGRATED populations usually not care or want freedom. Only want living undisturbed with food and shelter. No care who provides. Nothing to gain by destruction of masses, further not ethical. Must delete ones at top and middle who desire at top. On bottom, masses follow strongest leader. Not care for motivation or beliefs, only to survive."

Win nodded knowingly. "So what's our plan to take back newly INTEGRATED regions? Covert ops, internal sedition?"

"Not know," Igni said.

"Wonderful," Dirck muttered, ignoring Win's brief glare of disapproval.

"No," Igni clarified. "Not need to know. Duty of Strategic Planning, highly classified."

"Oh."

They stooped uncomfortably low as they entered another low tunnel, stretching gratefully when they exited on a vaulted vestibule that bowed into several separate paths. Igni chose the one farthest to the right, the narrow passageway inclined enough to induce noticeable exertion by the time they reached an area designated as Intelligence Processing and Synthesis, commonly referred to as IP&S. Comcons, datacoms and processors busily attended by a multitude of personnel filled the cavernous hollow beyond. Green input streams, yellow standbys and red alerts flashed from the equipment, monitored by uniformed attendants. Dirck's energy ebbed lower as another confidence crisis rolled through. No wonder his father believed what came out of Apoca was more credible than what they'd had in the Caverns.

"Commander Brightstar directed you with authority to reorganize IP&S," Igni said.

Dirck blinked, wondering if he'd heard correctly as he followed Win and the insectoid to a hollow off the main area that served as a briefing chamber. They sat at a naturally formed stone table, its eroded surface smooth and polished to a rich, mirror-like sheen. Igni lowered to all six, enormous head seeming to float above his reflection, accentuating his compound eyes which were drilling into him as the Arcturian awaited his response.

Dirck considered his words carefully, not wanting to say something incredibly stupid if he'd misunderstood. "The last time I talked to 'Merapa in Cira City he told me you had everything here. That our work at the Caverns was redundant and in some cases obsolete. What can we possibly do to improve all this?" he asked, waving his arm in emphasis.

"You're forgetting something, Dirck," Win interjected. "We did have information they didn't, on those hostile takeovers and use of lasoclear weaponry. Remember how they thought they were peaceful acquisitions?"

Dirck scowled pensively, remembering. Win was right. They had known, but he'd been so distracted by Bryl's intentions that he'd acquiesced to 'Merapa's assumptions that Clique conclusions were correct.

"Right," he agreed. "At the Caverns we'd known it from the start. The only thing we'd initially failed to identify was Eta's position as a covert INTEGRATION asset as opposed to being a Neutral territory. Creena had noticed how they'd been shipping food to INTEGRATED areas, but we both assumed it meant nothing since everyone needed to eat. Afterwards, we discovered Eta was nearly giving it away to them, compared to what they charged Neutrals and Clique members, which would have been a dead giveaway if we'd checked."

"Concede," Igni replied. "Cavern process superior. Apoca capability volume only, cannot integrate. When intelligence item you call double-i arrive, you not miss. Cliquers miss many. Not confirm drogues. Do not sort or tell difference between true and false information. With less hardware, less persons, you found double-i's here missed. Methods you developed good. Efficient. Accurate."

"One problem," Dirck said grimly. "A large part of that was Aggie, who filtered and categorized what came in. She grouped and sequenced key words in a way that often indicated intent more clearly than single data points. 'Merama and Creena screened the ones with the highest probability and sometimes tied even more facts together. And they're all back in the Caverns."

"Processors available, much capability. Only must code," Igni stated.

"We can do that," Win responded. "Aggie was a great package and we miss her, but we can work around it. I know enough about her primary algorithms to duplicate them. And there are plenty of people here we can train to perform the same function as Sharra and Creena."

"Concede," Igni agreed. "You are powerful team. Must determine why double-i of invasion and strategic weapon violations here not found. More mistakes, we fail."

Dirck's heart dove again with self-imposed inadequacy. He'd had all the double-i's in the world, plus a veridical dream, and still missed Eta.

Igni's huge eyes fixed upon him, a few crackles escaping his translator at what he probably sensed as disagreement, but the insectoid didn't comment. "Follow and will show where data stored," he said, and led them to a chamber filled with crystal cubes a few centimeters square. Roll-out shelves from floor to ceiling filled the room, their stacked contents glistening in the dim light.

"Double-i's all here, include dates and source, etched on outer edge. Advise what be needed to have process like Caverns. Improved process most needed if Clique to survive."

Dirck remained silent, still absorbing the realization they'd done a better job than the existing IP&S team. But only to a point. The most vital information had slipped past, overcome by emotion disguised as intuition. How could he have been so stupid?

"Okay, we're on it," Win replied before Dirck's lack of response became awkward. "We'll set things up like they were at the Caverns, review the data, and compare it to archived results so we can figure out why they missed it."

Igni nodded approval, casting Dirck a lingering look before dropping to all six to head back.

"All right, this we can do," Win stated, eyes boring into his as if scouring his mind and not liking what he saw. "I'll find a terminal and start coding an Aggie substitute while you find someone to retrieve our hardware from stores and configure it like it was at the Caverns. I knew we needed it here for some reason, and now it makes sense. Is that okay with you?"

Dirck stifled a sigh, knowing Win was right, as usual. "Yeah," he replied limply, awash in a renewed sense of inadequacy. "Sounds like a plan."

Win's gaze lingered another moment, then he took off to find an unoccupied terminal in the busy workroom beyond. Once he'd found one, he turned and looked back, folded his arms and gave Dirck a look when he saw he hadn't moved from the archive room entry.

"All right, all right," Dirck muttered to himself, and looked around half-heartedly for the team lead, trying to figure out what to do first. A moment later Win was back, hand planted on Dirck's chest and shoving him back inside the room.

"What's the matter with you?" he hissed. "You've been acting like a total snurk since we got here. What's going on? I know you're still upset about your father, but we have work to do and you're as spaced out as a planet with a hyperbolic orbit. What's going on? What am I missing here?"

Dirck buried his face in his hands and sighed, then dropped his arms to his sides and studied the stone ceiling. "I never told you the real reason I went to see 'Merapa in Cira City," he replied.

"What are you talking about?" Win replied. "You went to tell your father what we'd found with those takeovers. He convinced you our interpretation was wrong and then wound up being ambushed on Nifeir."

"Yes, but there was more."

Win scowled, anger still firing his eyes. "More? What do you mean, more?"

"Creena and I had another one of those weird dreams. You know, like the one I had with 'Merama about rescuing my father from prison."

Win's scowl deepened. "Why didn't you tell anyone else? Or did you?"

"No, we didn't. It was too, well, too personal. And we didn't want 'Merama to know. She would have completely flipped out."

This time Win rolled his eyes and stared at the ceiling. "What are you talking about? What could be more traumatic than fighting a war?"

Dirck's heart pounded in his ears as the dream replayed through memory in all its sordid detail.

"Well?" Win prompted.

Dirck sighed heavily as he cautiously met Win's blazing eyes with his own. "It was about Bryl. She tried to seduce 'Merapa. Not only that, but she was going to claim him as her bondling under Eshonian Law. Her government rank combined with them both being Eshonian citizens made it legal."

Win's jaw dropped. "Whoa! So that's it! I knew there was something bothering you, just didn't know what."

"The worst part," Dirck went on, "was that the dream included the information about the Eta TG. Bryl mentioned it in the dream, about setting up a meeting, but Creena and I were so torn up over the bonding part, we didn't catch it. When I went to see 'Merapa, I told him about Bryl's plans to snag him, so he did everything he could to change what would happen when she showed up. He even put himself on Argo's schedule!"

"So what are you saying, Dirck? I don't get it. He had bad data, didn't believe what you told him, and fell into their hands. What does this dream about Bryl have to do with anything? Her intentions don't matter anymore. So what's your point?"

Dirck closed his eyes, heart once again weighted with defeat and failure. "My point is that I'm no good at this. Even with the help of a veridical dream, plus our supposed superior intelligence methods, I missed what was going on with Eta. I was distracted and so was Creena. We focused on losing 'Merapa to Bryl and wound up losing him to the INTEGRATOR instead, because we were so stupid. How can I help get this place in order when I made such a horrible, deadly mistake? I'm not even a decent Miran, anymore, Win. Mirans may be boring, but they're objective. They weigh the facts. They maintain control. They're—"

"Oh, shut down, Dirck," Win cut in, shaking his head in dismissal. "There's no reason to feel guilty."

"Of course there is!"

"No, there isn't. Your father's the one who failed. Whether he was your Miran superior, father, or Clique Commander, you followed Miran protocol by not defying his reasoning. He wouldn't even accept what we had on those military coups."

"But I should have warned him about Eta! I didn't! I even mentioned it without realizing that meeting needed to be avoided, just like the one with Troy when he was in prison. Between the double-i's and the dream, I should have understood what was going on. They were sucking in Neutrals with one strategic strike after another, yet Eta was unscathed. How could I miss something so obvious?"

"Look," Win replied. "Everything always makes sense afterwards. Shoulda, coulda, woulda. You did the best you could with what you knew at the time. You're human, like everyone else, including your father. It was his fault as much as yours.

Even if you'd caught the implications regarding Eta, there's no guarantee he would have believed that, either, since he didn't recognize INTEGRATION's increasingly overt aggression for what it was.

"Peaceful acquisitions, yeah, right," Win went on. "No doubt INTEGRATOR interests were covering up their methods to avoid scrutiny by the HIO until they'd achieved the two-thirds majority they needed to take over the planet with the galactic organization's approval. If the HIO had known what they were doing, INTEGRATOR proponents would have been in a huge fix. Your father was wrong, didn't catch it, probably because he was distracted with getting this place set up, but you were right. You did nothing wrong. Why can't you accept that?"

Dirck's shoulders drooped. "I'm not sure. Maybe it's because I don't want to admit that he was capable of making such a huge mistake. I always thought he was perfect. When they hauled him off to prison the first time from the ballome, the hardest part was realizing it was his own fault. I had a bad feeling about him having that lasomag and told him as much. By the time he got around to realizing I was right, it was too late. I was furious when he left us like that, in such a bad situation. Then, at some point I started to understand a little, and then I thought he was perfect again, but in a different way. So I don't know if I'm feeling guilty myself or having trouble accepting he failed to respond correctly. I don't know who I'm madder at, him or me."

"One way or the other you need to get over it," Win stated firmly. "What is, is, and all we can do is learn from it. Here's what we need to do. Before we set things up, we need to determine why we didn't discover what was going on with Eta based on what we had, other than the fact they weren't invaded. We could have dismissed it assuming limited INTEGRATOR resources or any number of things. The main thing is it's doubtful they could have kept anything of that magnitude secret.

"We all missed something, that's all there is to it," Win continued, his tone softening. "We paid a huge price for it, but feeling guilty isn't going to change a thing. Beating yourself up is a waste of time. Pull yourself together, Dirck. Indulging in a pity party prevents you from using what you've learned to make sure this doesn't happen again. One lesson we can take from it shows emotional involvement can fog your reasoning. That's true of anyone. It's a matter of being human."

"I suppose," Dirck admitted.

"Exactly. And that's why we need to set up the computers to filter out important information the way Aggie did. They don't get distracted by feelings. Then we need to make sure anyone with a personal or emotional interest in a situation isn't the one interpreting the data, much less making key decisions. They'll immediately be relieved of duty, perhaps even furloughed, because they could make a mistake somewhere else as well when they're worried and upset. There's a lot to learn from this. Lots. And that's the value of experience. Meanwhile, you need to let it go and focus on the present. Things are extremely critical right now and missing something else could cause the Clique to fail entirely, plus send us all to Bezarna, right behind your father."

"You're right," Dirck sighed. "It's just not that easy to forget how badly I goofed up."

"I know," Win said solemnly. "But you really didn't, you just convinced yourself you did. Next time, don't hold all that crap inside. I just thought you were grieving. But I also thought losing your father should motivate you to be more determined than ever to defeat them. Now I can see why you were so distracted. Let it go. Focus on the present. Other than figuring out what we missed and why, we can't afford to look back. The future is the only thing we can influence. The past is history. Gone forever."

"Yeah," Dirck agreed. "I suppose the future's all that matters now."

"So is there anything else you want to talk about? Is that it?" Win prompted, keen blue eyes searching his expression like ionizing radiation.

Dirck emitted a deep sigh. "Actually, there's one more thing."

"What?"

"More about Bryl. I don't know what happened with the bondling angle, if she ever approached him or what. 'Merapa said she wouldn't take well to rejection. If he refused, no telling. For all I know, she set up that ambush. Maybe she knew what was going on and hid it from him. He reported to her, you know."

Win's eyes widened and jaw dropped. Finally he blinked and swallowed hard, more rattled than he'd ever seen him under any circumstances. "No," he said finally, shaking his head. "No. I can't believe she'd do that. No. Uh, uh."

"Why not?" Dirck asked. "Then no one else could have him, either."

"No. Absolutely not. She's one of the original founders of the Clique, even before your father came onboard. She wouldn't jeopardize its success over something like that. Never."

"But when they arrested 'Merapa on Nifeir, he asked if she knew. So he must have thought she had something to do with it."

Win shook his head, ponytail flying in emphasis. "No. I don't believe it."

"I hope you're right," Dirck said grimly.

Win blew out his cheeks and exhaled heavily, still shaking his head in denial, but with a slightly different rhythm. "Me, too, man. Me, too."

PSICOM

I miss him. A lot."

Creena jumped, startled, concentration so focused that she hadn't even noticed that Deven had joined her in the niche they used as a lab.

"I do, too," she answered absently, attention already back on the demodulator.

"You do?" Deven asked, surprise highlighting the round-eyed face staring into her own, eyebrows lifted so high in surprise they were hidden beneath his bangs.

"Of course I do! Why wouldn't I?" she replied, meeting his questioning gaze.

"Oh, I don't know," Deven shrugged. "You only met him once."

She scowled, confused. "Who are you talking about?"

"Enoch! It just hasn't felt the same since he left. We always felt good when he was here, never sad or worried."

"Oh. I thought you meant 'Merapa."

"I miss him, too. It's lonely here by ourselves, almost as bad as when it was only me and 'Merama in the ballome, when you were missing and Dirck and 'Merapa were looking for you. I miss Dirck and Win, too."

Creena bit the inside of her lip, not wanting to get into that statement for anything. Win, maybe. But Dirck? Deven's statement about things changing when the bnolar left had some truth to it, though. Their presence kept the negative energy at bay, whereas ever since their departure it had escalated to a frenzied peak until Igni came back, his need for consensus reducing, but not quite eliminating, the contention. Nonetheless, the barrier was still there, along with a host of persistent bad vibes, even with her elder brother gone.

Deven stood on tiptoe to see the test results on Aggie's readout panel. "Anything?" he asked.

"No, not yet."

"I have a surprise," he said, dark eyes sparkling with mischief. Heartstruck by their bittersweet resemblance to 'Merapa's, she blinked hard and quickly looked away.

"What?" she asked, trying to smile as she cautiously reconnected with his expectant stare. "Another cave lizard?"

"No. Better. Sorta."

"What?"

"Come on, I'll show you."

Taking her by the hand, he led her down the luma-lit passage to behind the comm-room, where Dirck and Win had stored excess equipment. Since their departure, he'd taken it over as his fort, numerous rock samples stacked in neat piles around the perimeter. The Caverns were replete with more minerals than could be studied in several lifetimes, their beauty often irresistible, from sparkling calcite's iridescent radiance to brilliant crystals that projected a perfect prism.

If she weren't so intent upon unraveling cristobalite's secrets, she could have easily been taken up by admiring such specimens herself. She'd gathered numerous samples from the Think Tank, always careful to remove them from an area near the entrance outside the circumference proper. Her rationale to avoid the interior assumed the loss wouldn't affect its ability to reflect energy, which seemed valid. Nonetheless, every sample had lost its luster upon removal, reverting instead to seemingly simple silicon crystals, pretty but unremarkable, indicating a strong synergistic relationship within the Tank as a whole, which was perhaps related to its unique properties.

Deven went straight to the far side and picked up one of several dark samples reposing in a small heap. Many were phosphorescent, some translucent, and a few of a form and color she'd never seen before, but this one's appearance indicated it was more than another simple variation. He came closer, holding what appeared to be a large yet perfect twelve-sided dodecahedron crystal about two centimeters in diameter. Its color was deepest violet, revealed only as light struck its facets, each of which glistened with an animated prism that twisted outward from its depths like Miran fog.

He held it toward her, rays liberated from its depths swooping and diving in random paths as if searching for something. Or *someone,* for as Creena moved forward in awestruck wonder, the energy sensed her presence and shot toward her, light now focused in a single, coherent beam with one end forming a dot above her heart, the other end similarly connected to Deven. Most lasers she'd seen were green or red, but this one, like its source, was purest violet, visible in patches where dust particles crossed its path.

Isn't it beautiful? Deven asked, grinning.

"Yes," she replied, then froze with the realization that her brother hadn't spoken aloud.

Pretty neat, huh? You can hear me, can't you? Just like Enoch! Is this cool or what?

"Deven! It's..." Her response trailed off as she wondered if it worked in reverse. *Deven. Can you hear me, too?*

Of course! What do you think? Will this help your research?

"Will it ever!" she cried, excitement seizing her in a sudden, optimistic wave. "Let's see if we can talk to 'Merama!"

"Here," Deven said, handing her the crystal, the link between them retreating back to random swirls.

Creena took it carefully, surprised when its surface felt warm as she held it out in front of her.

'Merama? Can you hear me?

The violet beam appeared again on her chest, the other end extending instantly in the direction of their grotto. When no reply came other than a sense of confusion, she tried again, then again. A few minutes later, 'Merama called her from where the comm equipment had once been, her voice echoing in the now empty chamber.

"Over here!" Creena cried aloud. "In Deven's fort!"

When 'Merama reached the back room she had a puzzled look on her face. "So you're way back here. That's strange. I thought for sure I heard you call."

Creena held up the crystal, its beam again retreated, and grinned. "You did."

Her mother's green, Miran eyes grew wide and her jaw dropped. "You figured it out?" she gasped, smiling.

"No, not really. Deven found these, in another area. Where exactly was it, Deven, and how many more were there?"

"I found them in this niche, quite a bit smaller than the Tank. It's completely lined with these. They practically jump into your hand."

'Merama switched her attention from the crystal in Creena's outstretched hand to her son, looking him square in the eye. "So where exactly is this niche, Deven?" she insisted.

The boy's expression fell into that sheepish look he always got when he'd done something he shouldn't have. Creena stifled her smile, knowing that he'd seldom done anything that was actually wrong in his life, and every time he came even close, it always turned out to be incredibly lucky, like meeting Enoch, who'd welcomed them to the Caverns when the heat exchanger blew up, saving their lives.

"Well," he started hesitantly. "It's kinda around where, well, you know, like sorta by where the transport went down."

"Where?" Creena asked.

"Yes, Deven, where?" 'Merama echoed. "You know I don't like you all the way down there by yourself."

The boy swallowed hard, eyes fixed on the floor. "I thought I should check the tunnel once in a while, to make sure it's still closed. You know, so no one from Dununda finds it. I was down there checking and found this place near the end, around where the tunnel walls had collapsed. I had this funny feeling it was important, so I dug through it a little ways and found the niche on the other side. I'm sorry, 'Merama."

'Merama looked anything but angry. "Deven, you know I don't like it when you wander off alone because I worry about you. And I really don't want you down there by yourself again. But I think you've helped us a lot."

"I know you have," Creena agreed. "My first thought is that they're either more pure or maybe a different isotope than Tank crystals. I'll have Aggie run some tests and see if we can figure out what makes them work, since they don't lose power when you remove them, like the ones from the Tank."

"Who cares how they work?" Deven commented. "Why does it matter? Can't you just see what they can do instead?"

Creena paused, mouth agape, dumbfounded by his simple, yet profound, logic.

'Merama shrugged. "Why not?" she said. "Makes sense to me."

He's right, Creena thought. It doesn't matter. Just because they didn't know how the Think Tank connected thoughts with a specific location, much less teleported them there, didn't make it any less effective.

"Good idea," she agreed. "Let's test it out, see what it'll do. First of all, let's check its range. You and 'Merama stay here and I'll go back to the Grand Cavern." She grabbed another crystal from the pile on the floor and dropped it in her pocket.

"Great!" he replied. "I'll count to two hundred, which should give you plenty of time."

During the walk back, Creena pondered how she'd often wondered if she'd ever know how the cristobalite worked, specifically within the confines of the Tank, since the samples she'd removed always lost their properties. It was such a strange concept that thoughts were things, miniscule energy packets transmitted as psi waves that traveled faster than the speed of light. Both she and 'Merapa assumed that cristobalite somehow reflected and amplified them, behaving in an analogous manner to electromagnetic radiation.

Yet, tests so far hadn't shown that to be true, and now she suspected maybe it wasn't. She still hadn't been able to detect or transmit a signal, psi or otherwise, even after purifying the crystals using a technique 'Merapa told her about. The method was called zone melting, which was why she'd needed the laser, to slowly heat the sample and melt an area which gradually captured and removed impurities. In spite of all the effort she'd put into that, nothing changed, as far as she could tell. Furthermore, Aggie explained that the instruments they were using were primarily sensitive to electronic signals, not psi packets, their new term to avoid thinking of them as light, the nontechnical term for electro-magnetic radiation in the visible range.

The hard part was breaking out of her familiar beliefs in favor of something entirely foreign, so unlike anything she'd ever heard of that it not only exceeded her knowledge base but her imagination as well. Thus, Deven's idea made sense. Just see what they could do, regardless of whether they understood why or not.

When she got to the Grand Cavern, she looked around the magnificent stone gallery, awed by its beauty yet again. Pillars, columns and rivers of frozen stone stood peaceful and still in the soft phosphorescent light of luma plants placed in a multitude of locations. She sighed, wishing she'd never have to leave this magical place, yet knew that day would come, the thought interrupted by Deven's telepathic voice.

Hey, Creena. Ya there yet?

"Just got here, Dev. Can you hear me?"

Barely. Are you talking out loud or thinking back at me?

"Out loud. Why?"

I can barely hear you, but 'Merama can, too, real faint like. If I wasn't listening for you I probably wouldn't notice. Try thinking.

How's this?

Yeah! Perfect! As clear as if you were right here. But 'Merama's shaking her head, so now she can't.

Great! Let me go a little farther, back to the grotto and see if that works.

Okay. I'll give you a minute. One...two...

The path ahead was riddled with ruts and bumps, so Creena made her way carefully, not wanting to trip and fall as she walked purposely along, chuckling to herself that it felt as if they were playing a game of hide and seek, like they did back on Mira III.

It does feel like that, doesn't it, Creena? This is fun, isn't it?

Much to her astonishment, she not only heard his words, which were unexpected enough since he'd read her mind, but also felt a burst of pure joy that she knew was his.

Deven! she thought back. *That was amazing! You read my mind, plus I could feel your emotions! Wow!*

In reply, she felt his preemptive giggle. *I can feel yours, too. You're really happy. This is so much fun!*

In the meantime, she reached their grotto and wound her way down the twisted path beyond their respective sleeprooms to where it ended abruptly against a wall of granite, the place she thought would be farthest away.

How about now, Dev? Can you hear me okay?

No difference at all. It's perfect. The musical ripple of another giggle soared through her heart. *You're really excited about this, aren't you?*

Creena laughed this time, remembering how hard it had been to keep her feelings and emotions hidden on Mira III, where control was expected. *Yes, I am,* she admitted. *But communicating like this sure wouldn't be appreciated by anyone trying to keep a secret, would it?*

More laughter, then, *Nope. Sure wouldn't.*

Okay, Dev, I'm on my way back. This is fun, but I really need to get to work and see what else I can figure out. "Oooops!"

As much as she'd tried to avoid it, somehow she lost her footing and tripped, barely catching herself as one knee hit the stone path.

Ouch! That hurt!

Deven responded. *What happened? Is your knee okay?*

"Yes, I'm okay," she replied aloud, as she sat down to examine the damage. "Just a little scrape."

Creena? I can barely hear you. Are you okay?

Yes. I forgot and said it out loud.

And then she noticed that whenever he psied, the purple dot reappeared on her chest, as it had in his fort.

What is it? Deven asked. *Are you sure you're okay?*

Yes, I'm fine. But guess what? That purple dot is on my chest whenever you talk! How could that be, with all the rock between us? Wow!

She got up and brushed herself off, mind racing as she hurried back to the lab. *I think the range is unlimited, but we'll have to test it farther than we can within the Caverns and we probably shouldn't do that until we know more, just in case. Maybe when you're holding a crystal and just thinking about someone, it'll send you their thoughts. Or maybe they could hear yours! That's pretty scary!*

Yikes! I hadn't thought about that!

Yeah. If a bad person had one, it could be very, very dangerous. Her thoughts wandered to the INTEGRATOR and his various intrusions into her mind, especially while she was on Terra. In a flash, it was as if she were there all over again, cool grass beneath her feet, a multitude of stars above, the fresh smell of summer rain, the starcraft hovering before her like a giant bird of prey. With a quiet gasp she returned to the

Caverns, a horrific thought consuming all others. Maybe they already had it!

Where was that, Creena? Terra?

Her heart raced with the realization that Deven had shared her brief excursion back in time. She swallowed hard, unsettled even more by the implications.

Y-Yes.

Who's the INTEGRATOR?

The one we're fighting, Deven. And they not only want to read people's minds, but control them, too. If they got a hold of this, it would be very, very bad.

That really scares you, doesn't it?

Yes, Deven. A lot. More than anything else in the whole, entire galaxy.

* * *

Apoca Canyon

While Dirck coordinated setting up their old equipment in a grotto off the main equipment room, Win developed an Aggie substitute that comprised a layered data interpolation synthesizer algorithm that they quickly abbreviated to L-DISA. In addition to the sorting and filtering Aggie had done, his version checked past events similar to those detected, to help extrapolate what the action or results might be. By the time L-DISA was in beta testing, they were ready to compare the data they'd gathered at the Caverns with Apoca's archives, starting a few weeks before the Neutrals were seized.

The next day, an unexpected difference commanded their attention—the timestamps. As the two sat at the stone table in the briefing chamber comparing Cavern data to Apoca's, they discovered they'd obtained the data in the Caverns *before* it was received there, sometimes by as much as three days. In checking further, they determined that the dates in the archives were true, not posting dates, so the discrepancy remained. They continued the comparison, wondering if Apoca's server was off, then even more mystified when the data they gathered in the Caverns *after* his father's arrest turned out to *lag* Apoca's by nearly a week. A quick check with the section's lead confirmed the server hadn't been down, the timestamps accurate. Ultimately, they confirmed they'd received identical data, but at entirely different times.

"So what's going on?" Dirck asked, scowling.

"I don't know," Win replied, getting up to lean pensively against a datacom unit. "Aggie's internal clock confirmed our timestamps, so it wasn't our power issues distorting the results. They could have been purposely re-broadcasting disinformation, but most of it turned out to be accurate, so I doubt that's the case. And if they'd rebroadcast it, we would have received it twice. It was also amongst the most deeply encrypted, unless that was to throw us off, make us think it was something important when it wasn't, but it was."

"I don't think it had anything to do with re-broadcasting, even though we did receive some of it twice," Dirck mused. "The frequencies were the same, the content identical, the only difference the time of receipt. It wasn't even consistently early or late. It's kind of weird that it was earlier before 'Merapa's exile and later afterwards. But we don't even know which one was correct, us or Apoca."

"Something mighty strange is going on, all right," Win agreed, worry creasing his brow. "I don't like this at all. It looks like we have bigger problems than we ever imagined."

Dirck drummed his fingers on the console. "Yeah. It's like we were in a timewarp or something. How about we start from the present to see if it's our equipment? Let's look at what's come in since we hooked up versus theirs. If any of the transmissions were tachyonic, maybe our transformation to local spacetime was off."

"That's worth checking," Win agreed. "There's also a chance that Aggie's date reflected the day we said it came in. Without having her here, I don't know if it would have been our comsystem's date or hers."

In spite of the tempting morsels beckoning them to the messhall, the pair had barely taken time to eat, their determination to identify the problem subduing their appetite for anything but a viable explanation. By the end of the next day, their efforts were rewarded in a sordid kind of way. While they didn't answer their primary question regarding the time differences, they did at least resolve something else. At last, for the first time since 'Merapa's arrest, their processor regurgitated new significant data, nicely sorted and sequenced by L-DISA.

Dununda fairly leapt off the monitor from one of INTEGRATOR Central's bulletins known as *Technical Breakthrough Advisories,* generally referred to as TBAs. Dirck and Win focused intently on the information that followed, anxious to solve the mystery once and for all. As Igni had suspected, an undisclosed mineral hit had occurred at one of the local mines. Whatever it was, it was obvious that the INTEGRATOR had a keen interest in it, based on elaborate evacuation plans for the residents and the high clearance level of military personnel that moved in.

Win coded additional queries into the processor and even more information followed:

More deposits suspected. All magnetometer data including that confiscated from most recent acquisition being scrubbed for more potential sources.

A treble-encrypted double-i, which translated into a work requisition for a scientific research director was next, obviously linked to the recent discovery in Dununda. Anyone successful in recruiting a suitable candidate was promised significant, unnamed rewards, at which they could only guess. The training and experience desired was general, yet specific, vague, yet clear, and the meaning penetrated Dirck's mind with the force of a lasoclear blast:

Experience must include extensive research in semiconductor applications such as induced conduction bands and energy generation, advanced quantum-based communications theory, exotic tachyonic transmission alternatives including psiband receipt and translation, as well as photon acceleration and entanglement techniques.

It was too familiar, made too much sense, and ironically was a perfect match for his father's qualifications. The materialization of Dirck's gravest concerns had come to pass yet again, the downward spiral of expected events as terminal as 'Merapa's trajectory to Bezarna. His eyes met Win's, anxiety well-founded and escalating as more bone-chilling information followed.

Somewhere in the vicinity of Dununda, the INTEGRATOR had found cristobalite. A heartbeat later, L-DISA's interpolation function confirmed Dirck's greatest fear: Discovery of the Caverns was no more than an S3 tomographic scan away.

DEVENITE

By the time a few days had passed, Creena found some important differences between cristobalite and Deven's crystals, which she'd named devenite. Her brother's discovery displayed a different bonding scheme at the molecular level, which explained its unusual multi-dimensional shape. While cristobalite formed in layers, each molecule a planar hexagon, devenite formed independent crystals, resulting in their geometric shape. Other than that, they seemed to consist of similar elements, simply bonded in a different way, which was common in nature and sufficient to explain why they were more powerful, including the ability to function independently rather than as part of a larger whole. It was certainly possible given the example of carbon's diversity, which included coal and diamond as well as the basis for much of organic life.

Devenite was so powerful, in fact, that she worried that random experimentation could cause trouble. Big trouble. If the Think Tank left magnetometer blooms, there was no telling what devenite might emit, which could alert the INTEGRATOR, not only to where they were, but the existence of devenite itself, either of which would be disastrous. Each of them kept a single crystal for emergency communications, just in case, with Deven securing the rest in a safe place near the Tank, where they could grab them quickly if they had to evacuate on a moment's notice. He and 'Merama had returned to the discovery site, gathered a few more, then filled in the area as much as possible, hoping to hide what remained in the event the Caverns were invaded.

After several more days with no specific progress, Aggie was at her limits, needing more input before she could produce new results. While the 'troid had been able to process 'Merapa's mathematical interpretation of cristobalite, she lacked the capability to extrapolate what it implied. Creena's main concern was understanding what Aggie called a "collapsed time tensor" and how it could be used. So far it explained why thought and transport capabilities were instantaneous, yet didn't reveal how to control, much less apply it, to communication functions like those perfomed by radio waves.

Finally, Creena told the 'troid to take a break and pensively made her way back through the Grand Cavern and down the steep passage to the Tank, hoping for inspiration which had been noticeably absent. So far her efforts to understand how cristobalite's teleportation properties worked had met with one disappointment after another, finding a solution in time to help 'Merapa less likely with every passing day.

Yet something inside wouldn't let her give up, reminding her that she might only be one idea away from the solution. What if she quit too soon? She'd come close several times lately and couldn't help but realize how much Deven's discovery had brought new hope, even though it was balanced with risk. Actually, in spite of all the cautions it had spawned, its promise had nonetheless dissipated the last of the gloom. Oddly enough, it was as if Dirck had taken a large measure of the negative vibes with him.

She paused outside the Tank's entrance, watching living walls of energy shift and roll within, pondering how the fact her older brother's negative node was located in the briefing room had made things worse, since that was where they did more brainstorming than anywhere else. Identifying it hadn't been as helpful as she and 'Merapa had expected without likewise knowing the location of his positive node.

Before she'd started thinking in terms of psi packets, while she'd been stuck in her light wave paradigm, she'd naturally assumed, as had 'Merapa, that the positive node, or peak of the wave, would be either halfway between the Tank and the negative node, or twice as far away. Neither had proven to be the case, however, putting them back where they'd started.

So where was his positive node? Or maybe he didn't have one. She admonished herself for the unkind thought, knowing it, too, was negative energy that she couldn't afford to generate, especially in there. Since they'd never found any evidence for anyone else's nodes, perhaps it wasn't his node at all, but something else, which had caused his exaggerated reaction that day.

She stepped inside the Think Tank and sat on the ledge of the center rise, trying to empty her conscious mind and open her subconscious to inspiration. Unless a breakthrough came soon, she'd never be able to help 'Merapa. She'd considered trying to contact him using devenite, yet felt the risk too great. The crystal's undetermined range was further complicated by the fact her father was traveling at warp speed. Something told her neither distance nor velocity was a problem, but that actually made it riskier if the transmission could be traced. For all she knew, it could leave magnetometer blooms like the Think Tank and reveal their location, even though it appeared the message itself was limited to the intended recipient. How the INTEGRATOR had found her on Terra she didn't know and didn't dare take any chances.

Energy swarmed around her, a reminder to consciously blank her mind to avoid generating any unwanted magnetometer blooms, but the sadness at the prospect of failure refused to budge. If she could get in touch with him, maybe it would be worth the risk, but that brought her back to the question that had plagued her since the start: Why was the Tank's range limited to Cyraria only?

If psi packets traveled faster than light and permeated solid stone, why would their range be limited? Thyron's telepathic range wasn't limited, at least when he was healthy. If only he could have contacted 'Merapa. Unfortunately, after a brief rally from the light panel, he'd succumbed to complete dormancy, awaiting a lighter season in the corner of Creena's sleeproom back in the grotto, where he'd gradually wilted into a compact package of leaves no more than a half-meter tall. By the time he awoke from hibernation, it would be too late. Placing him in the Tank hadn't worked, the vegemal complaining it was too "noisy." Interesting, she thought, and probably meaningful in some way. But how? Old thoughts bouncing around?

Igni's telepathic powers were also limited ever since arriving on Cyraria, but they'd never figured out why. He'd stated that its energy felt denser than most worlds. Did that mean that psi could be affected by energy but not matter? She stared at the walls pulsing around her, noting that their energy felt less vigorous, almost tired. The swirls moved slower and didn't extend as far beyond the walls as she remembered. Maybe because there were fewer people now and less mental energy to reflect.

Or perhaps it was because the bnolar were gone, the benevolent creatures whose influence had probably activated the Tank in the first place. Her heart warmed as she recalled her first and unfortunately last encounter with Enoch, when he'd welcomed her home with an inrush of loving emotion she'd sensed physically. There had been nothing frightening about him in spite of his towering size, multiple limbs and weird billowing layers of skin which protected his species from Cyraria's harsh environment. To the contrary, she'd felt nothing but concern and kind sincerity.

For what seemed the thousandth time, she studied the chamber's walls, the stepped rise in its center, then the domed ceiling shaped similar to an inverted dish antenna. Obviously, it wouldn't broadcast upward so much as down, with some random scatter from the vertical walls.

There she was again, reverting to electromagnetic radiation, but as much as her efforts to relate the two had failed, this made sense. Maybe that was why it was limited to Cyraria, unless there was some other inherent limitation.

So what would happen if the dish were pointed outward, toward the place offworld you wanted the psi packets to go? One cristobalite sample didn't have much power, but what about several? The walls responded to her thoughts with increased activity, the spectra dancing hypnotically before her in prismatic twists of light. Not knowing where the threshold for unwanted transmission might lie, she got up and returned to the lab, determined to at least give it a try.

She stopped by their grotto to join 'Merama and Deven for a bite to eat, voiced her theory, then took the hollow shell from a bowlbush root back to the lab to see what she could do, Deven and her mother tagging along to help. Her brother gathered up the best and most uniform cristobalite crystals she'd removed from the Tank and together they secured them inside the bowl, taking care to focus them at a point slightly beyond the sides. When they finished, she asked 'Merama to go to the farthest point again beyond their grotto to see if the new concept worked.

Creena waited long enough for her to get there, then pointed their makeshift psitenna in that general direction. She shrugged at Deven, thinking they had nothing to lose by trying, then concentrated on transmitting her thoughts to 'Merama.

'Merama, can you hear me?

Barely. Are you speaking aloud?

No. But this is more than we had before from just cristobalite. Stand by a moment.

A phrase she'd learned on Terra popped into her mind: *Nothing ventured, nothing gained.* She sighed and set her jaw, removing the chunk of devenite from her pocket and securing it in the center of the psitenna, hoping the cristobalite sides would focus the transmission and keep it constrained to line-of-sight.

'Merama? How about now? Is this better? Like before, a violet beam shot from the devenite, toward her as well as the recipient.

Wow! 'Merama replied. *I'll say! If that had been audible, it would have hurt my ears!*

Deven met her wide-eyed, elated look with one of his own. "Did it work better?"

"Apparently! Let's try something else." She extended the psitenna once more and spoke aloud. "'Merama? Can you hear me now?"

Yes, but not as clearly. Did you do something differently?

"I'm speaking aloud," she replied. "I just wondered if it worked that way, too."

Apparently. Just not as well.

Then she pointed it in the opposite direction. *Can you hear me now, 'Merama?* Nothing.

"Look!" Deven exclaimed, pointing at the makeshift device in her hand.

A miasma of purple swarmed at the bottom of the psitenna as if trying to get out, yet apparently held captive by the cristobalite lined sides. Gradually, the glow faded and she smiled at the implications. Her idea worked; knowing where the recipient was located, the devenite had tried to connect, but the cristobalite stopped it, which was even weirder, considering devenite alone typically penetrated everything, further confirming cristobalite reflected psi.

"Awesome!" she said, then lowered the device and turned to Deven. "Should we try to reach Dirck?"

"Why not? We know the general direction of Apoca Canyon and there's not much between us, anyway. Besides, it seems to know where the person is. The only problem is other people in that direction might hear it, too."

"That only seems to happen if I speak aloud. Think there'll be any magnetometer blooms?"

"Nah." he reasoned. "It's going horizontally, mostly below ground."

"Okay," Creena agreed. "Here goes."

Again she pointed it, eyes closed, and concentrated, putting some effort behind it like she had on Terra when she'd communicated with Thyron.

Detailer, she thought, using the code name he'd chosen sometime back. *Voyager. This is a test. Do you read? Over.*

"Try Win, too," Deven suggested.

Code Master, do you copy? she psaid. *This is Voyager. Do you read?*

The purple beam didn't appear so she peeked within, discovering the beam was swirling inside like before, apparently trapped.

"Aha," she said. "Wrong direction." She turned slightly and repeated her calls until the beam projected outward as expected.

The expression of complete surprise hit before the words, enveloping her with not only the uttered exclamation but feelings as well. Win's reaction was pure excitement, confirmed by an outflow of avid congratulations. Dirck's, on the other hand, while equally surprised, carried something else. Shock, perhaps, that her efforts had at long last succeeded. But there was more than that, something that didn't feel right at all.

"Well?" Deven asked.

Creena lowered the psitenna, other hand over her heart.

"What's wrong?" Deven prompted again.

"Wow," she whispered. "The feelings really come through, don't they?"

"What happened? What feelings?"

She sighed and shook her head, as if it could cast off the emotional blast. "Dirck," she said. "His reaction. Win was excited and happy. Dirck wasn't."

"He wasn't?" Deven gasped. "Why not?"

"Because he's jealous. And then he felt guilty," she explained. "And then he was grumbling because I make him feel so dumb! Snurkles," she breathed, the only adequate expression of what she was feeling herself. "So that's why he gets so reeked!"

Shaken by the sudden revelation, it took her over a minute to realize she hadn't sent back a reply.

Thanks to Wee One we've made a breakthrough, she replied. *So how's Apo—I mean the new location?*

Fine, Dirck replied, *But that's not where we are. We're coming to get you. Start gathering up what you want to bring. You need to get you out of there, now. They've found cristobalite outside Dununda and are taking magnetometer readings to locate more. Whatever you do, don't do anything to generate blooms. Don't go near the Tank! The slightest variation right now will tip them off for sure.*

Creena lowered the psitenna toward the ground so as not to transmit the groan gathering inside. Of all times to have to leave. She swallowed hard, then lifted it once more.

Roger that. We'll tell Starfire and get ready. What's your ETA?

Within a few minutes.

Okay. See you then. Voyager over and out.

She looked at Deven, arm falling to her side, then lifting the device to admire their work one more time.

The crystals glowed with an aura of approval that offered their own congratulations for persistence and a job well done. Yet it wasn't done, far from it. She'd only barely started and there wasn't much time left.

"Deven," she said urgently, wanting to perform one more test. "Deven, which way's Bezarna?"

Her brother looked at her dumbly for a moment, as if struggling for the context of her question. Its meaning gradually dawned, much as Zeta's light eventually would on the planet's dark and desolate surface. His eyes sparkled nearly as brightly as their recent invention, then clouded again in stupor of thought.

"I don't know," he replied. "I don't know what time it is and we don't have an ephemeris. You'll have to ask Dirck."

Creena felt a cold wave of intimidation at the prospect. Dirck would think she'd entirely lost her orbit, maybe even gone nova if she asked something like that.

"I know!" she exclaimed. "Aggie! She'd know!"

She started for the commroom where the 'troid was recharging, Deven on her heels, then stopped dead in her tracks. "What are we doing?" she said. "The psitenna knows where 'Merapa is!" But before she could try, 'Merama rushed into the lab, horror etched on her face like a mask of stone, Aggie bumping along close on her heels.

"Someone's coming!" she whispered urgently.

"Who?" Creena whispered back.

"I don't know, but it's a large group, just outside the Grand Caverns. You know how voices echo through those passageways, long before anyone arrives. We need to get out of here!"

"Dirck's on his way," she said. "Are you sure it's not him?"

"Yes! The entrance he uses comes in at a different place. Whoever this is, they're in the main tunnel leading from the front entrance. The one we used when we came here during Peak Opps."

"C'mere, Aggie, let me code you for survival strategy. Think you can get them all?" Creena asked.

"Most likely," the 'troid replied, photoreceptors flashing stand-by. "I've still got enough toxic gas to snuff out all life in the Cavern's entire underground network."

"Just like an yraglian lizard," Deven commented dryly.

"I suppose," Aggie sniffed, "Though I don't appreciate being compared to an organic. Unfortunately, however, without protection, all of you will be among the victims."

Creena sighed, berating herself for being so careless. Good thing the 'troid was protective in her own, digital way. "Look, there's probably time to get to the Tank," she speculated. "Deven, grab the samples, quick!" She thrust the psitenna into 'Merama's hands. "Here. Tell Dirck we're using the Tank, then all of you head down there, including Aggie."

"*Where are you going?*" 'Merama gasped.
"To the grotto," she replied with grim determination.
"*Why?*"
"To get Thyron. We can't leave him behind."

A Knick of Time

Ignoring any further protests, Creena sprinted as quietly as she could toward the Grand Cavern, stopping to listen just short of its entrance. All was quiet and still. She tiptoed forward, ears tuned, as the path continued beside a culvert, the stream's normally friendly gurgle damping any sound.

She hunkered down behind a mound of limestone tentacles and listened, thankful stalactites and other formations offered numerous hiding places. She proceeded a few more steps when above the water's chatter she heard distant voices, source and direction disassembled by confusing echoes.

The final stretch to the grotto involved approximately twenty meters of unprotected path, presenting the choice of speed versus sporadic jumps to concealment behind various floestone formations between her and the intruders. Before she could decide, the voices grew louder until a burst of volume reverberated through the huge chamber. As expected, the awesome spectacle of nature's design elicited a swell of admiration and a momentary hush. Taking advantage of their distraction, Creena crouched low and crept forward.

The intruders' conversations ebbed and flowed, apparently speculating where to go next. Creena peeked over the rise, holding her breath. The group was larger than expected, a handful of men and women in civilian dress accompanied by a band of commandos. Her breath caught in her throat, knowing no pleasant surprises lurked behind yellow armor this time, as it had when Win and Dirck rescued her on Mira III.

Their attention seemed diverted toward another tunnel on the far side, guarded by a huge column of precipitated stone. Counting on their continued inattention, she crept toward the grotto, grateful its entrance wasn't visible from the Grand Cavern.

Once inside, she went straight to her sleeproom. In deep hibernation, Thyron didn't stir, continuing his repose as a dormant cluster of tightly folded leaves. She picked him up carefully, grateful he wasn't too heavy and more compact than usual, and returned to the greatroom, where she crouched behind a towering stalagmite to steal a look.

Much to her horror, the civilians had dispersed in a curious mass while the troopers set out in groups of three toward each of the Grand Cavern's passageways, one of which led to their living quarters. One trooper paused a few meters away, helmeted gaze riveted in her direction. The trio froze briefly then broke into a run in her direction.

"Halt!"

Horrified, she tucked Thyron under her arm and dashed back into the grotto.

Neither her sleeproom nor any of the others had so much as a decent niche, much less an escape route to the caverns' network of tunnels, so she flew down the narrow passage beyond 'Merama's sleeproom to where a small waterfall collected in a deep pool. Mechanically amplified voices of armored troopers demanded surrender, footfalls heavy on the rocky floor. The rumble of rushing waters rose around her, muffling their approach as she reached her destination.

The waterfall's source high above was confined and hard to reach, so Creena edged her way around the narrow ledge rimming the warm, meter-deep pool to behind the cascading water to where she'd discovered a large cavity while washing her hair. It had taken her a long time to find it, so with luck the troopers wouldn't suspect it existed. If they thought to look behind the small waterfall, hopefully the cavity was deep enough to get out of sight. Once she got close enough to reach inside she crouched down, braced her right leg against the wall and leaned forward, blinking against the persistent spray as she carefully set Thyron inside the opening.

The ledge was precariously slippery and narrowed to only a decimeter wide before it reached the niche, Creena holding her breath as she edged along. One leg slipped, her foot touching the water, the scramble for balance which followed a mad tangle of arms and legs that ended with a tremendous splash.

Knowing she'd certainly betrayed her location, Creena felt her way beneath the water to behind the falls where she surfaced, startled and gasping for air. She wiped her eyes and listened, any indication of her predator's presence obliterated by the thunder of tumbling water. Senses tuned, she pondered climbing inside the niche when a telltale yellow reflection crept across the falls.

She sucked in a hasty breath and lowered beneath the surface, the falls' thunderous roar now an eerie gurgle. Distorted by the huge conglomeration of bubbles where the falls broke the surface, a yellow blur moved from side to side, then remained in place for what seemed like forever as her hungry lungs strained.

Her mind raced, capture and drowning scoring equally. Darkness enclosed her like a shroud, decisions deadlocked, when Deven's voice exploded in her mind.

Creena! Where are you? Are you okay?

No! she psaid frantically. *I'm in the bottom of the pool with three commandos a meter away. They're all over! I need to breathe and don't know if I dare!*

In the pause that followed, the sound of distorted voices echoed above her. The mumbles continued another long moment, then retreated. She emerged slowly, trying to catch her breath without coughing as she wiped her burning eyes, then peered around the falls and listened. The voices were distant, possibly in the greatroom, maybe beyond.

Carefully, she hauled herself to the ledge and crawled into the niche where she huddled as far back as possible, dripping wet and shivering, Thyron cradled on her lap.

Deven. I'm out. In the niche.

Did you get Thyron?

Yes.

Good. We're on our way to the Tank. Go ahead and imagine yourself there.

Dirck had told her how he and Win had teleported numerous times by creating a psilink to the Tank, though she'd never had reason to try it. With no other choice, she hugged the vegemal to her chest and willed herself there. She opened her eyes a moment later, knowing that still hearing rushing water was not a good sign. As expected, the dim light reflecting from the falls mocked her efforts.

Deven, are you there? Why didn't it work?

I'm not sure. There doesn't seem to be enough energy. We never did this without Enoch around. Maybe the Tank's losing its power. Or maybe you need to start here, to build the link.

Great! Where's Dirck?

We sent him back, said we'd meet him in, uh, you-know-where. We were afraid they'd get caught, too.

Well, get them back! If the Tank won't work, we're dead!

I wonder what would happen if I used the psitenna?

Creena scowled, unable to imagine what would happen with the combined effects. Her train of thought halted as the niche's pale illumination suddenly darkened. The water's cadence shifted then exploded in an angry splash; she screamed as the keen beam of a high powered portalume blasted her in blinding assault. A moment later, the trooper was in the pool, water crashing from his helmet in defiant protest.

Deven! They're back! Just do it, anything, but get me out of here!

Two hands shrouded in yellow armor reached toward her. She shrunk back, terrified.

Okay, Creena. Concentrate. Here goes...

She closed her eyes, hugged Thyron to her chest, and again concentrated on the Tank. An instant later, she was consumed by a brilliant flash of violet. The silence that followed seemed interminable, as if she were outside herself and somehow forsaken by space and time. It stretched and expanded, nothingness closing in as if absorbing her into the void.

Deven! What's going on? Deven! Where are you?

Then, without warning, she was in the Tank, Thyron stirring ever so slightly in her lap. She scrambled to her feet and whirled around, shivering with cold and fear. She was alone. Had they left without her?

Deven, where are you?

The subtle sound of multiple footfalls rang softly from the descending pathway beyond. She picked up Thyron and backed against the wall in the crook of the entrance, relieved when Deven, 'Merama and Aggie filed in, arms loaded with sacks and datadisks.

"Creena!" 'Merama exclaimed. "How did you get here?"

Creena blinked and shook her head. "Deven brought me here."

"I did?" her brother asked.

"Yes! You brought me here! Remember? I was trapped in the pool back at the grotto and you used the psitenna. Don't you remember?"

"There's nothing to remember!" Deven explained, shrugging while 'Merama's expression silently confirmed his assertion. "We've been gathering up everything we could and just got here. I tried to get you on the psitenna right before we left, but you didn't answer. We were really worried."

"Snurkles," Creena whispered, eyes wide. "I was just talking to you. You were leaving for here when you called, then I tried to teleport to the Tank like Dirck and Win used to do, but it wouldn't work. A commando found me and you used the psitenna as a booster. The next thing I knew, I was here."

"This is too weird," Deven said. "I haven't even talked to you yet!"

"Yes, you did!" Creena insisted.

The realization of what had happened hit everyone at once, its significance occulting the fact the Tank's usefulness was apparently impaired.

"Do you think I went back in time?" Creena gasped.

"There's no other logical explanation," Aggie stated.

"You call that logical?"

"Logic ceased to exist the day we left Mira III," 'Merama said with a frown.

"*Shhhhh!*" Deven said. "Listen."

Eager footsteps echoed through the passage, their amplitude rising, drawing closer and closer, as they eyed each other in a state of marginally contained panic.

"C'mon," 'Merama said, stuffing datadisks in every available pocket and clutching their bagged belongings. She motioned for them to huddle on the room's center rise, Aggie in the middle. "Concentrate on Apoca Canyon and let's get out of here!"

Voices from the entrance disturbed their focus but a moment before survival drove their thoughts back to their intended destination.

"Everyone ready?" 'Merama asked.

"Yes! Let's go! On three: one, two, three!" Creena stated. But as she somehow expected, nothing happened.

"*Halt!*" The armored figure of a commando filled the entrance, followed quickly by two more.

Creena grabbed the psitenna from Deven's hand and aimed it toward Apoca Canyon.

"*One more time!*" she cried. "*One, two, three!*"

Violet swirled, reflecting from the chamber's walls, then time and space collapsed on a dark and empty void. She knew she wasn't alone, yet couldn't feel or hear a thing except the rush and surge of tremendous energy.

The sensation reached a thunderous crescendo, then all was still. Something solid materialized beneath her feet and Thyron's green mass settled into her arms. Air filled her lungs and with an explosive gasp she opened her eyes.

* * *

The Bezarna Express

Eventually Laren allowed himself to wonder what Bezarna would be like. In theory, life could exist on a blackhole, it just couldn't leave. Ever. Light, either, which prevented any transmissions in the electromagnetic spectrum, such as radio waves, from getting out as well. Tachyonic transmissions, maybe, but it was highly unlikely such equipment would be provided for the galaxy's most notorious criminals. Receiving; now that might be possible, except it would take extremely sophisticated hardware to filter out the shifting effects.

Light couldn't escape, but that begged the question of whether it could even exist. If not, it would be quite literally a living hell, particularly in view of the unknowns regarding the passage of time. If it stopped, which it certainly could, he could live forever. He shuddered, more shaken by that than the thought of death. He could always hope death would come quickly from gravitational effects.

Death didn't scare him. Not anymore. Any residual concerns had vaporized during his infamous prison break. Though he'd never admit it to his family, it actually hadn't been an easy decision to come back. Left to his own, he probably wouldn't have; Win left him no choice.

No, there were worse things than death, some of which he'd seen. And his life wasn't over. Yet.

His fellow passengers on the *Bezarna Express*, however, were far from at peace with their fate. Since departure, he'd somehow assumed his usual place as commander and now he found himself looking upon them as his crew sharing an ill-fated mission rather than fellow prisoners. Oddly, nearly all of them at one time or another had confided their deepest feelings about their fate and he found that, more than ever, he was grateful for the consolation it was to trust in the *Benefics*. Now that he'd accepted his fate, that and the *Order* were all that mattered.

He'd always known that Ledorians had another side to their call, but had never anticipated using it outside his family. Yet, as time progressed, he found himself leading in a different sense, helping those around him find comfort in the inconsolable. As the others realized what privileges he had, they did everything they could to get him to request a miracle. He refused. Not because he couldn't, but rather because he felt inclined to turn the situation over to the will of fate. Once he'd determined that mechanical intervention was impossible, it had been easy. Worrying had never done any good whatsoever.

Furthermore, resisting, protesting or pleading often did nothing more than interfere with unseen forces that could provide assistance. If some sort of rescue was attempted by the Clique, the last thing he wanted was to compromise their efforts with his own actions.

He'd lost track of how many chrons had passed, neither did it matter, but he suspected they were probably at least halfway there. Even small accelerations were detectable to a seasoned spacer and he felt them more and more. With what could be the end apparently in sight, the next few chrons were spent recording his hopes and admonitions for his children on his c-com, grateful he could do so via psilink so he at least had that much privacy. While they would probably never receive them, the *Benefics* would, and he knew they'd be passed along somehow, even though he couldn't deliver them personally. He'd miss Sharra and his children horribly, especially if he survived. If he didn't, there would be far too much to do in the next dimension to think about it.

He paused, chagrined by the fact that time wouldn't exist in either of his two possible destinations.

* * *

<table>
<tr><td colspan="2" align="center"><h1>Integrator Central</h1>

<h1>TBA</h1>

Technical Breakthrough Advisory</td></tr>
<tr><td>TEAM:
Communications</td><td>PROJECT:
Encephalographic Access/
Reception</td></tr>
<tr><td>Date: DDW-108</td><td>Clearance: Top Secret</td></tr>
<tr><td colspan="2">Breakthrough/Milestone: Remote detection of specific encephalographic activity</td></tr>
<tr><td>Schedule Impact: Y/N? N</td><td>Days: NA</td></tr>
<tr><td colspan="2">SUMMARY: Cristobalite application beta testing indicates ability to detect and identify specific types of brainwave activity (e.g. sleeping, conversing, reasoning, creative endeavors) has been achieved. This constitutes a major step toward further refining the process to allow specific invasion techniques related to covert access of subject thought data based on cerebral location of synaptic activity.

BACKGROUND: Upon perfection of this technique knowledge of a subject's precise location will no longer be required when mindprint data are available.</td></tr>
</table>

Purple Haze

irck cleared a small patch of condensation from the shuttle's window with a gloved hand, startled yet again by how frigid it was. He'd never dreamed anything could be worse than dual suns at Peak Opps, but Dead Drop Winter offered stiff competition. The bone-chilling cold was as lethal as heat, draining resilience from everything, be it batteries or people but, as the season dragged on, what gripped him most tightly in the icy fingers of gloom was the darkness. He stared past his own troubled reflection to the frozen waste beyond, unable to see anything save the distorted image of Nifeir, stars long lost to a persistent haze as the atmosphere's moisture precipitated from sub-freezing temperatures. The window fogged anew, then flash-froze to etched crystal.

It didn't take long for the cold to penetrate the vehicle's conductive structure, then move through the interior in icy waves that threatened to suck the will from Dirck's weary body. He folded his arms close, the black, navy and grey shadowed fatigues well-insulated against normal temperature inversions, yet didn't protect against those invading his heart. The transport shuddered as Win activated the fuel cells, both to charge the batteries and throw some heat to defrost the window. The defogger cleared a small arc that edged upward by millimeters then reached steady-state just below eye level, refusing to progress any further.

He didn't know what he was watching for, only that something wouldn't let him leave. Deven's directive had made sense, that they'd use the Tank and meet at Apoca Canyon, but something wasn't right. He couldn't identify it, only knew a deep and ominous fear churned inside.

The past week or so had been rough. With all the resources they had, his predominant impression of Apoca Canyon had evolved to that of acute entropy. There were too many people that didn't know what to do. On top of that, there were different opinions, different cultures, different languages, and even different equipment incompatible with the rest.

There were plenty of Cliquers, such that they should have been a formidable opponent, but instead it was a covey of confusion, contention and contradictions. Even he and Win had been swept into it, disagreeing more than ever before, primarily over the weapons issue. Nearly two-thirds promoted the development of offensive weapons, the others preferring an emphasis on defensive. Dirck could see the necessity of both, and was thus in trouble with everyone, more often than not. The constant arguing had driven Igni to distraction and he hadn't seen the Arcturian in days. Storm did well supervising operations, yet lacked the ability to instill unity within the troops, something his father had done effortlessly.

"What are you beating yourself up over now?" Win asked, arms slung behind his head.

"Nothin'," Dirck replied, not moving his eyes from their distant focus. "I'm just worried, that's all. I should have never let them stay, alone like that."

"They wanted to, remember? As I recall, they refused to leave. If anything goes wrong, it certainly won't be your fault."

Dirck didn't answer, the issue of blame far removed from his greatest concern. What had really gotten to him lately was loneliness. He'd never thought much about it before, but he'd never been away from his family like this, ever. There'd always been someone there, either 'Merapa or 'Merama and Deven, and for the first time he had a glimpse of what Creena must have experienced when she'd jettisoned in the pod. No wonder she couldn't accept the fact 'Merapa was gone. A deep and poignant longing had begun shortly after his arrival at Apoca, one he'd dismissed previously by telling himself they'd be together again soon. Now he wasn't so sure, loss creeping through him like the frigid air beyond the window.

He couldn't stop thinking about Creena. He'd never made peace with her, as 'Merama had requested, which nagged him constantly. What if he never saw her again? His excuse that he'd been too busy and distracted preparing for the move fell flat, not even enough to convince himself. Then, during that brief flash when she'd first contacted him with whatever she'd finally come up with, it was as if a part of her had implanted itself in his heart. For the first time he realized how badly he'd misjudged her. He'd always known it with his mind, but now he knew it with his heart. He'd actually felt her eagerness to make contact and share her success.

Maybe that was where his own loneliness originated, in that longing he sensed in her for everyone to be together again. A longing that with 'Merapa gone could never be fulfilled.

His stare focused back to a slight depression occluded by shadow where their ballome had once stood. He'd never imagined that those horrid days of sweat and hard labor when he and 'Merapa had been building the water distiller would rank among his happiest memories. But they'd been together then, most of them, anyway, and there was hope that Creena would join them shortly. So what did he do when she got back, but immediately start in on her again. What was the matter with him anyway? The energy sink deepened with the ominous feeling he'd never see anyone again, period.

As he stared outside wracked by premature grief, a ghostly purple haze formed above the ground about a few hundred meters away, at first seeming no more than another air pocket traumatized by cold. It gathered intensity and crept outward, the brightening glow an apparent chemical reaction or energy field.

The location was where he thought the Think Tank should be, yet 'Merapa had insisted that there were no visible emissions, only magnetometer disturbances. The wave continued its radial motion, edge aglow as it swept frozen ground.

"Hey, what's that?" he asked, pointing.

Win straightened in his seat and scowled, reaction abrupt and decisive.

"We're outa here, man," he said, not even taking time to warm up the vector disks before throttling to full power.

"*What is it?*" Dirck asked, holding on as the vehicle screeched in protest, then entered a sharp climb and banked toward Apoca.

"There's only one thing I know of that moves like that," Win answered, a rare edge in his voice.

"*What?*"

"Radiation from a lasoclear weapon."

Dirck buried his face in his hands as the implications consumed his mind.

Oh, 'Merapa, I'm so sorry...

Win's hand rested sympathetically on his shoulder. "I'm sorry, man," he said quietly. "I'm really, really sorry."

As the initial shock ebbed, denial drove hope to a vain surge, and by the time they got back to the base, Dirck had convinced himself that it had been no more than Tank blooms ionizing hypo-chilled air.

Not wanting to contradict Win or set himself up for an argument he was sure to lose, he'd kept his theory to himself, fully expecting to find Creena, 'Merama and Deven at the outpost awaiting their return. After all, when Deven had told him to go back, he'd described his quarters so they'd have a reference for the Tank's telekinetics. They'd be there, waiting, that was all there was to it.

Win had barely docked the transport in its sling when Dirck flew out the hatch and raced down the winding passages, by now certain he'd find a welcoming committee in his room. He slapped the palmlatch and fairly dove through the opening, his presence activating low level lighting. He stopped and spun around, frantically seeking any sign of their arrival. His sleep cyll, comcon, scattered clothing and a few packages of dehydrated fruit stared back from their repose, the configuration identical to how he'd left it, comcon still set to the channel which had alerted him to the potential for a raid. He turned again, unwilling to accept the truth, then slowly sank down on his cyll, staring at the door.

And thus he spent the entire sleepzone, drifting back and forth between grief and denial, eyes open but unseeing, until Win came to get him in the morning. His friend said nothing of events recently passed, only made a fast stop at the messhall where he insisted Dirck eat, then each returned to what they'd been doing when so rudely interrupted by the contingency at the Caverns.

* * *

Too distracted at first to get anything done, Dirck gradually slid back into the work at hand, finding at least a partial escape from a reality too horrific to accept. Unable to solve the timestamp discrepancies other than a vague correlation with his father's arrest, Win finally decided they were wasting their time, that processing current information had priority, and they set to work accordingly. Synthesizing real-time intelligence data wasn't much different than at the Caverns, except there was so much more.

All the task comprised was determining what data to match together to maximize yield, which L-DISA handled beautifully. There were more sources than before, but several were bogus, spewing disinformation like spickle trees threw spikes. Before long it was easy to see why Apoca hadn't caught the Eta acquisition or the force involved with the others. They'd misidentified drogues specifically designed to hamper their progress and ignored prime sources, exactly how the

INTEGRATOR intended, while Aggie's sorting combined with Creena's and 'Merama's watchful eye had caught key subtleties, making the difference. Apoca's haphazard methods entirely missed what had been intuitively obvious to them. Apparently he was smarter than he thought, even though 'Merapa hadn't listened to him, either.

In the days that followed, he found himself morbidly drawn to prisoner listings, yet their content was benign. While 'Merapa's name appeared in the *Permanently Detained* category, Creena, 'Merama and Deven never showed up. Mention of activities at Dununda was nonexistent, its code name elusive or too classified to access through any means. Nonetheless, the fact the INTEGRATOR had cristobalite was intuitively obvious, how long it might take to develop potentially lethal applications no more than a guess.

The one thing neither he nor Win ever mentioned was the loss of crystal technology. While it was apparent Creena had achieved a major research milestone, to speak of such would have cheapened the loss of something far more precious. Comm problems persisted, particularly due to hypofrozen temperatures. Semiconductors were inhibited, conductor efficiency increased, imposing general havoc with external electronics. Storm had one of his engineering crews working on a heat pump to warm the antennas' surface components, even at the risk of detection by S3s, knowing loss of comm would be worse. Hopefully they could disguise it to look like a fumerole, a natural hot spring bubbling with mud, which were all over the place, except where needed.

Endless activities continued to keep him from dwelling on his loss, but the vacuum inside his heart persisted. Getting *Intelligence Processing and Synthesis,* or *IP&S*, on a keener track felt good, but the only real consolation he had was Win. His friend understood, having lost his own family, and knew when to talk and when to shut down, when to push and when to back off. While Dirck wanted to give up and die, the example before him beckoned otherwise and motivation gradually returned. A week later, with their first assignment successfully completed, including the launch of the final version of L-DISA and the completion of training of Clique personnel, Dirck and Win consulted Igni once more, this time about their next assignment.

"Decision of Storm," he replied, antennae gesturing that they follow. Together they left the intelligence bay for a desolate pathway off the main corridor.

"Where is he?" Dirck asked, following.

"On work for power plant."

Lighting was sparser than other areas, the air's moisture content increasing as they followed a tunnel that branched off the transport bay and proceeded deeper within the base's depths. Condensation dribbled from surrounding walls, graduated to trickles and small streams, then expanded to rivulets until eventually the throb of momentous energy pulsed around them, the amplitude of a low frequency growl rising as dramatically as the humidity.

Past another sharp bend, a thunderous roar greeted them as the tunnel ended overlooking a raging river troubled by rapids, rebelling against the constraints of imposing stone walls. A narrow path, slick with continually replenished puddles, hugged the wall beside it, the aquifer's surface three meters below. Dirck swallowed hard, uncomfortable with the height combined with the slippery path and the fact he couldn't swim. A kilometer of nerve-wracking footsteps later, the aquifer widened to a grumbling volume of swiftly moving water, rapids gone. Gradually, the path widened until it spread into a gaping area stacked with oversized equipment which dwarfed a nearby group of workers.

It wasn't hard to spot Storm. Usually Zinaanians were of medium height, but their acting commander towered above the others, almost as tall as Igni, who stood a decimeter above Dirck when upright. His shoulders were broad, arms well-muscled, scaled skin a rich bronze. Typical of his race, his head was broader at the top with spherical eyes of a reddish hue on either side which could rotate independently and thus attain a three-hundred-sixty degree view without moving another muscle. Other facial features included protruding cheeks separated by a thin, bony nose and a relatively wide lipless mouth above a powerful, pointed jaw. Seeing them approach, he came forward with long, yet graceful strides that defied his size, expression difficult to read while his posture suggested one of concern. When he got there they saluted, which he returned with a three-fingered hand, then ordered them at ease.

"We're grateful you're here," he yelled, his booming voice blending with the din. "There's much to do, much more than we can finish on schedule. Did you complete your initial project?"

"Concede," Igni hollered back, translator crackling with increased volume. "*IP&S* operative, much improved."

"Good. Now you can move on. Your talents are needed elsewhere. Dirck, I need you here. Win, they can use you in communications."

Dirck and Win exchanged glances, not necessarily in disagreement so much as surprise at their impending separation. Storm's sharp eyes caught the exchange as did Igni's translator, which crackled with the usual sound it made when he perceived a lack of consensus.

"Would you prefer to work together?" Storm shouted.

Both shook their heads in quick denial. "We're prepared to follow orders," Dirck yelled, contradicting his sinking heart. "We'll work wherever we're needed most."

"Agreed," Win said.

With no further ado, the insectoid signaled for Win to follow him back to the main base, Dirck uncomfortably aware of numerous eyes upon him.

"We're having problems with the turbines," Storm explained, gesturing toward several metal monoliths near the rear of the chamber. As they got closer Dirck could see water spilling from a huge opening in the stone wall like a giant faucet ten meters above their heads. Storm led him past the turbines through a door which led to a small chamber, walls too square and precise to have formed naturally. Storm closed the door and the river's roar faded, the volume of his voice lowering with it to reveal a slight accent peculiar to his race which exaggerated the pronunciation of vowels.

"The magnetite here is brittle and can't handle the rotational speed necessary to generate the power we need. Our forging capability is limited, so we need to come up with something else to deal with the problem. If you're anything like your father, I expect we'll have our answer by tomorrow." The huge Zanaanian smiled, revealing pointed, yellow teeth as he placed a heavy arm around Dirck's shoulders.

"Yes, sir," he replied, though his heart threatened to fail him.

No measure of success with *IP&S* could compensate for the fact he knew no more about hydro-engineering than the origin of the universe.

Storm granted him comcon access to the current design specifics, then explained the schedule, dismissing him when he didn't have any questions. Dirck stepped outside the chamber and stared vacantly at the raging river, not knowing whether to go back inside and tell Storm the truth, or remain quiet in favor of making a fool of himself later when he failed. The unpleasant choices rattled around inside his head for some time until a third introduced itself as slipping off the path into the waters below suddenly held undeniable appeal.

Vortices

irck lay in his cyll, the cold, unyielding stone on the opposing wall an unbidden reminder of his dilemma. Discouraged to say nothing of frustrated, he'd retreated to his quarters from the plant site with the excuse he needed to check some data, but now all he wanted to do was sleep. His concentration was shot anyway, thoughts jumping from one junction to another like a short circuit. When he'd been working on the intelligence problem he'd easily averted grief through distraction, since he knew what he was doing. Now, whenever he got stuck, which was every minute or so, his mind took the path of least resistance to the depths of despair.

He turned from his side to his back, staring through the transparent cyll cover to the rocky ceiling beyond, its closeness as imposing as the task before him. Coming up with a new design for the turbine magnets was so totally beyond him he didn't know where to start. Manipulating known data was one thing, something that came naturally, but hardcore engineering required high order math skills and creativity, both of which had seemingly come up missing on his list of talents and abilities.

He glimpsed his reflection, taken aback by the grief-stricken, worry-lined image that stared back, one he'd never seen on Mira III. Neither had he ever felt like this physically nor emotionally, much less comprehended its possibility. It felt like someone had kicked him in the ribs, pain echoing through his chest as if part of him had been wrenched out. If only he could get the indelible image of that pulsing violet shockwave out of his head. It was always there, just beyond awareness, deep purple flashes haunting his vision at random times when he'd least expect it. What had happened? Would he ever know? So far nothing significant had shown up, or so he was told by *IP&S*. He still couldn't believe they were gone, denial notwithstanding.

It just couldn't be. No. Couldn't. Absolutely not.

It was simply too much. Overwhelming. As he'd done a thousand times or more since that horrific day, he pushed it forcefully from his mind. What little functionality he had would be gone if he confronted it. Another burst of purple flashed inside his head as if refusing to be ignored. He closed his eyes and sighed with frustration.

A moment later, his fingers curled into fists which he lifted, then slammed to his sides, impacting the soft bedding which absorbed the dual blows. He had to get a grip. Recapture the cool logic he'd possessed on his *naterra*. If there was one thing he'd learned on Mira III, it was going with the flow. Unquestioned, immediate, complete compliance. He didn't think, he didn't argue, simply acted as directed, a method which had served him well all his life.

Until Cyraria. Where he'd learned that resisting was sometimes appropriate and persistent effort could make a difference, not unlike the cryptofluvial forces which had formed the bulk of their fortress, twists and turns directed according to the strength of its rocky opposition.

Similarly, opposing INTEGRATION was like going up against a granite wall. A river with enough volume when faced with such an obstacle would dam up behind it, eventually surging over the top. A stream might find a small weakness and burrow its way through or perhaps beneath, given enough time. Such an analogy suggested the Clique had a chance.

Then again, maybe not.

The analogy broke down even further, given his current circumstances. Their existence was based on resistance, yet within any military organization it was necessary to follow orders, not unlike his *naterra*. Oddly enough it made sense, but with all due respect to the merits of authoritative command, one fact was increasingly clear:

Storm had the wrong man.

The man's comment about his father hadn't helped. Trying to take 'Merapa's place was impossible, even when he knew what he was doing. He thought back to when his father had been designing the heat exchanger and tried to explain the efficiencies of thermoelectric cooling. He'd explained that instead of a working fluid going through phase changes, thermoelectric cooling used a direct current to drive electrons from one semiconductor to another, then dump the energy to a heat sink.

As if!

'Merapa may as well have been speaking in Erebusian, his explanation of acoustic cooling even more incomprehensible. Sure, transferring energy from one form to another was easy enough to follow in principle, but another thing altogether in practice. No, Dirck wasn't an engineer in any sense of the word.

If only I could talk with him for a few minutes, he could tell me what to do.

But that, of course, was impossible. And his father's technical skills weren't the only thing he missed, leading him back down the same dismal road he'd tried so hard to escape.

When 'Merapa had been taken, the grief had been devastating, but the pain of losing his mother far exceeded it. Whenever he'd get discouraged she'd always known what to say, or do, sometimes no more than a gentle hand on his arm or shoulder. She was the only one who came even close to understanding him and now she, too, was gone. Furthermore, he never would have imagined it possible to miss Creena like this, or Deven, but he did.

Or in the case of his sister was it simply guilt for how he treated her?

No, he decided. *I actually miss her, too. A lot.*

Without Win he'd shrivel up and die, yet he'd seen little of him lately as each pursued their respective assignments.

I should have told Storm we wanted to work together. He even asked!

Yet, if he went back and asked for that now, he'd look like either a quitter or a fool. Or, as Creena always said, a snurk. He covered his face with his hands, continuing to question the situation's connection to past decisions.

I wonder if I'll ever know what happened to them? If there was anything I could have done? And what about the Order. Could I have used that? Win said I'd know, but will I? I know one thing. I never should've left them alone. Never. I should have insisted they come with us. Why can't I ever do anything right the first time? Why do I have to learn everything the hard way?

He sensed movement, dropped his hands to his side and turned his head. Win stood in the door. It was seldom closed, his quarters situated in a low traffic area where others rarely came and claustrophobic even with the door open. Dirck sat up slowly and swung his feet to the floor.

"Hey," he said limply. "What brings you here?"

"Nothing much. Just wondered how you're doing." Win sat beside him and echoed his wilted pose, chin propped in his hands.

"How're you doing on the comm network?" Dirck asked evasively.

"All right, I guess. Kinda slow. We've been trying to get a signal scrambler together that modulates at random, making it tougher to trace." Win sighed. "Nothing else we can do. The INTEGRATOR knows where we are anyway, but this will make it harder to target the hardware and wipe it out."

"Hmmmmm," Dirck agreed absently.

"We're going out tomorrow to set it up."

The words clung to his mind like a requiem, bringing Dirck to full alert as violet again strobed his mind. His posture straightened, fingers gripping the edge of the cyll. "Where's the dish?" he asked.

Win shrugged. "A few kilometers away. On the opposite plateau."

"Our side?"

Win's pause said it all. "Not exactly."

Dirck swallowed, waiting for him to laugh and deny it. "You're kidding, right?"

"I wish."

Dirck looked at him directly for the first time, but Win's gaze remained fixed on the floor. His throat closed with unbidden fear. "Be careful," he said hoarsely. "I mean it."

"Yeah," Win replied, frowning. "We will."

* * *

The Bezarna Express

Laren slumped back in his seat, staring blankly at the seamless curvature of the passenger compartment. An unpadded bench followed the perimeter, except for the alcove that led to the sanicube and where they picked up their twice-daily rations. Sleeping cylls were stowed in the domed ceiling above, deploying automatically at sleepzone onset.

Whoever had designed it for Bezarna runs had been an obvious master at psychology as well as engineering. Six passengers remained including himself, three having already resorted to their captor's supposedly humane alternative to commit suicide via the airlock. If all prisoners opted for a fate that was known versus one that wasn't, then a perfectly good space vehicle would go to waste.

He straightened as a new thought chain developed. No doubt they were being watched, even with escape impossible. A successful escape you survived, he thought grimly, or it was pointless. Knowing the likes of Spoigan, Troy and Argo they probably tuned in using tachyonic video on a regular basis for entertainment purposes. They could even use such transmissions to scare others into submission by seeing how convicts en route to Bezarna dealt with their imminent demise.

Undoubtedly witnessing someone choose the airlock rather than never-ending yet meaningless life on a blackhole made for good INTEGRATOR motivational material.

So what if everyone resorted to that? What if they had an empty spacecraft worth nearly as much as a small battleship on a heading toward Bezarna? Would they kiss it goodbye or bring it back?

He'd been around long enough to know that finances were seldom a driver for a dictatorship. Nonetheless, the quality of the vehicle made more sense if it was retrievable. And if that was the case, if he could fool them into thinking everyone had checked out, preferring to explode their earthly remains in deep space rather than face an unknown and possibly worse fate, maybe there was roundtrip possibility after all.

His eyes met those of fellow Clique member, Jirhod Rhodus, seated on the opposite side. Rhodus was quite a bit older than Laren, perhaps even old enough to be his father, his once-blond hair interrupted with splatters of grey surrounding rounded features set with penetrating ice-blue eyes. An imposing man built more like an Erebusite than typical human, he'd lasted as long as he had because no one dared confront him. His demise had come when he'd insisted on an audit and recount from the election that brought INTEGRATION to Pi, one of only two remaining Neutral regions. As Deputy Territorial General he'd been vocal and effective, too much so, because he'd suddenly disappeared, a former Clique mystery now solved by his presence.

"You're thinking, Brightstar," the man said, his voice deep and resonant. "That's dangerous, you know."

Laren held his gaze and smiled, trying to figure out how to communicate, based on the premise they were being monitored. A moment later, he extracted his c-com from his breast pocket and psied his thoughts to it, then did the necessary coding to grant Rhodus access.

"Just playing a little mind game," he said innocently, handing over the device. "Want to play?"

* * *

Dirck's sleepzone alternated between fitful sleep and tense wakefulness followed by a taunting invasion of disturbing dreams. They weren't veridical, only vivid, ranging from undefinable abstractions to his sudden presence back in the Caverns.

A desolate silence echoed around him, no sign of previous occupation by anyone, human or bnolar. Even the luma were gone, forcing him to use a dim and heavy portalume, its desultory violet beam striking the blackness with weary reluctance. The paths were unfamiliar, winding in strange and unexpected directions, the passageway to Dununda gone. The grotto was barren, likewise the lab and commroom. What had once been their comfortable home had transformed to an underground hole haunted by shadow.

He wandered about the Grand Cavern, then from place to place, searching, calling, the surroundings familiar, yet not. At last, desperation rising, he ran to the Tank, hoping to find them or some evidence of their whereabouts. The chamber itself was gone, replaced by a bottomless pit, walls dark, absorbing light rather than reflecting it, not a shard of cristobalite in evidence. Eyes and heart aching, he cupped his hands and yelled into the depths, calling their names, the sound swallowed by silence.

He knelt at the edge and reached inside, but when he withdrew his hand it was gone, no longer attached to his arm. Horrified, he reached inside with the other, which disappeared as well. His attempt to throw himself into the abyss resulted in his body's complete disappearance, yet consciousness remained. From deep within, darkness resolved in an eerie glow that swelled upward and out, swamping him with purple waves that filled the Caverns with hideous fingers of irrevocable doom.

He knew he was dreaming, yet couldn't wake up, his consciousness locked in an endless, timeless, meaningless void until his sleepzone ended with activation of the cyll's built-in lighting. He opened his eyes and sighed, unrested and far from ready to face another day. He dressed reluctantly and dragged himself to the messhall, expecting to see Win, as always. They'd kept their mealzones consistent, regardless of where they were, their work schedule, or what they were doing, such that meeting was the norm more often than not. His friend never materialized, however, and he assumed Win and his work team had left early for their assignment.

Suddenly welcoming the distraction of work, he reported to the plant site and checked in, then told Storm he'd be in the commroom checking datalogs for fracture control methods for rotating machinery. It sounded good, though he wasn't sure what it was himself. The day passed quicker than expected, his attention lost in calculations for centripetal force versus rotational speed and its affect on structure.

Unfortunately, the relationship between the radius, mass and velocity was so complex he found himself hopelessly tangled in force, energy, and torque calculations until nothing remained but a miasma of confusion. At least velocity was based on the river itself, the mean speed more or less constant. Unless they wanted to move the site or change the diameter of the incoming channel, which oddly enough was a possibility, if all else failed.

Mind totally annihilated, he wandered off once more for the messhall, head pounding. There were no empty tables so he took his food back to the commroom and ate at Win's workdeck, logging in to review what he'd calculated so far. He scrolled through it vacantly, finally logging out in weary submission, too braindead to do any more. After finishing some stew concocted from an unrecognizable source, he wandered over to the duty officer to find out if Win had gotten back. The woman could have passed for half human, half Erebusite, but he knew the mix was genetically impossible, the latter silicon-based versus carbon. She was probably fifty, rigors of a hard life engraved on her face.

"Did the field team make it back yet?" he asked.

She studied him a moment with dark, deep-set eyes. "They're recalibrating the receiver now," she said, voice deep and gravelly. "We're scheduled for two more tests after that. If all goes well, they should be back within a few hours."

Noting the time on the digichronometer, Dirck nodded thanks and returned to his quarters, memories of the previous night's visions returning unbidden. A while later he left for Win's, needing the distraction of a change of scenery plus knowing he'd want to talk when he got back. His friend's place was cluttered, even more than his, mainly components and test equipment. Bored, he logged in to scan the day's double-i's.

Overt fighting had broken out in a few isolated areas, but troop movement was stable and logistics relatively quiet. He switched to S3 reports, finding nothing of note other than severe weather warnings along the terminator, the planet's light/dark interface. With one side in Dead Drop Winter and the Trailing Lats in their version of Opposition, the temperature differential drove tremendous convection currents that spawned huge PVs which sometimes traveled well into their region before dissipating. Fortunately, being underground they were relatively safe.

The prisoner listings still didn't contain any family members other than his father, concurrency reviews for the trigalactic region too remote to sustain interest. Fatigue weighted his eyelids first, then, after nodding off a few times, he curled up in Win's cyll, intending no more than a quick nap to rest his eyes, the unit's cushions humming in protest at the unfamiliar occupant. He woke up with a start after what seemed moments later, startled to see it was the time he usually excylled. Finding no evidence of Win's return, he went back to his quarters for clean clothes, then headed for the shower.

By the time he got to the messhall, he felt better, sleep having renewed body and mind alike. Ravenous, he ate a hearty breakfast, stopped by the nearest comcon to notify Storm that he'd be a few minutes late, then returned to the commroom.

A different duty officer was on console, a man with dark hair surrounding an expanding bald spot at the crown who appeared several years older than his father, deep worry lines permanently etched in his brow. Each of the people clustered around him stood quiet and somber. A few glanced up as Dirck approached, then dropped their gaze back to the projected image, postures a grim essay in body language.

"What's going on?" he asked.

"Weather," the DO answered, scowling as he adjusted his headset and maxed the volume.

"How'd the tests go?" Dirck asked.

No one answered.

"Is the test team back?"

The DO's steel-colored eyes silenced him as the man entered coordinates on the keypad embedded beside the console. The numbers on the monitor were converging to the location of the dish antenna and Dirck automatically assumed they were part of a test uncompleted the day before. The divergent numbers were erratic, jumping around in a way impossible for radio signals, scrambled or not, before eventually diminishing. The DO dropped his headset around his neck.

"The PV's been verified," he stated. "Sixteen-point-five kilos diameter, altitude twenty-three. Its eye crossed the worksite about o-six hundred. No evidence of life or hardware within twenty kilos."

One by one the group dispersed, leaving Dirck alone with the DO. Finally, he forced himself to voice the question lodged in his heart.

"The test team?" he asked.

The DO turned slowly and met his gaze as if it required supreme effort to do so.

"Affirmative, Captain."

* * *

<table>
<tr><td colspan="2" align="center">Integrator Central

TBA

Technical Breakthrough Advisory</td></tr>
<tr><td>TEAM: Communications</td><td>PROJECT: Encephalographic Access/Transmission</td></tr>
<tr><td>Date: DDW-112</td><td>Clearance: Top Secret</td></tr>
<tr><td colspan="2">Breakthrough/Milestone: Evidence of brain activity response to artificial stimulation from a distance exceeding a kilometer</td></tr>
<tr><td>Schedule Impact: Y/N? N</td><td>Days: NA</td></tr>
<tr><td colspan="2">SUMMARY: Use of available test subjects indicates potential for remote influence on thought queue via artificial stimulation in specific frequencies derived from individual's mindprint. While such effects have been accomplished at close range, cristobalite potentially extends this ability to a distance of 150 kilometers.</td></tr>
</table>

Many Happy Returns

irck didn't remember walking to the plant site, much less anything that happened along the way, only that when Storm met him inside the power station's cavernous beginnings, he meant it when he said he was okay and didn't need any time off. With that, he'd headed to his workdeck in the next cavity beyond Storm's office and pulled up everything he had on magnetic induction. He stared at it, trying to concentrate on where he'd left off the day before. His throat ached and chest still felt as if someone had kicked him, hard, the sense of loss momentous, but something inside drove him on.

His thoughts, however, refused to cooperate and wandered back to when he and Win had first met at the Supply Depot, back when he and 'Merapa were building the distillation unit to filter silt from the water at the ballome. He'd immediately been drawn to his confidence, decisiveness and quick wit, to say nothing of his rebellious attitude, antithetical to Dirck's propensity for Miran compliance. Back on Mira III, all Dirck and his friends ever worried about were how to have fun without getting caught, staying off the NCR Board, and passing the next exam. No wonder he didn't miss them. Such trivial concerns no longer mattered.

In comparison, he and Win had shared life and death situations from the start, between putting together the heat exchanger after his father's first arrest to orchestrating his subsequent rescue from territorial prison. He shuddered at the memory of their wild ride through Guipure Canyon when Win's piloting skills evaded the patrol veke which ultimately crashed, providing critical components for the heat exchanger. He smiled as he remembered Win's hysterical laughter when Dirck didn't recognize the compressor for what it was. What a day that had been, one of the worst of his life, yet oddly enough, somehow one of the best. What would he ever do without him?

The comcon blurred as tears filled his eyes and an emotional tsunami swelled in his chest. Then it was like he could hear Win yelling at him to man up and deal with it. And as always, even in his imagination, Win was right. The admonition's irony triggered a bitter laugh, which erupted sounding more like a snort as it released the sob caught in his throat. He wiped his eyes on his sleeve and dug around in one of the compartments in the workdeck for something to blow his nose on. Finding nothing, he got up and retrieved a rag from his toolbox, put it to good use, then took a series of deep breaths to clear his head.

Giving up would not be acceptable to anyone he was grieving. Not 'Merapa, not 'Merama, not Creena, not Deven and definitely not Win. Without his friend to kick him in the butt, he'd have to do it himself. So be it. If he was the only one left, then he'd have to work hard enough to make up for their loss. Giving up simply wasn't an option.

Concentration finally focused in resolve, he uttered a silent call to the *Benefics* for inspiration then tackled the turbine dilemma with renewed vigor. If the magnetite was too brittle for the radial stresses of high rotational speeds, then it would have to be designed within specifications. The heat exchanger had taught him something about the consequences of breaching such limitations. But knowing precious little about how they got electricity from mechanical energy in the first place, he changed tactics and buried himself in the basics of electromagnetic induction. How a conductor moving through a magnetic field could generate a current, or, conversely, how an electrical current could create a magnetic field, teetered precariously on the edge of comprehension, threatening to fry his brain even worse than before. He read on, determined, finally stumbling on a concept that struck like ten thousand volts.

It didn't matter which was the prime mover, the armature or the magnetic field. Meaning the magnetite didn't need to move at all.

Guardedly optimistic, he read on until he'd confirmed the premise beyond a doubt, then oscillated between feeling stupid and the elation of success. The struggle was far from over, the revelation necessitating an entirely new design, but at least the primary problem was partly solved.

He hunted down Storm, finding him in the fabrication area on the other side of a short tunnel a dozen meters beyond his makeshift office. The aquifer's thunderous roar replaced the clatter of machinery as he stepped inside, unable to restrain his smile.

"Hey, guess what?" he said, so consumed with excitement that he forgot to salute.

Storm's reddish eyes looked him up and down as if he'd grown an extra arm or maybe two. "What?" he finally responded, scrutinizing him as if he'd lost his orbit.

"I think I solved the magnetite problem."

Storm's huge mouth dropped open revealing a double row of incisors lining his lower jaw. "How?" he gasped.

Dirck explained, apologizing for taking so long to figure out something that turned out to be relatively simple. The congratulatory slams to his back would hurt for days and he wasn't sure what he thought of his superior's renewed expression of confidence, reiterating that he knew all along that he could do it, but over all he hadn't felt so good since longer than he could remember; probably when 'Merapa had been sworn in as Bryl's Minister of Regional Development.

The two sat down to sketch out preliminary plans for the new design and by the time he followed the precipitous path back to his quarters, tired but satisfied, it was far beyond the normal start of his sleepzone. The roaring aquifer surged beside him, the path less frightening from familiarity as he dodged wet spots and dark pools, pondering his progress.

While he wished 'Merapa were there to validate his theory plus help with the redesign, there was a certain pride in knowing he'd figured it out on his own. 'Merapa had always emphasized that assuming full credit if it was right was impossible without assuming full responsibility if it was wrong. But as he thought of 'Merapa some more, he realized he couldn't take all the credit after all.

His acknowledgement to the *Benefics* for their help was cursory, to the point, and directed to whomever or whatever might be listening. Too much intimacy with the divine in his current emotional state would most likely result in either uncontrollable anger or inconsolable grief, neither of which would help finish the job at hand.

He stopped by the messhall to grab a bite, finding it picked over, but still better than anything they'd ever had at the Caverns, then went to his quarters and cylled out. Sleep came quickly, overtaking him with a comfortable and welcome release from the day's cares. Conscious mind released from the rigors of scientific theory, it retreated to allow his subconscious to deal with the searing hurt. Again his dreams were vivid, but abstract and populated by those he never expected to see again. He tossed and turned, dream/wake interface unstable, psyche not sure where it was when the blackness changed texture.

He sat up, blinked hard and stared into the darkness, noting the LEDs on his comcon were burning undisturbed, the chronometer indicating he had a little over an hour remaining of sleepzone. He lay back down and stared into the dark as color gradually introduced itself, at first no more than the uncomfortably familiar violet glow, then gradually filling the room, increasing in intensity until he knew it wasn't a dream.

He sat up on the edge of his cyll, listening, but it was as if a wall of silence had invaded the room. The light escalated abruptly, flashed in a burst of energy, then disappeared as quickly as it had come.

Sound resumed, void gone, and in the darkness he sensed a presence; a stirring, the sound of breathing, a subtle whimper. He hit the light control above the cyll, braced for the unexpected, but was still astounded by what was there. For in his tiny room, as startled by the light as he was, were three familiar figures, a 'troid, and a vegemal, releasing their huddle on one another with a startled, disoriented gasp.

"We made it!" Deven exclaimed, first to recover. "And right on target, too! Hi, Dirck! You beat us back."

Seeing three of the people he loved most in the universe appear from the grave would have been a shock, even if he hadn't just come back from a dark and troubling dream. All he could do was stare and blink while facts struggled to resolve. Deven's hug brought him to full wakefulness and soon he found himself overcome while embracing each in turn with an intensity born of suspected loss.

"Where have you been?" he finally exclaimed, wiping his eyes with a shaky hand. "Do you have any idea how worried I've been? I thought you were all dead!"

"It was close, but we got away just in time," Creena answered. "What do you mean, where've we been? We came here straight from the Caverns."

Dirck gathered the implications in the context of his own cristoviatic experience and came up blank. "Just what I said," he replied. "When Win and I used the Tank it was instantaneous. I've been back for over a week. What took so long?"

The trio's expressions became delayed reflections of what his had been a moment before. Creena examined a strange device in her hand that looked like a bowlbush shell lined with a mosaic of crystals, then sat down on the edge of his cyll, staring alternately between it and him.

"What *is* that?" he asked finally.

"Our psitenna. What we used to talk with you earlier. But it looks as if it does more than transmit psi. It apparently has a fourth dimensional element, too. We left the Caverns right after Deven sent you back."

"What? You traveled forward in time?" Dirck gasped, the query at once a statement and a question.

"That confirms why you didn't remember talking to me!" Creena said to Deven. "I *did* go back in time!"

"What's in that thing? Cristobalite?" Dirck asked.

"Not entirely. Most of it is, but the crystal in the center is something new we call devenite. Deven found it in a cavity near the downed transport. It's a lot more powerful than ordinary cristobalite."

"No kidding."

"Let's get Win. He needs to see it and help figure out the time phase element."

"We can't," Dirck replied, staring at the floor.

"Why not?" Creena asked. "He won't care if we wake him up for this."

"It's not that simple, Creena." He took a breath and looked her in the eye, not sure he was ready to admit it to himself much less anyone else.

"Why not?"

She had that look of determination that he hated, yet this time it triggered compassion. "Because he's not here," he said softly.

"Where is he?" she persisted, caution gathering in her eyes.

"No one knows."

Silence settled like precipitated lead. "What do you mean, *no one knows*?" she asked slowly, expression gathering into a frown.

He shoved down his rising emotions, trying to ignore 'Merama's hand on his shoulder. "He and the entire comm setup team are missing. A PV crossed the worksite. The S3s found no sign of life for twenty kilos."

"Oh, Dirck, I'm so sorry," Creena said softly. Her horrified expression lasted but a moment before shifting to hope. "If he's still alive, maybe we can reach him with the psitenna."

"Good idea," 'Merama agreed. "At least then we'll know."

"Which way's the site?" Creena asked.

Still stunned, Dirck pointed toward the door. Creena positioned the device accordingly. A violet vector materialized from within what looked like a crystal-lined bowlbush root, but it was hitting the side. She adjusted its position until the beam shot out in the direction it apparently wanted to go.

"Code Master, this is Voyager. Do you copy?" She paused for a moment then looked pensive, probably mentally repeating the call.

Everyone jumped when a response blared into their minds.

Copy that, Voyager! Where are you? Are you okay?

I'm at the base, Code Master, and doing fine. How 'bout you?

A little chilly, Voyager.

Dirck signaled for the psitenna and Creena handed it over. "How do I use this thing?"

"Just hold it in front of you, make sure the violet beam isn't hitting the sides, and either talk or think what you want to say. Thinking works a little better."

"What's your bearing from the worksite, Code Master?" Dirck asked aloud.

Hey, Detailer. Good to hear your voice. About thirty seven kilometers at two-seven-four degrees.

Dirck grinned. "We'll be right there. How many are there?"

Three of us.

"How much life support is left?"

Around an hour. Maybe less.

"On our way, Code Master."

Copy that. And hurry!

Dirck switched on his comcon, but before he could enter Storm's code, the Zinaanian was at his door wearing the expression of someone who'd been awakened in a less than pleasant way. He wore a night-camo t-shirt that clung to his muscular shoulders and scale-covered arms, then fell loosely below his waist, pants askew, as if donned in a hurry.

"What's going on?" he demanded, scrutinizing the others with less than friendly, red spherical eyes. "Who are these people?"

Dirck snapped to attention and saluted. Their relationship had been casual before, but this time there was no question he was acting commander. "My family, sir," Dirck said. "They just got in."

Storm's expression didn't soften. "How? Why didn't they come through security?"

"Cristoviatic teleportation, sir. And we've made contact with Win."

"I know," he said. It wasn't always easy to read a Zinaanian, but Storm was clearly shaken. "I heard every word. The entire base did. What's going on?"

Dirck held up the psitenna. "Experimental technology, sir. A research project my father started that my sister and Win continued after he, uh, left." He introduced everyone, then nervously awaited the next directive. Storm's posture relaxed slightly, anger ebbing.

"There's one problem, Dirck," he said, "Who else heard your transmission? That site was outside our boundaries. I'm not sure we can risk deploying rescue vehicles when the entire planet may know what's going on, right down to the coordinates."

Creena waved her hand, anxious to speak. Storm folded heavy arms and nodded consent. "Its direction is fairly focused. If anyone else heard it, they were probably within only a few degrees. When you speak aloud, it isn't private, but it is with telepathy. The only ones who should have heard it besides Win would probably be line-of-sight. He must have spoken aloud when he responded so the entire base heard it, but it should have been confined to a few degrees."

Storm took the device from Dirck, frowning, as his spherical eyes examined it closely, moving independently across every millimeter of its crystal-lined interior. "What's the range?" he asked.

"We don't know," Creena said. "We haven't been able to test it yet to see if there's any attenuation with distance."

Storm rotated the psitenna pensively for several moments, then stared past them with a frown of heavy consideration.

"I'll be happy to go get them myself, sir," Dirck volunteered.

Storm's shoulders relaxed, but his scowl remained. "Denied. Our usual team will handle it. They're trained in high-risk rescues, emergency medical procedures and damage control." With that, he sent the summons via the comcon, then set his attention on his newest recruits.

"I apologize for my entry and formality. That was no way to greet the Commander's family," he said, smiling at last. "Welcome to Apoca Canyon. We'll discuss your research at our next briefing. I want to know everything about this technology's current status." Then he nodded farewell and left as abruptly as he'd arrived.

"Your commander?" Creena asked.

"Yeah. Acting, anyway. Yours too, now. He's usually not like that. He was just shaken up."

"He had a right to be," Creena replied. "Comm research involves a lot of risk."

"Yeah," Dirck said dryly. "So does war."

After giving 'Merama and Deven directions to the messhall, he and Creena turned on the comcon to compile Storm's briefing. A little over an hour later, Win returned. They stopped long enough to hear about his rescue, which had been uneventful with no indication the opposition was aware of the operation. After a brief round of rejoicing at their unexpected reunion, they returned to task, Win to check in officially while Dirck and Creena continued putting together the briefing.

Dirck leaned back in his chair, watching his sister as she noted everything they'd discovered so far about the crystals. Her dark hair was shiny, falling past shoulders which looked much straighter than he recalled. She didn't look like a kid anymore, act like one, either. He cringed when he thought of what his reaction had been when she'd first contacted him from the Caverns. During his brief conversation using the psitenna to talk to Win, he'd experienced more than words. In addition, he'd felt his friend's relief and elation that rescue was imminent. Beyond a doubt, that first time Creena had felt his negative reaction. If there had ever been a time he deserved to be called a snurk, it was then. But she'd never said a thing.

He watched her enter a few more lines of data, then prop her chin in her hands, brow tense with deep thought. An irresistible urge to hug her, even apologize, moved through him, but he let it pass, unheeded. After that, gratitude for everyone's safety warmed within him until his happiness was nearly tangible, a living entity he'd never experienced before.

The previous day he'd had no one besides the other Cliquers, most of whom he didn't really know. During that time he'd found unexpected peace in at least having them, knowing he was part of something important, and for the first time since his arrival, actually feeling comfortable in his uniform. He might not have been capable of saving Cyraria single-handedly, but he could do something no one else could to defeat the INTEGRATOR. Alone and hurting or not, he would honor his family's name.

And now they were back, unharmed, trailing hope in their wake. There was only one shadow remaining, the one irreversible failure he expected to follow him the rest of his life.

Unless, perhaps...

She'd never given up, he could tell, in spite of all the hassle he'd given her at the Caverns. His pride uttered a momentary protest, a reminder that if she was right, then he was wrong.

Again.

But as he watched her panning through 'Merapa's notelog a different facet of pride came forward, trailing sincere admiration. She had courage, enough to pursue what she believed in, regardless of any pressure to do otherwise.

Just like 'Merapa.

He'd never seen it as a virtue before, only another noncompliance. But if she could figure out a way to get their father back, he'd owe her forever. Because no matter how hard he'd tried to suppress it, he knew the longing for them all to be together again would never go away.

R&D

The chamber that served as their lab was so huge their voices echoed. Electrical cable that delivered power to racks of hardware criss-crossed the stone walls, then snaked upward to an array of lights secured to the ceiling with large hooks. One table along the far wall was loaded with test equipment, another at the room's center stood empty, except for 'Merapa's notelog, a comcon, the psitenna, and the small pile of devenite crystals they'd fortunately brought along. While this lab was much better equipped than the niche at the Caverns, its resources were useless until they increased their understanding, which so far hadn't occurred, as evidenced by the three individuals surrounding it in pensive silence.

Creena's mind was uncomfortably blank, unsure what to do first. Whether it was leftover stress at her commando encounter, space lag from being lost in time, or simply the fact her arrival didn't coincide with her zones didn't matter, there was too much to do to indulge in a nap. They'd been there only a little over an hour, yet it felt like days, making her wonder if the experience had entirely skewed her sense of time. She propped her feet on the stool's top rung, elbows on the table, staring at Win and Dirck across from her, hoping they'd have some idea. She straightened attentively when Win shook his head and sighed.

"Talking aloud versus using psi seems to control who receives the transmissions, which is great, assuing that's always the case. Teleporting is another matter entirely, especially with that time-shifting element," he stated, eyebrows cocked in one of his this-is-impossible scowls. His hair hung loose to his shoulders, stringy and damp after showering to warm up upon his return. He shook his head in emphasis, tucking a limp strand behind his ear. "If we can't figure out how to control the time factor, it could do more harm than good."

She fought a smile, encouraged. Win had a strong instinct for whether something was feasible or not and didn't waste time on things that weren't, yet he always started out the same way, declaring it couldn't be done. Maybe his skepticism was a form of weighing the odds starting with the cons. If they couldn't be eliminated, then it wasn't worth the effort; not a bad approach. Everything he'd attempted so far had succeeded, including surviving sub-freezing weather during a PV. It could easily be explained as luck, but Creena knew he didn't believe in that, either. He, like 'Merapa, thought everyone determined their own destiny, an opinion she was beginning to share. If a solution existed, it wouldn't just appear. They'd have to find it.

Or else.

"And I haven't the foggiest notion how to analyze something that isn't electromagnetic," he went on. "We don't even have a solid theory. Of any kind! No idea whatsoever why or how these crystals work. Which leaves trial and error. And errors could be fatal."

"Not trying will cost us, too," Creena said quietly, glancing at Dirck. His eyes met hers and held, more pleading than defensive.

Win's fingers drummed the workdeck, frown gradually relaxing. "You're right," he said. "But if the INTEGRATOR finds out what we're using to contact, much less bring back, your father, it'll be disastrous. In this case, R&D doesn't stand for research and development. More like risk and destruction."

Creena stared at the heap of devenite, knowing at this point it was the only possible advantage the Clique had. As if sharing her thoughts, Win reached over and picked one up, caressing it pensively between his fingers.

"So what do we do first?" Dirck asked. "I've held this up long enough. We need to get started and quit worrying about whether or not we can do it. We'll never know until we try."

"Quit worrying? You?" Win said. "Ha! If we were still at the Caverns I'd think you were standing in your positive node or something."

Dirck's eyes met his. "Maybe I've learned a few things."

"Maybe I have, too," Win replied, his mouth taut and eyes distant. "You know," he added quietly. "There were six on that test team. Only three of us made it back."

He exhaled sharply, as if to expel the harrowing experience, after which his demeanor slid from troubled back to his usual determination. "All right. Enough of that. What is, is. Okay. The first thing we need to do is sort and classify our data. Let's see what we have."

A short time later a simple table stared back from the notelog.

CRYSTAL TYPE	CHRONOVIATIC (Time Shifting)	CRISTOVIATIC (Real-time Teleportation)	PSICOMM
cristobalite	?	yes	yes
devenite	?	?	yes
combined	yes	?	yes

"So. What do we have?" Win asked.

"It's hard to tell," Dirck answered. "We don't have enough information."

"Maybe, maybe not," Win said. "Something about it suggests synergy. The combination gives more than either component alone."

"Whenever we used the Tank we never time shifted, so we can be reasonably sure cristobalite isn't chronoviatic," Dirck said.

"Not necessarily," Win argued. "Maybe if we'd focused on a different time it would have worked, but it never entered my mind. Transfer was instantaneous, but that was what we expected. If it responds entirely to thoughts, maybe it can timeshift. So we don't know."

"When Aggie looked at 'Merapa's calculations back at the Caverns she said they had a collapsed time tensor," Creena commented. "Which explained why transmissions were instantaneous. But it also implies they could go forward or backward as well."

"Good input," Win acknowledged. "This could also explain the timestamp discrepancy we discovered when Dirck and I first got here."

"Right," Dirck agreed, quickly giving Creena the rundown on what they'd found earlier, which they'd eventually abandoned for more pressing matters.

"It's certainly apparent the combination can be chronoviatic," Win stated.

"Definitely. But when we left the Caverns we only focused on the place," Creena stated. "All that mattered was getting away from those commandos." She shuddered at the memory, which was still too vivid for comfort.

"When you used the psitenna outside the Tank what happened?" Win asked.

"It worked for psicomm," Creena answered.

"That's all?"

"That's all. As far as we know. That's all we'd used it for at that point. We didn't even think of trying anything else."

"Then what happened? When did it go chronoviatic?"

"When Deven was in the Tank and psiported me over."

"What was different?" Win asked.

She closed her eyes, recalling every detail. "I was wet. Cold. Scared. I was trapped and didn't know what to do. Deven used the psitenna and the next thing I knew, I was there. But he wasn't. And when he got there, he didn't remember the conversation, much less bringing me there. The only explanation was that I went back in time."

Dirck entered 'Merama's code into the comcon. "Let's get them in here and see if they remember anything else."

The two arrived moments later. Win filled them in, then directed another question at Creena. "You're sure you didn't intentionally think of the past or future?" Creena shook her head "Okay. It apparently wasn't your focus, at least consciously. How did you feel right before it worked?"

"Scared! I just wanted to be somewhere safe. A commando was right there!" Her heart accelerated with a fearful adrenaline rush at the recent memory, hand instinctively on her chest. Her mother stepped over and put a comforting arm around her.

"A negative emotion," Dirck stated. "So I wonder if that means the chronoviatic effect also went in the negative direction?"

"But we went into the future when we came here," Creena noted.

"How did you feel then?" Win asked.

"Both excited and scared. But somehow I knew everything was going to be okay. And we were going to be together again. At least most of us."

"How about you two?" Win directed at 'Merama and Deven.

"Pretty much the same," 'Merama replied while Deven nodded in agreement.

"Positive emotions for the most part," Dirck said. "And you went forward. It looks as if there could be a correlation."

"Maybe. There's also the fact that the Tank wasn't working right," Win added. "We don't know why that happened, either. Maybe there was something wrong with it that caused the time shift "

"I think it lost power because Enoch was gone," Deven suggested.

"That, plus there could be another reason," 'Merama said with a sigh. "All the negative energy. There'd been a lot of contention for some time."

Creena eyed Dirck solemnly as the statement struck like a meteorite, his expression reflecting her own. If they hadn't been arguing so much, everything could have been a lot different, more so than she cared to consider.

"That's right," Deven agreed, dark eyes wide. "Enoch said something about that, too."

"Right. That's probably why the bnolar wouldn't do anything immoral or illegal," Dirck commented. "Negativity must neutralize the positive energy and inhibit its functionality. The fact it lost power was undoubtedly our own fault."

"Okay, what is, is," Win said, again using his favorite phrase, sparing them any further condemnation. "Is-squared. It's important information, but there's nothing to be gained getting all whiney and sorry about it. Let's just look at the data. Positive and negative energy are probably a factor, plus it appears that both crystals respond to psi. Based on experience let's take a guess at those blank cells."

The results brought neither surprise nor revelation.

CRYSTAL TYPE	CHRONOVIATIC (Time Shifting)	CRISTOVIATIC (Location Transfer)	PSICOMM
cristobalite	no	yes	yes
devenite	yes	no	yes
combined	yes	yes	yes

"It looks like a basic synergistic relationship," Win stated. "What we really need right now, though, is secure comm with the other bases and psicomm has definite possibilities. The first thing we need to know is how the sender and receiver tune into each another."

"When we used the Tank for psicomm it was always private," Dirck said.

"So what limited the band?" Win asked.

Dirck shrugged. "It went to whomever we wanted it to. No one else. At least as far as we know."

"Why don't we ask Thyron and Igni?" Creena suggested. "Since they're both telepathic, they may be able to shed more light on it."

"Good idea," Win agreed.

"What about Aggie?" Dirck asked.

"Where is she?" Creena asked, looking around. "She's usually here."

"She's verifying the L-DISA code I wrote for the surveillance people," Win replied. "But if you think she can help, I'll bring her back."

Creena frowned, thinking. "She might. She couldn't hear Thyron until he put her back together on Terra when he did something to her communications package. Finding out what he did might be helpful. But we can just ask Thyron, if she's too busy, since he did the mod."

"That would be pretty useful information," Win stated. "What she's doing is pretty important, though, so let's see if Thyron can explain it. At least to you, since I can't hear him, either," he added with a hint of sarcasm, then frowned, looking dejected. "I'm probably the last person who should be working this, since I'm apparently not psi-sensitive."

"Don't be a snurk," Dirck replied. "You heard us with the psitenna."

"Yeah, but only then, when everyone else heard it, too."

"Whatever," Dirck mumbled, then left to fetch the vegemal, who not only didn't have a pager code but would take too long to shuffle there on his own, anyway.

Meanwhile, Creena and Deven recounted their earlier experiments with the devenite for Win, which had established that messages were private, except when spoken aloud, the same as when they'd contacted Win after he and the test team had been caught in the storm.

By then Igni had joined them, Dirck arriving to set Thyron on the workdeck a moment later, where the vegemal settled with a somewhat dramatic flutter. Now that he had a steady source of light he'd come out of hibernation, but a trace of limpness lingered at his leaf tips.

"We need your input about how telepathy works," Win directed at Igni. "How do you tune into a specific individual?"

"Formicidae culture broadcast to all of colony. Thoughts merge and exchange as group, then operate as single intelligence. No cause to limit," the insectoid replied. "Individuals in colony virtually do not exist."

"Can other telepathic beings tune into a colony?" Dirck asked.

"No. Psi frequency hardcoded in colony DNA."

"But you can converse with other telepathic beings, like Thyron," Creena said. "How did you do that? Or could anyone or anything with psi ability pick up the conversation?"

"Can receive focused information outside colony frequency if beckoned. Outside contact, when accepted, creates ability to connect in same range."

"Why do you think your telepathic powers are limited on Cyraria?" Creena asked. "I thought psi waves obeyed different laws and could penetrate matter."

"Multiple factors," Igni responded. "Psi not affected by matter, but distorted or neutralized by negative energy. Adapted psi not as strong as colonial, where each individual contributes to network strength."

"So if your colony were here you could hear them, even though you can't hear anyone else?" Dirck asked.

"Concede," Igni replied. "Genetics key factor. Common DNA. Those in family similar to colony, more susceptible to each other. Or sometimes those with emotional bond."

The *flora peda telepathis* rustled his leaves, the usual preamble to speaking on any issue.

> [When on Terra we were stuck
> Getting off entailed some luck.
> Inspections by the HIO
> Led the way for us to go.
> If that had not been possible
> More options were available.
> A single target need not be set
> Or sent to someone I had met.
> The plea could ping the cosmic soup
> To any psi receptive group.]

"Interesting," Dirck said pensively. "I wouldn't think you could do that."

"What did he say?" Win prompted.

"Sorry," Dirck said. "He said that when he needed to send a help signal from Terra, he could have transmitted a generic one, to anyone who was psi-sensitive."

"That's kind of scary, actually," Creena said, frowning. "That could have alerted some bounty hunter. Or the INTEGRATOR."

> [Only friendlies would be invited
> Them alone their psyches lighted.]

"So that suggests you can send a message to anyone receptive to psi, say even a group, which can be limited, possibly by their energy or frequency level. Apparently the sender decides," Creena said, getting nods from everyone except Igni, whose translator crackled and Win, who was more direct.

"Would someone *please* clue me in?" he pleaded and Creena complied.

"Wow!" Dirck responded. "Apparently there are open channels, private channels or a combination of both, all determined by the originator. Interesting. If that's true, then limiting who receives it is not only theoretically possible, but could be easier than we think."

"That's certainly good news," Win agreed.

"Do you filter it consciously?" Creena asked. Thyron fluttered his leaves in an obvious negative response.

"So how exactly do you send a message?" Win asked.

"Telepathy operates under force of will," Igni said. "Focus thoughts on target, then project. Target senses psychic nudge and tunes in. Cannot describe, hard to teach, must feel and connect."

"So you either have it or you don't," Win suggested. "And apparently I don't."

The Arcturian's huge head nodded. "Concede."

"What do you think, Thyron?" Creena asked. "Is that how it works for vegemals, also?"

> [Telepathy is psi connection
>
> mind to mind without deception.
>
> Some receive it, others not
>
> Depending on the mind you've got.]

"Okay," Creena said. "That confirms what Igni said, that you either have it or you don't."

His leaves whispered again in apparent protest, dissent in his orb-like eyes.

> [That's not exactly how it be
>
> Is not all heredity.
>
> Your mind can be by you controlled
>
> Reception can be made a goal.
>
> Implants also do exist
>
> Psi reception to assist.]

Before Win could ask, Creena explained. "He said it's not just genetic. It can be learned. And there are implants to help, too. Right, Thyron?"

> [Any conscious entity
>
> Can build susceptibility.
>
> Receiving psi can thus be done
>
> With training and some practice runs.]

"It can be learned, but you need training and practice," she translated.

Dirck snickered. "Right. Like when Creena was learning mutogueronian."

She groaned and covered her face, embarrassed again by the humiliating mistakes she'd made when she'd first met Bryl, accidentally saying she had to use the sanicube instead of greeting her properly. Win, meanwhile, was grinning, while 'Merama and Deven wore questioning looks, having not been there at the time.

Dropping her hands, she quickly pushed the discussion back on track. "Do vegemals communicate with each other like formicidians do? Or is it more one to one?"

> [Vegemals' ingrown ability
> Works with any sensibility.
> Animal, mineral or vegetable
> All that matters is its will.
> Can broadcast news to all concerned
> Or limit to a single fern.
> Life will always find a way
> To transfer what it wants to say.]

"It sounds like they can communicate with just about anything, plant, animal, or even rocks, one way or another," Creena translated. "Apparently the only limit is the ability, or perhaps willingness, to receive the message."

"That explains how little plants can move big rocks!" Deven stated. "They tell them to get out of their way!"

Before anyone else could comment, Thyron fluttered, eyes round with enthusiastic agreement, leaving everyone momentarily stunned.

"I don't understand why I could hear you and Dirck with the psitenna, but I can't hear Thyron," Win stated, a puzzled look on his face. "Isn't it all the same?"

"Frequencies and amplitude not same, like radio waves," Igni stated. "Hear some, not others, depend on channel, but can develop sensitivity. Psitenna amplifies to awareness range."

"Cristobalite and devenite are apparently compatible with psi. Somehow they operate in a complementary way," Win mused aloud. "But don't forget the energy originates with the sender, not the crystals. They just reflect, amplify, and transmit it."

"Focusing may be the key factor," Creena noted, remembering the violet beam's behavior. "Psi transmission is probably omnidirectional. It's stronger when sent in only one, finely tuned direction. When I first contacted you, Win, did the others hear me, too?"

"Yes." He laughed. "We looked at each other as if we were losing our minds. The fact we all heard it was actually a good thing, though, since it confirmed it was real. Did you intend to send it to everyone?"

Creena frowned pensively, trying to remember. "I was mainly thinking of you, but realized there could be others. But the main thing is that I spoke aloud, at least the first time." Her frown deepened. "But on Terra, Thyron couldn't hear me very well *unless* I spoke out loud. Why was that?"

> [Just as air carries sound
>
> Energy to psi is bound
>
> No two planets are the same
>
> So technique will often change.]

"Oh, that reminds me, Thyron. What did you do so Aggie could hear you?"

"Hello?" Win grumbled, arms akimbo.

"He said it varies planet to planet, based on its energy, which explains why Igni's isn't working here," she explained. "Go ahead, Thyron."

> [Since the 'troid could talk to bugs
>
> It only took a tiny tug
>
> To add a channel to her rece ver
>
> Making her a psi believer.]

She quickly explained it was a simple mod based on the 'troid's ability to communicate with insects.

Igni nodded. "Makes much sense," he stated. "Many of Hymenoptera order use psi, such as wasps and bees."

"Besides DNA, like Igni mentioned, there must be some inherent intelligence or ability that psi has to find the recipient," Dirck mused. "Or perhaps encrypt it, so only the person on the receiving end can understand. I suppose all thought energy is lurking out there somewhere in the cosmic soup. If we picked up all of it, it would just be a lot of psychic noise."

"I wonder how psi ties in with the concept of positive and negative energy," Creena mused aloud. "If, like Thyron said, you can send it on an open channel to several in a given frequency range, there could be a correlation."

"Seems like it would, since there are positive and negative thoughts," Dirck replied.

"If that's the case, that could explain all the negative spikes we encountered coming here from Mira III," Creena said. "They could indicate how the INTEGRATOR is gaining power across the galaxy."

"That makes a lot of sense," Win stated. "And if these crystals have the power to control or perhaps increase that energy, it's critical that we develop the technology first, so we understand it well enough to develop countermeasures."

"It would be especially dangerous if they figure out a way to broadcast to large groups all at once," 'Merama said, the worry crease between her eyebrows punctuating her statement.

"Yes," Igni agreed, nodding. "Mass transmission could develop strength of colony with all on same frequency. Much control be gained."

Creena noticed that everyone's expression reflected her thoughts regarding the consequences if the INTEGRATOR perfected the technology first; Igni had vocalized a very real concern.

"Well, at least with the psitenna it seems to be private, making it safe to contact 'Merapa," she said, wanting to end their session on a more positive note. But before they aimed it toward Bezarna, there was one more thing they had to do:

Convince Storm.

* * *

<table>
<tr><td colspan="2" align="center">Integrator Central

TBA

Technical Breakthrough Advisory</td></tr>
<tr><td>TEAM: Communications</td><td>PROJECT: Encephalographic Access/Reception</td></tr>
<tr><td>Date: DDW-123</td><td>Clearance: Top Secret</td></tr>
<tr><td colspan="2">Breakthrough/Milestone: Keyword reception in response to remote stimulation</td></tr>
<tr><td>Schedule Impact: Y/N? Y</td><td>Days: Unknown - Favorable</td></tr>
<tr><td colspan="2">SUMMARY: Remote stimulation of test subjects in mindprint specific frequencies has resulted in the reception of keywords based on psi frequency of cerebral activity. Progress expected soon with regard to detecting and translating entire thought chain.</td></tr>
</table>

Discoveries

The Bezarna Express

Laren was convinced he was on to something that gave him a chance. A small one, perhaps, but a chance nonetheless. It wasn't like he had anything to lose or better to do. Furthermore, he'd always believed few things, if any, were impossible.

Fortunately, Rhodus bought into his scheme. Unfortunately, two others had taken the airlock option, bringing their number down to four, but that could work to his advantage as well. Using his c-com, he'd been able to hack into the ship's sensor system and record the jettisons. All he had to do now was fool the video and audio into thinking the passenger compartment was empty, then repeat the signals. If his theory was correct, at that point the ship would automatically change course and return to Cyraria. If he was wrong, he was no worse off than before.

Or was he? He paused when a flash of doubt fired in his gut, but dismissed it as quickly as it came. How could things possibly get worse? Furthermore, it simply wasn't in him to sit there and die quietly like a martyr. That wasn't who or what he was, never had been.

If only he knew whether he could trust the ones who remained. Rhodus he knew was a loyal Clique member. He was no problem. The other two, he wasn't sure. For all he knew, one or even both could be guards, making sure no one onboard did exactly what he planned to do. Neither had confided in him earlier when they were all in the acceptance phase regarding their fate, which was a clue in and of itself. But neither had interfered when he was tearing the instrument panel apart, either.

One of them seemed too emotionless considering their impending demise, a Pyxisite named Sa'ata who was stocky, not as big as Rhodus but probably younger. Like others of his race, he had skin reminiscent of tarnished copper, little hair and lashless, deepset, round, feline-like amber eyes that missed nothing. He'd never said much about why he was there or what his offense had been, only implied he'd gotten on the wrong side of someone high up the political food chain. Where his loyalties might lie was unknown. If he was pro-INTEGRATION, he could conceivably turn on him once they got back, perhaps to redeem himself and get reestablished in his former position. The man clearly hated certain individuals within INTEGRATION leadership, but never spoke against the political structure or ideology. He could easily be a guard with a phony story.

No, he couldn't trust him.

The other one, a whiney little human named Merik, paced too much, all the while wringing his hands. Somehow he doubted anyone of that caliber was capable of doing anything worthy of exile; however, he didn't seem a likely guard, either. He, also, had never fully 'fessed up to what he'd done. Everything about him screamed coward. But cowards were dangerous. Or maybe it was all an act and overdone at that. Physically, he was no challenge. Laren knew he could take him out with a swift kick to the jaw. Then hopefully, he and Rhodus could handle Sa'ata. Unless he had a concealed weapon, which was a definite possibility.

Clearly, this was not a simple operation. Getting back to Cyraria was only half the battle. They still needed to get out of the ship in one piece. But he'd have time to worry about that once it changed course. With luck, maybe he could redirect it to a remote location, perhaps within retrieval distance from Apoca Canyon.

Sure, why not? Dream big! The probability of success was pitifully low, but would definitely be zero if he didn't try.

So he had work to do. Like figuring out how to upload the video and audio feeds to indicate an empty cabin along with more jettisons. But how many? If the other two were guards, he might only need to fake two, his own and Rhodus', not four. But that was a gamble without knowing.

Would the ship change course on its own with two more gone or would one or both of these two, assuming they were guards, execute a failsafe code to initiate return? He could always fake two more and see what happened. Furthermore, if the other two *were* guards, what was their contingency plan if everyone didn't check-out early? Would they be forcibly escorted to the exit? Sa'ata was certainly capable of that, especially if he had some sort of weapon. As far as Laren was concerned, being magged was preferable to self-annihilating in deep space, anyway.

No, this was definitely not simple with so many unknowns and variables. And time was running out. Sitting there worrying about all the things that could go wrong could easily occupy him until it was too late. Until Cyraria, his instincts had always served him well. Now that he was off that miserable planet, maybe they would again. If nothing else, his mind was amazingly clear. Almost too clear. It had amazed him all along that he'd remained so calm in view of the circumstances. Was he still in denial? Or, like the prison break, was this also simply not his time?

A new wave of optimism fired through him, as if to validate the thought's truth. If that was the case, the only thing he could do wrong would be nothing. He made eye contact with Rhodus and snuck him a dim smile as he extracted his c-com from his breast pocket, grateful that it hadn't been in its usual place on his workdeck when he'd been arrested and hauled off. After that, Argo had been in such a hurry to get him onboard the Bezarna Express that the man hadn't even checked him for weapons or anything else.

The TG probably thought that nothing Laren could have on him while working in his lab on Nifeir could cause a problem, once his prisoner was secured on the ship, which had some level of validity. In fact, Laren actually did have a lasomag there, but it was locked away under the assumption that if he needed it he would have had some warning. It wasn't like anyone could really sneak up on him at the moon base with its transparent dome and airlock entries controlled from the inside. He'd been expecting Argo and welcomed him in, expecting to recruit another Clique member, rather than being arrested on the spot for treason. He frowned grimly, berating himself again for assuming their intelligence methods were superior and thus not listening to Dirck's report more carefully.

But he hadn't, and regrets changed nothing.

His c-com, however, might. At this point it held as much promise as anything, even if it did no more than keep his mind off his impending fate.

Long before his arrest, his clearance level had allowed him to download Epsilon's numerous databases, which knew everything about everyone. All he needed was the passenger manifest and flight plan for their vehicle. Then figuring out who or what the others happened to be would be like downing Lemitini. He set his jaw with determination, then focused on what he might be able to discover.

* * *

Deven was so excited he could hardly stand it. Another cavern! How cool was that? He'd loved exploring their previous home, all the niches, cavities, and weird formations, especially when Enoch was around, plus naming them according to how they fired his imagination. He wasn't sure what he'd find in Apoca Canyon, but couldn't wait to find out.

Breakfast in the messhall had been absolutely awesome. All his favorite foods were there, plus some he'd never heard of or seen before. Genour was pretty boring after a while and so was bowlbush root, but this was spectacular! He'd wanted to try everything, until 'Merama had reminded him it would still be there tomorrow and he didn't have to try everything at once. He couldn't remember the last time he'd felt so stuffed, but it felt good. And now he got to explore!

'Merama, Dirck and Creena were busy talking to Win in that big lab not far from where their quarters were being set up down from Dirck's. They were obviously occupied talking about the crystals, which was the perfect time to slip away, after telling 'Merama he'd be looking around, of course.

"Okay, sweetness," she'd said, "Don't go too far."

He nodded solemnly yet smiled inside, knowing her definition of "too far" differed greatly from his. He grabbed a portalume from Dirck's quarters and then paused in the doorway, deciding which way to go.

He already knew the way to the messhall, so the next most interesting place would be in the opposite direction. The main base was loaded with people, vehicles, military stuff, noise, funny smells and light. Nothing interesting there, especially since much of the immense cave had been further expanded with machines that melted rock or dumped it outside in the canyon, making it more like a monstrous building and therefore boring.

It was much more interesting to see how the caves looked in their natural state. 'Merapa had told him quite a bit about what it was like to be a terralogist and to understand what made planets work. Mira III was basically a big rock, but most planets were alive with a variety of forces that made life possible. And life was what made them interesting. There had been a few creatures in the Caverns like lizards and fish that glowed in the dark. It amazed him that those in the deeper sections didn't have eyes, yet seemed to get around just fine. Bats and birds that lived inside the Caverns, yet spent part of the day outside, went into long-term hibernation during seasons with extreme weather, which on Cyraria was most of the time. But creatures that lived in the caves exclusively never knew the difference whether it was light or dark, hot or cold, wet or dry. Their environment never changed.

The path heading away from all the activity looked as if it had been widened and smoothed out a little, but other than that, undisturbed. Power cables littered the floor, lighting placed at intervals with only a few steps of darkness inbetween. It was harsher than luma, the phosphorescent plant they'd used in the Caverns, but easier to see, too. He felt the portalume shift in his back pocket, grabbed it and clipped it to his belt. So far he hadn't needed it, but knew he would when things got interesting. None of the good stuff would be out in the open. People always scared it away.

There were lots of hollows off the main pathway, most of which looked as if they'd been expanded to room size with electrical and communication cables roughed in. Apparently they were expecting a lot more people.

Boooorrr-iinng.

He walked for what seemed a long time, walls smooth and uninteresting compared to the formations he'd expected. Once he got beyond the range of equipment and people, it smelled about the same as the Caverns they'd left behind. A short time later, it got a little warmer. He'd wondered why they had huge fans and ventilation shafts all over and now he knew. This underground network went deeper, much deeper, and Dirck said it was formed by an aquifer or underground river. What little moisture remained on the planet's surface evaporated or froze solid during Cyraria's harsh seasons. The majority of the planet's water existed in a life-sustaining liquid state beneath the surface.

Eventually, the path split, continuing much the same in a tunnel to the left with a narrower one going off to the right. A few steps in he knew he was on the right track when the lights ended. He smiled at his small victory and unclipped the portalume, sending its white beam dancing along the pathway ahead. The ground shot upward abruptly for a few meters, leveled off, then twisted and turned amid gentle rises and falls. He watched carefully for any branches off the main track, assuring he'd be able to find his way back. So far there weren't any. Good.

A swarm of winged insects danced in the darkness several meters away, their luminescent glow visible beyond the range of his light. He saw something move, pointed the portalume in that direction and saw a lizard similar to the ones in the Caverns. He heard water dripping and noticed the smooth path beneath his feet was wet.

The path dipped suddenly and began a sharp descent, forcing Deven's attention to what lay ahead. Most of his exploring in their previous underground home had been done with Enoch, his bnolar friend, who'd assured his safety, so he knew he needed to be careful. He scoped out the path with the portalume, noticing it continued downward for as far as he could see. The surface was smooth and got so steep he finally sat down and scooted along on his rear, dampness seeping through his pants until they felt nice and cool. It really was pretty warm now, but nothing like Peak Opps.

Before reaching the bottom the path widened, then opened up, light bouncing off more solid rock on either side that formed a series of smooth, rolling bumps. He giggled as he slid over them, then the surface leveled out enough that he scrambled to his feet, excited to survey what lay beyond.

After descending gently for a few more meters, he found himself in a chamber at least twenty meters in diameter. His portalume cast strange shadows on the surrounding walls which were deformed with bulges similar to where he'd come down on his butt. Other than the soft gurgle of meandering water, it was quiet, a reverent hush embracing the space as if keeping an important secret.

He swept the light slowly in a huge arc, barely able to see the domed ceiling above, which was as high as the room's diameter. Eerie shadows followed him as he strolled along the perimeter, driving him to examine the walls' strange surface more closely. He smiled when he discovered that each rocky swell was edged by a trickle of water, explaining their lumpy appearance as well as the rivulet following the circumference. Just past halfway around he jumped, startled, when the light's moisture-laden shaft revealed a gaping tunnel, its ceiling high enough for a man to walk upright. He wondered where it led, but decided he'd save that for another day.

When he got back to where he'd entered, he swept the portalume throughout the area again, the resulting sense of awe everything he'd hoped for. This is what he loved about exploring, finding places like this, different than he'd ever seen before. Maybe even *anyone* had seen before.

"Wow," he whispered. There was something very strange about this place, something he could feel deep inside. It felt familiar, as if he'd been there before. A quiet glow embraced his heart and he thought of those he loved and how important they were to his happiness. He could somehow feel them here, all of them. Including 'Merapa.

Water sparkled across the surface of iridescent stone, making it shine as if it were moving and alive. He turned off the portalume and waited for his eyes to adjust. As expected, a soft glow of luminescence gathered around him, crevices eroded by liquid producing an odd texture that yielded the impression he was inside a giant brain.

"Wow. This is awesome," he whispered, gently breaking the profound silence. "I will call it Cranium Cavern."

Contact

Storm sat tall and solemn behind his workdeck in a enormous chair that not only accommodated his size but contributed to it, increasing the intimidation factor, whether intentional or not. Creena, Dirck, Win, 'Merama and Deven waited nervously on the other side, hoping he would understand the urgency of their request. For what seemed like hours he examined the cristobalite, devenite, the psitenna, their data, and the crystals, again and again, over and over, until at last his orb-like eyes gleamed with cautious enthusiasm.

"This is monumental," he said. "Unfortunately, with the breach at the Caverns, it's very likely that the INTEGRATOR is also onto this technology, or will be soon. From what I can tell, it has tremendous upside potential."

"Yes, sir," Creena replied.

"Tell me what you've found so far."

First she gave him an overview of what they'd determined about the two types of crystals, their individual properties and then their combined effects. Next, she explained when transmissions were private versus public.

"We'd like to figure out how to control the chronoviatic properties so we could get my father back," she concluded.

"I see," Storm replied. "I agree. If there's a way to bring Commander Brightstar back, we'd all benefit greatly." He rotated his eyes back to the notelog and did a few quick calculations. "By Cyrarian time, we have less than a week before he reaches his destination."

He paused, as if carefully considering what he was about to say.

"I'm a builder, not a scientist or electrical engineer," he continued. "I have limited experience in technical applications. However, that experience has taught me some hard lessons. I've never known a single technological advance of this magnitude which has occurred without direct or indirect loss of life. From what you've explained, these crystals have that potential on a frightening scale. The risk is formidable. The benefits, however, are equally staggering. And if the INTEGRATOR perfects the technology before we do, it will be catastrophic." He paused long enough for the full impact of that possibility to settle.

"They could use cristoviatic properties to invade us with no warning, easily breaching any security or barriers," he went on. "Strategic planning would be entirely vain since the enemy could predict our every move with encephalographic access. And what might be missed could always be recaptured through chronoviatic transfer. While all these properties could assure our victory, in enemy hands they could silence us forever. Even as we speak, the INTEGRATOR has some of the best scientists in the universe working on it. If they harness their properties before we do, it will seal our fate." He looked at each in turn, his penetrating gaze eventually landing on Creena. "So tell me, how are you going to assure that we get there first?"

"I can't," she replied. "I'm not even sure that 'Merapa could. I can promise to give it my best efforts, but I'll need lots of help, especially from Win. And help or not, there aren't any guarantees."

Storm nodded, as if satisfied with her answer. "If you'd said it was a sure thing, you'd either be lying or overconfident. Then I wouldn't expect you to come even close. But your honesty and humility should bring success. With that, you can access the wisdom and power of the Universe. Inspiration doesn't visit the arrogant. When you become obsessed with your own knowledge and ability, you lose it. That's the edge we have over our opponents. Probably the only one, except maybe time, assuming we found them first. I want regular updates on your progress and absolutely no actual experimentation on this or anything else without explicit permission. Is that clear?"

"Yes, sir," she replied.

Storm nodded, the initial caution shadowing his eyes yielding to new hope. "Okay," he stated. "When will you be ready for your first test?"

"We're almost ready now, sir," Creena stated.

"What do you plan to do?"

"Try to contact my father. If it works, maybe he could help figure a few things out."

"So what are you waiting for?"

"Your permission, sir," she said hopefully.

"Permission granted," he replied.

Surprised by the ease of their victory, Creena was ecstatic but speechless.

"It's just about time for mealzone two," Win noted. "We can put the details together while we grab something to eat."

With no further discussion, everyone headed to the messhall, then a short time later assembled in the Comm Division conference chamber, which offered some privacy.

No discussion had been necessary to appoint 'Merama to make the transmission. As much as Creena loved 'Merapa, and she knew her brothers did, too, it was still no match for the bond between her parents. Once inside, Dirck pulled down the door then they all helped move the table as well as all but one of the chairs to the far side, opening up a large area in the room's center. The walls were shiny and dark, every sound reverberating from their hard, slick surface.

Win placed the chair in the center where 'Merama sat facing Bezarna, psitenna gripped tightly between her hands while the others formed a circle around her, the grouping designed to lend additional strength and backup power to the primary contact. Each placed one hand on their neighbor's shoulder, the other on

150

'Merama's, duplicating the configuration the bnolar had directed them to assume when they'd resuscitated 'Merapa following the prison break. Everyone was there, including Storm as well as Aggie and Thyron, though the 'troid and vegemal only observed. Any negative feelings or doubts were forbidden. Creena watched Dirck place his hand on their mother's shoulder, still awed by his change of attitude. His eyes met hers, confirming his hopes matched hers.

"Are we ready?" Win asked. Everyone glanced around the circle and nodded. "Okay, Sharra," he said. "Give us a moment to focus, then go ahead on the count of three. One...two...three."

'Merama spoke no words aloud, but Creena could feel when the transmission began. The usual violet beam snapped into place as before, requiring only the slightest adjustment to keep it centered. The warm outpouring of emotion that followed was nearly tangible, originating in her arms and hands, coursing through her body and down to her feet. Hope and optimism cleansed her mind of all darkness, every good feeling she'd ever locked up inside released, engulfing her in a wave of hope. After what seemed an endless yet instantaneous span of time, the feelings dimmed until nothing more than a warm afterglow remained.

One by one everyone exchanged questioning looks, but didn't move until 'Merama sighed heavily and lowered the psitenna. Their hands withdrew slowly, then, one by one, each person moved to the back and sat down, waiting.

"It worked," 'Merama finally whispered, then stopped, covering her heart with her hands. Creena's eyes filled with tears, not only because her suppositions had been vindicated, but because they'd actually contacted 'Merapa. She glanced over at Dirck, whose eyes were closed, and then Deven, who was grinning ear to ear.

"He's glad we're together and safe and of course wishes he was here, too," 'Merama eventually went on. "The prison ship will enter Bezarna's gravity field within a week and after that it will accelerate rapidly. He tried to access the guidance, navigation and control system, but discovered that the instrumentation in the passenger compartment wasn't connected to the systems as he'd hoped. The bulkheads are impenetrable, so getting to the flightdeck is impossible. As far as he can tell, there's nothing he can do to change course." She closed her eyes and sighed, pain etched in her expression before taking a deep breath and going on.

"I told him what we've been doing. He's concerned about the risks and insisted that nothing be done that could jeopardize us, the Clique, or any of its members." She stopped, closed her eyes again, and bit her lip for a moment before continuing in a voice modulated with emotion. "He emphasized that rash decisions could cause a greater loss than his life. He doesn't want any attempt made to rescue him. He relinquished his post as commander to the Council. He's accepted his fate and wants us to do the same."

'Merama blinked hard, then added that he'd given her messages for each of their children as well as Win, which she'd deliver privately. Then she just sat there in silence, expression pensive, eyes focused infinitely far away.

As everyone else's shoulders slumped with the unexpected let-down, Storm's straightened with decision. "Since Commander Brightstar has retired command to the Council, they are now officially the governing body. I'll call an emergency session so they can be told what has transpired and either validate or veto his wishes. Until then, you're all dismissed to resume your primary duties."

Creena couldn't believe how quickly the warmth she'd experienced only moments before had evaporated to a cold void of momentous loss. Something inside cried out in agony, refusing once again to accept the fact they'd never be together again.

She tried to silence it, tried to be compliant, and tried to give up what had driven her forward up until now, when all her hopes had experienced a sudden and violent death. She tried to let go with all her heart, she really did.

But she couldn't.

* * *

Clique Base
Nu / Theta

Bryl Woeyel jumped as the hatch to the evac vehicle sealed with a thump, then lifted effortlessly to the vacuum of space. Through the small window beside her, she watched the lights below shrink and gradually disappear within Drop Dead Winter's chill-induced haze. She closed her eyes and sighed, still trying to comprehend her escape. So much had happened the past few days she'd barely had a chance to put all the pieces together.

Since her confrontation with Troy following Laren's arrest, her determination to build the Clique and continue their fight had grown, her recruiting efforts increased an hundred fold. How Laren had gotten the idea she'd known about the ambush, much less betrayed him, had haunted her to near distraction, her frantic efforts to build the Clique directed toward vindication, even if he'd never know.

Theta had been clearly neutral, weapons long surrendered with resources focused on non-military industries. They were rich in agricultural assets and aluminum deposits, nonaggressive and nearly self-sustaining. Where the INTEGRATOR found the audacity to move in with a blatant display of strategic hardware and blow the settlement that housed their peaceful government off the face of the planet was incomprehensible. She cringed and closed her eyes as the scenes of destruction and death staged an unwanted replay. Even on her war-torn *naterra,* respect was maintained for civilians and government authority, most battles related to clan territorial disputes involving control over land, water rights and minerals. Such an immoral tactic on Esheron was unthinkable.

As the shock dissipated, however, she'd found a new emotion crowding out the determination she'd maintained since Laren's arrest. Truly her opponents were far bolder and stronger than she'd ever imagined. The icy fingers of vulnerability closed around her, reminding her how very alone she really was. They'd even stolen her research team, skilled scientists she'd mentored and trained with Woeyel Industries funding.

There was only one place left on the planet where hope might remain. The place where his physical presence might be lacking, but his plans and hopes would live on. Maybe there she could not only find safety, but renewed hope. He never gave up and she shouldn't, either. What else could she do, go back to Esheron? That was always an option, but if things had been satisfactory on her *naterra,* she never would have left in the first place. She came here because she wanted a new challenge.

I got that, all right, she thought, exhaustion gradually relaxing her tense but weary muscles until she slumped wearily into the seat.

But since when did she back down from a good fight? In spite of the increasing blare of a headache, she set her jaw, determined to make this thing work if it was the last thing she ever did. If there was one thing she'd never done, it was give up and now was hardly the time to start.

ETHICS

The network of niches and cavities allowed for plenty of expansion room and by the end of the day Creena as well as the others had settled into their own quarters. Its simple stone walls were darker than the Caverns and less ornate, but it was reasonably comfortable. By the next day, she'd even have a comcon. Meanwhile, she'd have to share Dirck's, his niche a few meters away through a low, convoluted tunnel.

It was kind of weird how silence could be different, yet it was. Or maybe it was simply the energy difference between the Caverns and Apoca Canyon. That and a plethora of other things occupied her mind, racing wildly from synapse to synapse as she lay wide awake in spite of the fact it was well into her usual sleepzone. As tired and weary as she was, sleep eluded her. The cyll was trying its best to help via gentle massage and stress-blasting aromas, but she was so wound up they barely breached her awareness. So much had happened that her mind raced trying to comprehend it all. In her mind a mere day and a half had passed, yet she felt as if the time Dirck had experienced was an imposing gap she somehow needed to grasp.

It was incomprehensible that it had taken so long to arrive versus when they'd left the Caverns. Where were they while all those things were happening to Dirck and Win? The trip felt instantaneous, yet clearly hadn't been. Time had obviously ceased to exist during transfer. And then there was the matter of going *back* in time, when Deven brought her to the Tank, to the point he didn't even remember doing it, or hadn't done it yet. How could that be? And what if they could figure out how it worked and how to control it? What if she could go back in time to the *Aquarius* and not get lost in that escape pod? How different would their lives be now if she could? Her excitement at such a possibility was almost too much to bear.

Then there was the change in Dirck, which likewise boggled her mind. It felt so good, she wondered if maybe it was a dream. Or maybe that trip through time had brought them to another dimension. He was being so incredibly nice and it didn't seem fake at all. Actually admitting he'd been wrong to interfere in the crystal research was beyond incredible. He was like an entirely different person, and a better one. All of a sudden she had the brother she'd always hoped for. His personality was largely intact, but how he treated her and how it felt to be around him had totally changed. Had he really learned all that while the rest of them were lost in time? Who or what had arranged it so he would go through such an amazing transformation?

From nowhere, Terra flashed through memory, of when Allen Benson had told her about his attitude changing when his sister, Tammy, got sick. The similarity was amazing and she remembered how hard she'd wished at the time that Dirck might have a similar epiphany. And he had. *Wow*. If thoughts became things, had that somehow precipitated their delay in passage? Would she ever know?

The personal message from 'Merapa echoed through her mind as well. 'Merama had recorded it in a notelog and as she'd read the words, she could almost hear his voice. He'd cautioned her to be cheerful and forgiving, to let go of the past and work diligently toward a bright future. He told her to be obedient and comply with righteous laws, yet not hesitate to fight against oppression in any form. She was to be patient with her family, especially Dirck, and be a comfort and joy to 'Merama.

She had a great work to do, which she was to pursue in all diligence, secure in the knowledge that she was greatly loved and that with perseverance, her fondest wishes would eventually come true.

She read the words over and over until each and every one was etched in her mind and heart. Still, comfort eluded her, the message yet another painful reminder of how much she wanted her family back together. If her wish for her and Dirck to get along had come true, why couldn't that one? If nothing else, 'Merapa would be so happy they were finally getting along. How could her fondest wish come true with him on Bezarna forever?

She read it yet again, looking for clues. Perseverance basically meant to never give up, yet he'd forbidden any rescue attempts using untested technology.

But what if they knew what they were doing? What about devenite's chronoviatic properties? What if they could go back in time, say to Nifeir, and save him before the arrest occurred? More excitement fired through her with the realization that if they could control time itself, there were no limitations on the rescue possibilities. It wouldn't matter if he'd arrived on Bezarna or not.

What she really needed was to talk to 'Merapa herself, obtain the answer to her questions first hand, and know for a surety what he meant. The resolve triggered a wave of guilt as if she doubted 'Merama's conveyance, which would hurt her deeply. But there was more to it than that. If there was anything 'Merama didn't need right now, it was to know how deeply her daughter was hurting; surely she had enough grief of her own.

Yet, the words haunted Creena and contacting him herself was the only thing that could solve her dilemma. But it would have to be entirely without the others' knowledge. And there was no time like the present, when the others were fast asleep.

Ex-cylling with renewed determination, she pulled her overshirt over her unispan and crept around the first turn in the passageway to listen. The cave's silence prevailed, disturbed only by the rhythmic groan of a generator a few meters away. The psitenna was in the lab, so she set out in that direction, hoping she wouldn't encounter anyone along the way. The base was still, *Intelligence* and *Strategic Ops* the only divisions with continual shifts, both of which were located on the other side of the messhall.

Once inside the lab, she turned up the lights only long enough to find the psitenna before dimming them again and sitting on the floor in the far corner, back against the stone wall. An unbidden lump formed in her throat as she wrapped her hand around the psitenna. What would she say? What if she really didn't want to hear his response? And what if 'Merama or Dirck found out? On the other hand, what if she didn't and gave up when she shouldn't? Especially since 'Merapa's message had told her to persevere.

No, this was something she had to do. She took a deep, shaky breath and concentrated with all her might, raising the psitenna, then adjusting it until the purple beam shot forward at full amplification.

'Merapa. It's Creena. Can you hear me?

The usual violet beam implied the link had been made, so she waited expectantly, then repeated the call with increased concentration. *'Merapa, please. Are you there? I need to talk to you. Please.*

Nothing.

Maybe she couldn't do it on her own; when 'Merama had contacted him, they'd all been there, lending support. Desperation drove her onward to another level of will, a shift she could feel in her heart as she tried again.

'Merapa, please answer. I have to talk to you. I know this works better with help, but I can't do the power-boost thing like we did with 'Merama because I don't want anyone to know. C'mon, 'Merapa. Please.

She waited what seemed like forever, struggling to accept failure, then trying one last time in what she had decided would be her final attempt.

'Merapa, I don't know if you can hear me or not, but I can't hear you. If you can, I want you to know I love you. And I can't stand the thought of us never being together again. That's all I ever wanted. That's all I still want. And I can't give that up. If I do, nothing else will matter. I'm sorry, 'Merapa, but I just can't. You said to persevere, so that makes me think I shouldn't give up. So I'm confused. I just don't know what to do.

Emotions welled inside her in a rising wave, heart aching as she started to lower the psitenna, when a sudden warmth enveloped her in spite of the cave's persistent chill. A moment later, words and feelings resolved in her heart and mind with an overwhelming sense of her father's presence, as if she were being held again as a little child, safe and secure in his arms. In her mind's eye she could see him, looking tired and in serious need of a shave, but so close it was as if she could reach out and touch him. Still overcome with emotion, words failed her, but her heart assumed the task until control returned.

It's okay, Creena, 'Merapa said. *I love you, too. But there's a time for perseverance and a time for acceptance. Sometimes things happen we don't like or understand, but are really for our benefit. It just takes a while to figure things out.*

I miss you, 'Merapa, she sobbed, words erupting simultaneously from both mind and heart.

I know. And I know how you feel. When my father was killed, I didn't think I'd ever get over that, either. But it also motivated me to achieve things I never would have if he'd lived. If he had, I probably would have been killed years ago in the Esheronian wars. I'm not dissatisfied with my life. I've made mistakes like everyone else, but I also feel as if I've done everything I could to make a good life for our family while still standing up for what I believed was right. I never wanted it to end like this, but apparently this is how fate would have it. There's something about it that's right, something we may not know for a long time. You have to accept that, Creena.

Why? she pleaded. *We've made lots of progress with the devenite. Without it, we couldn't even talk. And it has chronoviatic properties, we know it has. We just don't know how to control it yet. But when we can, why can't we go back to Nifeir and rescue you before your arrest? Then we'll return to whenever we left from, or any other chronplace you say, but we'll all be together again.*

If we're going to do that why don't we just go back and destroy the INTEGRATOR before he gained so much power? her father responded. *We could go back and undo every mistake, remove all the pain, and have perfect lives.*

Exactly! she responded.

No, Creena. Chronoviatic transfer for reasons like that is morally wrong. It's the ultimate in cheating. We'd never learn anything, because we'd never have to live with the consequences. We'd never develop any strength of character or wisdom, learn obedience or discipline. Not only would we get away with everything, but there would be utter chaos. What one person liked, another might not, making change and total unpredictability a constant threat. No, that's not what life is about.

She bit her lip, trying not to cry as her heart imploded with disappointment. *So you don't want us to rescue you? You want to go to Bezarna and that's that?*

No, of course not. I don't want to go to Bezarna, Creena. I just don't want you tampering with dangerous and potentially immoral technologies to do it. If you could have brought me back via the Tank, or some other form of cristoviatic transfer, that would be fine. Likewise, if you pulled up beside this ship in the Volition, I certainly wouldn't refuse to go. But it doesn't look very likely that either of those options is going to happen within the next five chrons, does it?

No.

Okay, then. It's not worth it to waste your time on it any further, is it? Not when there are more important things to do, all of which have a much higher probability of success. You're dealing with a very real enemy out there, Creena, one that you must defend against and conquer. What if the INTEGRATOR *obtains those technologies first? Morals aren't exactly high on his list of priorities, but unrighteous power and dominion is. I don't want you wasting your time trying to save me while the entire planet is consumed.*

You have an important work to do that must be pursued immediately, one that can save thousands, maybe even millions of people. I'm just not worth that much, Creena, not my life at the expense of all those others. I've done my work. Besides, if the INTEGRATOR *wins, that's not a life I'd want anyway. So let me go. Get on with your life. There are a lot of people depending on you right now, so don't waste your time and energy grieving. It's not good for you or anyone else. Okay?*

Her mind wouldn't answer but her heart did, agony spilling through it like liquid fire. All she ever wanted was to be together again, no more, no less. How could he tell her to let it go?

Creena, there's more to life than you realize. I understand how you feel. I don't like this, either. It's not what I would have chosen, yet my actions dictated this fate. I chose to oppose the INTEGRATOR *and now I'm paying the price. It's not that I was wrong, I just opposed a powerful entity that won this particular battle. But I wouldn't change what I believe in. If I were willing to do that, I could have probably saved myself. But the cost would have been much higher, because I would have gone against everything I know to be right.*

But you'd still be here, she protested.

I'd rather be dead than betray myself like that. I know you don't want to hear this, Creena, but right now you're being incredibly selfish. This isn't easy for anyone and you're making it even harder. For me, for yourself and certainly everyone you could be helping if you'd accept it and move on. Please, Creena. I know it's hard. But won't you please try? For me?

Her will was trying but her heart resisted, still not ready to let go.

Creena, please, he pleaded. *There's nothing you can't accomplish. You've made remarkable progress with the crystals that's essential to the Clique's survival. Anything I may have done can live on through you, if you'll just accept it. Okay?*

The slightest hint of willingness softened her heart, desire following in its wake until gradually one by one the tears ran dry. *Okay,* she agreed, composure returning. *I'll do it for you. But at least help me a little. Tell me this much, 'Merapa, what should we be working on first? Everyone seems to think we should stick to the comm applications, but I'm not so sure. I think we ought to start in on some of the cristoviatic transfer stuff. If you were here, what would you do?*

Follow orders, he said. *Unless there's something you know that the others don't that could influence their decision, in which case you owe it to them to explain. But remember, in most cases your commander is working with a much broader knowledge base than you are. You may not always understand or agree with his decisions, but there's a reason behind them. If I were there and still your commander, I'd also direct you toward comm. Don't underestimate its importance. Without it, we wouldn't even be having this conversation.*

No, we wouldn't. Okay, 'Merapa. That's what we'll work on.

Good girl. Are you okay now?

Sort of.

What are you going to do first?

I'm not sure. It shouldn't take much to come up with a realtime psi-based comm system. I'd also like to figure out what caused those veridical dreams.

Sounds good to me.

I miss you, 'Merapa.

I miss you, too. Good luck on the comm work. Is Win on your team?

Yes. He always starts out a skeptic, then comes around.

A lot like you.

I suppose.

Bye, Creena. I love you.

I love you, too, 'Merapa. Thanks for everything. I'm proud to be your daughter.

And I'm proud to be your father. Now say goodbye.

At the very thought, an insurmountable wall closed around her.

Creena? C'mon, tell me goodbye.

She tried again, but couldn't. *I, I can't,* she responded, eyes refilling with tears.

You have to, Creena. Goodbyes are part of life. You can either say it now, when I can hear you, or later when I can't. It's up to you.

All the resolve and acceptance evaporated into a final burst of sorrow. All the days of hope and longing, her best efforts that weren't quite enough, all the dreams of being together, all collapsed in an avalanche of soul-wrenching grief. The psitenna slipped from her hands, violet thread still attached while her hopes collapsed.

Gradually regaining control, an unexpected peace replaced the emptiness as she raised the psitenna one more time.

Okay, 'Merapa. G-Goodbye.

Bye, Creena. I love you.

I love you, too, 'Merapa.

The violet beam evaporated and Creena lowered the psitenna, its weight heavier than before. Her head bowed in defeat, the stone floor's cold, unyielding surface matching the chill of endless silence.

* * *

<table>
<tr><td colspan="2" align="center">Integrator Central
INCIDENT REPORT # # # #</td></tr>
<tr><td>TEAM: Communications</td><td>PROJECT:
Encephalographic
Access/Reception</td></tr>
<tr><td>Date: DDW-125</td><td>Investigator: Rohlnach</td></tr>
<tr><td>Injuries: 16</td><td>Fatalities: 14/16</td></tr>
<tr><td>Schedule Impact: Y/N? Y</td><td>Days: +10</td></tr>
<tr><td colspan="2">SUMMARY: Attempts to refine reception to word chain level based on mindprint specific remote stimulation model has resulted in cessation of brain activity (brain death) in several test subjects. Cause currently believed to be related to excessive amplitude of stimulating frequency. The two survivors remain in a catatonic state.</td></tr>
</table>

* * *

Integrated Territorial Tower
Cira City

Troy could tell by Spoigan's expression that he thought the information on the latest *Incident Report* was unfortunate. He and his superior had this ongoing argument related to dealing with dissenters. Spoigan hoped to use mind control methods to win them over or, at the least, neutralize them from pushing the issue, while Troy felt eliminating such individuals would be more effective in the long run. He had no patience for those who disagreed with him or his ideologies, preferring to spend resources on weapons research as opposed to psychological mumbo-jumbo.

"This could come in handy for executions," he ventured. "It would save the cost of hunting down enemies to our cause and even allow their disposal in a covert manner which wouldn't be easily traced to INTEGRATOR sources."

Spoigan's apparent concern at the unfortunate accident quickly escalated to resolute determination to the contrary as demonstrated by squared shoulders and the usual sharply truncated snort.

"Absolutely not," he growled. "I don't know why you have such difficulty recognizing the importance of citizen resources. This technology has the potential to change their mindset to whatever we want. This is all about people, Troy! Can't you see that? What good will it do if we win by indiscriminately killing off all opposition? I agree that some must be eliminated, like your buddy, Brightstar, but certainly not the masses. People are resources. They work. They produce."

"What if they can't be convinced? Then what? Then the masses you're so fond of will rebel and cause all sorts of disturbances which will distract us from larger acquisitions, both in time and resources."

Spoigan's glare bore through him, yet Troy didn't flinch, having become accustomed to his superior's intimidation tactics. "You're out of order, Troy," he snarled.

"I thought the point of having a deputy was to present other views," he retorted without apology.

"Point taken," the man replied, glare diminishing ever so slightly. "But our disagreements must remain within the confines of this office, is that clear? Otherwise you may be the one meeting with an unfortunate accident."

Troy winced, having failed to consider the possibility that he could become such a target.

"Yes, sir," he replied evenly. "I'll keep that in mind. By the way, did you see the report from the team that raided the cavern where the Brightstars were holed up over High Opps?"

Spoigan's expression shifted slowly from annoyance to pensive to curious. "No. What about it?"

Troy stifled a smile, satisfied to be one up on his superior yet again. "Two troopers reported an interesting incident whereby the people occupying the cave escaped."

"Hmmmph," Spoigan grunted. "Probably some wild tale to explain their incompetence."

"Maybe," Troy said evenly. "But it's interesting if true."

"All right, Troy. What happened?"

"The troops involved have favorable records and appear trustworthy. Both claim in identical stories that a small group, including at least one child, a 'troid and two females, teleported from a cylindrical chamber lined with cristobalite using some strange, primitive looking device."

Spoigan straightened with interest. "Indeed. That's definitely interesting to say the least. Are researchers following up on it?"

"Of course."

"Good. Keep me posted."

Troy smiled. "I will."

CONNECTING

The Bezarna Express

They bought it. Every one of them. Whatever they'd used to communicate had conveyed emotions as well as words, allowing Laren to sense everything from their heartrate to the resulting despondency. Yet somehow the realization was bittersweet.

Accept his fate indeed! *Ha.* Didn't they know him better than that? Apparently not. Furthermore, he'd gotten himself into this mess and should therefore get himself out.

But the good news was that apparently they hadn't tuned into his feelings. Why they'd failed to do so had a variety of possibilities. Maybe their own were so strong they were overcome, excluding his. Or perhaps they felt his optimism and interpreted it as acceptance. And possibly, which could also be the case, he'd succeeded in shielding them, thanks to practice attained in the Sigma section of Epsilon Territorial Prison.

Not that he was proud of what constituted lying, albeit by omission. He'd never done so before, but this time it was necessary. He didn't have a choice. For one thing, he had no idea what they were using to contact him and whether or not it was secure. For all he knew, Dirck might find a transcript of their conversations on INTEGRATOR Central a few hours later. Nonetheless, their grief lingered in his heart and part of him regretted having to hurt them like that. But it was better that they think he was going peacefully, not only for security reasons, but if his efforts failed. False hopes could be more devastating when they crashed than no hope at all.

Or were they? Were his false? Or did he simply have nothing to lose? Trying to figure out whether it would work or not was wasting valuable time. Time was definitely running out and there was much to do. He finally consoled himself that at least they had closure if his plans didn't work out.

He took his c-com out of his pocket, trying to remember where he'd stashed Cyraria's databases. He'd secured them where no one else could find them, perhaps even himself, judging by his luck so far. He queried via psi with no results. He switched to manual mode, hoping for some visual reminder. An unfamiliar screen came up, vivid and somehow cryptic, asking again for his validation code.

He psied the code and waited.

The results were entirely unexpected and he consciously veiled what he was sure was a puzzled expression, knowing Sa'ata was watching from across the craft. Since acquiring the device on Esheron, he'd used it primarily to record his thoughts and communicate, first with Dirck to convey instructions on constructing the heat exchanger and more recently with Rhodus. Its capabilities were remarkable to say the least, the technology a few steps beyond anything he'd seen before. C-com was short for *cerebral companion*, implying it augmented its user's brain, but exactly what that constituted, other than the obvious function of recording thoughts and intuitive data searches, he didn't know. He'd never taken time to explore what was there because he'd been too busy and had other more familiar technologies available. That certainly wasn't the case now, giving him nothing to lose besides time.

So where was he in this thing, anyway? He thought he understood its workings, all its various complexities, but clearly he'd somehow entered a different space. And that was essentially all he saw, quite literally, a tiny, slowly rotating spiral galaxy hovering just above the device in the usual holographic format. There was something beckoning about it, so he projected his thoughts into its depths, having no idea what, if anything, to expect.

Much to his surprise, he slipped through a portal and found himself in virtual reality, a room of sorts. So it was reciprocating, *i.e.,* connecting back to him somehow, not just accepting input. In the past, he'd always extracted data via video or audio, not a direct brain dump. Such capability made him a little nervous, especially after all those mind games they used on him in prison. He looked around, seeing avatars for two familiar figures, his brother, Jen, and Bryl. Why them? The device sensed his query and responded. They were the only ones he had connections with who were part of his network.

Of course! Jen had gotten one the same time he had, and Bryl would have one since she was from Esheron, owned a business there and thus had access to their technology. Esheron was rarely involved in intragalactic trading, which had interesting implications. In other words, except for those who'd been onworld or hailed from there, c-coms were unheard of and inaccessible. Even if they'd checked to see what he had on him when he was arrested, it was doubtful they would have taken it away. They probably would have thought it was a simple communications device that wouldn't operate beyond Cyraria.

Were they right?

He focused his attention across the virtual room to the image of his brother, wondering if Jen knew everything the device could do. He'd certainly had more opportunity to become familiar with it than he had. A voice came into his head.

Do you wish to contact Jen Brightstar?

Yes.

The words "Time Synching" flashed in his mind. Of course; he was traveling at warp five and Jen was stationary by comparison.

Connected.

Jen? Are you there?

A sudden emotional blast of uncontained surprise washed over him along with the vision of his brother consulting with a patient in the office of his Physical Assistance and Remediation Center or PAR. His brother was, as could be expected, entirely flabbergasted, blue eyes wide as if he'd experienced an unexpected electrical shock. He ran both hands through grey-spreckled hair, mouth agape, as he stared dumbly at his patient.

It's okay, Jen. Tell him you just got an urgent call. It's me, on the c-com.

Laren? Is that you? Are you back?

No, but I'm working on it and need some help.

Jen got up from behind his desk and offered what had to be a rather flimsy excuse, but the patient left, looking back over his shoulder as if his physician had clearly lost his mind. Laren laughed, the vision fading enough for him to see Sa'ata giving him a suspicious look and reminding him where he was, at least physically.

"Gaming again, Brightstar?" the Pyxisite asked coldly.

"Yeah, Sa'ata. Gaming," he replied. He focused back on the device, finding his brother back at his desk talking to himself; he couldn't hear a word.

Psi, Jen, he prompted. *It's a clever little feature of the c-coms we got on Esheron.*

Sweet Benefics, Laren, what's going on?

Right now I need information. I thought I'd downloaded everything, but can't find it. Maybe I'm out of range or the link requires tachyonic data receivers, which I would think this ship would have, but I don't know. It's possible if they're monitoring us. Anyway, I did find you. I need background information on two others on this trip. A Pyxisite named Sa'ata, the other a human named Merik. I need to know if the charges against them are legit or if they're spies.

Once again Jen looked astonished and he felt his doubts. *Can I get to that data?* his brother asked.

If you can't through the medical portal then try your c-com.

A sudden commotion snapped Laren's attention back to his current location just in time to see Merik dive into the airlock.

Never mind Merik, he psaid. *But send everything they've got on Sa'ata. I'll check back later. Gotta situation to tend to.*

He exited to the main menu just in time to record the sensor data for the jettison, then dropped the c-com in his pocket. He folded his arms and gave Sa'ata a wry smile. Their eyes connected but no humor softened their darkened depths.

* * *

Apoca Canyon

What's wrong?"

Creena looked up from her notelog into Dirck's searching, green eyes. The two were alone in the commlab, reviewing crystal data she'd gathered at the Caverns while Win worked at decrypting a particularly difficult double-i with Igni.

"Nothing," she answered.

"Yes, there is," he argued, pulling his stool over to sit beside her. "You look awful."

"Thanks."

"It's 'Merapa, isn't it?"

She looked away as tears glazed her eyes, hurt and disappointment from the conversation with her father still fresh and too painful to confront. The next thing she knew her brother slid off his stool and was standing beside her with his arms around her and she realized he wasn't in any better shape than she was.

"I can't believe he's gone," she sobbed into his chest.

"I know," her brother replied, holding her tighter. "Maybe if we ever perfect the chronoviatic—"

"No!" she protested, shaking her head. "He doesn't want that. He thinks it's immoral."

Dirck stepped back, expression laden with questions. "How do you know that? All 'Merama said was we weren't supposed to rescue him, and I assumed that meant using untested technologies. Once it's fully developed—"

"No! He said no timeshifting."

"When?"

"Never mind." She bit her lip, knowing she'd said too much.

"Hey, I have a right to know," Dirck insisted, eyes locked on hers. "Was it in the message he sent through 'Merama?"

Creena sighed and looked away then cautiously met his eyes again. "No. I talked with him myself."

Dirck's solemn expression broke with the dawn of a dim smile. "Oh," he said. "Good. So did I."

"Didn't he tell you the same thing?" she asked, not overly surprised.

"No, not exactly. He just said there was a reason behind all this and that we had to accept it and go on. That and a bunch of man-to-man stuff."

"Such as?" Creena pried, smiling herself.

"Oh, just the same old stuff about how it's my responsibility to take care of the family now and all that."

"I asked him specifically what we should be working on," Creena replied. "He said stick with the comm. But I'd really like to figure out what caused those veridical dreams. Wherever they came from, they brought useful information, even if we didn't always understand correctly. Maybe we could induce one that would help with our research."

"That would be great," Dirck agreed. "I think they were related to the Tank, and without that it'll be hard to test."

"Maybe. I'm thinking it's got a lot to do with the devenite, since it relates more to time."

"I think you're right," Dirck agreed. "And there's another thing, too. The Tank worked, or at least used to, for location transfer based on thought, but devenite transmits emotion. It's like they have similar yet entirely different baseline functions."

"Yes!" Creena agreed, suddenly remembering what she'd felt him projecting during that first contact. "Words come through, but you can completely sense what the other person is feeling." She looked him straight in the eye but thought better than to bring it up.

"Right," Dirck replied after a moment's hesitation, apparently understanding but not wanting to discuss it. "So you agree, it's like the Tank relates to thoughts, more specifically that thoughts become things, and devenite to feelings."

"And memories, too, it seems," she added. "But of course the two are usually connected. The clearest memories are the ones tied to strong emotions. And it's like they're timeless."

"I think we're onto something here, another data point," Dirck said. "Think about it. Some people you connect with mentally and others emotionally. They must be two entirely different psi types or frequencies. Now that I think about it, that's when I first heard Thyron, when I was trying to figure out what to do when the heat exchanger blew. It wasn't mental, it was emotional."

"That makes sense," Creena agreed. "And the psitenna beam shows up on your chest, right over your heart."

"The veridical dreams, both the one about 'Merapa in prison and the one we had about Bryl had a strong emotional element. So much so, we didn't recognize the true message." He paused and shook his head. "I don't know if I'll ever forgive myself for that."

"I know," she said quietly. "I missed it, too, along with several references to Eta providing supplies to INTEGRATED regions that should have given it away. That was also when I was working on the crystals during my sleepzone. So I'm at least as guilty or more than you," she admitted, heart again laden with guilt.

"Look," he said, hand resting gently on her arm. "We both made mistakes. Big time. But there's nothing we can do about it now. We need to forgive ourselves and not let it distract us any further. Okay?"

She nodded. "I know. But it's pretty hard to forget that it's the reason 'Merapa isn't here, right now."

"Yes and no. I blamed myself for a long time, until Win helped me realize it wasn't that simple. But whatever part we played is all the more reason we need to concentrate on what's possible with the crystals and whether we can possibly get him back. If you want to figure out which one of us carries more guilt, just think how I feel about keeping you away from researching them during workzone, forcing you to do it when you should have been sleeping."

She shook her head and rolled her eyes, not so much at him but the two of them for being so foolish. "We both messed up, that's for sure. So you're right, let's let it go and see what progress we can make now. Too bad we can't use them to buy some additional time."

"Who knows? Maybe we can. Let's see what we've got. Maybe devenite gathers information beyond the limits of time that would have an emotional impact. And that could be why it's difficult to interpret their message, because emotions, as they told us repeatedly on Mira III, aren't logical. And it's the same with veridical dreams."

Creena laughed. "You sound like Aggie. I can't tell you how many times we had that conversation. She'd get so frustrated with me when I had a feeling about something since a 'troid has no emotions."

"I don't know. I've seen her get pretty reeked before," Dirck commented, laughing.

"True. But anger was probably programmed in as a response to frustration when she can't analyze something using her logic circuits. That's pretty simple, just another way of expressing an error message."

"Probably," Dirck agreed. "So, back to our theory that cristobalite operates on the principle that thoughts become things and devenite operates emotionally. Empathically, actually. Let's figure out how we might be able to induce a

174

veridical dream. One that would bring us something we need to know."

"Right. Like how to control chronoviatic teleportation."

Before they could decide how to test their theory, a messenger arrived with a directive from Storm. The boy was slightly younger than Dirck with shaggy dark hair, olive skin and intense blue eyes. He stood straight and saluted, Dirck acknowledging with a nod.

"What is it, Corporal?"

"We have a ship coming in with about two hundred evacuees from another base, Captain," he explained. "Some of them must be mighty important, because Storm wants quarters defined immediately for four individuals with complete intelligence and comm capabilities."

"Any specific location?" Dirck asked.

"Fairly close in was all he said."

"There are a few more rooms off our passage that should work. I was planning on using them for work areas, but we don't have time to identify somewhere else at this point. Where's Win?"

"He's coming, with the hardware," the boy replied.

"All right. Thanks, Corporal," Dirck said, nodding his dismissal, then turned to Creena. "I'll be back as soon as I can. Why don't you stay here and work up a plan for the experiment design?" She nodded and waved him on.

She tried to turn her attention back to her notelog, but wound up staring blankly at the stone wall across from her instead. How much Dirck had changed was still registering as his behavior backed it up. Truly that was the kindest he'd ever been to her, ever, not only holding her while she cried, but listening and even talking about emotions without being derisive. The only other time she could remember him being nice was when he'd found her on Mira III. But this time was different, somehow deeper, as if a defensive barrier had fallen that would finally allow them to be friends as well as siblings.

She smiled to herself as a warm feeling enveloped her. It was like a miracle, one she didn't understand in the slightest, much less recognize in its significance to all they were trying to accomplish.

News

Creena closed her eyes and tried to remember if they'd done anything special before she and Dirck had had that dream about Bryl. Nothing came to mind. As she continued to ponder what the trigger might be, she knew the Caverns had played a major part. It could have been the presence of both cristobalite and devenite, but the peace and quiet they enjoyed were probably factors, too. Where they slept was also free of any equipment, which could cause interference, except perhaps their notelogs. So the first thing they needed to do was find somewhere less saturated with noise and technology. Knowing that her little brother was always exploring, he was a likely candidate to find such a spot. She quickly paged her mother to see if he was with her, which he was. He arrived at the lab a short time later, breathless.

"Hi, Creena! What's up?" He stood before her grinning, trying to catch his breath.

"Dirck and I want to see if we can cause another veridical dream," she said. "I think our quarters and all the equipment might interfere, so we need to find somewhere that's big enough for all of us to get away from the main base. Want to help?"

"Okay," he said, taking a deep breath and letting it out in a big sigh.

"I know how you like to explore, Deven. Do you know of anywhere like that?"

Gradually his pensive expression gave way to that sneaky little smile he got when he had a secret he wanted to share.

"Cranium Cavern would be perfect, but it's a little far and kinda hard to get to."

Creena scrutinized him carefully, knowing he was inclined to gross understatement. "Just how hard are you talking about?"

"Oh, it's like, well, probably around a kilometer past our quarters, down a passage that climbs a little, then goes back down, sorta, then through this big long tunnel that finally opens up on a big lower level."

"Is it being used for anything else?"

"Nah. I don't think anyone knows it's there. There isn't any power or stuff around at all, and it's a little warmer."

"Okay, sounds great. Actually, being that far away is perfect. Why don't we get 'Merama in on this, too? She probably wouldn't like us down there alone, so let's get her so we can check it out. Are you sure it'll be big enough for all of us?"

"Don't worry, it's big enough," he said, grinning. "It's like a giant hole. With another tunnel off one side, where I couldn't even see the end."

Creena met his gaze as he peered up at her with his big, brown eyes, surrounded by dark, shaggy hair. So often he was wise beyond his years while at other times he seemed no more than a typical little boy, but something about his expression this time bespoke the former. Wondering what he could have found, she blinked away her suspicions in favor of the task at hand.

"Okay. Great. I guess," she said. "Let's get 'Merama."

Creena summoned her with the lab's comcon and she arrived a short time later, anxious to hear about their discoveries and plans. Creena had no sooner started explaining the premise for their research when she realized she'd made a tremendous mistake.

"Dreams?" 'Merama asked. "I thought that only happened once, the one Dirck and I had when your father was in prison. You mean you had one, too?"

Creena's heart accelerated, horrified at what she'd done. Having to deal with 'Merapa's loss was bad enough, much less fresh consideration of who may have betrayed him, much less why. She'd had never been any good at hiding her emotions, anyway, and, as usual 'Merama sensed something was wrong. Concern etched her expression with weariness as she lowered herself onto a stool, green eyes fixed firmly on hers.

"There's something you haven't told me, isn't there?" she asked softly. Creena nodded painfully. "I think it's time you told me, don't you think?"

Creena's mind raced as she tried to decide how much she could tell her without compounding her grief. "Dirck and I didn't want you to worry," she replied shakily.

"Was it about your father?" Again, Creena nodded painfully. "Am I safe in assuming that whatever it contained came true?"

"Not exactly," Creena replied. "Only part of it. I guess. I really don't know. We like, well, didn't catch part about 'Merapa's meeting on Nifeir with the Eta TG, and didn't warn him in time."

"So the message wasn't that obvious?" 'Merama asked. Creena swallowed hard and shook her head. "I'd really like you to tell me about it." 'Merama's eyes were sad and pleading, making it even harder.

For what seemed a very long time Creena just stood there hanging her head, unable to speak until finally her mother got up with a sigh and turned away.

"It was about *her*, wasn't it?"

Creena cringed and nodded, then looked up and realized her mother was facing the other way. "Yes," she whispered.

"What...happened?"

"No, 'Merama. No. It wasn't like that. Well, not exactly. As far as we know."

"What *do* you know?"

"She, she, well, she wanted to claim him as her bondling under the ECL. But he was going to do everything he could to stop her!"

"How do you know that?"

"Because Dirck talked to 'Merapa about it when he went to Cira City."

"In other words he'd stop it if he could."

"Yes. If he could."

'Merama's sigh of relief was deep and soulful. "I see," she said, then displayed an artificial smile. "So. Have there been any others?"

"Others?"

"Dreams. Have you and Dirck, or you and Deven, or Win, or whoever, had any other dreams?"

"Not that I know of," she said truthfully.

"So tell me about your experiment. You think you know what causes them?"

"We're not sure. We're just thinking that there's a connection with either the cristobalite or devenite. Especially the devenite, since it timeshifts. Maybe it brings information about future events through veridical dreams."

Before she could get any further, a clamor arose in the passageway outside, echoing amidst the clatter of numerous footfalls. She and 'Merama exchanged a startled look as Creena moved toward the door to see what all the noise was about, colliding with Dirck as he came flying in.

"Hey! What's going on?" Creena asked, startled as well as concerned.

He started to speak then noticed 'Merama, confusion clouding his expression. "What's wrong?" he asked.

His mother walked over slowly and rested her hand on his shoulder. "I understand you and Creena had a veridical dream about your father," she said.

Dirck's eyes shot to Creena questioningly to which she smiled sheepishly.

"I appreciate that you were both trying to spare me from something painful," 'Merama continued. "Your father used to do it all the time. But I really need to know these things. Please. Don't do it again. Okay?"

He glanced back at Creena briefly. "Okay, 'Merama," he agreed gently. "We just thought—"

"I know," she interrupted. "You didn't want to hurt me and I appreciate that. But I want you to tell me about anything that important, painful or not."

"Okay," Dirck agreed, unsuccessfully stifling a sigh that was heavy enough to echo.

"So what's going on now for you to come racing in here like that?" Creena asked, eager to change the subject.

"I just thought you ought to know, before you find out some other way," he replied, the set of his jaw putting her on full alert. "You know that group of dignitaries they brought in?"

"Yeah, what about them?" Creena prompted.

"Well, you're not going to be too happy about one of them. Especially now."

Creena's eyes widened. "Bryl Woeyel?"

"I'm afraid so."

They both glanced at their mother whose eyes were closed while a pained expression claimed her features.

"And it gets worse," Dirck went on.

"How?"

"She's our new commander."

* * *

Bezarna Express

By the time Laren recorded the sensor data from Merik's airlock egress, a datafile showed up from Jen. He opened it anxiously, hoping it would answer his questions about Sa'ata. If it came right out and said he was a guard he'd know what he was up against. If it had a list of offenses worthy of exile it would be less clear since it could be fabricated, not only for fellow passengers but future ones. If others knew there was a guard onboard, they'd also know the ship was not on the expected one-way trip.

Jen had forwarded all the databases he could access including the Planetary Law Enforcement Database or PLED.

Sa'ata, as expected, was in there with a variety of charges, mostly what he expected for someone of his size and heritage such as public disturbances, petty theft, licensing violations, and grand larceny involving government equipment. The last one, while serious, certainly wasn't a capital offense. In an organization as corrupt as INTEGRATION such behavior was often viewed anywhere from business as usual to a personal recommendation. This really wasn't going in the direction he needed. Perhaps political enemies of INTEGRATION were recorded somewhere else. But where? Maybe that one was so secure he couldn't get into it. He read over the list, frustrated, then mentally kicked himself.

Query it, you idiot, he thought.

Search null for 'it you idiot,' the device responded.

Query Sa'ata Kwortuya political alliances, he psaid back, stifling a laugh.

A heartbeat later, the requested data was before him. Supposedly Sa'ata had been a Lieutenant to the Regional Governor in Gamma/Theta, the territory bordering Epsilon to the east and one of only two remaining Neutrals. He'd been convicted of conspiracy in an assassination attempt on their INTEGRATION-sympathizing Regional Governor.

Laren's suspicions swirled like a PV. Everything the man had said favored INTEGRATION. Why would he go after the Governor unless he simply wanted his position? Possible, but unlikely given he seemed to lack ever marginal leadership ability.

Verify data, he psaid.

In response, a flashing banner obscured the entry with an ominous red glow: "Unverified: Probability 89% data contains disinformation."

So. That implied it was entered through unusual channels, probably fabricated and making it likely he was a guard.

That speculation confirmed the vehicle would return, which was good. However, it also implied that anyone who didn't voluntarily head for the airlock would probably be forcefully escorted in that direction sooner or later. That could be done in a variety of ways, the simplest being to render dissenters unconscious followed by a rather hostile heave-ho into the cosmic void.

Nice.

Now the question was when, how, and what to do to make sure Sa'ata was the one who didn't return.

ORDERS

“I absolutely cannot believe you won't do everything possible to get him back. His own family! I thought for sure I could count on you.”

Creena shrunk back with her mother and Deven as Bryl stood glaring at Dirck and Win from behind what had so recently been Storm's workdeck and prior to that, her father's, in the commander's office. The woman emitted an exasperated sigh, then collapsed in her predecessor's padded chair. Mouth in a thin line, she shifted her attention to her c-com, apparently checking for messages, giving everyone a brief respite.

In uniform, she looked and acted like an entirely different person than Creena remembered. She recalled being awed by the woman's luxurious strands of raven hair twisted into exotic Pleidonian braids fit for royalty, which in a sense she had been as Delta's Regional Governor. Now her wave-turned locks were neatly restrained at the nape of her neck and twisted into a knot, lacking any style besides efficiency. Clearly, she'd assumed the mantle of commander and had no problem exercising its authority.

“It's not that we don't want to,” Dirck explained when she looked up, frown still creasing her forehead. “He told us not to make any rescue attempts, specifically stating chronoviatic methods were out. He said they're immoral and he'd rather die. I suppose you could accuse him of being too philosophical, but there weren't any alternatives, either. He said it was pointless to direct all our efforts toward a rescue that probably couldn't happen, especially at the expense of developing other strategies.”

"That man has the worst tendency to underestimate his worth," Bryl muttered, voice edged with unexpected emotion, which she tried to mask by clearing her throat. "Well. I don't happen to believe his rescue is impossible *or* that chronoviatic transfer is immoral. This is war and he's one of our most valuable players. We absolutely can't afford to lose him. He's the only reason we've made it this far. I'm not about to let him go."

Creena cringed as she recognized one very valid reason for allowing 'Merapa's fate to proceed, undisturbed. 'Merama wore a rare frown while Bryl acted as if she didn't exist, directing her comments primarily at Dirck with an occasional searing glance at Win, both of whom stood at awkward attention while, as civilians, Creena, Deven and her mother cowered silently behind them.

"If we had any practical options we would have used them," Dirck repeated.

"But what about that chamber in the Caverns, the one he used to go home several times? "Why can't we use that?" Bryl demanded.

Win cut in, giving Dirck a chance to catch his breath. "First of all, it was limited to on-world teleporting only and second, for some reason it lost power and wouldn't work, even locally. Furthermore, the Caverns have since been occupied by the INTEGRATOR."

"Wonderful. What about that new device? The psitenna?" she queried, eyes back on Dirck. "Storm told me you've already achieved some chronoviatic effects with that. What's holding that up?"

"We don't know how to control them," Dirck replied. "Sometimes it goes forward in time, sometimes back, and we had orders from both Storm *and* 'Merapa to work comm apps first."

"Well, be advised that I'm your commander now and I'm ordering you to change priorities." She folded her arms in emphasis.

"We *will* get him back, at any cost, by any means, and as with other Clique campaigns, victory is our only option!" Her statement was firm, but a hint of sadness softened her eyes before she could extinguish it. "And if you either won't or can't do the work, I'll get someone who can. I've already sent for more of my researchers from Esheron, who ought to be here within a day or so. They may be a little unfamiliar with this technology, but they know how to run a research project to get something done instead of jumping around from asteroids to comets at every shift of the stars in some sentimental stupor. Meanwhile, you're ordered to abandon the comm aspects and concentrate exclusively on cristoviatic and chronoviatic transfer. Do I make myself clear?"

"Yes, sir. I mean ma'am," Dirck corrected himself, expression taut.

"Sendori?" she prompted. "Do you understand?"

"Yes, ma'am," Win replied stiffly.

"I assume we all agree the sooner we get Commander Brightstar back the better." She paused and smiled at 'Merama sympathetically, but Creena couldn't help but notice she didn't smile back.

After that they were all summarily dismissed with the directive to report to the lab and get to work. They walked the passageway back slowly, making certain they were well beyond Bryl's earshot before assuming any conversation.

"Wow," Deven finally stated, looking up at Dirck through his bangs with wide, questioning eyes. "Do you think she ordered 'Merapa around like that?"

"Are you kidding?" Creena snorted. "She kissed up to him so bad it was disgusting."

"I'll say," 'Merama said grimly. "In more ways than one. If she'd acted like *that* I wouldn't have had a worry in the world."

"At least it's pretty clear she didn't betray him," Dirck commented.

"Right," Creena agreed, wondering if that veridical dream she and Dirck had shared ever played out. "But we still don't know what 'Merapa meant when he asked if she knew about his arrest."

"Maybe he was trying to find out if she'd been arrested, too, without being too obvious," Win suggested. "They probably would have said so if she had."

"Yeah, that makes sense," Dirck agreed, then threw up his arms in frustration. "'Merapa tells us to do one thing, then she turns around and tells us the exact opposite. If we follow *her* orders, we're betraying 'Merapa, and if we follow his, we'll be insubordinate or worse. Talk about a classic lose-lose dilemma. *Hmmmph.*"

"I think I already know," Creena responded unhappily.

"What?" Dirck and 'Merama asked in unison.

"He said to follow orders. That's what he told me when I asked what we should work on."

"I can see that," Win agreed. "And since he's retired his post, he wouldn't intrude on the ruling authority with his own opinion."

"She was right about one thing," 'Merama admitted.

"What?" Creena asked, surprised she'd agree with Bryl about anything.

"Underestimating his worth. Not only professionally, but to the family as well. I really don't think he has any idea how much we need him, or anyone else for that matter."

"But if we bring him back using chronoviatic transfer when he told us not to he'll be extremely reeked," Creena reminded them, a dark swell of gloom accompanying the thought. "He said it was like cheating, that he'd rather die honorably."

"Maybe so," Dirck stated, "but if we go back in time to before he told you that, he won't have any knowledge of ever saying it, like Deven when you met him in the Tank. So how can he be mad? Meanwhile, we'll have him back. And how could he get *that* upset if we were just following orders?"

"Good point," Creena agreed, smiling in spite of herself. Then all of them stopped simultaneously and stared at one another, eyes wide, as logic took its natural course.

"So what are we waiting for?" 'Merama finally asked, eyes brightening with hope.

And with that, they took off for the lab at a dead run. When they got there everyone stood around, dumbfounded, gaping at the numerous work centers, each cluttered with a different project at some stage of development.

"So where do we start?" Creena asked, arms flung wide in frustration. "Everything we've done is so preliminary it's impossible to tell which one holds the most promise."

"The surest method is chronoviatic transfer," Win stated. "Going back to warn him before his arrest. But it's also the most dangerous, and undoubtedly the hardest to test, much less control."

"But cristoviatic transfer would only work if we could get it online before 'Merapa reaches Bezarna," Dirck mused. "So time's against us on that one, considering we're not even close to duplicating the effects and the Tank's inaccessible, even if it would work for off-world teleportation."

"And inoperative anyway, even here," Creena reminded him.

"So we're dealing with the challenges of innovation versus known but unavailable technology," Win went on, sitting down on the nearest stool and tapping his fingers on the workdeck.

"Plus the psitenna," Dirck added with a pensive look as he picked it up from the table and rotated it almost reverently between his hands. "Don't forget it was the combined effects with the Tank that triggered the chronoviatic aspects."

"The devenite is obviously more powerful and since the quantities of both may be limited, it looks as if it's our best bet," Win stated. "We'll just have to deal with timeshifting the best we can."

The risks, however, were overwhelming, bringing to mind Storm's admonition about the lethal potential of technological breakthroughs. At least their experience thus far indicated that the destination was predictable with only the timing unknown. Creena had gone from the pool to the Tank on target, likewise all of them from the Caverns to Dirck's quarters. The primary unknown was what determined the ETA, *i.e.*, estimated time of arrival.

"I'm glad Bryl's research team is coming in to run this thing," Win stated. "Maybe they'll be able to put everything together. They'll have an advantage, coming in cold. We may have missed something that they'll pick up on right away."

"So what do we do until they get here?" Dirck asked.

"Brainstorm," Win suggested. "Let's just figure out exactly what we know versus what we don't. Then we'll at least be able to give them a coherent briefing when they get here, so we don't look like total morons."

"There's still one thing that bothers me about this," Creena said awkwardly.

"What's that?" Win asked.

"The fact that 'Merapa will be on Bezarna real soon, meaning our success is entirely based on perfecting something we know hardly anything about. And he specifically said not to use timeshifting."

"That's two things," Dirck stated.

"Sorry."

"Let me put it this way. Do you ever want to see him again?" Dirck's tone was a mixture of empathy and persuasion.

"Of course I do," she replied. "You know that and I assume you do, too."

"Exactly. And like both Bryl and 'Merama said, he always underestimated his worth. And like you said yourself, he'd want us to follow orders. So it's simple. We do what we were told to do."

"Sometimes it's easier to get forgiveness than permission," Win added with a wry smile. "It's worked for me, various times."

"I suppose," Creena agreed reluctantly. "But I still don't like doing exactly what he told us not to."

"Do you have any other alternatives?"

"Not that we can finish in a week."

"Actually, if we figure it out, we can go back in time to get him, so we're really not limited to a week," Dirck added.

"Maybe," Win said. "There's no telling when a blackhole is involved. Time may not exist and thus not be reversible."

"Good point. So we'll shoot for a week, and if it takes longer, hope for the best." Dirck set the psitenna back on the table and nodded firmly in emphasis. "Chronoviatic transfer it is. Let's take a look at what we've figured out so far."

* * *

Integrator Central
Sub-Level 9
Cira City

"Something's not right onboard the *Bezarna Express,* General."

Troy braced himself, glad the contact was being made remotely from the relative safety of his office as Spoigan's image looked up, frowning. The Quadrumvirate's second in command turned slowly toward his comcon, his huge form nearly obstructing the holomap behind him as he glared, furious, with that look he got when a problem he thought was resolved returned with full force.

"What could possibly be wrong?" his superior growled. "It's secure and automated. Only two prisoners remain, with a contingency plan in place if they don't self-dispatch."

Troy flexed his jaw, knowing Spoigan was right, yet also acutely aware there were no guarantees everything would go as planned, especially with Brightstar involved. "There have been several intrusion alarms indicating someone's been accessing those systems," he said. "We've also detected psi activity in both directions."

"We know Brightstar talked to his family," Spoigan admitted. "No big surprise. It's how we determined their location and confirmed they're alive. Having his and his daughter's mindprints on file made it a simple matching exercise. They're apparently making progress with psi comm, which we're monitoring. Anything of value they discover will benefit and accelerate our efforts. So what's the problem?"

"This is different. This psi traffic had an entirely different signature, mostly uploads. Encrypted. Highly encrypted, using some advanced scheme we've never seen before. He's up to something, I know he is."

Spoigan emitted an exasperated sigh. "Troy, your obsession with this man is unacceptable. There's nothing he can do."

"You don't know him like I do, General. I'd feel better if we locked the trajectory. The return option is a gateway with tamper potential. If it can't be altered, then anything he does will be ineffective. We could deactivate the nav system once gravity takes over and just let it follow a ballistic path to its supposed destination."

Spoigan straightened, studying his face for a long moment. "What about the escort?"

"What about him? He's a guard. Compared to Brightstar coming back, an insignificant sacrifice."

Spoigan's forehead creased with thought as he pursed heavy lips. "Okay, I suppose the guard's expendable. But losing that vehicle is of greater concern. It's a valuable piece of hardware, Troy, and we don't have that many configured for that function. There's a reason we bring them back, you know. You need to change that mindset of yours that assets are all expendable, whether flesh and bone or alloys and electronics."

Troy held his gaze as his mind switched to less expensive alternatives. "We could depress the cabin," he suggested.

"A bit messy, don't you think?"

Troy laughed. "I suppose, but it'd send a strong message to the prisoners tasked with cleaning it out."

Spoigan laughed as well, a short burst that brought an unexpected break in his usually flawless control. So beneath that iron façade lurked a sense of humor after all, albeit a dark one.

"Just cutting off the oxygen generator would eliminate the mess," Troy went on. "If we did it during sleepzone, they'd never know the difference."

Spoigan looked pensive then slowly nodded. "Sounds like a plan, Troy. It could be explained as a malfunction and even has a humane twist, as executions go. That I can buy into. In fact, it's really quite brilliant. Maybe we ought to handle all of them that way in the future."

Troy smiled. "Always glad to be of assistance, General." He leaned back in his chair and smiled, already looking forward to witnessing the final result via tachyonic video feed. "And by the way," he added, "We've been able to pick up another team of researchers with excellent experience which should accelerate the efforts of our comm team."

"Excellent. Where from?"

Troy chuckled in spite of himself. "Esheron."

"Indeed. Good work, Troy."

"Thank you, sir," he replied, disguising his arrogant sneer with a snappy salute before terminating the transmission.

* * *

<table>
<tr><td colspan="2" align="center">Integrator Central

TBA

Technical Breakthrough Advisory</td></tr>
<tr><td>TEAM: Communications</td><td>PROJECT: Encephalographic Access/Reception</td></tr>
<tr><td>Date: DDW-128</td><td>Clearance: Top Secret</td></tr>
<tr><td colspan="2">Breakthrough/Milestone: Acquisition of Additional Research Assistants</td></tr>
<tr><td>Schedule Impact: Y/N? Y</td><td>Days: Unknown/Positive</td></tr>
<tr><td colspan="2">SUMMARY: A team of researchers skilled in psi communications has been detained in immigration incoming from Esheron. Individuals lack proper visas given sensitivity of their knowledge base and have been turned over to Integrated authorities for reassignment as opposed to deportation.</td></tr>
</table>

MOTIVES

Sharra sat in the back of the messhall, forcing her thoughts to something positive. The first thing that came to mind was how good it felt not to worry over where the next meal was coming from. The return to order quietly nourished her Miran roots, food availability one of the few circumstances in her life that she could feel comfortable about. That, and the fact her children were back together, almost giving an illusion of normalcy reminiscent of Mira III when Laren was deployed. The reality that this time he was unlikely to return, however, forever lurked just within the bounds of conscious thought.

She wasn't sure whether she was glad or not she hadn't been given an assignment. As the commander's bondling she wasn't expected to work, nor allowed, as Storm had told her when she'd initially requested involvement. While sorting through intelligence data in the Caverns had been stressful, it had also distracted her from reality. She hated being alone most of the time, yet didn't want to bother the others, so usually found herself in *Intelligence* seeing if she could help or sitting at that same table in the messhall, sipping a cup of sennulian tea.

As she thought back over the past several years, she had to admit she'd done better on her own than she'd ever imagined possible. Courage was not something she'd needed on Mira III and she'd never given much thought to whether she had any or not. Yet somehow, fear notwithstanding, she'd faced each day and gotten through, for her children if nothing else. Admittedly, her introduction to Laren's Ledorian beliefs had come at a good time, when she surely needed to believe that some infinite power of goodness existed somewhere. Regardless of all that, however, there was still one thing that never changed, that his loss left a void that could never be filled.

She watched as others wandered through in a steady stream that dwindled slightly between scheduled mealzones but never stopped. Currently, there were four others, two humans at separate tables and a pair of Erebusites making their selections, *videras* angled to checkout the menu options. Movement caught her eye and her frame stiffened as a tall female figure of substantial rank entered; Bryl Woeyel. Her long, dark hair seemed incongruent with the military fashion statement, heavy locks held by a single restraint at the nape of her neck from which numerous strands had escaped to cascade halfway down her back.

If one individual, other than the INTEGRATOR and his insidious cronies, was responsible for Sharra's sorry situation, Delta Region's former Governor was certainly the best candidate. She thought back to the first time they'd met at Jen's subterre, back when the woman gave Laren asylum after the prison break. Even then she hadn't liked, much less trusted her, with less reason to do so now than ever before. She and Laren had hit it off just a little too well, and it wasn't hard to recognize the look of a predator in the woman's dark eyes.

Neither Dirck nor Creena had told her much about their dream, neither had she asked. She'd always trusted her bondling implicitly, even on Mira III where such offensive behavior was commonplace. He'd promised to be faithful and she knew he was. But that was before she'd encountered the intricacies of the ECL.

No matter how much sense the Esheronian Contingency Law made on that world, before she'd be party to it she'd rather die. It sounded too much like the very thing their *Promises* vowed to shun. It was abhorrent when it was to her advantage, licentious for what that dreadful woman had in mind.

Share her bondling, indeed! *Over my dead body*, she thought.

Life on Mira III had been so perfect, her only concerns incident to his safety during offworld assignments. All that had faded in bland obscurity with their arrival on Cyraria, where his absence was punctuated by fear, for both her own as well as their children's very existence. It hadn't taken long to realize how much she really needed him simply to survive in ways she'd never before imagined, neither could have. She shuddered with the memory of when she and Deven had been nearly out of genour and she had no idea if, much less when, he and Dirck might return.

Each reunion after that had been sweeter than she'd ever thought possible, but the price had been steep. Each subsequent separation had been harder to bear, her only consolation the fact he'd been hers entirely, mind, body and soul. And if his belief in eternity turned out to be true, he'd be hers there as well.

Or thus it was until Governor Woeyel entered the scene. When they'd first bonded long ago, Laren had teased Sharra about multiple bondlings being legal on his *naterra*, knowledge that had impaled her heart. His reassurances that it would never happen had been fiercely insistent and eventually accepted, until gradually the fears diminished. Until Cyraria. The doubts had been fleeting at first, constant thereafter, evolving to a gaping wound of insecurity. As much as she longed to hear it was unfounded, she likewise feared confirming the worst.

Not that it mattered anymore. And as much as she wanted to believe they'd bring him back, something inside resisted.

The very fact her bondling was gone, however, introduced yet another element. No one knew whether Dirck and Creena's dream had ever materialized or not. For all she knew, maybe that woman had already laid legal claim to him.

She watched as the woman gathered her choices from the dispensers and arranged them on her tray. Or maybe she did betray him, adamant orders to recover him notwithstanding. Maybe she'd done so in a moment of rage, perhaps at his refusal, only to regret it later. She stifled an angry sigh, continuing to watch from the corner of her eye as her assumed rival selected some biscuits and, like herself, sennulian tea. Then, much to her horror, the woman threaded her way between the empty tables, straight in her direction, making a hasty retreat out of the question.

Grateful for her years of practice with Miran composure, Sharra took a deep breath and met Bryl's gaze, which she held as the woman approached, hoping her eyes wouldn't betray her thoughts. The woman's face was entirely unreadable, intent unknown, defying Sharra's usually astute feminine intuition. And then she was there, eyes locked on hers, as she stood on the other side of the small table.

"Hello, Sharra," she said amicably, tone entirely different from the one in her office. "First of all I want to tell you how sorry I am about Laren. His loss is a tragedy to us all, but most certainly for you and your children. I am truly sorry."

Thrown somewhat by her kindness, it took a moment before Sharra realized she was staring, mouth agape. "T-thank you," she finally stammered. "Would you like to sit down?"

Bryl scowled at the digichronometer on her sleeve before answering. "Yes, thank you, I would, but I don't have much time." She sighed and took the seat across from her, expression still unreadable. "I'm glad you and your family got here safely," she went on. "You're all tremendous assets to the Clique. Are you comfortable with not having an assignment? If so, that's not a problem, but I thought you might need to get your mind off things."

Sharra smiled in spite of herself. "Governor Woeyel, I, I'm sorry, I mean Commander Woeyel, I would love to have an assignment, but I was told that I couldn't because I was the commander's bondling."

"First of all, please call me Bryl," the woman replied. "And as far as an assignment is concerned, much has changed since then. Laren relinquished his post to the Council and they appointed me, so he is no longer in command. If you would like to be involved, it can be arranged. We need all the help we can get and there's probably no one here, except perhaps your children, who would be more dedicated to INTEGRATOR defeat."

Sharra eyed her closely for any sign her comments were sarcastic or insincere. Seeing none, she allowed herself to absorb the woman's words at the emotional level. Even her Miran upbringing was not enough to keep her eyes from filling with tears. She tried unsuccessfully to blink them away, annoyed with herself when one escaped and dribbled down her cheek.

"Thank you for understanding," she said softly. "I would be honored to serve in any capacity you choose."

"Let's make that any capacity *you* choose," Bryl replied. "Storm can show you the open billets via his comcon. Look them over, then let me know which one you want and it's yours."

In spite of her best efforts, everything Sharra had either suppressed or denied the past week slipped their bonds. She buried her face in her hands and tried to hold back the sobs, which only served to make them worse. Before she knew it, Bryl was in the chair beside her, arm around her shoulders in attempted comfort, head resting against hers. When Sharra finally got herself back under control and looked up, incredibly embarrassed, she could see that her assumed nemesis was tearful, too.

"Sharra, there's something I really think you need to know," Bryl said, unashamedly wiping her eyes, moisture clinging stubbornly to her dark lashes. "I don't know how often Laren told you how he felt, but he told me once how you owned his heart, that he was so lucky to have you, and would do anything, including die, for you. Knowing that, I feel as if he would want me to take care of you and your family in any way I can. If you or any of your children need anything, please let me know."

Sharra bit her lip as a new wave of emotion roiled through her, questioning the harsh and bitter feelings she'd held toward the former Regional Governor.

"Thank you," she whispered. "For everything."

"No. Thank *you*," Bryl replied. "And I really do intend to do everything possible to bring him back. For both of our sakes." She glanced at her sleeve again and sighed. "I'm sorry, but I have to go. Remember," she went on, touching her hand, "don't hesitate to contact me if there's anything I can do."

"I will," Sharra replied, then watched her leave through different eyes than those that had dreaded her approach only moments before. She took a deep breath and sighed, then glanced around the messhall, noticing that the number had increased by an order of magnitude and every one of them was watching. She straightened in her chair and smiled, picking up her tea for a final sip with a shaky hand, amazed how everything she'd originally felt about their commander had apparently been wrong.

Or was it?

She froze as another possibility slipped into her mind. According to her understanding of the ECL, as Laren's first bondling she had to grant permission for any additions. Was it possible that allowing that woman to share her bondling was what this show of compassion, sincere or otherwise, was all about?

She sighed, suspicion rekindling the dark emotions so briefly put to rest.

* * *

INTEGRATOR Headquarters
Cira City

Rohtik Spoigan examined the small device confiscated from one of their most recent albeit reluctant recruits, acutely aware of its owner's indignation as he did so. Its elliptical shape fit his hand comfortably, metal case cool, yet somehow alive, as if checking him out in some weird, covert way. He set it back on his workdeck cautiously, not trusting it. For all he knew it could kill him.

"You can either tell me what this thing does and how it works, Professor Denale, or join others who have defied command," he said coldly.

The young woman on the other side of his gleaming stone-topped workdeck met his gaze with a look of contempt rarely seen in either gender. Her blazing eyes, emphasized by short dark hair, high cheekbones and anger-flushed olive complexion, possessed an intensity which charged the air, evoking a reaction unlike any he'd experienced before.

"As you well know, I'm lead scientist of this expedition, which you so rudely detained," she stated, matching his tone. "Kill me and my knowledge goes with it. Clearly you're unfamiliar with Esheronians, General. We don't fear death. It surrounds us on our world. Dying is but part of life. The end of one cycle and start of another. To die without honor is by far the worser fate."

Her words echoed in the marble chamber, as cold as its polished walls, something about her demeanor sending a chill up his spine. Never had he seen such strength and determination in the face of such formidable odds, especially in someone so young, as near as he could tell probably not much more than twenty. That, combined with the knowledge she had, was certainly a testimonial to Esheron's education system. He made a mental note to study their culture more thoroughly so they could learn how to instill the same in INTEGRATED youth. With an army with as much integrity as she displayed, they could conquer the galaxy.

"So you have no problem condemning the rest of your team to the same fate?" he asked, eyeing the small device, then cautiously picking it up once more. "Over this?"

"Over anything that could benefit your insidious cause," she replied, stoic posture unchanged.

"You realize, of course, that our own people can reverse engineer this device with no assistance from you or your team. You are, indeed, dispensable."

"As we all are, General," she replied, eyes unwavering.

"Indeed."

He shifted his attention back to the small metal case, wondering what secrets it could hold worthy of claiming its owner's life, much less the entire entourage. He examined every millimeter again, finding no distinguishing marks, means for activation, or any clue whatsoever related to its function, other than the odd feeling that it was somehow intelligent or even alive.

Was it his imagination or was its surface getting warmer? Vibrations, at first subtle, then demanding, followed, until he thought it would leap from his hand. He set it back on the workdeck's stone surface, mesmerized as it repeatedly faded from view, then reappeared. He blinked, rubbed his eyes, and instinctively leaned back cautiously, as again he met the woman's icy gaze. Her expression had evolved from ironclad resistance to defiance, yet bespoke genuine amusement as the object evaporated, leaving not the slightest trace of its existence behind.

"Where'd it go?" he asked, flabbergasted.

"Home," she replied, still smiling even as her eyes bespoke successful retaliation.

For a moment, he retraced the day's events, seriously wondering if the entire experience was a dream, and braced himself for her to likewise disappear. She didn't, convincing him the experience was real, yet failing to remove his consternation. Disappearing entryways and other illusions created by energy fields were commonplace, but he'd never seen a piece of hardware do so before. Either it had passed into another dimension, making it multi-dimensional, or converted from mass to energy, a feat typically requiring lasoclear reactions to achieve.

Gradually, control returned as he scrutinized the female before him with different eyes. Her black hair framed remarkably delicate features including a straight nose, deepset eyes the color of lemitini cocoa and full lips which continued to maintain a satisfied simper. Never had he seen such strength residing in such an attractive and delicate package. He'd always been impervious to female wiles, viewing women as weak and inferior or, at best, a nuisance, but this one was indeed a different breed.

Admittedly, he didn't know much about Esheron besides the fact Woeyel hailed from there, the paternal half of Brightstar's heritage as well. Troy was certainly correct in thinking the likes of them could be their greatest asset or most formidable opponent. That integrity factor was what consistently got in the way, however. But like gravity, there was more than one way to use or reverse it to one's advantage.

Deciding upon an alternate approach, he leaned back in his chair with folded arms, gaze fusing once more with hers, but this time with an entirely different frequency.

"Good one, Professor," he admitted, punctuating it with a rare smile. "I'm impressed. Obviously your *naterra* has achieved a level of technological expertise that ours currently lacks. I've never been to Esheron, but you've certainly piqued my interest. How would *you* feel about likewise going *home*?"

A MATTER OF TIME

By the next day, Creena wasn't sure whether they'd accomplished anything or not. She sighed, frustrated, and shifted on her stool at her lab workdeck, facts ricocheting inside her head so fast she couldn't capture a single one. Whatever would make controlled chronoviatic transfer reality was there, but putting the information together was like trying to assemble a starship with a lasoclear bomb.

They certainly hadn't found anything significant enough to report to Bryl, who came by so often that using her for a test subject held more appeal every hour. The fact that roughly five days remained before timeshifting was their only option didn't help, shoving them forward along a precarious path they'd barely begun to map.

Meanwhile, Deven and 'Merama were busy hauling their cyllmats to Cranium Cavern for the dream experiment. The odd chamber definitely deserved its name, walls bulging and heaving with what looked like boiling stone set in time, the resemblance to a giant brain unmistakable. It was mostly grey, darker in the network of crevices which outlined its bubble-like surface. But it was more than that. It seemed to glow, displaying a subtle iridescence that tickled the back of her mind with similarities to the Think Tank's trapped photon emissions.

The lab, on the other hand, where she sat alone, possessed walls which were smooth and stratified with shades of brown and black, their overall impression dark, but not oppressive. It was definitely austere, offering no distractions to the work at hand, at least not by appearance, any inherent natural beauty disrupted by the miasma of wires and cables cluttering the surface.

Her thoughts wandered back to the dream experiment since it also related to warping time. Clearly one, or perhaps both, crystals together facilitated a connection between sleeptime brain activity and some other dimension. How devenite physically transported someone to another point in time, however, was much more complicated; chronoviatic transfer wasn't simply a vision, it was real.

Cristobalite manifested thoughts into reality; devenite manipulated time, apparently based on feelings of different frequencies that covered the emotional spectrum.

But how?

Any theories that resulted from the dream experiment could expedite progress, especially since it didn't require any extra time. They had to sleep sometime, whether they wanted to or not. If there was one thing she'd learned back at the Caverns, it was that going without sleep didn't help. Rather, it compromised judgment and thinking to the point of being self-defeating.

She forced her thoughts back to the basics, that cristobalite was sensitive to psi generated by a person's mind, and devenite to psi from a person's heart. She frowned, recognizing they really needed to come up with a term for each to avoid confusion. Something simple. Like c-waves for communication, brain-based psi, and e-waves for empathic heart-based psi.

Yeah, that would work. If nothing else, it made it easier to visualize the two interacting, especially when she thought of them in different colors.

Obviously, cristoviatic and chronoviatic teleportation were closely related, or became such when cristobalite and devenite worked together. So how could she test the concept without jeopardizing someone with an inadvertent time shift?

Unless, of course, Commander Woeyel was willing to volunteer. She sniggered at the thought, indulging in its implications for a few moments before finally refocusing on her work.

Veridical dreams so far involved the future, reaching forward in time to extract information that could be used to avoid an emotionally devastating event. Both emotion and time were involved, which further confirmed they were related to devenite.

She pondered everything she knew about time travel, mostly related to space and objects moving near the speed of light or using warp harmonics, technologies that manipulated gravity waves to bend and shorten distances in the spacetime continuum. All such influences resulted in different reference frames, different accelerations, and different clock rates. Her thoughts turned to 'Merapa, who was probably moving close to lightspeed as well as some warp harmonic, each one shrinking space by an order of magnitude, like a logarithmic scale. Igni would probably know which one, since the prison ship was the same model as the *Volition*. She'd have to ask him about that.

As she recalled, time onboard a starship moving at warp speed proceeded at a different rate than an inertial reference frame, a fancy term for something that wasn't moving, like a planet. Of course planets moved, not only by rotation on their axis causing day and night, but also along its orbit around its host star. Except for rogue planets which had gotten lost someway or another and just roamed about interstellar space at the mercy of any gravitational fields. Nonetheless, planets weren't moving even close to the speed of light, so relativity didn't apply, at least in most cases, since the effects were miniscule.

She thought back to when they left Mira III onboard the *Aquarius*, remembering 'Merapa explaining how hundreds of years would pass on Mira III while they traveled for what seemed like about a month. Starships adjusted their time backward to the appropriate Galactic Standard Time defined by the Hostii Intergalactic Organization or HIO upon arrival to maintain continuity as well as avoid the misuse of chronoviatic effects. Which definitely indicated that the HIO had the ability to manipulate time; too bad they couldn't convince them to help. Furthermore, how did they do it? Devenite? Not likely, manipulation of space-time probably achieved through some other means, probably gravitons.

Slowly, a subconscious whisper broke the surface of awareness. If time was going that much slower onboard 'Merapa's craft, then they should have more than a few days. Could Storm have been mistaken when he made those calculations?

Hardly daring to hope, she sent an urgent message to Igni, asking what the average intragalactic velocity and warp rate was for a spacecraft like *Volition*. She'd spent enough time on the vessel she should have known, but simply hadn't paid attention, her focus on getting to Mira III, then later to Cyraria. The insectoid responded quickly and she entered the information into the comcon to calculate relative time.

She gasped at the result, realizing Storm had done it backwards. It was approximately a week onboard the prison ship, not Cyraria. They actually had *years* to work the problem before 'Merapa would arrive on Bezarna.

Her head and heart raced with hope at the implications, not knowing whom to tell first, Dirck or 'Merama. But what if she was wrong as well? She needed someone to check and make sure it was correct before revealing something with such emotional impact. That narrowed it down to Win or Igni, the latter the obvious choice, given he'd provided the input.

She fired off another urgent message with the results of the calculations and requested verification. This time the response didn't come as quickly as hoped. As minutes dragged by, she finally got down from the stool and paced impatiently. She laughed at herself, recognizing the irony of being in such a hurry to tell everyone they may have all the time in the world, perhaps their entire lifetime, to find a solution. At worst, they would all age at the usual on-world rate while 'Merapa wouldn't, meaning he could come back younger than she was or even Deven. She smiled at the thought, trying to imagine what that would be like.

Impatience flared again and about the time she was ready to hunt him down, she heard the distinctive clickity-click of multiple feet in the stone passageway, coming her way at an accelerated pace. She stepped outside the lab, fidgeting until he came into view. At that point she could tell by the angle of his antennae that the news was positive.

She covered her mouth, stifling laughter punctuated by tears as he closed the space between them and bestowed a congratulatory pat on her back.

"Concede results. What thought had you to check such things?" he asked.

"I just started thinking about everything I knew about time travel, including how relativity affects a starship. I thought I remembered that lots of time passes on a planet when someone is traveling in space and took it from there."

"Genius, young one!" Igni said, enthusiasm coming through the translator with a few sounds she'd never heard before. "Have you given news to others?"

"No, I wanted to make sure I didn't make any mistakes."

"Calculations correct. Those who travel much in space forget effects as adjusted on arrival by HIO. Remember addition of time assist father only. Still must develop chronoviatic technology before INTEGRATOR."

"Oh," she said, somewhat crestfallen. "You're right. Time is still not on our side."

"Concede. But can hope similar victories follow."

"Too bad we can't find some extra time here as well."

"Concede."

* * *

Integrator *Headquarters*
Cira City

"Tell me, Troy, how much do you know about Esheron? Or more specifically, their technology?"

Augustus Troy sat on the other side of his superior's marble workdeck and studied his face, wondering what prompted such a question. There was something about the look in the Territorial General's dark and deeply set eyes that suggested an ulterior motive, which put him on alert. Just because he felt as if he knew Brightstar inside out didn't mean he was an expert on the man's cultural roots, much less his *naterra's* technology.

Yet, it was considerably flattering that Spoigan would ask him anything. He certainly never had before. Conversely, if he couldn't satisfy his expectations it could conceivably drive him down a notch in the promotion listings. Perhaps this was some sort of test. One he needed to pass to assure his current status as Deputy Territorial General wasn't compromised.

So what did he know? Not much. He thought of his nemesis and tried to remember anything that could relate, even in the remotest way. The man had certainly been more resistant than most to prison interrogation techniques. And then there was the matter of that prison break. How they so cleverly faked the man's medical death was definitely an enigma. But surely, as closely as he'd followed Brightstar with the original intent of recruiting him, he had to know something useful.

"Well, Troy?" Spoigan prompted. "Surely you must know something, considering how determined you were to bring this man, or even his daughter, over to our side."

"They definitely possess superior intelligence," he answered pensively. "Largely because they excel at integrating the right and left hemispheres in their brains to synthesize information, combining logic with intuition in a powerful way. Which must be related somehow to being a hybrid. Both human, but entirely different gene pools from diverse planets."

"I'm not interested in Brightstar, Troy," Spoigan stated with an impatient sigh. "At least not in this context. I'm interested in Esheron's technology."

"Right." Troy bit the inside of his lip, hoping his scowl looked pensive as opposed to reflecting the irritation he felt at the put-down. "They're mostly self-contained as a planet. Few imports or exports. Their culture is so given to wars and disputes it's hard to say how much time and effort is given to develop anything other than weaponry."

Spoigan adjusted his posture impatiently. "I'm not talking about weaponry, even though a military focus would undoubtedly relate to having advanced skills in tactical and strategic planning."

The General's expression relaxed slightly in spite of the fact the man's coal-like eyes still drilled into Troy's, suggesting his superior was about to reveal something important.

"As you know, we recently detained another research group Woeyel brought in," the man went on. "The first team reluctantly helped us develop a theoretical model for a psicomm bandpass filter. That's the reason we're as far along as we are in developing controlled individual encephalographic access, at least when we have a mindprint. When that's fully implemented, which should be soon, we'll be able to input as well as listen to anyone's thoughts at the turn of a dial and ideally, at some point, access and store everything in their brain as well."

Troy nodded, remembering well the exuberated feeling he'd enjoyed on that momentous occasion when a TBA had shown up on his comcon making the bandpass filter announcement. After that, all they needed were the right materials, which they'd since also acquired, suggesting total victory was within reach. But Spoigan's frustrated expression didn't support such an outcome.

"However," the general went on, "when the second team got here, we made the mistake of letting them work together. We figured they'd make faster progress if we allowed them to collaborate. Big mistake. Since that time, they won't cooperate.

Any of them. Apparently, they've become aware that their efforts are in direct conflict, literally and figuratively, with their original employer. I don't know if it's loyalty, nationalism, the ethics of revealing Woeyel Industries' proprietary data, or what, but if they don't get with the program soon, they'll be the next passengers on the *Bezarna Express*."

"What are you saying, General? Have they sabotaged their previous work?"

"Not entirely. Fortunately, our own scientists were involved enough that we haven't lost our grip. But the final application of screening mindsets and integrating individual mindprints into the propaganda machine has stalled."

"That is, of course, very unfortunate," Troy answered sympathetically. "But I don't understand what you think I might know about the engineering specifics. My work on Spectra was at a much broader level and didn't involve individual access, only collective influence on the masses plus it involved simple radio waves. They influence the brain, but are entirely different from psi, which isn't part of the electromagnetic spectrum."

"I know, Troy. Frankly I'm beginning to wonder why I'm even discussing this with you. You apparently don't have a clue how to deal with this, either."

Troy shifted uncomfortably in his chair and bit his thumbnail nervously, knowing if he didn't come up with something incredibly brilliant soon he'd either be demoted or on the same one-way trip with Woeyel's recalcitrant scientists.

"I wonder what was causing that psi traffic detected on the *Bezarna Express?*" he mused aloud. "It had some new technology behind it, considering the complex encryption scheme involved. Even with Brightstar's mindprint we couldn't break it."

For the first time Spoigan looked interested. "Did you ever see Brightstar use a small, handheld device? One with no visible markings, obvious functionality, or power source?"

"Not that I recall," Troy replied. "We could always pull up the video feed from the Bezarna Express to see what it shows."

Within moments the general downloaded archive recordings of cabin activities, quickly answering the question.

"Just what I suspected," Spoigan stated. "A few days ago I confiscated a similar device from the lead scientist we detained. She refused to tell me what it was and somehow made it disappear right here on my workdeck, right before my eyes. I asked her where it went, and she sarcastically told me it had gone *home*. Apparently, it's some sort of psi-driven communication device and probably exactly what we need for the next phase. Ironically, now that we have the needed components, they've refused to go any further."

"Does anyone else on the team have one? If we could get our hands of one, I'm sure our people could back-engineer it, especially given the work previously done."

"As far as we can tell, they've all *gone home*," Spoigan said sarcastically. "Originally, as near as our own people recall, all detainees possessed one, but now there are none to be found and they've all refused to discuss the issue any further. She and everyone else are willing to die before revealing anything about it."

"The device's disappearance suggests they're capable of operating in at least two dimensions of either time or space," Troy speculated aloud. "Interesting. Which explains why it could transmit psi on universal as well as localized time."

"Good point, Troy. I think it's important enough that I'm considering a short trip to Esheron to see about acquiring one directly."

Troy frowned pensively. "A bit dangerous, don't you think, General?"

"Not necessarily, if I have the rather, uh, pleasant looking team lead along as a facilitator."

Troy chuckled. "More like hostage."

Spoigan almost smiled. "Right. Furthermore, I'd be interested to see what kind of welcome she'd provide to her *naterra*."

Troy laughed. "Knowing Esheronian women, it may not be what you expect. I may have a safer but certainly less stimulating alternative. The *Bezarna Express* should have the capability to analyze anything onboard. We may be able to get enough information remotely to back-engineer the thing without actually having one here."

His superior's expression brightened, reassuring Troy he was back on the promotion list, provided he could actually deliver the promised information.

"I'll get my people on it immediately, General," he stated confidently. "Meanwhile, you may want to book some seats on the next Bezarna run, don't you think?"

The general's sneer was cruel, his intent clear. "I do believe I will," he replied. "But not before I extract a bit of amusement first."

The man stood up behind his desk and saluted sharply, something he'd never done in all the years Troy had worked under him. He returned it with equal enthusiasm, at once excited and relieved.

"Am I correct to assume I've provided the information you were seeking, General?" he asked.

"You certainly did, Troy," he replied. "You certainly did. Assuming you can indeed provide what we need to fabricate one. If not, then I at least have an alternate plan. Either way, we'll get back on schedule."

"Yes, sir," Troy responded, a small knot of trepidation forming in his gut at the prospect of failure until he realized he couldn't lose. "If nothing else, when the vehicle returns, we'll have one in hand," he stated.

"Right. Along with Brightstar's dead body," Spoigan added.

Troy smiled, eyes gleaming with anticipation. "Yes, sir," he replied with another snappy salute. "We certainly will."

WAVES

The others took the news concerning the timing issue much as Creena had, *i.e.*, elation quickly followed by an abrupt tumble back to reality. It was still necessary to defend Apoca, the Clique's last remaining stronghold, before the INTEGRATOR used the technology to annihilate them. Storm was apologetic, repeating again that he wasn't an engineer or scientist. Commander Woeyel was pensive, giving careful consideration to the implications before changing any directives. For the present, they were to continue as before, except for Win, who was assigned back to his post in *Intelligence* to see what they could flush out regarding how the opposition was progressing technologically.

Meanwhile, Creena and Dirck sat in their usual places in the lab and resumed their quest regarding if and how c-waves and e-waves interacted to activate chronoviatic transfer.

"So we're pretty sure that e-waves trigger the timeshift," Dirck stated, meeting her gaze from the other side of the workdeck. "We just don't know how the timeframe is determined."

"Right," she agreed. "The person decides where, and cristobalite delivers. But there has to be similar logic behind the timeshift, even if it's at the emotional as opposed to the mental level."

"I like that," he said. "It's as if the heart's looking for safety and somehow the Universe knows when that will be."

"Yes! That feels right! It's like devenite reads your heart and taps into the future to determine when that might be. Either that, or the Universe reaches back in warning, which comes in the form of a veridical dream."

"That fits," he said. "Apparently e-waves are timeless, so accessing the future would be a simple matter."

"I wonder if it's the Universe or our subconscious," Creena speculated.

"Could be," Dirck agreed, pensively tapping the workdeck. "It ties in with the concept that thoughts become things, which was how the Think Tank operated. Our thoughts, either conscious or subconscious, are the primary driver."

"Based on that, why did we arrive when we did instead of immediately?" Creena asked. "What happened during the eleven days or so we were lost in time that related to emotional security?"

His rhythmic rapping continued for a while, almost hypnotic, then abruptly stopped. Creena exited her own ponderings, unable to tell if her brother's expression reflected shock, horror, revelation or all three.

"Holy holocubes," he said, half under his breath. "Holy holocubes. That's it."

"What?" she prompted. "What happened?"

He let his breath out in a clipped sigh, looking at her as if she'd sprouted a few additional eyes or limbs.

"Holy holocubes," he whispered again.

"Dirck," she stated firmly, eyes locked on his. "You're making me crazy. Have you figured something out or lost your orbit? Talk to me, bro!"

"All right," he said, swallowing hard. "All right. Here, uh, here goes. That was the, the worst time of my entire life. The absolute worst. Everyone I cared about, everyone, was gone. *Everyone.* 'Merapa, of course, plus you, 'Merama, Deven and then even Win. I was a total wreck. I'd never felt so alone."

He sighed heavily, as if even the memory was hard to bear. "At first I wanted to die, too," he said, voice heavy with emotion. "But then I realized how cowardly that would be. Facing everyone in that state, assuming we'd meet up somewhere in another dimension, was horrifying. So I decided I had to do everything I could to help the Clique as a memorial to what the rest of you died for. I still hurt, a lot, but I made up my mind to do something everyone would be proud of, whether they were here or not."

He smiled slowly as he finished the tale, eyes reflecting the change he'd experienced. "That was when I solved the magnetite problem at the power plant. I shifted to a more positive energy, for one thing. But beyond that, my feelings toward everyone, especially you, went to an entirely different level. I understood things I never had before. I realized why you were so obsessed with getting the family together again. I knew what it felt like to be alone and abandoned. And then *Boom!* You all got here that night."

Creena's eyes glazed with tears as she realized what had occurred. "Oh, Dirck!" she exclaimed. "That's so amazing! Here's what else I think happened. I was the one with the psitenna and was thinking of you here at Apoca, so that set the place through the cristobalite and probably was assisted by the Tank. But my heart also must have connected with yours through the devenite in the psitenna, which brought me here at a time that would be best for us both, which was only after you'd discovered what it felt like to be completely alone."

"Right," he said, nodding agreement. "That's what it seems like, all right."

"That is so awesome," she commented. Her eyes widened with another realization. "And you know what? This is even stranger. Getting along wasn't ever on my mind in the Caverns, only getting here. But I'd wished for that back on Terra!" She quickly recounted her experience with Allen Benson, when he'd told her about his feelings toward Tammy. "So that's the original reference point. The Universe remembered the past and connected it to the future when the opportunity arose."

"Wow," Dirck whispered again. "That's incredible."

"But there's still a problem," she went on. "If e-waves match past intent with a suitable future reality, we still don't know how or if we can control the timing."

"Sounds logical," he replied.

"But what if the intent is negative?" she speculated aloud. "It's pretty obvious the INTEGRATOR isn't interested in anyone's well-being, emotional or otherwise. Their goal is to dissolve everyone's identity into one that obeys."

"Which is negative energy. And we don't have any idea how devenite reacts to that. If it operates based on what your heart wants, it could theoretically take a person back in time to a point where they could achieve complete control. Or they could use c-waves to make people think whatever the INTEGRATOR wants them to, making everyone like 'troids that simply do what they're programmed to do."

"Exactly," Creena agreed. "I know what that feels like, too. When I was on Terra, someone or something tried to control my mind and make me go with him or someone he sent."

"What did you do? Obviously you resisted. How?" Dirck asked, eyes wide.

"I couldn't, or at least I didn't think I could. I called Thyron for help and he coached me out of it. If he hadn't responded, they would have had me."

"When we use psi, or c-waves, to communicate, we just concentrate on the person or place and it connects automatically. How do you think the INTEGRATOR knows you? Or how to contact you, specifically?"

"I don't know," she replied, mystified. "I guess we have some unique identifier that can be defined. Like a mindprint." Her eyes widened with the realization she'd made an important discovery. "Yes, that's it. Somehow they can figure that out. And if they had that for enough people, they could broadcast to them all at once, and take control, like they almost did for me."

"My impression, Creena, is that you have a better understanding of what they're trying to do than anyone else, except maybe 'Merapa. Since the deadline to save him isn't that urgent anymore, it sounds like figuring out how to stop them from accessing people's minds in specific groups may be more important."

"I agree," she said.

"I think we need to talk to Bryl, uh, I mean Commander Woeyel, and tell her what you've experienced. That might help her decide what we should be working on. And she may have some other ideas as well."

"I suppose," Creena sighed, less than happy about sharing experiences that had been quite frightening and very personal with someone she still wasn't sure she could trust.

"Has the INTEGRATOR bothered you since that experience on Terra?" Dirck asked, deep concern lining his expression.

"No," she said. "I guess they figured out that I meant it when I said I wouldn't go with them. Just like 'Merapa."

"Good," he replied. "If they're not bothering you anymore, hopefully they don't know where you are, either."

"Exactly. I certainly haven't missed those encounters."

* * *

The TL-87's interior was beyond luxurious, the passenger compartment resplendent with fine fabrics, exotic wood furnishings and of course, food and drink fit for nobility. Antara Denale pondered the planetscape projected on the artificial window with feelings as diverse as the holographic scene before her. She hoped her outward appearance was one of calm, controlled confidence, while inside her mind and heart raced. She took a careful sip of sennulian tea, hoping it would calm her nerves as she purposely ignored the man lounging in a leather chair on the other side of the cabin. Whatever resulted from this unexpected turn of events had volatile, perhaps even deadly, potential, the question, as usual, being who would survive?

She realized now that commanding her c-com to skip to universal time on Spoigan's workdeck was impulsive and dramatic. The satisfaction it wrought had been priceless, but so doing had revealed technological capabilities she should have kept underwraps. At least she'd been able to instruct the others to dispose of theirs in more discrete fashion before these insidious fools got their hands on them. A sigh escaped before she could stifle it, its message to Spoigan entirely misread. Esheronian women had a low regard for men, even without provocation, and this Spicadian bull was certainly no exception.

"Call me Roy," he said, once again attempting conversation.

"Why would I want to do that?" she replied, refusing to meet his lascivious gaze.

"That's an order, not an invitation, Antara," he said coldly. "This little excursion will be more successful for both of us if our, uh, alliance, appears friendly."

"Indeed," she replied, matching his tone and look with one of her own. She tucked a stray lock of dark hair behind her ear and folded her arms, again facing the faux window.

Antara had strong reservations about their supposed deal and whether or not he could be trusted to fulfill his side of the agreement. He'd offered to release the remainder of her research team in exchange for acquiring c-coms for himself and various others. However, she had serious doubts whether or not that would (or even could) occur. It wasn't only a matter of *if* he would follow through with their release. It was unlikely a high ranking INTEGRATED official would be approved to receive such a powerful device. The c-coms were manufactured and issued by monks belonging to the Ledorian religious order who would undoubtedly have strong objections to his political beliefs. So far, INTEGRATION had left Esheron alone, which would hopefully continue if they cooperated with his request. The implications if they refused were another story.

She shuddered at the thought of him as well as his evil cronies having c-com technology at their disposal. In spite of her earlier comments about sacrificing her team, that was the last thing she wanted, returning them safely to Esheron the part that had enticed her to agree to what was an increasingly risky excursion. If the Ledorians refused to accommodate him, it would not only spell doom for her teammates, but perhaps her and anyone else involved as well.

"As soon as we're onworld, you'll contact the manufacturer and request a tour for an important Woeyel Industries client," he stated.

"I don't have the clearance or authority to do that. Such a request must be made by the chief operations officer or higher," she stated truthfully.

"I'm sure you'll find that no more than a minor task."

"Possibly. It depends on my supervisor's availability as well as the manufacturer."

"Let's say it's up to you to convince them to cooperate, my dear Professor, or our deal is off. Not only will it mean the execution of your team if you fail, but I'll use the fact I have your mindprint to disable your ability to control your bodily functions."

She turned her head enough to meet his dark eyes with her own, unintimidated, at least visibly, knowing that showing any form of weakness would be like the smell of blood to a predator.

"I told you before, General, that I'm not afraid to die."

"Roy."

"Whatever."

"Maybe I didn't make myself clear. I'm not talking about death, Antara. I'm talking about being trapped in a lifeless body."

She rolled her eyes defiantly and resumed staring at the pseudo-landscape beyond glass as she took another sip of tea.

"When will we arrive?" she asked, hoping it would be soon. In spite of the luxury surrounding her, she knew it was a military craft capable of maximum warp. At that rate, they should get there within a few hours, unless he planned to purposely delay arrival until her behavior met specifications.

"Don't worry, my dear," he replied. "I see nothing to be gained by delays. I'm sure you can be quite reasonable if properly motivated."

She stiffened inside with the realization he'd apparently read her mind. Maybe this would be more difficult than she expected.

* * *

<table>
<tr><td colspan="2" align="center">Integrator Central

TBA

Technical Breakthrough Advisory</td></tr>
<tr><td>TEAM: Communications</td><td>PROJECT: Encephalographic Access/Reception</td></tr>
<tr><td>Date: DDW-132</td><td>Clearance: Top Secret</td></tr>
<tr><td colspan="2">Breakthrough/Milestone: Technology identified to refine encephalographic reception to word chain level.</td></tr>
<tr><td>Schedule Impact: Y/N? Y</td><td>Days: Unknown/Positive</td></tr>
<tr><td colspan="2">SUMMARY: Under interrogation Esheronian scientist divulges key data with regard to refinement of cerebral stimulation technique for extracting specific word chain from cerebral storage. Using individual mindprint as access key requires validation with aura signature. Encephalographic tapping of individuals for whom such information is on file to proceed immediately</td></tr>
</table>

* * *

Sharra's eyes were fixed on the job billets hovering above the workdeck in the common area off the messhall, but her mind was far away. Her logical, Miran mind insisted that Bryl Woeyel's offer to have any position she wanted was generous and based on consideration for her personal well-being. Yet another part of her, which had unfortunately been awakened upon arriving on this horrific rock of a planet, somehow refused to believe her. It wasn't that she thought the woman was lying, no that wasn't it at all. No, it was more a matter of what her motivation might be in being so nice.

It just didn't make sense why she would be so considerate if she didn't have an ulterior motive. Even though the woman was aware she had the legal right to steal her bondling, she probably knew that wouldn't sit well with Laren. Thus, if she could cozy up to Sharra such that she would welcome her into the family, he would be more inclined to accept it. Assuming, of course, that they brought him back.

She closed her eyes and groaned silently, emptiness expanding as the feelings rumbling inside mixed as reluctantly as oil and water. Thinking she may not ever see him again took her breath away. If there were any means to rescue him and bring him back, she'd give anything for that to happen. Yet, the thought of sharing him was so offensive that it brought similar discomfort, almost to the point that she'd prefer the status quo.

What kind of person am I? she thought. *How can I even consider that sharing him is worse than doing without him completely?*

When she tried to even imagine such a situation she nearly got sick to her stomach. What kind of horrible place was Esheron to allow such uncivilized practices? And whatever possessed Laren to renew his citizenship there? The consequences of that action had reverberated in ways he'd admitted he hadn't considered, when he'd found her and Deven on the threshold of starvation in that horrid ballome. And now that action opened him up to being snatched away in another way as well. How much power would Bryl have? As far as she was aware, Esheron was largely a matriarchal society. What if she could insist upon their entire family returning there?

Another jolt hit as she realized that, very possibly, Esheron was a better place than where they were at the moment. She buried her face in her hands and laughed softly at the irony. But her dilemma was no better for it.

* * *

INTEGRATOR Headquarters
Cira City

Augustus Troy leaned back in his chair, glaring at the null results of the vehicle scan. Whatever that thing was, there was no evidence that it existed onboard the *Bezarna Express*. Yet it wasn't his imagination, both he and Spoigan had seen it in the video feeds.

Great, he thought. Just when he thought he was making progress getting into Spoigan's favor. The thought of telling him he'd failed twisted his stomach into a knot, yet time was of sufficient importance that the longer he waited, the worse the consequences could be. Admitting failure in person was out of the question. The more casual he acted about it, the better. Maybe he could blame it on the vehicle itself, a malfunction caused by Brightstar's tampering while trying to compromise the system.

Yes. Perfect. That would do it.

Before he lost his nerve, he commed the General, mustering his most indignant and confident look as the connection went through. A moment later he blinked, startled, when the face that filled the space before him was familiar, but not the one expected.

"Where's the General?" he asked Spoigan's response avatar.

"He's on a brief excursion abroad," the image replied.

"To where?"

"He didn't say."

"When will he be back?"

"A day or two. He said it was somewhat unofficial, that's all. Would you like to leave a message?"

"No," Troy replied, barely able to contain his smile of relief as he commed out. Maybe by the time he got back, he could figure out some other way to obtain one. If Spoigan went where he thought he did based on their last conversation, the man should come back in a much better mood, if not with the device itself. Meanwhile, he couldn't believe how good it felt to know his superior was off-world.

A Bit of a Break

Creena wasn't sure what to think of her commander's expression after briefing her on their latest theory, which included conveying her experiences with the INTEGRATOR. The woman's dark eyes were hard to read, much like 'Merapa's, their slight upward tilt sometimes giving the impression she was scowling, even when she wasn't. She glanced at her brother, whose idea it had been to meet with her in the first place, projecting a look of suspected betrayal, but his gaze was fixed on their leader, straight and commanding behind her workdeck, numerous comcons filling the walls with incoming information and various video feeds.

Finally, the woman took a deep breath and let it out with a sigh, an action Creena remembered all too well from Mira III as the precursor to being issued a noncompliance report or NCR. She held her breath, braced for the worst.

"Thank you," Bryl said at last, eyes softening. "I appreciate you sharing what must have been very traumatic experiences. I had no idea you'd been through anything like that. How many others have you told?"

Creena blinked, somewhat taken aback that she wasn't in some sort of trouble. "Uh, o-only 'Merapa and Dirck, b-besides you," she stammered. "I really, uh, don't like to talk about it. I feel kind of, well, guilty, in a way, that I must be a bad person or something for him to be so interested in having me on his, uh, side."

"Oh, Creena, don't feel like that!" she said. "His original intent was probably to use you to get through to your father.

That and you probably have abilities they'd like to use, for testing purposes, if nothing else. You're obviously extremely intelligent, as you've proven with all your work on the crystals. If they could have gotten you to go with them, they would have scored a major victory in a variety of ways. But thank the *Benefics* they didn't, and that you're here, safe with us."

"I wonder how safe any of us could be if this is how they plan to use cristobalite?" Dirck commented.

"Absolutely," their Commander agreed. "We should switch our focus to defeating INTEGRATOR efforts to achieve mass mind control. Chronoviatic transfer is less urgent, now that you've discovered time is not a factor for retrieving your father. It also gives us time for the HIO to approve our application for chronoviatic transfer research. Defensive measures to prevent such nefarious tactics should clearly be our top priority."

"When is your research team going to arrive?" Dirck asked. "We could certainly use their help."

A troubled look clouded her expression. "They should have been here by now," she said, removing her c-com from the breast pocket of her uniform. The woman frowned with concentration, obviously extracting information from it, when her jaw suddenly dropped, color draining from her face.

"Oh, no," she whispered, looking up in horror. "They're here, onworld. Arrived over a week ago."

"So where are they?" Dirck asked, puzzled.

"They were detained at immigration. Their visas weren't accepted and they were remanded over to local authorities. INTEGRATED authorities. They've done it again, stolen my people!" she exclaimed, sighing angrily. "I should have been more specific about what's going on down here and instructed them to come onworld under more anonymous pretenses. Great. Well, not much we can do about it now. Looks like we're on our own."

"How exactly does that thing work?" Dirck asked, gesturing toward her c-com. "My father has one and, as I recall, it operates using some sort of psi link. Whatever technology it employs might help our research."

Commander Woeyel looked at it as if seeing it for the first time. "That's a good question," she replied. "It's a relatively new invention and I haven't had time to exploit all its features. I've primarily used it as a communications device and to store and extract information. We don't export our technologies, so there shouldn't be any around, except those brought onworld by Esheronian natives. I guess we'd better figure it out, though, especially since the INTEGRATOR has them now, too, thanks to abducting my research team."

"Maybe they won't recognize what they are," Dirck said hopefully. "Or suspect their capabilities."

"It also depends on how willing my people are to help them. They may face death if they don't come up with something within a certain amount of time. That can be a pretty strong motivator." She paused a moment, focusing on the device with a pensive expression. Her eyes widened a moment later, gaze shifting back and forth a few times from Dirck to Creena along with an expectant smile. "I should be able to communicate with my team using this. And if they've managed to keep them confidential, it might be very, very useful."

"Maybe the technology we're trying to develop already exists," Dirck commented. "But that may not be a good thing in the wrong hands. The main thing we need to figure out is how it works."

"Let's get Aggie in here to check it out," Creena suggested. "She should be able to tell us without taking it apart."

"Good idea," Dirck agreed, Commander Woeyel already entering the 'troid's pager code into the comcon.

Aggie arrived a short time later, a combination of suspicion and pride in her photoreceptors.

"Hi, Aggie," Dirck greeted her. "How'd the audit of L-DISA go?"

Aggie ignored him, reporting directly to the commander. "You summoned me, ma'am?" she asked.

"Yes, I did," she responded. "But you may address Captain Brightstar's question first."

The 'troid rotated her photoreceptors toward Dirck as if seeing him for the first time. "The L-DISA audit went well. I was somewhat amazed how precisely Captain Sendori understood my algorithms, even improved upon some of them with the interpolation code, which I've assimilated."

"Great," Dirck replied.

"Aggie, we'd like a technical analysis of this device," Commander Woeyel stated, holding it up for the 'troid to see. "I assume you can do so without disturbing any of its settings or files?"

"Yes, of course, ma'am" Aggie replied. "I'm already in *Technological Assessment* mode so let's get to it."

"First of all, let's quit all this *commander* and *ma'am* formality business," she replied, reaching over to set the c-com on the other side of her workdeck where Aggie could scan it. "I think we all know each other well enough to dispense with titles and salutes, at least when we're in private. Please, call me Bryl. Okay?"

"Yes, ma'am," Dirck and Creena said in unison, then laughed awkwardly when Bryl rolled her eyes.

Aggie focused her sensors on the device, emitting a brief burst of green, then red, as she scanned its components. Her photoreceptors froze momentarily while she analyzed the data and prepared her assessment.

"Okay, got it," the 'troid stated. "Who wants the analysis?"

"Me, Dirck, Creena and Win," Bryl replied. "We'd like a briefing now as well."

"Of course," the 'troid agreed. "It's a communication device that operates by connecting and synching with the encephalographic glial cells of the brain via quantum photon entanglement. Those cells are encoded genetically by the individual's DNA, making them unique, thus limiting access to any incoming psimissions to that person alone. It also utilizes a small crystal of the substance you call devenite, which validates the identification process via cardiac emanations in a slightly different psi band, making it one fault tolerant. If one or the other fails for any reason, the crystal maintains security.

"The device communicates with others via a cristobalite chip that amplifies the psi signal to a range that exceeds the recipient's consciousness threshold. In other words, it'll be loud enough to breach their awareness as much as if someone was speaking directly in their ear. Even if a person had no natural telepathic abilities, they could receive such messages. It can also record and organize them automatically. It has data storage and gathering capabilities as well."

"That much I knew," Dirck commented. "When 'Merapa was designing the heat exchanger, he stored all the information there and coded it so I'd have access. It was literally a lifesaver when he wound up in prison. With the information he left, Win and I were able to build the heat exchanger, even though we had to substitute several of the components, which was why it eventually blew up. What kind of signal is it? RF?"

"No," Aggie replied. "It's not radio frequency or any other wavelength in the electromagnetic spectrum. Quantum entanglement is interdimensional and instantaneous. If a photon is split, anything that subsequently affects one, affects all of its parts. Cristobalite has this property. It interacts with all dimensions, and is thus not limited to the speed of light or subject to time or other relativistic effects."

"So it's similar to tachyonic communications used on starships?" Creena asked.

"No," the 'troid replied. "Tachyonic transmissions travel at approximately two-hundred-eighteen times the speed of light, a finite speed that, while fast, isn't instantaneous. Time has two functional dimensions. The one we're in, which flows in one direction toward the future, and one that's universal, which encompasses all directions, past, present and future, simultaneously. Since psi operates through all dimensions, it accesses universal time and is thus instantaneous. That allows it to synch up with the inertial frame of both sender and receiver, even if one or both are onboard spacecraft moving in opposition directions near the speed of light under warp acceleration. Time and space essentially do not exist. Thus, it can deliver information from or to the past or future."

"How are new recipients added?" Bryl asked. "Is personal contact required? Can someone else access the device from a remote location?"

"No one else can access the device, unless permission is granted by its psi-linked owner. If you want to contact someone, they have to grant permission, in which case their DNA signature is downloaded so the device can transmit to them and vice versa. After that, they'll be included in your list of recipients. You accept those from whom you will accept messages in the same way. However, the device has a high level of intelligence. If you've had repeated voice contact with someone, it can make a command decision, based on your trust level as determined by the devenite chip, to add them to your authorized recipients, if they're in your network. But you still have to approve it or that person cannot contact you without user validation and vice versa."

Creena, Dirck and Bryl met each other's startled gaze in a shared flash of unexpected hope. "Would it be possible to hack around those restrictions?" Dirck asked.

"I don't think so," Aggie replied after a moment's hesitation. "If the device senses a threat, it shuts down. The owner has complete control over incoming and outgoing communications. Whether or not the owner is already telepathic, they can forward all incoming messages through the device for recording and screening."

Bryl's eyes were wide, excitement animating her expression. "In other words, if we provided one of these to every Clique member and sympathizer, they would be immune to any propaganda coming in from the INTEGRATOR?"

"Theoretically," Aggie said. "Its capabilities and functionality depend on the user. It can do virtually anything it's told to do, but won't offer options without being queried. Each unit is initially personalized by its owner's mindprint, their subsequent queries and commands making it entirely unique."

"Does your written report include build-ready schematics?" Bryl asked, intent crystal clear.

"Yes, of course," the 'troid replied with the haughty digital expression she wore when she'd been insulted. "A complete user manual is there as well."

Bryl was on the comcon a heartbeat later, summoning the supervisor of their manufacturing division to her office. "Clearly, we can't import these from Esheron because they'll be confiscated on arrival," she explained. "But hopefully, we can make them here. All we need to do is find enough cristobalite and devenite." She looked at Dirck, then Creena hopefully, awaiting a reply.

Creena and Dirck looked at each other. The only source they were aware of, other than their few samples, was back at the Caverns, which, as far as they knew, had been overrun by INTEGRATOR forces.

"Aggie, how much cristobalite is needed for each unit?" Dirck asked.

"A slice that measures three centimeters square by two millimeters thick," she replied.

Creena cringed, knowing how difficult it had been to secure samples half that size without crumbling or splitting.

"And how many will we need?" he asked, noting Creena's expression as he turned toward Bryl.

"For everyone, at least eight thousand."

"Aggie, can cristobalite be synthesized?" Creena asked hopefully.

The 'troids circuit indicators flashed, photoreceptors momentarily in standby as she determined the answer. "Yes and no," she finally replied.

"Please be more specific," Bryl stated, impatience shadowing her eyes in spite of her even tone.

"Yes, it can be manufactured, given the correct elemental material contained in its molecular structure is available. However, unlike naturally occurring cristobalite activated by the recipient, it needs to be primed by a strong, natural psi source."

"Such as?" Dirck asked.

"The bnolar."

"The who?" Bryl asked, frowning.

"The bnolar," Dirck explained with a sigh. "Indigenous creatures native to Cyraria and the original occupants of the Caverns. When it was likely we'd be found, I warned them and they disappeared. I don't know if we could find them or not. Maybe Deven could contact them, but it might take a while."

"Which explains why the Tank lost its power when they left," Creena stated.

"Right," Dirck agreed. "Which means the cristobalite in the Tank may be useless, anyway, without the bnolar."

"Okay, this is important enough to pursue, by whatever means necessary," Bryl declared. "We need to contact these bnolar somehow, as well as analyze our existing samples to determine what molecular substances we need to synthesize it."

"There might be some complications," Dirck added, visibly wincing. "Conditions are, well, involved, with bnolar assistance."

"What are you talking about?" Bryl asked, scowling.

"They have a strict non-interference policy. They'll help, but only to a point. They have strong moral and ethical guidelines they won't violate. In other words, they won't do anything illegal, combative or confrontational."

"Who do they think they are, the *Benefics*?" Bryl commented sarcastically.

"Actually, that's probably not too far from the truth," Dirck responded seriously.

"You know, we most likely don't have a choice but to work with them," Creena stated. "There's a chance the crystals we have won't work, either."

"You have samples here, don't you?" Bryl asked.

"Yes," Creena said. "But only a few that would be big enough."

"Let's build as many prototypes as possible with what we have as quickly as possible and see if they work," Bryl suggested. "If so, then maybe the crystals are still active. It's also possible that the owner of the c-com is the one who charges it. There aren't any bnolar on Esheron and that's where they were invented. I'll get in touch with someone there who can tell me how it's done. I did something to connect with it initially, but it's been quite a while and I can't remember exactly what."

About then the manufacturing supervisor arrived, a jendak whose uniform looked somewhat askew except it was actually the round body and short legs natural to his race that made it look that way. His complexion was the usual violet, though some of his race were a deep shade of blue, which implied a slightly different heritage.

He saluted sharply, round yellow eyes fixed on his commanding officer, pointed ears straight in attention, demeanor professional and competent. "Major Zebatohn reporting be for duty, ma'am," he said.

"At ease, Major," she said. "We have a device here we need to reproduce, but there may be some problems obtaining the needed materials. Nonetheless, we should have enough for a few prototypes. How quickly do you think you can get them off the line?" She gestured to her comcon holoscreen and brought up the schematics. He studied them carefully, rotating the diagrams to several different views and positions before responding.

"With materials proper we should be to build a few prototypes by thirty-nine hours," he replied at last. "Most critical are crystals, cristobalite and devenite, in proper proportion."

Creena nodded, fascinated by his huge, yellow eyes, which reminded her of the Benson's cat back on Terra. "Stop by our lab on your way back and I'll give you what we have," she said.

"I'm not exaggerating when I say that our survival depends on this device, Major," Bryl stated solemnly.

"Yes, ma'am," he replied.

"Okay, here's the plan," Bryl concluded. "Major Zebatohn will pursue fabricating as many units as possible from available materials, then investigate synthesizing what's needed for the rest. Hopefully, we have enough to at least provide one to each of you. I'll take an action to see if I can get in touch with my science and engineering team to find out the status of INTEGRATOR research efforts. I'll also find out how to initiate the c-coms by charging the crystals. Meanwhile, I want the rest of you to resume research into chronoviatic transfer. We may not need it immediately to recover Laren, but we could conceivably use it to rescue my S&E team before they were hijacked. I suspect their future is far from secure as long as they're detained by the INTEGRATOR. Any questions?"

"Not really a question but a comment," Creena said.

"Go on," Bryl replied with a nod.

"There really aren't that many crystals. That was part of our problem with pursuing chronoviatic transfer. We didn't have enough to conduct any large-scale tests. All we have is what's in the psitenna and a few loose ones we were going to use in our dream experiment."

"Dream experiment? You haven't told me about that. What's the objective?"

"To see if sleeping in the vicinity of devenite would result in any veridical dreams."

Bryl scowled pensively. "Veridical dreams? I don't recall you mentioning them before, either." The woman was looking at her with an intense look that combined confusion with curiosity as she awaited further explanation.

Creena almost choked as she remembered the last dream she and Dirck had shared had involved Bryl putting the moves on her father, to say nothing of the resulting debacle of misunderstanding. Certainly she couldn't tell her about that. Fortunately, Dirck jumped in, allowing her to regain her composure.

"I guess we didn't. Right. So, when we were in the other caverns, 'Merama and I had a prophetic dream about my father. It warned us that Troy was about to make his final offer. That was when we came up with the plan to rescue him from prison."

"The prison break," she said pensively. "So that was the result of a dream?

"Yes. Without it we wouldn't have known that he was in danger."

"Have you received any other prophetic revelations?" she asked, head cocked to the side as she assimilated the information.

After a short pause, Dirck spoke up again. "We had one from Zahra, the jendak who managed the comcenter," he replied. "She told us about those eclipses and that they probably meant trouble, which they certainly did."

Creena closed her eyes and stifled a sigh of relief, grateful that Dirck's Miran heritage had kicked in and diverted the subject without having to tell a blatant lie.

"With only one data point, it sounds like your experiment is based on conjecture. Given the circumstances and the crystals' importance to developing c-coms, which we know will provide substantial protection and benefit, I don't think reserving the crystals to pursue veridical dreams is that urgent, considering the need to establish a means for protecting us from INTEGRATOR intrusions. Can't you conduct your experiment without them?"

"I guess so," Creena replied. "We didn't have them with us for the other one, but we thought having all those crystal deposits around us might have had some influence."

"Then I'd say try it without them and see what happens. Then, if we get some synthesized, you can have some of them to use to see if it makes a difference. Trying without them first can serve as a control."

"Okay," Creena said, reasonably satisfied. "We'll do that."

"The psitenna was also our only means of communicating with 'Merapa," Dirck added, a slight catch in his voice.

"That's true, but the c-coms should provide that ability as well, assuming he still has his. I realize that devenite has more potential for chronoviatic transfer, but that's already on hold and we may be able to synthesize it. So does everyone agree that we should proceed with fabrication?"

Creena and Dirck exchanged pained looks, then nodded their heads.

"Okay, then let's proceed," Bryl said decisively.

Major Zebatohn saluted and left with Creena while Dirck disappeared in the tunnel ahead to brief Win on the latest developments. Creena slowed her steps to that of the jendak as the pair headed for the lab.

"You must be daughter of Commander Brightstar," he said, still hustling to keep up with her long-legged stride. "Are you she who was lost?"

"Yes, I am," Creena replied, slowing some more.

"It is with great pleasure to meet you," he said. "Sister mine has spoken much kindly of your family."

"Your sister?" Creena asked. "Really? Do I know her?"

"Is known by family yours. My sister be Zahra. She lead communicator be in Sigma/Epsilon comcenter. She has been much worried about family yours and relieved very to know you be well. Except for father, of course."

"I never met her," Creena answered, "but my brother, Dirck, and mother have mentioned her. My mother said she was a dear friend and my brother was very impressed with her knowledge and ability to predict events. Is she okay?"

"Yes. She some days ago arrive with small group of settlement others. We would be much pleased to meet with you and family yours."

"That would be wonderful!" she exclaimed.

Upon arrival at the lab, Creena dug through the small pile of remaining cristobalite samples, hoping that maybe there'd be enough, which wasn't the case. Furthermore, Deven's cache of devenite only contained two tiny crystals which appeared usable, if each of them kept one for the dream experiment, which she still wanted to do, regardless of Bryl's directive. Her heart fell; their only choice was to dismantle the psitenna.

She found herself nearly overcome as she picked it up, holding it to her heart and caressing it, remembering. Tears she'd managed to hold back in Bryl's office glazed her eyes as she reluctantly placed it in Major Zebatohn's extended hands.

"This should be enough for the prototypes," she said, avoiding his gaze. "Will it be a problem to split the large devenite crystal into several smaller ones?"

She could feel the jendak eyeing her strangely, not speaking until she looked up.

"Can notice device has much caring," he said gently.

"Yes," she said, wiping tears from the corners of her eyes as casually as possible. She swallowed hard as memories besieged her. It had even contributed to mending her relationship with Dirck, probably the greatest gift of all. And now, they'd never uncover its secrets regarding chronoviatic transfer, which they still might need to rescue 'Merapa. But orders were orders, as her father had emphasized himself. She swallowed hard, then squared her shoulders with resolve.

"It saved our lives and, like Dirck said, it also allowed us to contact my father," she explained. "And hopefully, its crystals will allow us to do so again," she added, firmly meeting his eyes as she forced a smile.

"I will take care much to use only what be needed," he promised, placing an understanding four fingered hand on her arm.

"Thank you, Major."

"Will convey to Zahra location yours," he said as he departed. "She will have much joy to know your safety."

"Yes," Creena replied. "I'm sure my family will be equally pleased."

* * *

Bezarna Express

Laren handed his c-com to Rhodus with a wry smile. "Here. See what you think of this move," he said, still maintaining the illusion they were playing a game. And indeed they were, albeit a deadly one.

Matching his expression, his comrade took it and logged in, listening to what Laren had determined so far with regard to their situation. He pretended to interact via the virtual screen as he psied a response, which the device recorded. "Good luck, Brightstar," he said, handing it back.

He agreed with Laren's speculations that procedures in the absence of their voluntary descent into the void would involve something like being knocked out and jettisoned. How and when they'd be rendered unconscious was the question. Since there were two of them, they'd have to be dispatched simultaneously or there'd be a fight, something their captors surely anticipated. He was confident the two of them could overpower Sa'ata, but it would undoubtedly be picked up on video. No telling what authorities could do from the ground, if they sensed trouble. At worst, they could probably blow up the entire vehicle, at least, have a rather unfriendly welcoming committee awaiting their return to Cyraria.

Unless he could hijack the video feed. He'd been working on that, anyway, *i.e.*, faking their jettisons before he knew for sure Sa'ata was a guard. He and Rhodus had already faked their approach to the airlock in a pensive manner, hand hovering above the release, then supposedly changing their minds, which he'd captured then spliced with the electronic signals associated with the actual occurrences on the part of the others. Theoretically, if he could control the video feed and mimic the airlock expulsion signal, they'd be free to do just about anything they wanted, possibly even assume control of the vehicle itself.

But how much time he had to get things together was a matter of when and how they planned to immobilize him and Rhodus. If Sa'ata was getting suspicious, he might be able to accelerate the process timeline.

So far, the c-com hadn't failed him as far as the vehicle's sensors and wiring were concerned, so on a long-shot, he queried the vehicle's upgrade specifications and software algorithms for prisoner contingency procedures. He found the command queue with amazing ease, read through it carefully, noting a recent modification that also precluded future changes. *Not good,* he thought, but he'd seen such things before and was confident he could find a workaround. It would take precious time, but should be possible.

He perused the code further, unable to contain a horrified gasp at what was coming up, far sooner than he cared to acknowledge.

ACTIONS

Apoca Canyon

As soon as everyone left her office, Bryl started working her action items. First she needed to see if she could contact one of her hijacked team members regarding their status, both at the personal and research level. As important as the activation issue was, her first concern was the welfare of her employees. Woeyel Industries was not a huge operation and she'd always done her best to know everyone. That had deteriorated since her extended absence, but her Science and Engineering, a.k.a., *S&E,* team had been around for a long time and she was reasonably sure she knew most, if not all, of them. Nonetheless, considering their circumstances, composing a coded message was a delicate operation.

According to Aggie's analysis, no one but the original owner could access information sent to their psi address without permission, but her team members could have been coerced or forced into doing so. It was also possible that INTEGRATED sources had discovered how to get around that feature, motivated by how useful c-coms could be for conveying propaganda. She definitely didn't want to inadvertently reveal Clique status or plans in the process, either. Since INTEGRATED forces had undoubtedly discovered both cristobalite and possibly devenite, they already had at least one major advantage, an abundance of needed resources. They also had her team who were familiar with c-com technology, not because they'd created, it but because they used it every day. Surely, as scientists, they were aware how critical it was not to reveal it to their imposing hosts.

So what could she say? It had to be innocuous enough that it could be dismissed as noise, a malfunction, or blanket transmission with no specific action required if intercepted. As sender, she would be automatically identified, so trying to send something anonymously was impossible.

Mentioning the technology specifically, much less the Clique's intended application to the war effort, was entirely out of the question. If their opponents hadn't already figured it out, it could tip them off to its potential as well. She didn't even know which members of her team had been dispatched for the assignment, making it nearly impossible to contact them herself, anyway. She'd sent for two teams since Opposition and both had been pirated away, not leaving many on Esheron to carry on. Who might have stayed behind, perhaps for personal reasons? She'd been on Cyraria for so long, she'd lost touch with the specifics of who worked or ran what, especially since involvement with the Clique had consumed all her waking hours.

Okay, let's think this through.

Getting in touch with someone working with the INTEGRATOR was urgent, but not necessarily the best approach. First of all, she needed to know who was involved, which could help decide whom to contact. She could get that information from the Chief Operations Officer she'd left in charge back home. If that person contacted a research team member, it would look less suspicious. The main thing she needed to know was the status of INTEGRATION'S efforts, so the team at Apoca would know how to counteract them.

As far as information on how to charge cristobalite was concerned, she should be able to obtain that directly from Esheron. She was reasonably sure that they were manufactured at that huge Ledorian monastery on the hill overlooking Twiozopa City. Maybe she should do that first. If they couldn't be activated by their primary user, they'd be useless, unless they could find the bnolar, which could be a daunting task. If done by the user, that was one major issue they didn't have to worry about, except it would make things easier for INTEGRATION proponents to use the technology as well.

She pulled up her contact list and found her chief operations officer, a dark and heavy woman thrice widowed, who'd worked for her many years. As she thought about how loyal and trustworthy Berenices Tucana had been running things in her absence, Bryl realized she hadn't made formal arrangements for what would happen to Woeyel Industries in the event she got herself killed through her Clique involvement. Her precarious escape from Nu/Alpha certainly illustrated that possibility was very real. If she didn't set things up now, then the company she'd founded and put her life's blood into for decades would simply fall under government control at her demise.

No, she thought. *I need to take care of that, too, just in case.*

To think that one of the reasons she'd left Esheron was to escape their perpetual wars. She rolled her eyes at the irony, then considered what she needed to do to assure her wishes would be followed. Her older sister was certainly incapable of such an endeavor, confirming that leaving it to Berenices, whom she'd always called Bernie, was the best recourse. As soon as she got this c-com issue taken care of, that would be the first thing she'd do.

Contact Bernie, she instructed the device. She waited for the usual sense of connection, that subtle twinge in her solar plexus that indicated the link had been established. And waited and waited. When more than a minute had elapsed with no response, she issued a *cancel* command and tried again with the same result. Trying to squelch the rising panic, she tried a simple query. Again nothing, its usual mind projection blank.

Her heart rate accelerated as she realized something was very wrong. But what? Remembering that Aggie had produced a user manual, she brought it up on the comcon and went directly to the troubleshooting section. She indulged in a preemptive sigh of relief when the first entry answered her question, the response in Aggie's voice.

Any perceived security breach will shut down the device and require recharging by the user.

Apparently, the 'troid's scan had been perceived as a threat after all. In a way, that was a good thing, assuming she could get it activated again. It also suggested that her science team's units would be safe as well. She quickly searched for recharging instructions, hoping the response would solve her immediate problem as well as answer her action item. Aggie's voice responded again.

Recharging: Must be accomplished by original user within 16 hours of shutdown or device will self-destruct. To reset comm function, position device over third eye in forehead and psi password. Device will acknowledge with brief flash of mentally perceived light. To reset empathic capability, hold device over heart and project prevailing feeling until connection indicated by violet beam. When accomplished, device is fully functional. Note that user can send an instantaneous self-destruct command, sending the device to universal time dimension, but this action is irreversible. Automatic flash backup option to home site is activated, however, as part of command.

Bryl took a deep breath, gradually remembering the procedure as she followed the instructions. The first part worked immediately, but it seemed as if it took a long time before the violet beam finally appeared and she felt the c-com come to life. She indulged in a huge sigh of relief, smiling with hope and satisfaction that initial charging by new users could be accomplished the same way, in which case that problem and one of her actions had been resolved.

Again, she entered the command to contact Bernie, the connection immediate.

Are you okay? The concern coupled with the words came through from the woman with tremendous urgency before Bryl could utter a word.

Yes, Bryl replied. *Why do you ask?*

I had a bad feeling something had happened to you for the last hour and couldn't get through.

My c-com shut down, but it's okay now, and a somewhat long story. Did you know the S&E team you sent was detained at Cyrarian immigration and ultimately turned over to INTEGRATED forces? Bryl felt the woman's heart drop and knew she'd been unaware of their abduction.

I need you to try to contact them and determine their status, Bryl went on. *If at all possible, we need to know what technologies they're working on so we can be one step ahead with countermeasures. If they're being threatened or coerced, we need to know as well. We may not be able to do anything to rescue them, but at least being aware of their situation will be helpful.*

Of course, Bernie psaid back, Bryl acutely aware that the woman did so through a lump of emotion lodged in her throat.

The highest order of discretion is required or it could create a potentially lethal situation, Bryl continued. *We know they want to develop a means to control the masses through mind control and c-com technology may be the best countermeasure. But they can't know that, or they could force our team to use their knowledge to work around it in some way.*

Got it. I'll let you know what I find out.

Bryl felt the woman's heavy-hearted concern for their team as well as herself and once more knew this woman was the right one to replace her, should she fail to return.

And Bernie, one more thing, she psaid. *How would you feel about being my primary heir in the event I don't survive this conflict?*

The complex emotional barrage that followed provided an immediate answer.

Good, Bryl psaid. *I'll get that set up from here. Namaste, my friend.*

The woman's tears were contagious and Bryl wiped away her own with gratitude, threw a huge blast of confidence Bernie's way, and ended the psimission, relieved and somehow at peace. She closed her eyes and relished the positive emotion for a long moment, trying to ignore the implications of feeling good about arrangements related to her demise, then sent charging procedural data to the relevant parties, hoping her optimism was justified.

* * *

"This is great!" Dirck exclaimed, quickly sharing Bryl's charging news with Win, who was at his console in the commlab. "At least that's one less thing to worry about. And it sounds as if this shutdown security feature can work to our advantage, too."

"Absolutely," Win agreed. "If they try to get to us through them, we'll know immediately. Now we just need to produce enough units for everyone. The only problem is if we have to synthesize the materials, then they'll need to be primed."

"Yeah," Dirck agreed. "That could be a problem. Nothing's ever simple."

"No," Win replied with a wry smile. "Only death."

Dirck held his gaze, knowing how close all of them had come to crossing its threshold too many times.

"Yeah," he finally replied. "Only death."

CUSTOMER SERVICE

Bernie hoped she looked calm and in control in spite of the fact she could tell by the evolving headache coupled with the tightness in her chest that her blood pressure had ascended to vast new heights. She grabbed a patch from a niche in her workdeck and slapped it on her arm next to the other one, knowing a quick meditation session to bring it down was out of the question. A large, imposing woman who didn't tolerate numerous things, especially disloyalty and incompetence, she nonetheless had a tender heart and loving soul. She knew what it meant to work and she knew the heartbreak of losing someone you loved, both of which were evidenced in the gathering streaks of grey adorning her temples. Such experiences were deeply etched in her face as well, yet life and optimism still managed to shine from her almond shaped, emerald eyes.

After the conversation with Bryl, she'd tried to get in touch with the research team, yet wasn't surprised when every attempt failed. All were trained in contingency procedures and being captured by enemy forces was something they'd been prepared for, especially since the previous group had met a similar fate. Whether they were dead or alive she didn't know, but knew there was little she could do without more information.

Thus, the message from Antara had been expected as well as the unmistakable code embedded within. On a world embroiled in perpetual war, the use of code words was a way of life. But it was the fact the team lead herself was back onworld that took her by surprise, so much so that she'd let fly with an expletive she'd sworn to delete from her vocabulary after letting it slip sometime back at the monastery during a quality inspection. She'd embarrassed herself as well as everyone within earshot on the factory floor and had promised the *Benefics* never to do so again. She looked heavenward, muttered a penitent, *"Sorry,"* and resumed dealing with the matter at hand.

Antara was more than the team lead. She was Bernie's protégé and like a daughter, the relief she'd felt that she was still alive nearly overwhelming. How safe she was, however, remained to be seen.

Within moments of their arrival onworld, Antara had sent a short and cryptic comcon message: *Back onworld in company of potential new customer. ETA 1hr.* To an outsider, including hopefully Antara's escort, it appeared innocent and to the point. However, *in company of* was the tipoff. When used instead of a simple *with,* that phrase indicated someone who couldn't be trusted to the point of being not only hostile but potentially deadly. She'd immediately notified the chief of security and made sure her c-com had adequate charge to serve as a defensive weapon, if required.

The unexpected contact had arrived approximately forty-eight minutes ago and since then she'd talked to so many people she took a moment now to go over the list, making sure she hadn't forgotten anyone. Most important had been her recent conversation with Bryl, which had fortuitously tipped her off regarding the abduction situation and provided suitable motivation for handling it. She hadn't had a chance to get back to Bryl, but certainly would when things settled down.

So now she waited, eyes fixed on the digichronometer on the opposing wall as another minute flicked by.

She jumped at the sound of muffled voices outside her heavy door, which included the deep booming tones of a male, rare to say the least in a woman-run economy where most men were on the battlefield. Her comcon pinged as her secretary announced their arrival, and Bernie hefted to her feet behind her workdeck to open her door and greet them.

246

Relief washed over her when Antara entered, looking tired but otherwise unharmed, the man with her not so much tall as built like a bull with a heavy crop of carefully groomed black hair with a splattering of grey which framed hard eyes as cold as space.

"Welcome back, my sister," she said, smiling as casually as she could. "I've been concerned for your safety when we lost contact."

"Thank you," Antara replied. "No need for worry, we've been well cared for."

More code, Bernie noted. Clearly her experience had been quite the opposite.

"This is General Spoigan," she continued, nodding toward the imposing man beside her, who was giving Bernie a rather disdainful look. "He's very interested in c-com technology and would like to acquire several units for his subordinates. In return, he's agreed to release the members of the *S&I* team who were detained along with myself upon our arrival on Cyraria."

"We've been working on a similar technology," Spoigan interjected, "but since you've obviously already achieved the objective, it will save us valuable development time and resources to simply obtain it from you."

"I see," Bernie said, heart racing at the prospect of a trade that could return the remainder of her hijacked employees. "Have a seat and we'll talk about it. We're only a distributor, not the manufacturer, but should be able to help. Have you defined your specifications?"

Spoigan settled his bulk into a lush leather chair as Antara did the same, discretely maintaining as much distance from him as she could.

"Not yet," he replied. "I'd like to see what options you offer first."

"Of course," Bernie agreed, bringing up the ones available to offworld customers and angling the holographic projection so he could see. He leaned forward to read them, her heartrate doubling as his expected disappointment flashed to anger.

"These are not the features I witnessed on Professor Denale's unit," he growled.

"I'm sorry, General," Bernie replied sweetly, "but these are all we can offer for export. Esheron has strict technology transfer laws, as I'm sure you're quite aware."

"This is not what I came here for," he said, volume of his voice rising as he stood up and rose to his full height. "I assume you're ready to take responsibility for the demise of your team. Furthermore, I represent an entity who can crush your miserable world, if necessary, to obtain it."

"I'm sure that neither of those actions will be necessary, General," Bernie said with a calm that even surprised her. "Perhaps you can make direct arrangements with the manufacturer, obtain an offworld license, and thus bypass export regulations."

"Yeah, that's more like it," Spoigan declared, sitting back down, but looking far from relaxed. "I assume you can set something up immediately."

"Of course," Bernie answered, smiling for any number of reasons, none of which involved keeping him happy other than possibly offering him one of her bloodpressure patches. On the other hand, if the man keeled over, it would eliminate the problem at hand. She retrieved her c-com from its niche, noticing Antara stiffened, perhaps thinking she intended to take him out right there. As satisfying as that would have been, it would undoubtedly set off an intragalactic incident that probably wouldn't end well for either side, especially those still captive on Cyraria.

"Excuse me while I contact the facility," she explained, quickly, selecting the needed contact at the monastery and establishing the connection.

The conversation, while silent, was nonetheless devoid of any incriminating information, just in case the man was telepathic or his cronies were further along with their research than he'd indicated. As previously arranged after Bernie received Antara's original message, the monk offered to see their alleged guest right away.

"You're in luck, General," she said, terminating the connection. "Considering how far you've traveled, they'll see you now, rather than cause you further inconvenience."

Spoigan's reply was but a grunt and Bernie had to bite the inside of her lip to preclude a smile as, with some effort, she got up from her chair and came around her workdeck to escort them outside to where a shuttle was waiting.

It was a clear sunny day, the azure sky interrupted by a few fluffy, white clouds banking the horizon, a stiff but warm breeze stirring early summer air. Bernie settled somewhat awkwardly into a seat that was clearly a bit small and coded in their destination. The craft lifted silently and effortlessly considering the load it was carrying and headed toward Twiozopa City, beyond which the Ledorian monastery sprawled atop a looming, grass covered hill.

As soon as they were airborne, Spoigan cleared his throat. "If you try anything, Madam Tucana, be advised that I have Professor Denale's mindprint and I will see to it that she is immediately dispatched at the slightest provocation. Do I make myself clear?"

"Indeed, General," she replied evenly. "If I should decide to *try anything* I will keep that in mind."

"Hmmmph. You people are really quite given to hyperbole, aren't you?" he added sarcastically.

"On a world where you never know which day will be your last, it's quite easy to keep things in perspective," Bernie replied. "Detachment is essential. I'm sure as a military officer you understand."

"Hmmph."

Their vehicle skimmed the domed rooftops of the city and proceeded through the smoke and dust of the manufacturing sector toward the ancient towering edifice overlooking the valley that stretched beyond. A short time later, they shuttle settled in an expansive stone-lined courtyard flanked by pillars that stretched skyward amidst a stand of sparkling holodendril trees, the musical tinkling sounds of its dancing silvery leaves filling the air. A terraced fountain graced the cloister's center, the soft rush of falling water mingling with the whispering breeze, which cast droplets along their path toward the entrance as if in welcome. At their approach, a flock of birds occupying the path soared away amid the flutter of several dozen wings.

Bernie stepped over to the security alcove, allowing the embedded biometric reader to identify her, then led them through a towering pair of double-high wooden doors that creaked open on ancient hinges as they approached, an odd blend of past architecture coupled with modern sensor technology. Their footsteps echoed in the vaulted corridor the same width as the walkway outside, more ornate yet unmarked doors widely spaced on both sides, walls and floor alike comprised of rust-colored sandstone. When they arrived at the far end, Bernie announced their presence by palming a small pad beside another over-sized door.

"Who is there?" an unembodied yet gentle voice responded, to which Bernie introduced herself and stated they were the party from Woeyel Industries.

The door opened slowly and was unexpectedly silent, revealing a huge, semi-circular room lined with windows that overlooked the city and valley beyond. Directly in front sprawled an intricately carved wooden workdeck behind which sat an ancient man clothed in a heavy, slate-colored robe, his head topped with a mass of unruly white hair.

"Greetings, my friends," he said, rising to bow. "It's my understanding you're interested in our product. I am Friar Johann. How may I help you today?" He gestured toward several straight-backed chairs and resumed his position on his own.

Spoigan sat on the edge of his, clearly impatient with the friendly protocol.

"I will eventually need several thousand units like the device Professor Denale had when we, uh, worked together on Cyraria," he said. "It's my understanding that we should be able to work around the export regulations with some sort of license agreement."

"I'm sure that can be arranged," Friar Johann answered graciously.

"Where's your manufacturing facility?" Spoigan asked. "It's my understanding that you make them here."

"But indeed we do, General. We have a secure facility underground," he replied, nodding toward the stone floor. "It wouldn't do for us to be disturbed by an itinerant bomb or other missile, should any battles come this way."

"I'd like to see it."

"Of course. But first I'd like to determine exactly what you're looking for. Each unit is custom manufactured for its user. They cannot be transferred or used by anyone else without explicit permission from the unit's cellmate, if you will."

"Cellmate?" Spoigan asked, thick eyebrows raised.

"Yes. The bond between the unit and its owner is at the cellular level. It's unique and matched precisely to your DNA."

"I see. Will that present a problem acquiring them for my subordinates? Or can that information be obtained remotely?

Friar Johann smiled. "There are various options. Remote acquisition, of course, is one. Or they can be fitted for you and transferred with your permission. That way you retain ownership and control of the devices and can access everything they contain which, of course, also means you can commandeer them at any time."

For the first time Spoigan actually looked pleased. "Yes, that would have many advantages," he agreed. "When can we get started? How long will it take?"

"How many do you need, General?"

"Initially six hundred eighty-four. I may eventually return for more, but that would provide a good start."

"We would need a day or two to produce them, since each is individually assembled by a few highly qualified residents of our abbey."

"I see," Spoigan said, frowning. "How long would I have to wait for mine?"

"We should be able to take care of you today, a few hours at most," Friar Johann replied. "When would you like to get started?"

"The sooner the better."

"Excellent. But first let us pray."

Again Bernie bit her lip at Spoigan's startled expression, then exchanged an instantaneous conspiratorial look with Antara as the friar came around from behind his imposing workdeck and bid them form a circle. Bernie bowed her head and closed her eyes, then snuck a peek when Friar Johann failed to speak. Spoigan was looking straight ahead until the friar gestured for him to do the same. He looked down with obvious reluctance, but kept his eyes open, which was apparently good enough because the priest immediately raised his voice in solemn prayer. Bernie quickly closed her eyes.

"Our trusted benefics of the Most High God," the monk began. "We request your grace and blessing as we prepare another of your children to commune through your channels for the most holy and righteous of purposes, to assure peace and harmony throughout our troubled galaxy. We ask that you guide this work and assure the safety of those who enter in at these sacred gates. In your most holy name. Amen."

Bernie and Antara clearly enunciated an emphatic *amen* while Spoigan scowled and pursed his lips, as if debating whether or not to acquiesce.

Friar Johann's gaze riveted on him, awaiting a response which eventually came out sounding more like a grunt than acknowledgement of divine petition. Apparently satisfied nonetheless, Friar Johann nodded and tucked his hands inside his robe.

"All is well," he said. "Follow me and we shall begin the cellmate process so you can be on your way as quickly as possible."

Spoigan waited for Bernie and Antara to go first, snarling under his breath, "Remember what I said about trying anything," as he took up the trek behind them.

"Indeed, General," they replied in solemn unison. "We remember."

This should be interesting, Bernie thought, eyes fixed straight ahead as they left the room. As she recalled, the cristobalite lining the area to which they were headed, coupled with her and Antara's natural telepathic abilities, could help them obtain additional insights into the General's intent. However, it was essential that they shield their own thoughts because it was possible, depending on his capabilities, that it could provide the same benefit to him.

* * *

Sharra was surprised herself by how excited she was about seeing Zahra again. The night before, when Creena told her the news, she realized she hadn't felt so happy since that day she'd gone to the ballome's front entrance to see Laren and Dirck appear through Zeta's searing light, returned at last following their futile attempt to bring Creena home. She was sitting at her usual table in the messhall, attention fixed on the entrance. She'd hardly been able to eat breakfast, being somewhat distracted by repeated false alarms, surprising her with how many jendaks were at the base. At last, her friend appeared, simple attire accented with a colorful scarf that trailed behind her as she headed toward the table as quickly as her short legs would carry her, stubby arms extended in heartfelt greeting.

Sharra got up and met Zahra halfway, laughing while tears dribbled down her cheeks. She stooped over to hug the one who'd surely kept her sane during those frightful days, when she and Deven were alone and running out of food, Opposition on the way with no hope in sight.

"Oh, my dearest, most precious friend," she said, holding her at arm's length. "You have no idea what a wonderful surprise this is."

"Of me as well," Zahra replied, her square, bluish teeth exposed by her grin. "I be so much excited, I think nothing of else since brother mine gave news. So where is daughter? Of her I want meeting! So much glad she be home at last."

Sharra directed her friend toward her usual table and sat down, the sight of the only friend she'd made since leaving her *naterra* delicious to behold. "Creena is busy working in the lab," she explained. "We can go by and meet her there. We're still hoping that perhaps we'll be able to save Laren. But apparently, due to the relativistic time differences, that isn't our most pressing problem. First we must make every effort to prepare against INTEGRATOR aggression, whatever form that may take."

Zahra's round, yellow eyes grew distant the way they always did when she was accessing information from some unknown cosmic source. Sharra still didn't understand it in the slightest, but had learned to respect it, based on the accuracy of previous predictions. She waited quietly, hoping it would validate their current plan and a positive outcome. A moment later the jendak returned to the present, expression troubled.

"As this time, bondling safe. But death looms."

"What do you mean?" she asked, puzzled. "Our calculations indicate he won't arrive on Bezarna for several seasons Cyrarian time. That should give us time to develop something to bring him back."

"Nay, not be," Zahra replied. "He be with scheme to alter course of fate. Those he resists know of attempting and plans stopping. Life's breath will be gone. This plan he be knowing, but stop cannot."

"What are they going to do?" Sharra responded, green eyes wide. "Blow up the ship?"

Once more, Zahra's heavy eyelids briefly covered her eyes.

"Not know. Command upped from ground of badness to ship systems."

Sharra's heart pounded with the realization that maybe they wouldn't be able to save her bondling after all. "Can't we do anything to stop it?" she asked, desperation escalating.

"Cannot tell. Chance of either, dead or live. Time most critical. Command execute sleepzone next."

Sharra closed her eyes briefly then looked upward beseachingly before finally expelling a horrified gasp. "How long does that give us to intervene?"

Again, the jendak's eyes fixed momentarily on another dimension. "For here, on world we be, days be three," she replied. "For him, soon. Minutes soon."

Any random thoughts Sharra had entertained earlier about letting him go evaporated with her horrified gasp. Somehow they had to save him, before all hope was lost forever. Again, the thought of Bryl claiming him collided with the thought of his return, her heart dropping from her throat to her stomach, leaving a well of emptiness in its wake.

Charging

Rohtik Spoigan entertained a variety of thoughts as he followed Friar Johann and the two women back along the stone corridor through which they'd entered the ancient building. From there, they proceeded out the double wooden doors, across the cloistered courtyard, and into what appeared to be a small chapel. The inside was filled with several rows of simple wooden benches with an altar and podium at the front, again tickling his suspicions. It wasn't that he thought their host was untrustworthy, so much as Spoigan's aversion to religion. Any with which he was familiar embraced a philosophy based on superstition which was antithetical to that of INTEGRATION.

Hands concealed within his robe, the monk led them down the center aisle, then behind the altar and past a red velvet curtain to an alcove, where a heavy door secured with a sophisticated palmlatch was hidden. It seemed oddly incongruent in the traditional building, yet somehow fitting for a high tech facility. The lock responded instantly to the friar's touch and opened on a stairwell that descended down a flight of stone steps to a brilliantly illuminated vaulted passageway at least fifty meters long that defied their other surroundings. The seamless walls appeared to have started as a natural limestone tunnel, which had subsequently been expanded and reinforced.

Spoigan's thoughts shifted from the vast contrast between the oscillating rear views he had of the two women to considerations of a more technical nature. At this point, the place was starting to look more like a high tech facility, which brought him a substantial measure of relief. On the other hand, that prayer had given him a deeply ominous feeling that made him feel as if he was being taken to some ancient torture chamber. Logic intervened, reminding him that Esheron had a favorable, non-aggressive diplomatic history, regardless of its own internal wars. Furthermore, it defied reason that such an insignificant planet so steeped within its own problems would mistreat, much less injure, one of INTEGRATION's top officials.

It appeared that both Antara and that bovine specimen beside her had called his bluff on his ability to eliminate the former through her mindprint. That also made him nervous. While it could be done back on Cyraria, he certainly had no means to do such a thing himself. The beta device he'd insisted upon testing allowed him to read her thoughts to some degree during their journey, but they were a bit cloudy and subject to misinterpretation. Since their arrival, it seemed as if she could cloak her mind in some way that blocked access completely. Conversely, in view of their apparent technological advances and the reason he was there in the first place, he didn't doubt that one or both could read *his* thoughts. He lambasted himself for his escalating anxiety, knowing the tactical advantage of sensing your opponent's fear only too well.

Nonetheless, it was impossible to halt his suspicions. He should have known better than to come alone, though at the time it seemed like a good idea. In his position on Cyraria he felt nearly omnipotent, the biggest threat the likes of Troy, but that feeling had fled the moment they'd egressed his TL-87. He reminded himself of the advantage such a device as the one he sought would provide and the fact Antara wouldn't have destroyed hers before his very eyes if it hadn't held secrets that would greatly benefit INTEGRATION.

Again, his eyes rested on the pleasant sight of Antara's shapely behind, remembering his elevated expectations fueled by what he'd heard about Esheronian women and their raging libidos. True or not, it certainly wasn't for her, whose response to his advances had been as warm as Cyraria's desolate moon,

Nifeir. He would have forced the issue except for being cognizant enough to recognize this was supposed to be a business trip to acquire their technology, not see to his own personal needs, demanding though they may be. Further alienating, much less violating her, when their destination was her *naterra,* was far from wise, leaving him no choice but to simply entertain himself with fantasies. That was what self-control was all about and the reason he'd risen as far as he had within the brutal hierarchy of INTEGRATED politics.

The release of Antara's remaining team members being contingent on his return with the desired device had been part of their deal. Thus, it was implied that their demise could result if that were not achieved, but he had not bothered to leave such instructions. At the time, he had no doubts that they'd deliver, even though his intent to fulfill his side of the agreement was less committed. Most likely, Antara would remain here, which wasn't good since she would undoubtedly relay the sordid tale of her team's unwilling diversion to INTEGRATOR interests. However, what could they do, other than complain to the HIO? Nonetheless, he probably should have told someone besides Troy where he was going, given the fellow snake-minded antagonist could benefit greatly if Spoigan failed to return.

He kicked himself mentally, realizing it was distractions related to that thing of beauty sashaying so enticingly before him, which had caused misjudgments and oversights with dangerous potential. He hadn't seen her as dangerous, simply a conquest and prisoner. Now he wondered if those roles had reversed and cursed his foolishness in the most brutal of terms, noticing that both women, as well as the monk, flinched simultaneously yet kept walking, seeming to confirm they were hearing his every thought.

Quit being paranoid, he admonished himself, balancing the fact that paranoia had kept him alive numerous times versus the inestimable benefit that acquisition of their sophisticated com devices would bring to INTEGRATION and thereby to his own position. Even if he only obtained one for himself, it would give him an incredible advantage over his peers, to say nothing of his charges.

They reached the end of the corridor and the friar opened another palmlock-secured door with a single, well-practiced swipe of his wrinkled hand. Beyond fell another narrow, dimly lit flight of stairs that once more reflected the ancient dwelling he thought they'd left behind. Ominous feelings returned until he pushed them aside when the two women smiled at each other, again following some covert exchange.

Benefics, indeed.

His gut told him he shouldn't trust these people any more than his vilest opponent residing at the Quadrumvirate level of the INTEGRATED Tower, yet he couldn't identify any show of aggression or threat, veiled or otherwise, to justify his mistrust. Furthermore, if Brightstar had one of those devices, then other Clique members undoubtedly did, too, making it imperative that INTEGRATED leadership obtain them as well. Determining their capability was essential, but more important still was the hope they could advance their strategic objectives relating to mind control.

The descent was long, at least three levels with each separated by a small landing and switchback. He was grateful for the reduced speed required by the sacred cow up front since his knees weren't what they used to be and he hadn't yet found time for replacements, not daring to turn his back to his cronies long enough for the needed injections to take effect.

When they reached the bottom, he took a deep breath and gazed down another nondescript tunnel-like corridor, this one broken up by numerous doors, all windowless and secured by more palmlocks. The only sound was their footfalls, a claustrophobic feeling teasing his senses in spite of the high ceiling and brilliant, yet seemingly sourceless, lighting. How much farther did they have to go, anyway? He set his jaw, what little patience he had waning, but said nothing, not wanting to let on that he thought he wasn't in control of the situation by complaining.

After more endless walking, the friar stopped by one of the doors, outside of which a dozen small cavities interrupted the wall. "Please remove your footwear," the man requested, setting his sandals inside one of the compartments. The women quickly slipped off their shoes and Spoigan grunted as he stooped over to remove his boots and do the same. Satisfied, the monk bid the palmlocked door open, stepping aside so the others could precede him into the room beyond.

The limestone interior was elliptical, walls gently arched to meet the domed ceiling above and, as far as he could tell, empty. It felt as if he were inside a giant egg, its interior only interrupted by an S-shaped enclosure to the far right.

Anger rumbled inside, but he forcefully maintained outward control.

"What is this, some sort of trap?" he growled, voice echoing in the empty room. "You realize, of course, that if I fail to return to my post, that you will have not only terminated the lives of your research team, but jeopardized your entire planet as well."

"Of course not, General," Friar Johann replied with a patient smile. "This is where we obtain your encephalographic signature so we can encode your device via our unique cellmate process. Without that, it couldn't be personalized for your use alone. Once we have that baseline, you can choose what other features you'd like us to install. From that point on, you can instruct it to do just about anything you want. Your own personal data collector, manager and synthesizer, if you will."

"Why's it empty? Where's the equipment needed to do this?" Spoigan asked, still suspicious. "Our mindprint collection devices are small, but based on psi frequency, not DNA. I assumed your process to be more sophisticated and thus require more extensive screening."

"Not at all, General," the friar replied pleasantly. "Ours is likewise quite compact. The purpose of the chamber is to shield the input from interference generated by other individuals, such as myself or your gracious hostesses from Woeyel Industries."

He gnawed the inside of his lip and scowled. "Okay, fine. So what do I need to do?"

The monk motioned toward the entrance leading behind the curved wall. "If you'll step inside, remove your clothing, including your undergarments, then have a seat within the acquisition chamber, I'll fit you with the recovery cap. You'll find a cubbyhole inside for your belongings. When you're ready, we'll leave and activate the collection process from the next room. Once we have a precise reading, we'll retrieve you from the chamber and proceed with assembling your device."

Spoigan walked slowly toward the designated direction on full alert, hair on the back of his neck standing up as he drew closer. He paused briefly at the flexed entry, then proceeded within, recognizing the walls as the same substance they'd discovered within the caverns where Brightstar's family allegedly survived Opposition. He removed his uniform and everything else, cool air sweeping over him in a chilling wave. Nonetheless, he felt less vulnerable naked than when they'd confiscated his weapons at customs, recalling with considerable irony how in the distant past he and Troy had allowed Brightstar to proceed onworld with his lasomag, only to use it against him later.

The chamber's luminescence changed frequency as he settled onto the sculpted seat in the depth of the curve, stone alarmingly cold against his bare cheeks. Colorful fingers of refracted light swirled toward him, almost tauntingly, as if he were being examined by some mysterious intelligence. The walls were polished and flawless, but the floor slightly pitted with tiny holes, probably damaged by previous occupants and the reason why he had to remove his boots.

"Are you ready, General?" the friar asked.

"Yeah, I'm ready. How exactly does this thing work?" he asked, trying again to subdue his recurring nervousness.

"Quite simple, really," Friar Johann replied as he entered, then placed on Spoigan's head what appeared to be a bowl-shaped object formed from the same material as the walls and secured it with a leather strap beneath his chin. "It operates on the age-old principle of quantum photon entanglement. Your mindprint, as you refer to it, is reflected by the cristobalite, which we capture in the lab. Any brain activity is then encoded within your personalized device, but of course you control what is retained and what isn't. You can protect the information to any level of security you choose, and you'll be able to communicate with those with like devices who permit you inside their network."

"That's it?" Spoigan asked.

"Yes. An interference pattern will be captured from your aura as well, the two being unique identifiers that assist in the location function. Are you ready, General?"

Was it his imagination or did the monk's enigmatic smile not quite reach those dark, knowing eyes?

"Yes, I suppose," he replied, still inexplicably uncomfortable, but determined to overcome his superstition-based fears and complete the process rather than waste the trip. If he came back empty-handed, he'd never hear the end of it from Troy. Again, he reassured himself that these people had a lot to lose if this transaction failed to go as agreed. He was willing to pay royally for the devices, plus they would get their team members back.

Unless, of course, Troy or someone else had disposed of them during his absence. If that were the case, they would delay such unfortunate news until he was safely back on Cyraria, com device in hand. At that point, anything the Esheronians might do could provoke an invasion by INTEGRATED forces, which would result in their entire planet's demise rather than the loss of a few worthless individuals.

"All righty then," the monk said with a smile, bringing him back to the matter at hand. The man patted Spoigan's shoulder in an apparent gesture of reassurance, then tucked his hands inside his robe's over-sized sleeves and exited the chamber. No words were exchanged with the others as he joined them, their footsteps silent as he and the two women left the main room, announced only by the soft click of the lock as the heavy door closed behind them.

* * *

Bezarna Express

Laren's eyes met Rhodus' across the cabin, the man immediately joining him upon noting his expression. He indicated the ship's command queue on the c-com without comment while his mind continued to race. The digichronometer on the wall indicated it was only a matter of minutes until sleepzone. They were as good as dead.

As always, Sa'ata was watching carefully from his own area. Doubts raged whether or not he was a guard or a fellow prisoner. If nothing else, it was time for total honesty; if he thought he had a round-trip ticket, he was sadly mistaken.

"Hey, Sa'ata," Laren said. "There's something you need to know."

The Pyxisite silently met his gaze with one that was cold and hard.

"I don't believe you're who and what you say you are. If you think this trip is going to end differently for you than the rest of us, you might be interested in what they have planned for our next sleepzone."

A flicker of interest appeared as his lashless eyes narrowed.

"What's that, Brightstar?" he replied, deep, raspy voice as friendly as the hiss of a snake.

"They're cutting the O_2 at twenty-two hundred hours, which is exactly twenty three minutes from now."

"Since you haven't cooperated so far, maybe that only pertains to you," he said smugly.

"Unfortunately for you, no," Laren stated. "The command is vehicle-wide, not cyll-specific."

"What has you done?" he snarled, glaring. "What has you been doing that caused them to do something like that?"

"What do you think I've been doing?" Laren countered. "You actually think I'm going to sit here and accept my fate when I might be able to do something about it?"

"I knew you was up ta somethin'. I shoulda eliminated you chrons ago."

"Yeah, well you didn't. And for whatever reason, they don't value your life any more than ours. So we can either work together or die together. Your choice."

"No, Brightstar," he snarled, pulling a compact service grade lasomag from the inside pocket of his jacket. "You and your buddy here is gonna die, but I's goin' back."

In a flash Laren realized his suppositions had been correct, that the ship would return as soon as the passengers were dispatched, cutting off subsequent commands. Which left one other solution, one he and Rhodus could possibly survive.

"Wait," he said calmly, raising his hands in momentary surrender. "What if we can get the return command queue to activate without the usual trigger?"

"What you talkin' 'bout?" the guard replied, face distorted with distrust tainted by confusion, lasomag still leveled in Laren's direction.

Not surprisingly, he apparently had no understanding of the ship's internal functions, much less what constituted a "command queue," only that when the last prisoner took the suicide option or he forced the issue, the ship returned.

Before Laren could explain, in a lightning fast move that defied both his size and age, Rhodus took advantage of the momentary pause and dove across the floor. He tackled the guard at knee level, which slammed the back of Sa'ata's head hard against the back wall. Right on cue, Laren snatched the weapon out of the air as it flew from the guard's grasp.

"My, how quickly things can change," Laren said, shoving the weapon in the Pyxisite's face as Rhodus hauled him to his feet. "Are you going to cooperate, Sa'ata, or head for the airlock?"

The man's raised hands were shaking, eyes wide with terror.

"Well?" Laren insisted, eyes locked on his.

"Yeah, yeah, man," he stammered. "Anything but nots the airlock, man. Anythin'. Mag me if ya gotta, but nots that."

"Twenty minutes," Rhodus reported, a quiet reminder that time was not on their side.

"All right, I've got work to do," Laren said, handing off the lasomag to Rhodus, who pushed Sa'ata into a seat where he secured his hands with wrist wrings built into the armrests.

He took out his c-com and brought up the file with the video and digital code he'd set up to mimic their supposed exit via the airlock. He read it over one final time, then switched to transmission mode to send it to the ship's systems. He waited for the device to respond as it had before, but nothing happened and a heartbeat later the holo went blank. A chill ran through him as what felt like some form of organic life drained from it.

His jaw dropped as his future became as dark as the mysterious device resting in silent repose in his outstretched hand.

Intrusions

Back in the lab, Creena immediately logged in to review what they'd already determined about cristobalite, devenite and chronoviatic transfer. She added a few more notes related to the mental and emotional components, then checked Aggie's c-com schematics for the ratio between cristobalite and devenite so she could compare it to the psitenna. As it turned out, the differences were substantial, the proportion of devenite in the psitenna about three times greater. She'd barely settled into studying the data further, when icy fingers of doom crept outward from her chest, weakening every limb. Her heart felt heavy, as if laboring with every beat, even while the hair on her arms and back of her neck rose in eerie warning.

She shivered, overwhelmed with the sudden sense of being watched, not by Bryl, Dirck, Win, or even Storm, but by a cold and sinister presence. She thought of 'Merapa's admonition again, wondering if what she felt was guilt, making all their rationalizations intrinsically wrong. Maybe the immorality of time travel went deeper than philosophical differences between 'Merapa and Bryl.

She purposely shook off the feeling and concentrated again, wondering if they could use an object rather than a person to test their progress. Sending people on what could be little more than random timeshift excursions was not only dangerous, but illegal. Bryl was working on a waiver from the HIO allowing them to conduct such experiments, but for now it was forbidden. Losing a member of their own research team wouldn't exactly move the project in a positive direction, either.

Her musings stopped abruptly as again darkness closed around her, triggering a fear that chilled her flesh, hackles staging an encore on her arms. She looked around quickly for an intruder, snagging Dirck's watchful eye across the lab.

"What's wrong?" he asked.

"I'm not sure," she replied. "I just got this creepy feeling. Like I'm being watched."

"By who?"

Even as she spoke, she realized she'd felt that way before, several times, and not just since they'd begun work on chronoviatic transfer. There'd never been any physical evidence to substantiate it, yet she knew with a surety what it was. Her expression must have given her away again, because Dirck set aside his notelog and came toward her, questions firing from his eyes. Before she knew it, Win was there as well.

"What is it? What's wrong?" Win asked, stooping over to look closely at her face. "You look scared to death."

"It's *him*," she whispered, as if revealing a horrific and terrible secret.

"Who?" Dirck asked.

Creena rubbed her arms nervously, looking once more toward the open door before she answered.

"Something's really wrong," she said shakily. "I don't know what's going on, but he knows what we're doing."

"Who?" Dirck asked insistently. "Merapa?"

"No," she replied, shaking her head adamantly in emphasis. "The INTEGRATOR."

The memories were unpleasant, all competing fiercely for the *Worst Nightmare* title. All shared a common thread, however, that dark and heavy feeling of doom, a negative energy spike that sapped both strength and hope.

Creena's previous encounters with the INTEGRATOR had ranged from mild enticements, which had beckoned her into the escape pod, to that ominous and threatening dialog on Earth.

Things had been quiet for so long she'd nearly forgotten them, the recurrence as surprising as it was unsettling.

Gradually, the intensity increased, escalating from the vague feeling of being watched to a sense of acute psychic invasion, as if her thoughts were on virtual display. She held her temples tightly, trying to will it away so she could work, yet knew from experience that she was incapable of stopping such intrusions.

"Why me? What does he want? And why now?" she wondered aloud, not expecting an answer.

"From what you told us, their previous contacts were aimed at getting you to work with them," Dirck said. "You made it clear you wouldn't, so they left you alone. Now they've either changed their mind, maybe because 'Merapa is gone, or somehow they know what we're doing. The real question is how did they find out where you are?"

"Good point," Win agreed. "As far as we know, we got you onworld without revealing your identity, so if cristobalite only works onworld they'd have to know you're here, but how?"

"But telepathy isn't limited by location," Creena argued. "It locates the person wherever they happen to be. Like the psitenna. Or Bryl's c-com."

"True," Win said grimly. "If they want to pick your brain, they may not need to know where you are. They also probably have devenite."

"Who cares how they found me?" Creena said, irritated. "They have and that's what matters. If they're reading my mind, then what?"

"Knowing how they contacted you is important so we can figure out how to shield it," Win said evenly. "It could even be to our advantage. But you're right, Creena, our immediate problem is that we don't know how much they can intercept, whether they only hear your conscious thoughts, what you deliberately project back via psi, or what. The last thing we need is for them to know what we're trying to do. Too bad we don't know how to reverse it, so you can find out what they're thinking."

"Right," she muttered, not sure she wanted to know.

"Apparently this problem can be solved with the c-coms," Dirck said. "Maybe we need to quit until Major Zebatohn produces them."

"I think you're right," Win replied. "Then we can figure out how they're encrypted and filtered. Positive identification of who's supposed to get any messages is critical, as well as preventing intelligence leakage."

"Merapa's c-com did all sorts of cool stuff," Dirck said. "And I assume it was all secure, or he wouldn't have included some of the things he did."

"All right," Win said. "Let's just call it a zone bust and quit until then. Once we have c-coms, Creena should be able to filter who comes in."

* * *

Ledorian Monastery
Esheron

As soon as everyone left Spoigan alone in the acquisition chamber, something changed. At first, it was just a feeling in his chest and Spoigan wondered if all the stress was giving him a heart attack. But it wasn't pain, rather a feeling of emptiness, more as if it were imploding. The light in the room, all provided by the chamber itself and its iridescent walls, was fading as well. He blinked, hard, wondering if it was real or he was getting ready to pass out, as he had as a young lieutenant the first time he'd seen someone ripped open by a lasomag, guts a tangled mass on the starship's deck.

He took a deep breath and blinked again. No, it was definitely getting darker, even though fingers of energy were still there, barely visible as dancing streaks of light. But rather than peaceful and wispy as they'd been before, they gathered into frenzied clusters of tangled knots; crackling, smoking fibers that disintegrated like burning fuses, then fell as ashes.

With the realization his neurons and synapses were annihilating, he tried to remove the cap, only to discover he couldn't move, scream dying in his throat. The last thing he saw was the floor rushing up to meet him before everything went black.

* * *

Before they'd finishing shutting things down, an emergency page rang through the lab. Dirck called it up and saw it was from 'Merama, immediately accepting it. Her face appeared in the space before him, her pale, worry-lined expression one he'd seen far too often.

"What's wrong, 'Merama?" he asked, the others crowding around, beckoned by the concern in his voice.

"I just talked with Zahra," she said, voice shaky. "She had some impressions regarding your father's situation which change everything."

"What?" Creena asked, wondering if her dark feelings had anything to do with him.

"She said he's been trying to compromise the ship's systems. They apparently found out and are going to make sure he doesn't succeed. If she's right, we have three days to do something, or he's dead."

Creena's jaw dropped in horror. *"Three days?"* she gasped, as Dirck mirrored her expression and Win muttered his favorite expletive.

"Does he know?" Win asked.

"Yes, but she said he couldn't do anything about it," 'Merama answered.

Dirck paged Bryl, who joined the holo a moment later, looking so tired he wondered if she already knew. "What is it, Dirck?" she asked.

He quickly summarized the situation, proposing they attempt contacting his father via her c-com.

"It's more private in my office than the lab," she stated. "Come on down and let's talk about it."

A few moments later, they were all in Bryl's office, including 'Merama, whose anxiety level was off the scale.

"I want to make sure I understand this correctly," Bryl said, addressing her comments to 'Merama as they all took a seat across from her workdeck. "Major Zebatohn's sister told you that Laren did something to the prison ship, which has been detected, and they're going to destroy it before it gets to Bezarna?"

"Yes," 'Merama replied stiffly. "That's what she said."

"How does she know this?" Bryl asked, frowning.

"She, well, just seems to know these things," 'Merama replied, expression defensive. "She's highly intuitive. Somehow she tuned into what's happening. I don't have any idea how she does it, but she's given us information before, which has always turned out to be correct. Always."

Bryl's eyebrows rose, eyes reflecting what appeared to be surprise, either at the information or 'Merama's unusual tone, then recovered quickly to her usual mien. "Is she telepathic?"

"No, I don't think so," 'Merama said after a moment's thought. "I would say she's clairvoyant. Or a strong intuitive."

"But you have confidence in her visions?"

"Yes. Of course. I wouldn't bother everyone like this if I thought she was crazy," 'Merama stated, defensive again.

"So apparently, we don't have as much time to bring him back as we originally thought," Bryl said, watching her carefully. "Whatever they're going to do will happen in three days, our timeframe, correct?"

"Yes," Sharra replied, emphasizing her answer with a nod. Her expression relaxed somewhat, apparently relieved Bryl believed her.

"Okay. Here's how I see it," Bryl continued. "If we perfect chronoviatic transfer, then it doesn't matter when, because theoretically we can always go back in time to rescue him. But that's a big *if*, especially if how far we can go back is limited. The main thing we need to do is synch up with when this destruction could occur, so we can precede it by sufficient margin when the time comes."

"But there's always the risk the HIO won't approve chronoviatic, even if we figure it out," Dirck stated. "Then what?"

A look of firm determination shrouded Bryl's dark eyes. "To borrow one of Win's favorite sayings, sometimes it's easier to get forgiveness than permission."

"What are you saying, Bryl? Defy the HIO?" Win asked, eyebrows raised.

"Absolutely," she said. "I don't see the INTEGRATOR worrying about permission, do you? There are provisions for defense in kind. And furthermore, I don't see the HIO helping us, either. As far as I'm concerned, that's not an issue."

"I think we should contact him," Dirck stated. "Even if we can't do anything now, we can at least let him know what we hope to do."

"But he was totally against chronoviatic transfer," Creena protested. "He'd probably just tell us again not to do it."

"Maybe not if Bryl told him," Win suggested. "He told us to follow orders and now she's the one calling the shots."

Bryl held his gaze for what seemed a long time, eyes active with thought. Then, without another word she got her c-com out of her workdeck and focused all her concentration on the job at hand. After entering a few commands manually she held the device between her hands, eyes closed in concentration.

Creena held her breath, eyes riveted on the woman's expression for clues to whether or not she'd made contact. Seconds stretched into minutes, Bryl's expression unchanged as if frozen in time. Creena exchanged hopeful, then worried looks with Dirck, then 'Merama and Win, all knowing the longer it took, the less likely it was to succeed. After what seemed an eternity, Bryl sighed and slowly placed the c-com on the workdeck in front of her, eyes still fixed upon it pensively for several long moments.

"Well?" Win prompted.

"No go," she said grimly. "Which could mean a number of things. Maybe he doesn't have it with him, it shut down because they tried to access it, or, well, or maybe we're already too late."

"Zahra said we had three days," 'Merama said, her expression an odd mixture of unreadable emotions.

"Have you used it to communicate with a vehicle before?" Dirck asked.

"Yes," she replied. "And there was no delay. None."

"Try Uncle Jen," Dirck said. "Maybe 'Merapa has contacted him."

Again, Bryl's concentration turned to the device, her expression quickly indicating contact. A full spectrum of emotions arranged her features in a series of unreadable looks, some hopeful, some not. At long last she looked up, as if surprised to see everyone still there.

"Well?" Win prompted.

The woman emitted another sigh before she answered. "Jen said Laren contacted him and asked him to upload a substantial amount of data. As far as Jen could tell, the communication was instantaneous, as it always was when I used mine. He hasn't heard from him for a while, and also tried to contact him to no avail. The logical conclusion is that some form of intrusion shut it down."

Left unspoken, yet reflected in the solemn looks exchanged, were the other reasons for silence.

"Did Jen say what he uploaded?" Win asked.

"Databases, primarily," she replied. "But he did inquire specifically about some of the people onboard. From what he could gather, the ship itself returns to Cyraria. Laren was trying to figure out how to remain on board for the return trip. Which means they have to dispatch the prisoners by some other means before the ship returns."

"That makes more sense," Win commented. "It's not a matter of when they arrive, because they never do. Rather, it's a matter of when they get rid of the passengers, which could be at any time, once they reach deep space."

As the implications settled 'Merama's horrified look said it all.

"There's gotta be something we can do before then," Creena said. "Gotta be."

No one spoke, expressions grave, collective hopes mingling plaintively with the substance of space.

Brain Storms

The three-day countdown dominated Creena's thoughts to the point of obsession. Drop dead dates were one thing, but this one held literal implications. There was no time for distractions, yet tuning into the task at hand was impossible as the psychic invasions continued. It was only barely past time for the midday mealzone, yet as she sat in her usual place in the lab she felt as depleted as when she'd been working through her sleepzone back in the Caverns.

She cringed as the dark preamble to another intrusion enclosed her mind.

"Again?" Dirck asked, hand resting apologetically on her shoulder when she jumped, startled.

"Again is hardly the word," she replied, holding her temples. "It's constant. I can't even sleep in peace."

He studied her with a look of genuine concern. "Why don't we grab something to eat in the messhall, then see how Deven and 'Merama are doing with setting up the dream experiment? Maybe we can start this sleepzone. If we're lucky, we might even have a dream that helps. On the way back we can check and see how they're doing with our c-coms."

Not wanting to waste any time, they simply grabbed a handful of genour bars, then headed for Cranium Cavern. They proceeded in silence, Creena keeping her mind as blank as possible. They'd already passed their personal quarters and were nearly to the main branch, where their conversation would of necessity dwindle, due to the physical demands imposed by the route to their destination. Just short of that point where it began a steady descent, Dirck stopped again.

"So you're sure it's the INTEGRATOR?" he asked.

"Yes."

"What exactly does he say?" he asked.

"Nothing! Absolutely nothing!" she answered, fists clenched in frustration. "There's just that awful feeling that he's there, listening. That and gloating."

"Gloating?"

"Yeah, *gloating.*"

"About what?"

"Everything. Mainly 'Merapa."

"How can you tell if he doesn't say anything?"

"I can feel it. Like comm using devenite, which they probably have."

"But no words."

"I get the impression of words sometimes, but not complete thoughts. Sometimes it's almost like background noise, as if there's more than one person there and they're talking to each other."

"So can you listen back?"

"Not really, it's too garbled. Like a bad connection."

"But you're sure he's talked to you before."

"Yes."

"During those other times, did you feel as if he could read your mind?"

Creena paused pensively. "No, I don't think so. Only when I deliberately said something back."

"Telepathically?"

"Yeah."

"So it's different now, because he doesn't say anything. At all."

"Right. I have no doubt he's spying on our research. We know they have cristobalite because they found the Tank, plus anything we left behind. They saw me, plus witnessed how we left. Apparently they had my mindprint from before, and have now figured out how to probe my mind."

Dirck's expression mirrored her own. "As soon as we're done here, we'd better get with *Intelligence* to see what we can find out," he said.

She nodded agreement, then followed in troubled silence as they cautiously made their way along the convoluted pathway to Cranium Cavern.

When they arrived, they paused before making the final descent to take in the strange scene below.

All previous visits they'd only been able to see small portions of the chamber, since all they had were portalumes. Handheld lighting would have been too awkward to get everything set up, so Dirck had requisitioned six battery-operated lumapoles, light tubes two meters high which emitted enough light to illuminate the average size room. They were set at equal distances apart, forming a hexagon which surrounded where the sleep stations were being set up. The lights' bluish glow cast weird shadows on the bulging walls until they gradually succumbed to darkness near the zenith, giving the impression of being inside a giant brain; truly Deven's name for the place fit.

Five rolled up cyllmats were scattered within the lighted area, which they'd just started to set up, allowing each unit to achieve its expanded configuration. Moving their actual cylls would have been a formidable task, plus they required an external power source, so cyllmats like they'd slept on back at the Caverns were the best option. Cylls were fully integrated, sound filtering domed enclosures with built-in temperature and lighting controls programmed to match its user's sleepzone; conversely, cyllmats had limited features, but were lightweight and rolled up easily, making them more practical to move, plus they had self-contained power derived from their occupant's body heat.

While they lacked the privacy afforded by the optional cover, they were just as comfortable with temperature control deriving from the soft lining while nanobots adjusted its support to accommodate their every move. Lighting capability was achieved by the unit's base, which emitted a fiber-optic channeled glow which was reflected throughout the mat, gently nudging its occupant awake as sleepzone ended. When deployed, each stood a half-meter high making them awkwardly low to sit on, yet high enough off the ground to feel reasonably secure.

Deven noticed they were there and waved happily. "Check it out!" he said with a grin. "Is this cool or what?"

"Looks great, Dev," Creena replied as she and Dirck made their way down to the main floor, marveling again how vast it appeared.

"We'll be ready to start tonight," 'Merama said, expression tightening when neither Creena nor Dirck showed much enthusiasm. "What's wrong?" she asked.

"Apparently the INTEGRATOR has encephalographic access," Dirck explained. "That's probably why 'Merapa's c-com shut down and why Creena keeps feeling as if she's being watched."

"How much do you think they've been able to find out?" she asked nervously.

"I don't know. We're on our way to see if *Intelligence* can confirm or deny it."

"The INTEGRATOR wins either way," 'Merama mused grimly. "If we stop our research, we'll never bring your father home. If we succeed, they'll have our technology to use against us."

Creena shivered as additional understanding fell into place. "That's why 'Merapa said he was against chronoviatic research," she said.

"That certainly makes sense," Dirck agreed. "But let's see what evidence we have before we decide."

* * *

Ledorian Monastery
Esheron

Friar Johann opened the door on the darkened room that housed the acquisition chamber, Antara and Bernie close behind. "Oh, my," he said. "I suspected this might occur."

"What happened?" Antara asked, expression puzzled. "Where'd he go? Why's it so dark?"

The monk sighed, pausing as the chamber gradually came back to life, filling the room once more with dancing light, before he proceeded inside the rest of the way.

"Apparently, the general was not a nice man," he explained sadly. "This happens when there's simply too much darkness in their soul to overcome."

Bernie had been around long enough to remember when this had happened before. In fact, she'd counted on it, but Antara was clearly confused. The older woman smiled and placed a comforting arm around her protégé's shoulders.

The Ledorian priest slowly entered the chamber, women close on his heels, as he examined the empty stone seat, the abandoned helmet, and then the floor. "Sometimes you can find the result," he stated, flicking a piece of what appeared to be sand with his finger. It skipped across slippery stone, stopping a few centimeters away. "Nope, too light," he said mostly to himself.

"*Sweet Benefics*, is that what I think?" Antara exclaimed, hands over her mouth in revulsion.

"Probably," Bernie explained. "He self-annihilated when bombarded with the positive energy inherent to the process. Sometimes you can find their remains, others not, depending on how perfect the reaction was. Thoughts become things and if they're dark…"

"They become a, a *blackhole*?" the other woman interjected, dark eyes wide.

"Yes," Bernie replied. "Thus the pitted floor." She patted Antara on the back in a comforting gesture, then sighed. "Too bad. He was actually a fairly decent looking man."

With that, she beamed with a deep, satisfied smile, gave Antara another reassuring squeeze, then set her hands on ample hips. "Well, our work here is done. Let's contact Bryl and give her the news."

"But what about my team?" Antara asked. "When he doesn't return…"

"Don't worry, child," Bernie replied. "I suspect Friar Johann might be able to do something about that, too."

When Bernie arrived in her office, the first thing she did was contact Bryl, whose reaction was best described as pure shock.

What? You vaporized Spoigan? Like TG Spoigan, down here?

Bernie laughed with hearty, soul-felt humor, which generated an instantaneous wash of affection from her *in absentia* boss and comrade.

Not anymore, she replied, still chuckling.

All right, Bernie. From the beginning. What's going on?

After Bernie explained the situation, she could tell Bryl was not as elated as expected.

I don't know whether that's good news or not, Bryl psaid. *Such an unexpected upset in* INTEGRATOR *leadership may or may not be to our advantage, depending on who takes his place.*

Where there's chaos there's opportunity, Bernie replied, leaning back in her reinforced chair.

True. But the person who's next in line is definitely not an improvement.

Bernie felt Bryl's rush of discouragement punctuate the statement. *Perhaps we can arrange a similar fate for him as well,* she psaid, chuckling.

Not likely at this point. There's also the matter of whether or not the authorities on Cyraria will believe your explanation of his unfortunate, uh, accident, Bryl went on. *Up until now*

INTEGRATION has left Esheron alone. If they perceive you as an accomplice of Clique forces, you could be next on their list of conquests. As if we don't have enough trouble with our own internal warfare.

Well, at least there's one less evil person in mortality, Bernie pointed out, disappointed that Bryl didn't see it as advantageous.

True, Bryl agreed. *But if it opens the way for someone worse to come into power, which is likely, it may not be a good thing.*

Time will tell, my sister, Bernie replied. *Time will tell. Sometimes all we can do is trust the Universe.*

ANTICIPATION

After Dirck and Creena returned from Cranium Cavern it took a while before they found Win and Igni holed up in a remote corner of the messhall. Dirck pulled over a couple chairs from an empty table, then sat down and proceeded to explain their conclusions based on Creena's experiences.

Win was visibly rattled by the possibility. "We need to check for any strategic troop movements or technological advances that mirror our activities," he said.

"Yeah, that would indicate whether they've been accessing individual sources," Dirck replied. "If only we could find out how their research is progressing more specifically. Know exactly what they can and can't do."

Win's face lit up like a star gone nova. "Remember when we discovered what was going on in Dununda? We found a bulletin, one that looked like a report up the foodchain, of how things were going with their research."

"Yeah, I remember that," Dirck said with a nod. "Short and to the point, yet exactly what we needed to know."

"They probably issue them on a regular basis, especially when they make significant progress. That way they keep the big guys happy and assure their funding continues."

"As well as their lives," Dirck added humorlessly.

"Right. We need to go back and see how we accessed that and whether we can get on distribution, so to speak." Win laughed. "I'm sure they're out there, we just need to find the right search code to filter them out, then break the encryption scheme. Should be easy for Aggie."

Win looked puzzled as concentration pulled Dirck's expression into a frown and Igni's translator crackled. "What's wrong?"

"Nothing. I'm trying to remember what they were called."

Creena smiled and nodded at both Win and Igni. "Dirck has always had a really good memory. I wouldn't be surprised if he could recite—"

"Got it!" Dirck exclaimed. "Technological Breakthrough Advisories. That's it. They were called Technological Breakthrough Advisories. Or TBAs."

"Awesome!" Win agreed, exchanging a Miran grip across the table, then with Creena and Igni. "We'll head over to *IP&S*, hunt down Aggie and see what we can do."

Dirck and Creena went back to the lab until about an hour later, when Win summoned them to the briefing room. They arrived moments later and viewed the results, which turned out to be both ominous and disturbing. There had been a fourfold increase in decisive Clique defeats since Creena first noticed the intrusions. In further confirmation, Aggie had accessed a series of TBA's that told the rest of the sordid story.

Even though it was lean for detail, what Aggie uncovered further confirmed their worst fears. Exactly what the INTEGRATOR had done with the cristobalite had been unknown before. Now they knew. Encephalographic access was their top priority and had been for a long time. Based on the fact the INTEGRATOR had found her on Earth, Creena suspected they'd been able to detect psi associated with specific mindprints based on quantum fluctuations, but not necessarily interpret them word for word. Understanding at that level involved more sophisticated technology. Apparently, now they could, at least to the keyword level. From that, a basic interpolation algorithm could fill in the blanks.

They wanted to use the crystals to bring 'Merapa home, the INTEGRATOR wanted to read their minds. A simple strategy, really—knowing their every tactic, every plan, every weakness, whether in battle or research, would yield easy victory. Without the crucial element of surprise, every action, whether defensive or offensive, was doomed to failure. And once they'd figured out time travel, it would be plundered as well, assuring the enemy a flawless victory that spanned space and time.

Creena looked at the digichronometer glaring down from the briefing room's far wall and moaned in defeat. "We won't get the c-com's until tonight at the soonest, if they even work, and right now we only have two days to save 'Merapa. Meanwhile we can't work on a thing."

Then, quick-thinking as usual, Win waved for their attention and continued in mutogueronian, nicknamed *mutog*, Esheron's sign language, which they'd used with 'Merapa in the Territorial Tower when they suspected audio monitoring.

||I don't know whether they can detect this or not, but it's worth a shot,|| he said. ||It should use a different part of the brain which could fog the message.||

||Concede,|| Igni agreed.

||Why's Creena the only target?|| Win continued. ||How can he tune into her but not the rest of us?||

Everyone looked at her as if she should know the answer. And something inside told her she did. ||He's had direct contact with me,|| she replied. ||Since the *Aquarius*. And on Terra. Somehow they can access me. But they don't bother any of you. Why?||

Win waved for attention. ||You're more sensitive to psi than the rest of us. They know you can hear them because you've responded. They may be trying to connect with all of us but we don't notice.||

Creena nodded in partial agreement. ||But Igni and Thyron are both telepathic and they're not picking it up, either. Why not?||

||They must be specifically targeting you,|| Win continued. ||We've already determined that sometimes psi is private and sometimes not. Maybe they can only hear you when you talk

aloud, when it's not private. When you're quiet they turn up the gain. We may not need countermeasures for everyone, just you. So if only one of the c-coms works you'll be the one who gets it. | |

| |Not necessarily, | | Dirck pointed out. | |Creena hasn't been working anything but the crystals. So whatever information they got on Clique strategic moves didn't come from her. They're tapping someone else as well. | |

He exchanged fearful looks with the others as the implications settled.

| |I don't doubt they hijacked our mindprints a long time ago, back when we were in your father's office in the Tower, | | Win stated. | |But we used fake identities whenever we were there, so maybe they haven't linked them with us. | |

| |Probably, | | Dirck agreed, | |But we're not working strategic moves, either. All we've been into besides research has been intel. *Their* intel, not ours. | |

No one spoke at first, the answer suddenly as obvious as it was horrifying.

"Bryl!" Dirck and Win said aloud in unison.

| |Right! | | Win said, signing again. | |She worked in the Tower, too, and Troy undoubtedly had her under surveillance. They could have grabbed mindprints from everyone in the building, possibly all of Cira City. No telling if security levels were as solid as we thought, either. | |

| |But I can feel it when they're listening, | | Creena added. | |Wouldn't Bryl know, too? | |

| |Depends, | | Igni replied, translator picking up a significant amount of interference since so far the discussion was inconclusive. | |Only if she's psi sensitive. | |

| |We need to alert Bryl, | | Dirck said.

| |I agree, | | Win said. | |From what Aggie told us about the c-com's, she should be able to block any unwanted psi signals. | |

||But we assumed it was INTEGRATOR intrusions that shut down 'Merapa's. If that's the case, why haven't they shut down Bryl's?|| Creena asked.

||Maybe they did,|| Win answered. ||Maybe it wasn't Aggie's scan after all.||

||According to Aggie's description, if the threat is identified, it can be blocked without shutting it down,|| Dirck stated. ||Let's get Aggie in here and find out how.||

He paged the 'troid who arrived a few moments later.

"You rang?" she asked.

||Yes, Aggie,|| Dirck signed in reply. ||Can specific psi signals be blocked on a c-com while maintaining its functionality?||

"What's with the signing?" she asked, tone somewhat norfed.

||We suspect the INTEGRATOR can access our thoughts and this may keep our conversations private.||

"Sounds like paranoia to me," the 'troid stated, rotating her photoreceptors in an electronic eyeroll. "If they've accessed our plans, maybe they did it the same way we do, monitoring transmissions. I'd start with a more complex encryption scheme instead of resorting to a bunch of hand waving, don't ya think?"

"Aggie's got a point," Win agreed aloud. "Let's at least drop using *mutog* unless it's classified. Besides, Creena might be the only one who needs to go mute."

"Maybe, maybe not," Dirck argued. "Creena can sense intrusions, so there's something going on. Maybe we're not psi-sensitive enough. We can't take a chance on compromising our research if they're picking up on everything we're doing."

"Thyron meditates to get away from telepathic noise. I wonder if it works in reverse?" Creena mused aloud.

"How? What do you mean?" Dirck asked.

"Maybe you can't be heard, either. From what he's told me, meditation is like an internal receiver mode versus transmitting. You consciously quiet your mind until it's blank, then wait to see what materializes from your subconscious."

"Yeah, but you won't get anything done if you mediate all the time."

"I wouldn't have to. Only when I sense an intrusion. Then, if he doesn't pick up anything, maybe he'd go away."

"That's not a bad idea. Hopefully by tomorrow Major Zee will bring us a few c-coms, which will solve the problem," Win said, dispensing another unsolicited nickname as he was prone to do. "For now, we need to check in with Bryl, let her know what's going on so she can block intrusions, and show us how when we get ours, hopefully tomorrow. After that, I say we call it another zone bust, get something to eat and what rest we can. We'll start fresh tomorrow, think about mindprints some more, and get Thyron to give us some meditation tips."

"Meanwhile maybe our sleep experiment tonight will bring something," Creena said. "At this point, we could sure use some help."

* * *

Creena lay wide awake on her cyllmat in Cranium Cavern, everyone else already asleep, judging by the steady blue indicators on their individual stations. Someone stirred, apparently Dirck, the sleep phase indicator lights on his mat flickering green, then resumed a steady blue concurrent with the soft sound of snoring. She smiled, the sound endearing, even though it brought another distraction from falling asleep.

Her thoughts wandered to her father and what he might have done to cause problems. She smiled, knowing she would have expected no less. Somehow it made her feel better to think that if he had to die, it wasn't without putting up a good fight. That story he told her that he'd accepted his fate and to let him go never felt right. Maybe he'd said that in case anyone was listening. The resulting jolt to her heart bore witness of its truth and she shuddered, trying to remember what she might have said that she shouldn't. Oh, well. What is, is, as Win always said. Is-squared.

Or was it? Not if they had chronoviatic abilities. They had the makings of it, if they could only control it. Devenite operated using some form of intelligence which calculated the time adjustment based on emotional comfort and harmony. Was the Universe itself controlling it? Perhaps the *Benefics?*

Who exactly were the *Benefics?* Were they individuals? Some form of consciousness? Or simply energy? Which then begged the question, what was the INTEGRATOR? Was he an individual or simply collective negative energy? Or maybe both, perhaps not one person, but several. There were all those negative spikes they'd detected when they'd returned from Mira III; maybe they were caused as people adopted or fell prey to the evil philosophy. As their minds turned to darkness, the negative energy increased, which was then harnessed by one or more individuals. If so, it made sense that good energy could overcome it, if there was more or it was stronger.

But how? Cristobalite reflected it, but they no longer had enough crystals to make a difference. Could devenite take them back so they could get more? Yet, since the INTEGRATOR probably had both, then what? Or maybe not. When they fled the Caverns they'd taken all the loose devenite and they'd buried the cache where Deven found it before that. If the enemy didn't have devenite, the Clique had an advantage. Yet, the fact she could feel them gloating indicated they did, because cristobalite only conveyed thoughts, not emotions.

She turned from her side to her back, noticing tiny sparks dancing on the ceiling. *Weird,* she thought, then discounted it. Probably they'd been there all along, but visible now since her eyes had adjusted to the dark. Like thoughts bouncing around.

Deven's name for the place was so clever. She smiled. He was such a great kid. And it was so cool that now she and Dirck were finally getting along. For the first time in her life. All thanks to devenite. Too bad it couldn't do that for the entire planet.

And with that final heart-warming thought, she finally fell asleep.

* * *

Igni shifted in her cyll, never quite comfortable within the confines of the purely human invention. Luckily she didn't require as much sleep as those comprised of flesh and blood, so time spent in such an unfamiliar device was limited. She switched to the floor, closer to what she preferred, but it was too flat and unyielding. At least the base was underground, which had a familiar, comfortable feel. She crawled back in the cyll, tucking her six legs beneath her segmented body and relaxing her antennae against the sides, realizing it really didn't matter. Adapting was simply part of life.

She wouldn't be so restless except she knew they were missing something. That was the problem with humans, they were too independent. In colonies such as the one on Arcturus where she'd been raised, the collective never failed to solve any survival issue. She knew she couldn't do it alone, and on her homeworld didn't have to.

A phrase she'd heard on Terra during one of her many HIO excursions, *All for one and one for all,* summed it up nicely. While achieving consensus with her fellows was a reasonable substitute for the colony collective, it wasn't the same. Yes, she was telepathic, but the ability was intended to be networked with others of her kind, merging their thoughts, ideas, ambitions and lives into a single consciousness. No individual was ever expected to do it all. If you missed something, it was irrelevant, because someone else would catch it. There was no competition, at least amongst workers, only within the worthless drones who competed for access to the queen, whom the rest of them protected, at any cost.

Her antennae trembled briefly with pride, knowing that she could likewise be queen, simply a matter of receiving the special nourishment required to activate critical strands of her DNA.

Yet humans thought of her as male, a source of unending amusement that she perpetuated, given that the males of some species were troubled by it, perhaps because she could lift and transport burdens fifty-seven times her own weight. No matter, it was usefulness that counted, not gender.

She still missed the crew she'd lost on Mira III and hoped they'd found a way home. She'd tried to bond with these humans and indeed felt concern for their fate, but their way of doing things was so foreign she marveled that they ever accomplished a thing. Unity and single-mindedness as they knew it was nothing like the combined mental energy of a swarm, all linked by unified psi and purpose.

Something tickled her mind, something one or more fellows of her kind could have brought to conclusion, but it lingered out of focus, awaiting input for clarification. The collective power of psi-linked intelligences was formidable, far exceeding collaboration. But lamenting its loss would bring no answers. The humans had taught her something about independent thought, even though it was uncomfortable and unnatural. But she'd bought into their cause and would do her part, whatever it took. If nothing else, she was the ultimate team player.

The *swarm* concept stuck in her mind, swirling within genetic memory of millions of her fellows operating in total harmony, deep beneath the surface for millions of years. Networks were the closest thing humans could relate to, technological linking of data, communications and ideologies. Her mind wandered back to her crew and the *Volition,* in a parking orbit somewhere above the planet. Hopefully, it was still there. Not that she'd ever return to exploration efforts with the HIO. The way things were looking lately, survival was less than assured.

She missed the *Volition*, her connection with it similar to that with her own kind. After all, Formicidae designed the vessel. She understood its capabilities and how to use them and it responded to her commands via psilink. Interactions with her crew were likewise seamless, her intent matched with theirs, issuing commands never required, because they simply knew intuitively what they needed to do.

She remembered her feelings of isolation while wandering about the galaxy collecting data and conducting inspections, knowing there was little hope of support should an emergency arise, whether it was a sudden negative spike, unexpected nova, or attack by hostile forces. She'd suggested to the HIO that all RA-681 intragalactic spacecraft be linked, so that in the event of such a contingency, others could be beckoned by a simple code transmission known only to captains. Activating *Swarm Mode* summoned the three nearest RA-681s to provide immediate assistance as well as alerting HIO Command, who would dispatch further support, such as a war ship, if required. Such a call superseded anything else in the command queue, survival of sister vessels first and foremost. Mission objectives were entirely secondary and, of course, it changed the affected ships' current trajectories.

Another thought lingered, inaccessible within her psyche, that her ponderings weren't random, but held place and reason to the grave situation in which all were bound. Maybe through some evolutionary mutation, she was bonding with these humans after all. Maybe that was why her telepathic powers had weakened on this planet. Connecting all the thoughts on her own was difficult, like understanding how humans could look at a grouping of stars and think it represented a person or animal. Yet that was how her kind operated, constellating thoughts into a coherent whole.

She felt a subtle nudge to her mind, unfamiliar yet friendly, and carrying a distinctive vegetative aroma. Tuning into it, she quickly recognized it as Thyron, the *flora peda telepathis* who'd requested assistance to deliver himself, the girl and 'troid away from Terra. As different as she and the vegemal were, nonetheless they had much in common, both having telepathic abilities and plunged into an alien culture far different from their own. Maybe this unlikely alliance could fill the blanks.

Straightening her antennae around the confines of the cyll, she pinged back to the vegemal, transmitting her disconnected thought train in a single burst with a request for input.

A moment or so later, a green bouquet responded, subtle but informative. She immediately recognized it as containing the clarifying link between the humans' dilemma and her seemingly random self-nattering.

> [There is a link distinct and real
> to aid Apoca's grand appeal.
> Your spacecraft saved them once before
> and can again, in peace or war.
> The craft where ex-commander lies
> is where he does expect to die
> yet can be helped by unique code
> within hard-coded swarming mode.]

The sweet feeling of resolve achieved through finding a viable solution with another telepath surged through her, bringing comfort at last. Now all she had to do when sleepzone ended was get consensus, then connect with *Volition*.

Ascending

Augustus Troy drummed his fingers on his workdeck, anticipation roiling in his gut. The feeling had awoken him earlier than usual, prompting him to check his comcon for any critical developments that may have occurred during his sleepzone. Finding nothing worth noting in the logs, his brow creased with concentration as he pondered what it might be. It didn't exactly feel ominous, yet he knew something was about to happen. But what?

Deep in thought regarding the possibilities, he jumped when an alert chriped from his comcon. "Display," he said, scowl of concentration unchanged as he read the summons ordering his immediate presence in the Quadrumvirate council chambers, deep in the bowels of the INTEGRATED Territorial Tower. He knew the four Territorial Generals who comprised Cyraria's INTEGRATED leadership met on a regular basis, or so Spoigan had indicated, but deputies were seldom included and as far as he knew, they met at a more civilized hour except during strategic ops.

"Do you wish to attend?" the comcon prompted.

"Accept," he said, puzzlement modulating his voice, to which the automated system paid no heed. The projection faded and he rose to his feet, curious what was going on. He went to the sanicube adjoining his office, combed his thinning hair and decided a quick shave was in order, considering the scruffy image staring back from the mirror. While Spoigan was off-world he'd let himself slide a bit, enjoying his absence, but showing up to a Council meeting in such a state was unacceptable.

As he ran the razor over his face, he continued to speculate on the reason for the summons. Spoigan must have returned with significant news, which could explain why he was being included in the conclave. Maybe his superior had obtained some of those devices he was so curious about.

He grabbed his jacket off the back of his chair, donned his hat and summoned the elevator to sublevel fourteen. As always, the cavernous hallway was empty, boots echoing sharply from the stone-tiled floor. When he reached the end of the corridor, he palmed in, the molecules comprising the heavy door dissociating to let him pass, then reorganizing as soon as he'd cleared the threshold. The room was multi-purpose, capable of supporting strategic operations, yet screens and consoles were dark as well as overhead lighting, except for a few spotlights illuminating a circular table. Some four meters in diameter, its polished stone surface gleamed uninterrupted, embedded comcons retracted. Three men sat on the far side, not the expected four; Spoigan was not among them, only Eulon Argo, the Eta TG, and his two counterparts from Alpha and Gamma.

The Alpha TG was several centimeters taller than Troy, muscular build apparent beneath the epaulets of his uniform. He was relatively young, blond hair cropped close, probably to draw less attention to the fact his hairline was receding at an accelerated pace in spite of his age. He fixed cold, blue eyes on him as if he were some sort of insect, nodding with the other two in response to Troy's sharp salute. Gamma's TG was oldest of the three, hair white and somewhat disheveled framing sharp features above a slight frame, though there was nothing weak about his glare.

"At ease," Argo stated, the light directly above reflecting on his bald pate such that it appeared as if it was housed in his skull. The man motioned for him to sit and Troy obliged, focusing his attention on the trio before him while hoping he'd have a chance to examine the strategic and tactical campaigns, past, present and future, represented in numerous holos on the surrounding walls.

"As you have probably already surmised, we have a serious situation in which you play a critical part," Argo stated, amber eyes boring into his. "You're a key witness, Troy, and this is a formal deposition to gather critical information. These interrogation proceedings are being recorded and, given the circumstances, you need to wear a truth disk."

"Yes, sir," Troy agreed, mind starting to race as Argo secured the disk to his forehead, then resumed his seat.

"Okay. First question. Were you aware that General Spoigan left four days ago for Esheron?"

"Yes, sir," Troy replied.

"Did he tell you why?"

"Yes."

"Why?" Argo prompted.

"He wanted to checkout a device manufactured there, which relates to mind control technology we're trying to develop. He hoped to acquire one or more so we could back-engineer it, and accelerate our research efforts."

"Isn't the research team we commandeered from Esheron?"

"Yes, sir."

"Why couldn't they provide this information?"

"They were not the original developers, plus not cooperating, to the point of defiance. While he believed that each of them originally possessed such a device, they all mysteriously disappeared. Rather than dealing with them, he felt it would be more efficient to go to the source."

"He was wrong."

"Sir?" Troy asked, puzzled.

"As you are probably aware, Esheron is not a very friendly place. We received notice earlier today that General Spoigan met with an unfortunate encounter with an incendiary device."

Troy's jaw dropped momentarily before he quickly resumed visible control.

"Is he…going to recover?"

"Not likely. He's dead. According to the official transmission, there were insufficient remains to identify, but there were three supposed witnesses to the incident. Do you have any reason to doubt that this is what occurred?"

"What are you inferring?" Troy asked, appalled they would ask such a thing.

"We need to know if he was assassinated. If so, it would warrant a full interplanetary investigation with strong diplomatic implications for our relationship with Esheron."

"Anything is possible, sir. It is highly likely that the individuals he met with had connections with Bryl Woeyel."

"What?" Argo responded, eyes blazing. "How is that possible?"

"The research team we commandeered was from Woeyel Industries and brought on-world to assist Clique objectives. We snagged them in immigration on a visa technicality."

The truth disk flashed green and blue at such a rapid pace that Troy noticed its reflection in one of the holopanels across the room. Good. They could see he was not only surprised by Spoigan's fate, but also telling the truth.

"You realize, Troy, the reason you had to undergo this interrogation is because you have much to gain from his demise."

"Yes, sir," Troy said solemnly, mind in warp drive at the situation's implications. "Of course."

"Fortunately for you, there is no indication of your involvement, other than indirectly through acquiring the Woeyel research team. Which was really quite fortuitous, if I do say so myself."

"Thank you, sir."

"However, if they've proven themselves useless, then they should be dispatched. It's dangerous to harbor such untrustworthy individuals, especially those of high intelligence, within our ranks."

"Of course, sir. We can always use more test subjects for our high risk experiments. We've been trying to fine-tune the probe frequency amplitude for encephalographic access to the word level. If it's too high, it tends to cause brain death. Which comes in handy for resistant individuals."

"You can do with them as you please," Argo replied. "Perhaps an unfortunate accident will occur for them as well." A few low chuckles rumbled from the others and Troy allowed himself to smile, noting how comfortable he felt to be around like-minded individuals.

"All right," Argo continued, shoulders relaxing slightly as he visibly shifted gears. "Now we can proceed to the second part of this session. As you have probably already surmised, as Epsilon's Deputy Territorial General, you are the primary candidate to be installed as Spoigan's successor, subject to the approval of Supreme Command. Assuming, of course, that you accept the position."

That eventuality had been dancing in his mind since the moment he'd learned Spoigan was dead. Its articulation, however, was almost more than he could contain in a dignified manner. Elation exploded within, which he fought to suppress, knowing an uproarious victory shout would be inappropriate, given the demise of his former superior. All that he'd worked for and aspired to for years had suddenly landed in his lap, bringing a sense of power and satisfaction such as he'd never felt before. His mouth twitched, resisting a smile, eyes wide as the truth disk betrayed his reaction in a rotating prism of color.

He couldn't quite contain the gasp as a small fraction of his excitement escaped, but quickly converted it to what he hoped would simply appear as his own surprise, which was certainly genuine. He wondered what they'd do regarding a suitable memorial for Spoigan. His first thought was more along the lines of a celebration. He had learned decades before that there were funerals at which you grieved and others at which you cheered.

While he'd never wished Spoigan dead, much less taking him out himself, being distressed about it certainly didn't fit, either.

"The Supreme Command is meeting in an hour and we don't expect their decision will take long," Argo went on. "Until your installation, which will take place for security reasons in a small, private ceremony immediately following approval, it's important that the news not be revealed. After that, it will be announced concurrent with Spoigan's death. As you're probably aware, such unexpected events can bring instability, which the enemy can exploit. Until then, you should be thinking about whom you'll nominate as your deputy."

"Of course, sir," he agreed. If there was anything he didn't want, it was any sort of delay. There was too much to do, starting with that treasonous research team.

* * *

When sleepzone ended, Dirck, Creena, Win, Deven and 'Merama remained in Cranium Cavern, discussing whether anything unusual had occurred. Each sat on the floor, backs propped against their cyllmats, silhouettes eerie in the sleep stations' dim glow. No one had any dreams worth noting with the only thing that seemed different a slightly more pronounced sheen to the walls accompanied by increased random sparkles.

"Do you really think they're something new?" Dirck asked, skeptical. "Or is it just because our eyes are adjusted to the dark?"

"I noticed the sparkles before," Creena admitted. "But I think there are more now. I'm not sure, though. I didn't really pay that much attention."

"There are lots more!" Deven declared. "When I first found this place, there were hardly any. It feels different, too. Way different."

'Merama's look was pensive as she peered around the huge chamber, the gentle glow of the cyllmats' wake cycle only enough to illuminate the floor between them.

"It looks like quite a bit more activity to me," she agreed. "I wonder why?"

"It's hard to say," Dirck said. "It could simply be reflections from the cyll lights."

"It's possible the electronics in the cyllmats are creating a disturbance," Win suggested. "There could also be some cristobalite embedded in the walls that's reflecting our thoughts. We should take a sample and figure out which minerals are present. There could be something valuable there."

Dirck nodded agreement and started to comment, then paused, listening. He caught Creena's eye, whose expression indicated she heard it, too. He wasn't sure, but it sounded like the distant echo of Igni's feet. The clicking got louder, Win's expression indicating he'd picked up on it as well.

"I wonder what's going on," Dirck mused aloud. "He's never come here before."

"Must be important," Win speculated.

"Maybe good news for a change," Creena added.

"Of course it is," Deven said, a hint of reproach in his young voice.

Before anyone could comment further, Igni's enormous head breached the entry, the click of multiple feet reverberating with a different tone as he proceeded down the incline into the vast chamber.

"What is it, Igni?" Win asked, walking over to meet him as the insectoid nimbled down the bumpy path his human counterparts executed with considerable trepidation.

"Good, all are here," he said, translator crackling, "I have what may be good news."

"Yes!" Deven exclaimed, grinning victoriously. "I knew it! I totally knew it!"

Dirck rolled his eyes and refrained from telling his younger brother to shut down, even as he tried to contain his own hopes.

"What is it?" he asked, everyone gathering around expectantly.

"May have ability to interact with prison ship," he said. "You certain was RA-681, concede?"

"Yes, definitely," Win answered.

"Yes, we were hoping it was the *Volition*," Creena added. "When it wasn't, we thought maybe if you knew the codes we could bring it back, but it was too late, anyway, since we didn't have a tachyonic transmitter to contact a ship traveling at warp speeds."

"Concede," Igni responded. "But if connect with *Volition* through psi and *Volition* contact prison ship, then is not problem."

"What are you talking about?" Win asked. "What exactly can you do?"

"RA-681 designed for Hostii Intergalactic Organization peaceful galactic exploration. Was good ship. After HIO had quota, builder made more, many more, to sell to others. Did not change design, except for minor specs requested by other buyers."

"Okay," Win prompted, impatience growing. "So what?"

"Exploring galaxy has many risks. Hostile forces, no defense with offensive weapons forbidden on HIO vessel."

"Go on," Dirck said, hanging on every word.

"For protection, assistance call hardcoded into vehicle. Known as Emergency Swarm Mode or ESM. Activation aborts current command queue of three nearest RA-681 vessels and directs to troubled ship. Or summoning ship performs automated return to home port, if closer than assistance."

Dirck nodded attentively, knowing Igni had the ability to direct the ship remotely, based on when he'd sent the *Volition* to a parking orbit following their arrival. But there was at least one problem.

"But what if 'Merapa's ship isn't close enough to be one of the three?"

"HIO vessels spread throughout galaxy. Probability favors prison ship one of three."

"Where's the home port?" Creena asked, cautious optimism lurking in her expression.

"Mira III."

"But Mira's now under INTEGRATOR control," Dirck reminded him, shaking his head. "What good would it do if the *Volition* returned there? We'd lose any chance of using it to leave."

Igni nodded in agreement. "That is true, going there not good," he said. "But can cancel. Can abort. When ESM cancelled, vehicle systems do power-off reset. Current command queue cancelled, and ship defaults to manual ops. Captain enter new order. If *Volition* break orbit, will know plan failed."

"From what Zahra told me combined with our discussion with Bryl," 'Merama said, "Laren tampered with the ship's systems. They must have discovered that, so they locked him out and entered some other directive, which relates to the three day deadline. If those could be stopped, it could buy more time."

"Concede," Igni replied. "Is true. If lethal command entered, ESM would abort sequence."

"So if 'Merapa's ship is one of the three closest, it would come back to Cyraria?" Dirck asked, optimism expanding with supreme caution.

"Concede. Unless feature removed, which not likely. *ESM* very secret, very remote, known only to builder, captains and HIO top officials."

"Sounds like it's worth a try," Creena said.

Dirck nodded agreement. "Let's tell Bryl and see what we can do."

Bryl looked up, startled, as the entourage barged into her office with enthusiasm she hadn't seen, much less felt, in a long time.

"It looks like Igni can buy some time," Dirck said, then quickly explained the plan.

"We certainly don't have anything to lose," she agreed. "What do you need? Is there anything we need to do?"

"No, ma'am," the ant responded. "Only concede."

"You've got it," Bryl said. "Do it."

"Yes, ma'am," Igni replied and immediately dropped from standing, as typically maintained when in the company of others, to his more comfortable ground position. Igni stood perfectly still, focus of his compound eyes far away. Dirck could barely detect a small vibration in his antennae as the *ESM* was sent. When it stopped, he awaited a report.

"It be done," Igni announced a moment later.

"Do we have any way of knowing whether it worked for 'Merapa's prison ship?" Creena asked.

"Not directly," the insectoid replied. "Will know didn't, if *Volition* break orbit. Or three arrive, but not prison ship. At some point will know from double-i's. Much confusion at all levels as captains check reason of swarm."

"That's true. The other captains won't know what's going on. Maybe once it's assured it could have worked on the prison ship, you should cancel. Then the others would simply think it was a false alarm," Bryl suggested.

"But then Laren would have to assume control of the ship," Win stated. "I doubt prisoners have that kind of access."

Creena shook her head. "True, but if he tampered with the systems before, maybe when things reset, he could again."

"How soon could you send the cancel command?" Win asked.

"No sooner of one standard day. Prison ship trajectory need time to reverse."

"Right," Dirck agreed, remembering what his father had taught him while they'd been looking for Creena in Troy's TL-87. "It needs to exit the warp run first, then either execute a huge return loop or reverse direction in a carefully executed sequence. Otherwise, they could experience a timebump."

"How soon would the *Volition* break orbit, if it was going to?" Win asked.

"A day or two, most, if other ships do not or cannot respond. Could do immediately, if no ships closer than Mira III."

"In which case we'll know it failed," 'Merama said grimly.

"Concede," Igni said, emphasizing his response with a nod. "If ship's orbit stable, have chance of success. But will not know for sure if prison ship was part of ESM."

"Ah, much good, all be here."

Startled by the unexpected voice, everyone turned to see Major Zebatohn in the Bryl's doorway with a handful of c-coms.

"Perfect!" Win said, extending a congratulatory hand which the jendak accepted. "Now to see if they work. How do you set up these things?"

"Here's what you do," Bryl instructed. "It's a two-step process." She then proceeded to walk them through the procedure, step by step.

Win, Dirck, Creena and Sharra each successfully charged theirs, after which they experienced a surge of joy they hadn't felt since any of them could remember.

"This is incredible," Creena said softly, reverently caressing its smooth surface. "So now that we're connected, now what?"

"First of all," Bryl replied. "Let's test them out for communications. You each felt your connection, so use that feeling to transfer something to it for storage. Then see if you can retrieve it on command."

When everyone had successfully completed that task, the next test was for psicom. One by one, they connected, creating a network between them, until they attempted to contact Bryl or vice versa.

"They work perfectly between us," Creena stated, confused by the unexpected failure. "Why can't we contact Bryl?"

Major Zebatohn's expression had remained reserved as they'd gone through the other processes, as if concerned there could be a glitch. He closed his large, yellow eyes for a moment before responding.

"I be afraid of such fail," he stated with a huge sigh. "Network derives of crystals. Must be of same source to properly link."

"At least they work," Win stated. "Apparently they retained activation from the bnolar."

"I'm not sure what might be required to integrate the networks. The crystals used for yours are from here, while mine are from Esheron and probably activated by the Ledorians," Bryl explained. "At least you can talk to each other. And you should be able to use them to block INTEGRATOR intrusion, especially you, Creena." She explained the process and each followed her instructions, even as a touch of sorrow dampened their previous elation.

Light and Dark

Bezarna Express

"There's nothin' I can do 'bout it, Brightstar!" Sa'ata shouted. "Nothin'! I don't have no authority or trainin'. I's just a guard, s'posed to keep yous people from doin' somethin' just like this. I can't get to controls, the ship's automated. They can do stuff from the ground, but I can't do nothin'. Nothin'. So now you's done got us all killed."

"No, only you," Rhodus said sarcastically. "We were already doomed. Welcome to the club."

Sa'ata glared back, his look preamble to either an attack or a scream, and Laren braced himself to defend his friend, thinking they'd made a mistake releasing the wrist wrings. He relaxed as the guard sat on the floor cross-legged and hugged his knees to his chest.

"I gots fam'ly down there, man," he said, rocking back and forth. "I gots fam'ly. What's they gonna do when's I doesn't come back?"

"Gee, Sa'ata, I don't know," Laren replied, unsympathetic. "What do you think mine or Rhodus' are doing?"

"But you deserved it, man," the pyxisite protested. "You did somethin' to get here. I didn't. This just my job. I was jus' doin' my job."

Laren's dark eyes flashed with long-suppressed anger. "All I did was fight the forces who sent us all out here," he snarled. "They're wrong and you know it. I'm not a criminal and neither is Rhodus. You might give some thought to the people you've been working for, Sa'ata. Clearly your life has no more value than ours."

With that the guard buried his face in his arms, shoulders heaving. Laren exhaled sharply and shook his head, unimpressed, then sat down in his usual spot and took out his c-com, hoping for a miracle. As before, it was dead and unresponsive.

"Well, I guess this is it," he said, trying to smile as Rhodus sat down beside him. "It was worth a shot, anyway. If nothing else, we gave them something to think about on the ground. You can bet this won't happen again."

Rhodus' only response was a grunt, eyes fixed on the digichronometer as it switched to sleepzone countdown. Lights dimmed as always and cylls lowered slowly from overhead stowage.

Laren took a deep breath, thinking it could well be his last, wondering whether to simply give in and enter the cyll or be defiant to the end and remain in the cabin. One thing he definitely wasn't about to do was head for the airlock.

"It's been good getting to know you, Rhodus," he said, offering him the Miran grip. "At least we didn't go down without a fight."

"That we did," Rhodus agreed, returning the gesture. "I'd always hoped to meet you, but certainly not like this."

Sa'ata lifted his head from his arms, eyes red and glazed. "I's cain't believe you twos are so, so..."

"Courageous in the face of death?" Laren finished for him, voice saturated with disdain.

"I s'pose," the guard said, voice barely audible.

"You don't fight for what you believe in without recognizing it could end this way," he replied. "Dying for a cause has some value when you reach the other side."

"What other side?" Sa'ata asked, puzzled. "What's you talkin' 'bout now?"

"Dying is just another beginning," he replied. "It's..."

Before he could finish the vehicle shuddered amidst a symphony of hums and whines as the lights abruptly went out without the usual fade-in sequence to sleepzone. Sa'ata let out an eerie wail, a suitable, albeit primitive, prelude to death.

"Well, I guess this is it," Laren said through the darkness with a calm he didn't feel. "See you on the other side."

* * *

Integrator Central	
TBA	
Technical Breakthrough Advisory	
TEAM: Strategic Weaponry	PROJECT: NECM (Negative Energy Creation & Manipulation)
Date: DDW-135	Clearance: Top Secret
Breakthrough/Milestone: Negative energy transport for psi invasion and consciousness annihilation	
Schedule Impact: Y/N? Y	Days: Immediate Access
SUMMARY: Beta testing involving refraction capability of cristobalite is complete. Results indicate negative psi energy can be generated and subsequently focused on specifically targeted mindprinted subjects, resulting in interruption of consciousness and removal from corporeal plane.	

* * *

Augustus Troy closed his eyes and sighed as the nanobots within the fibers of what had been his predecessor's chair targeted and massaged key areas of his back and shoulders. Apparently it had reprogrammed itself to fit his physique, at last noting that its former occupant had been replaced. A moment later he opened his eyes to sweep the stone-lined chamber which had previously belonged to Rohtik Spoigan from an entirely different perspective, literally and figuratively, versus when he'd been his subordinate.

He'd never particularly liked the man whose ideologies differed significantly from his own, yet Troy knew enough to render him respect as his superior in spite of his personal opinions. Thus, he'd provided enough obsequious responses to demonstrate his support, many of which left his gut in a knot, yet such were the man's due, simply by rank. But now he was gone, out of the picture not only entirely, but permanently, and Troy felt as if he had reached the pinnacle of mortal existence. As he'd done several times a day since his promotion, he stretched his arms overhead and luxuriated in the fact that this was now *his* office and that he possessed political power that comprised the better part of his fondest hopes and aspirations.

The tone announcing the arrival of a TBA chimed from his comcon, distracting him from his new digs back to duty. He ordered it to display, then read it repeatedly, word by word, allowing its message to sink in. As its full meaning registered, he straightened to full attention, nanobots pausing their massage so as not to disturb his train of thought.

Could it really mean what he thought? In the past, he'd acquired such information when it was released, always accompanied by fanfare and celebration across the INTEGRATED network. As he pondered its lack, he realized that indeed this was how such data were initially divulged, to those in high command. Now that he was the ruling member of the Quadrumvirate who monitored the technology sector, it was up to him to tout such accomplishments, much as Spoigan had announced INTEGRATION'S victory over the planet. Such a significant breakthrough deserved being released in an appropriately flamboyant manner.

The sense of power nearly consumed him as he pondered the incredible luck which had come his way in the course of a few days. Truly it was more than good fortune; it had to be fate. He'd always known he was destined not only for greatness but to be remembered forever as a driving force in galactic history. His ascension to power had come entirely unexpectedly. While it was what he'd worked for his entire life, now that it was within grasp, he still marveled at its reality, his destiny further reinforced by this latest status report from the Strategic Weaponry team.

What they'd accomplished made previous efforts at mindreading virtually obsolete, at least for his purposes. True, accessing others' brains could provide useful information from certain individuals but as far as spying or covertly tracking those opposed to INTEGRATION'S intent were concerned, it no longer mattered.

He now had the power to perform individualized strikes to eliminate anyone for whom they had a mindprint, which comprised the majority of people on the planet, at least anyone who had ventured into the Territorial Tower in Cira City.

Or did he? He frowned, lines furrowing his brow as doubts doused his excitement. Personal experience had taught him that such advisories inevitably involved restrictions or limitations, which they failed to report. As an engineer, he'd done it himself, inflating accomplishments to lessen the blow of failures. Such information typically only slipped out incidentally after kudos, bonuses and promotions had been doled out to those responsible for the supposed advance. In some cases, deliberate oversights resulted in lethal action, depending on how devious the omission was determined to be.

He took a deep breath as more euphoria diminished, replaced with a cold, practical demeanor suitable for conversing with the chief scientist, whom he summoned to his office as opposed to a video conference. He intended to look this man square in the eye.

The researcher arrived quicker than expected, as if he'd anticipated the query, as well he should. He entered Troy's chambers and stood at attention, but failed to salute while his expression showed more annoyance than intimidation. His stature was several centimeters shorter than Troy, his blocky build interrupted by a bulging belly which his lab coat struggled to cover, the bottom two fasteners undone. A disheveled mixture of grey and faded brown hair topped his head, the scruffy beard covering his face more appropriate for a vagrant from the City's immigration shelter than the project's chief scientist. The icy blue eyes that met his were piercing, confident and condescending. Such a demeanor could easily be offensive, but Troy immediately relaxed; such arrogance could only come from someone who knew what they were doing.

"You have questions regarding our latest TBA, General?" the man said, heavy lips barely moving as he spoke.

"Yes, I do," Troy responded, gesturing to a chair across from his workdeck. "Sit down. What's your name?"

"Bareuth Argo. Doctor Bareuth Argo."

"Related to Eulon?"

"Cousin."

The fact the man was related to the Eta Territorial Governor who was Troy's equal in the Quadrumvirate explained a lot. No matter how badly the man screwed up, it was doubtful he could be eliminated, explaining his attitude. Hopefully, his knowledge matched his arrogance. There was no room for incompetence, regardless of political connections.

"Tell me more about the latest TBA," Troy stated, gaze fixed on Argo's piercing eyes.

"What do you want to know?"

"Everything."

"You wouldn't understand *everything,* General."

Troy stiffened, irritated by his haughty response. "Try me, *Doctor,*" he replied, increasing the force of his frigid stare.

Argo almost smiled. "Oh-kaaay. Cristobalite's birefringent properties allow splitting of a subject's psi input to positive and negative components. Amplifying and refracting the latter, augmenting it with systemic negative flux, then returning it to the original psimission source result in neutralizing synaptic and neuronic activity, such that the subject's ability for coherent thought is permanently eliminated."

Troy's response was immediate, eye's locked on Argo's. "How focused does the transmission band need to be? Are you talking about targeting one at a time, or can it be used to annihilate an entire group?"

The frequency of Argo's glare shifted slightly with the realization Troy had actually understood what he was talking about, unlike Spoigan who'd lacked scientific training, much less acumen.

"The objective can be achieved with multiple targets, provided mindprint data are available. The effects take effect instantly, so a coherent beam can cover multiple psi frequencies in a short duration of time."

Troy tried not to smile. So far so good. "Sideband coverage?"

"Perhaps. Haven't tested to that level. But theoretically, it's possible."

"What about location? Omni-directional?"

For the first time Argo looked less confident. "No. Since the device must acquire the matching psi signal for the mindprint input, process it, and then return the augmented negative component, there are fairly narrow focusing requirements."

"How narrow?"

"Five degrees." Argo was starting to look nervous. "We're working on expanding it. I know that's not broad enough for an entire region much less territory, but it would be sufficient for known outpost locations where high concentrations of targeted individuals gather."

"Like military bases," Troy stated.

"Exactly."

Troy allowed a rather nasty smile to form as euphoria returned. "How long will it take to bring online?"

The man looked relieved that known limitations apparently weren't a problem. "About a week, give or take. We need time to gather, sort and encode the mindprints, then program and target the device. You have precise coordinates, I assume?"

"Most certainly, Doctor Argo. I take my job as seriously as you apparently do. By the time your equipment is ready, I should have the Quadrumvirate consensus I need to proceed."

"May I ask where the target is? With that, we can at least rough in the settings, then fine-tune the Vernier just prior to operation."

Troy leaned back in his chair, enjoying the nanobots resumed massage across his shoulders, which had stiffened with the hatred he felt for his opposition. Argo flinched slightly under the full force of Troy's glare, even though it wasn't directed at him.

"Apoca Canyon," he growled through clenched teeth.

"The Clique Base?"

"Yes. Most certainly. The Clique Base."

"Got it." Argo arose from his seat and smiled for the first time. "It's been a pleasure, General Troy."

Troy likewise stood and extended his hand. "Likewise, Doctor Argo. Good work."

"Thank you, General. Unlike some of the other teams, we're behind you one hundred percent."

Troy's expression darkened with thoughts of the one alluded to, reminding him he had unfinished business to attend to.

"Their day is coming as well, Doctor," he stated with a smirk.

"We can always use more test subjects," Argo replied mirroring his expression.

"Excellent idea. I see we think a lot alike."

"Apparently, General. Good day."

"Indeed. To you as well, Doctor."

As soon as the door materialized behind the exiting scientist, Troy tilted back his head, lifted fist-topped arms toward the domed ceiling and bellowed a victorious, *"Yes!"*

The outburst's echo reverberated for several seconds before the room became as still and silent as death.

NEGATIVITY

Onboard the *Intruder,* Captain Srikneif couldn't figure out what had happened. He stood at his usual post on the bridge staring at the control panel with cool grey eyes as an ominous feeling gathered in his chest. For the vessel to suddenly reduce power and yaw in an entirely different direction was an anomaly he'd never seen before, which wasn't good. They'd been conducting a routine patrol through their quadrant of the galaxy's Gamma Sector when all of a sudden the vessel changed course, which meant it was no longer under programmed command. His angular features were taut when efforts to resume control manually failed, making the situation even more serious. Sweat broke out on his expansive brow, each droplet reflecting the medley of multicolor lights flashing on the starship's bridge.

He ran both hands over the closely cropped remains of his greying hair, then gripped the back of his neck, heartrate accelerating. He cursed the powers which had yanked him from a comfortable retirement, then straightened his shoulders with resolve, activated the com, and ordered his executive officer to run a systems check. He held his breath, awaiting the results, which came back in the usual time, yet felt considerably longer. He frowned at the notice which was far from comforting. Some mysterious order had showed up in the queue. Simply identified as *ESM,* whatever it was had not only assumed control, but couldn't be overridden or deleted, regardless of what action they employed.

He blew out his cheeks with a forceful breath as if it could release his frustration. This definitely wasn't good.

Srikneif was an experienced spacer, but unfamiliar with the RA-681. When the INTEGRATOR commandeered the ships previously operated by the HIO, he'd been reactivated as the need suddenly arose for more ship captains. He wasn't happy about it, but that was the way it was. It wasn't like there was anything he could do about it, anyway, refusal likely to end his retirement as well in an even more unpleasant way.

The previous crew had been entirely dismissed, how and to where he didn't know and didn't care, the ship renamed when it joined the INTEGRATOR'S growing fleet. They hadn't changed anything else, the ship still unarmed and used strictly for exploration and surveillance purposes, something that should be a simple, routine operation.

The HIO had used the ships to maintain accurate charts related to astronomical events such as novas, blackhole event horizon changes, and energy flux differentials as well as their respective effects on local planets. His orders had changed these only slightly. While keeping track of cosmic events was still important, they were ordered to focus primarily on planets that offered expansion potential as well as any existing activity on their surface. Discovery of new worlds suitable for habitation was most desirable and accompanied by a generous bonus. Due to the similarity to the original HIO function, none of the ship's systems had changed. He would have felt more comfortable if there'd been at least minimal weaponry or countermeasures onboard, but it would be a standard year or more before it was retrofitted with armaments. Knowing how things moved it would probably be more like five.

He exhaled sharply, deciding this undoubtedly required contacting HQ. Maybe they'd instituted it, mustering the fleet for some recent development. INTEGRATOR activity had escalated recently and something was up, though he had no idea what. He disliked how they purposely kept captains in the dark with only minimal knowledge of their own missions, fully enforcing the "need to know" philosophy to maintain secrecy of their stragetic moves. As an unarmed vessel, he couldn't imagine why he'd be summoned back in the first place, much less in a manner beyond his control. Were they afraid that he'd abscond with his own ship? If they'd originated the directive, they might not even tell him why. But if they hadn't, then they needed to know something off-nominal had occurred.

He activated the tachyonic transmitter and sent a simple but urgent query: "*Intruder* off-nom ops. ESM cmd n cntrl. Pls cnfrm."

A response came back quicker than expected. As he scrutinized the answer his chiseled features gathered into a tight frown. The command's origin had not been sent from HQ and apparently they didn't know who'd generated it, either, since they were currently seeking its source.

Whatever was going on wasn't good.

* * *

Creena and Dirck spent the rest of the day in the lab getting familiar with their c-coms. While for the most part the devices were intuitive, similar to a very intelligent friend, there were apparently a vast number of other functions as well. They only became apparent when specifically requested or needed, however, so they were experimenting with the capabilities and sharing what they discovered.

Creena's mind had been so engaged with the device that her head was spinning. The interaction had been so intense it felt as if the c-com were downloading her brain, which was somehow too much like the INTEGRATOR for comfort.

She took a deep breath and disconnected, needing a break. Dirck looked up and lowered his device as well, apparently sharing the same overload.

"How's Win's new signal filter working?" she asked, attempting to get her mind focused somewhere else.

Prior to receiving their c-coms, Thyron had tutored them individually in meditation techniques as a defense against intrusions, which had also expanded their natural cognitive abilities. While it had helped Creena and the rest of her family deal with 'Merapa's unfortunate fate, the payoff for sharing them with Win had been dramatic. Numerous unorthodox filtering and encryption breaking schemes had revealed themselves, which he was avidly pursuing.

"It seems to be functioning pretty well. We'll know when this next batch is sorted." As he spoke, he got up to check the comcon on the far end of the table.

She watched his expression as he studied the data without any obvious reaction. He'd gotten pretty good at Miran bypass mode, that objective state of observation that absorbed information without generating any outward appearance. 'Merapa had always been good at that, too, reacting with deliberate intent only after all the facts were in. What her brother's expression may have failed to acknowledge, however, was growing increasingly evident in his eyes.

"What's wrong?" Creena asked.

"Plenty," he replied, entering Win's, Storm's and Igni's pager codes in the comcon.

The trio arrived moments later, gruesome expectations destined to be satisfied.

"Your decryption routine for those TBAs works like a charm, Win," Dirck stated. "Check this out." Everyone viewed the data dump suspended above the workdeck. "They've discovered cristobalite's refraction and amplification properties," he explained, bringing up the specific TBA and double-i's that supported it. "According to this, their next offensive will involve the strategic use of psi-based negative energy."

"Doesn't positive energy repel negative?" Creena asked.

"Not exactly," Dirck replied. "It annihilates it. But only if it's of equal strength. What I'm afraid of is the INTEGRATOR will generate more negativity than we can repel."

"Won't our c-coms work?"

"I doubt it," Win answered, shaking his head. "It's not neutral communication psi, it's combined with negative energy, which will be directed at each of us personally. It's similar to how we virtually killed your father for the prison break."

"Only temporarily," she replied, hopefully.

Dirck shook his head. "It wasn't that easy to bring him back. And there's a good chance a dose like they're talking about would melt our brain. Fry every synapse. No coming back from that."

Creena's thoughts wandered back to her numerous INTEGRATOR encounters. Its ability to control her had been staggering. Then there were all those negative spikes they'd seen from the *Volition*, specifically the negative energy field surrounding Cyraria when they'd arrived. If that was their energy source, resistance to an attack of that magnitude would require more positive energy than they could generate.

"What of evacuating?" Igni asked. "Is location needed to target?"

"I'm not sure," Dirck went on. "If our mindprints are in their datalogs the negativity can be directed against us personally. However, the TBA suggests it's focused. It probably has to be for it to be strong enough to have a lethal effect. They would probably direct it toward known concentrations of people they've identified as enemies. Like here. To answer your question, Igni, evacuating would probably work. But there are way more people here than we could possibly transport."

"How many?" Igni asked. "*Volition* hold few hundred. Moving vessel would cancel swarm, but initial alarm been sent. If cancel, vessel captain take control."

"That would be a good start, but require multiple trips," Storm answered. "We have thousands here, the bulk of what's left of the Clique. Only three outposts remain. Aren't there any other known defenses?"

"Only positive energy," Dirck reiterated. "But in quantities far beyond what we have."

"When do they plan to attack?" Win asked.

"They ran a successful test at an unknown site yesterday. Current intelligence indicates the offensive is likely to occur within a week."

Creena met her brother's gaze, the unspoken conclusion clear. "Who's going to tell 'Merama and Deven?" she asked quietly.

Dirck sighed heavily, shoulders drooping. "I will," he said grimly.

"I'll tell Commander Woeyel," Storm offered.

"Tell me what?"

Everyone turned simultaneously as their commanding officer entered. True to his word, Storm delivered a terse summary of their impending fate.

Creena waited for her response with a quark of hope that the indomitable woman would laugh off the offensive and inform them of some irresistible defense they had at their immediate disposal.

She didn't. Instead she collapsed wearily on the nearest stool, closed her eyes and sighed. When her eyes opened, any trace of her former determination and confidence were gone, her previously strong chin no longer set.

"There's nothing we can do," she declared, voice uncharacteristically quiet. "Our defensive weapons would be ineffective against such an attack. Unless you can come up with something in the next day or so."

"We're working on it," Win replied.

She met his gaze briefly, sighed heavily again, then got up and left, muttering that if anyone needed her she'd be in her office

"We can't just sit here, waiting," Win stated angrily. "We have to do *something,* even if it's wrong." When no one responded, even to argue, his fury grew, but whether it was directed at the others or the situation remained unclear. "Fine," he grumbled. "You can all just sit there and rot for all I care.

But I'm not going to run away or go down without a fight." And with that, he uttered an ancient Miran curse and exited the lab in a huff.

Unimpressed by his ire, neither Dirck nor Creena moved, each staring into space without a clue what they could do to avert it.

A short time later, 'Merama and Deven stopped by and heard the news. 'Merama said nothing, face frozen in a typically Miran blank expression. Her younger son, on the other hand, was more reactive.

"I don't believe it," Deven said firmly, pacing between the lab benches. "I can't believe cristobalite will work for them. No. It just won't."

"Why not?" Creena asked, too discouraged to argue, but curious at the commitment in her brother's young voice.

"*Because*! Think about it! When we were in the Caverns and you and Dirck were fighting all the time, the Tank quit working. When Enoch was there it was fine, because he and the other bnolar stopped it somehow. So if negative energy stops it from working, how can they use it to amplify it and send it here? It doesn't make sense. No, it won't work. It just won't."

"You don't understand, Deven," Dirck said wearily. "Negative energy neutralizes positive energy. When it wipes it out completely, then negativity takes over. Electrical charge can be reversed, magnetic polarity can be reversed, and energy can be reversed. The INTEGRATOR has some of the best scientific minds in the universe and can certainly accomplish this."

"But good isn't bad, and bad isn't good, and that's what negative and positive energy are all about," Deven insisted.

Dirck sighed and shook his head, hands flat on the table. "You just don't understand, Deven. When 'Merapa used to say nothing was impossible, he meant it. This is possible. We're doomed. That's all there is to it. We're doomed."

"If anything's possible, then why doesn't that work for us, too? Why can't we make enough positive energy to get rid of it?"

"Because we don't have the technology they do!"

"But we're better than they are!" Deven insisted. "We're doing what's right! If good's on our side, what more do we need?"

Dumbfounded, Dirck, Creena and 'Merama simply stared at him as if trying to muster the slightest hope he was right. The effort was too much, however, and reality quickly prevailed. Dirck knew what his brother had said was true, but also knew he didn't have what it would take to ask for anything of that magnitude from the *Benefics*.

It didn't matter whether he was in the Order or not, he couldn't bring himself to believe in a blatant miracle. He glanced at the others, seeing similar guilt and failings on everyone's face. Except, of course, his brother's.

"Because it's too late, Deven," Dirck replied. "We're out of time. It's over."

"I don't believe it, Dirck," Deven repeated, folding his arms in emphasis. "No. Absolutely not. I don't believe it. I just don't."

* * *

What had once been HIO Exploration Headquarters was now INTEGRATOR Space Survey Operations, typically referred to as ISSO. When that enigmatic query came in from the *Intruder's* captain, the blank looks it generated in Central Control, including its commanding officer, strongly resembled those of individuals used for unsuccessful psi research who'd been left with the mental acuity of an asteroid. Rather than providing an answer, tracing the source simply generated more questions.

Why would such an order have come from a vessel which had been listed as missing when INTEGRATOR forces assumed control from the HIO two standard years before? Lost in a time warp? Stranger yet, its location was determined to be a parking orbit around a planet where substantial INTEGRATOR activity was occurring in the form of psi and energy research. Contact with the relevant scientists denied any activity that could have resulted in such action.

Once the vessel was identified as the missing *Volition,* it was apparent that it was emitting some sort of emergency assistance beacon. Connecting that situation with the fact the *Intruder* had been effectively hijacked led investigators to quickly surmise the two events were connected. Fortunately, the *Volition* was not locked into some pre-determined command queue, making it a simple matter to retrieve it remotely when efforts to hail its captain failed. Once the vessel arrived in its berth in the space facility outside Mira III, technicians would conduct an investigation regarding the origin of the mysterious *ESM*.

As soon as the retrieval command was issued the *Volition* responded and Captain Srikneif's vessel returned to nominal ops, so at least part of the mystery was solved. Whether any other ships were affected by the mysterious order was unknown since no others reported any such disturbance. One of the prison ships apparently changed course about the same time, but it was reported that it was due to dispatch its passengers and return to base, so it wasn't considered part of the anomaly.

ISSO's CO shrugged, still wondering what had occurred. But until the *Volition* returned, there was nothing more they could do.

ATTITUDE

Deven didn't get angry very often but when he did it was all-consuming. Why wouldn't Dirck listen? Why was he so dense and totally stubborn? Just because he was older didn't mean he was smarter. Sometimes he really was a snurk.

He sighed with frustration, and stormed out of the lab, ignoring 'Merama when she called after him. She probably didn't believe him, either. How come when people grew up they got dumber instead of smarter? He hoped that wouldn't happen to him. Of course if Dirck turned out to be right it wouldn't matter because he'd be dead. But somehow he knew that wouldn't happen.

No. He was right and he knew it, with every fiber of his being. Feelings like this simply didn't lie. Why hadn't they learned to listen to him? Just because he was a kid?

Hmmmph, he grunted, feet stomping angrily along the stone path as he headed for Cranium Cavern. He hadn't done so consciously, at least not at first, but as he gradually walked off the anger, he kept going in that direction, as if drawn. Which wasn't surprising, since it was his favorite place. He stopped by his and 'Merama's quarters and grabbed his portalume, then resumed his trek as well as his unhappy thought train. He almost regretted sharing the location with the others. It wasn't his own secret hideout anymore, plus now it was all cluttered up with cyllmats and everything else. All he'd ever tried to do was help, and this time it had turned into a giant mess instead.

He got to the final descent, clutched the portalume to his chest, and slid down the well-worn path on his butt. It hurt a little, but didn't matter. He reached the bottom where he flashed the light around the space surrounded by their cyllmats to get his bearings, then set the portalume down on one and started to pace, frustrated. He followed the bluish beam, back and forth several times, finally stopping in front of his sleep station to catch his breath. He exhaled, hard, then sat down on his cyllmat, young stature making it a comfortable perch unlike adults who would've had their chin on their knees.

Geez, sometimes I don't want to grow up, he thought. But being a kid that no one listened to was no fun, either. What could he do to convince them? Of course if he was right, then they wouldn't die and he could rub it in. Or was it possible they were both right?

Sighing, he turned off the light, thinking he'd take a nap. The entire episode had tired him out and the darkness bid him rest. Before laying down, he took a moment to see if the sparkles were still there like when they'd ex-cylled. Nothing. He waited for his eyes to adjust; still nothing. That was strange. He'd been sure he'd seen them before, but now they were gone. Maybe Win was right, it was caused by the cyllmats. But no! He'd seen them before they'd even set them up. What was going on? Had everyone ruined the one spot he loved where he could remember the good stuff?

Suddenly overcome with a multitude of emotions he flopped down on his belly and started to cry. Everything had gone wrong, ever since they'd left the Caverns. He missed Enoch horribly and this had been the only place that had felt good, but now it was as empty as everywhere else. Defeated and abandoned, more heart-wrenching sobs echoed throughout the chamber as he bawled into his arms until he finally fell asleep.

Deven awoke a while later, trying to remember where he was. He sighed, anger gone, but a remnant of sadness remained. He turned to his side, staring into the darkness, sitting up abruptly when he saw they were back. Sparkles like he'd seen at the end of his sleepzone, all over the walls and ceiling.

Cool, he thought. *But weird.* Where had they gone? He knew they weren't there before. Why? Maybe because he'd been mad! If that made them go away, maybe being happy would make them come back. Lying back down he turned on his side, thinking of how much fun he'd had with Enoch when they'd first met. He remembered the bnolar pointing out the plants and wildlife, which had not only provided food for the family but something to barter with, so they could buy stuff. He'd felt like a hero and everyone had really appreciated what he'd done, even though he got in a little trouble, sorta, for wandering off into the wild alone.

He laughed when he remembered going there with Dirck that first time, when they'd made that deal to 'fess up to 'Merapa about their misdeeds. And of course the time when the heat exchanger blew up. He laughed, remembering when he told Dirck that the bnolar got through opposition just fine, not surprised at all when they wound up going to the Caverns where they were welcomed by Enoch, as if he'd been expecting them all along.

A wide grin stretched Deven's face to its limits, and he turned his gaze toward the ceiling, gasping when he saw not only sparkles, but the beginning of an actual glow at the domed ceiling. The sparkles had become wisps of light, dancing and dashing in circles as radiant fingers reached downward. Deven giggled, wondering what was going on. The lilting lights reminded him of the Think Tank, even though they were only on the ceiling. What was happening?

He certainly didn't have the answer, but somehow knew that it was good. It had to be the result of his happy thoughts. It felt really good in his heart, too, like it had at the Caverns, especially in the niche where he'd found the devenite.

"This is important," he said aloud. "I know it is. I need to tell the others. I'm not sure what it means, but it's important. Real important."

He felt around the cyllmat until he found the portalume, turned it on, then headed back up the rocky slope to the now-familiar path where he took off at full speed, grinning ear to ear.

Before he reached the lab, he skidded to an abrupt stop. They may not believe him now any more than before. But this time he had proof! Deven gnawed his lower lip, thinking. If they could see for themselves, then they wouldn't have to take his word for it. They would know, just like he did.

Yes, that's what he had to do. Prove it right before their eyes. Then they'd have to believe him! The grin returned and he took off running again, his plan falling into place.

* * *

The commander's quarters were simple but adequate, including a well-furnished command post that provided regular intelligence updates as well as strategic and tactical activities. Bryl checked the latest report, then closed her eyes and sighed. The damage assessment confirmed her team's instincts. If they stayed at the base, they probably wouldn't survive, much less prevail.

Her thoughts wandered to when she'd first come to Cyraria. Being treated as an equal combined with the preponderance of men had been a high in itself. She'd never dealt much with men before, and it had been more enjoyable than she'd ever imagined. The male mentality she'd learned to despise on Esheron had shown its more positive side, at least for the most part, and for the first time she'd seen how the strengths and weaknesses of the two sexes complemented each other. At least until they'd assassinated Krai and the Triumvirate had formed. Then each and every one of her newly formed opinions reverted to Esheronian skepticism.

Except maybe one. Laren. An exception to numerous rules.

Being the center of attention hadn't hurt her feelings one bit. Most had treated her like a friend, a few had other intentions. Every match had failed, leaving her in a state of rejection. She couldn't believe she'd nearly resorted to the ECL, a law she'd sponsored while called upon to serve a brief but mandatory senate term. At least she'd come to her senses before seeing it through, but for some odd reason, she felt as if everyone knew about her former intent. She'd confessed to Laren, but doubted he would have told them, especially since it had been resolved, so she had no idea how that was possible. Nonetheless, it was one viable explanation for how his family, especially Sharra, acted toward her.

Or perhaps it was simply her own guilt, not only for her original intentions, but for missing Eta's covert alliance with INTEGRATION, which ultimately resulted in Laren's arrest for treason. All due to the adolescent emotional turmoil she'd been experiencing at the time. Foolishness which had resulted in lethal consequences.

From what she'd seen of Laren's family, she could understand his loyalty and affection. At first, she'd been jealous of what they had, but now she felt genuine compassion for their loss. A loss she felt deeply as well, even if he was no more than a good friend. Except he'd been so much more than that.

Convinced their chances of survival were minimal, she tapped Storm's pager code into the comcon, emitted a heavy sigh, then stepped into her front office. Her arrival at Apoca flared from memory, of how he'd accepted her assumption of command so graciously. He was a good Zinaanian man who had earned her utmost respect.

The comcon chirped, his check-in swift, as always. His location and status appeared, likewise a query whether voice or face-to-face was required. His activities at the time were routine, so she opted for the latter, then leaned back in the huge swivel chair to wait. At one time it had felt good, even comfortable, but now she felt lost within its unyielding depths in spite of the nanobots' best efforts.

Moments later Storm's immense frame filled the doorway, features solemn and expectant.

"Thank you for responding so quickly," she said.

"Yes, ma'am," he replied, concern in his bulbous eyes revealing he suspected she had bad news.

"It's my understanding that our situation is far from ideal," she stated, then paused, shaking her head. "Who am I kidding? It's catastrophic. And it's my responsibility to do everything possible to assure everyone's survival. Based on the information we have, our only choice is probably to evacuate. We thought this place was secure enough we wouldn't need such a plan, but obviously that has changed. I want you to confirm the *Volition's* capacity with Igni and then develop a lottery scheme to select who'll be onboard, besides our usual command crew. The Brightstars, Sendori, you, and of course, Igni. There's a chance that anyone who hasn't been mindprinted is safe. My guess is that would be anyone who's never been to the Tower in Cira City. That can be your first cut.

"Then inventory the transports and other vehicles to see how many troops can be moved to a safe location. Identify suitable safe havens, either on or off-world, according to the vehicles' capabilities, so we can maximize the INTEGRATOR'S confusion regarding our destinations. The more the better. Plan to deploy the first set of vehicles within fifty-two hours, perhaps sooner. However, at this point, this is for your ears only. No one else. Since we may not be able to accommodate everyone, I don't want to start a mass panic. As far as I'm aware, few realize how bad the situation really is and it needs to stay that way a little longer. Any questions?"

"Am I correct in assuming I'm not to notify the Brightstars, either?"

"No, not yet. I don't want them distracted from their efforts to develop countermeasures."

"Yes, ma'am," he replied, then returned her salute and left, his only comment a pensive frown.

She inhaled deeply and blew it out in a sigh, acutely aware of the situation's lethal potential as she leaned back, barely aware of the nanobots' subtle massage.

Memories besieged her again, of when she'd first come to Cyraria; she'd never dreamed a simple consulting job would come to anything even close to this. Back then, it was exciting to be part of something so dynamic and feel as if, in some small way, she could make a difference. When Krai Laitselec, Epsilon's former Territorial General, appointed her as one of his regional governors, her excitement had been that of a dream come true. To think she'd be able to build a system of government that she believed in and then watch it grow was exhilarating. Giving Laren asylum had been the highest point of all. Having that kind of power felt good as well as meaningful, as if she'd done something that really made a difference.

Krai's assassination had been the worst shock since losing her father as a child, but Laren had gotten her through it. His ambush had been another blow, then witnessing the brutal attack of a defenseless Neutral first hand. Barely escaping on the last evac vehicle had given her serious pause regarding what she could possibly do to combat such evil forces. Her confidence had surged again upon arriving at Apoca Canyon where she had so many capable people backing her up. But once more, they were on the brink of not only defeat but annihilation, and all she could do was take action to assure survival for as many as possible.

She pondered whether not telling the Brightstars was a good idea. The last thing she wanted would be for them to think they'd been deliberately left out of the loop. Yet she had justification, if there was the slightest chance they could come up with something. Bryl bit her lip as she reconsidered, finally deciding to at least let someone in their close circle know what plans were in work. If they found out through the rumor mill, which was sure to start as soon as Storm started inventorying vehicles, it would be worse.

She set her jaw and entered Win's pager code, expression grim, then leaned back to wait, knowing his response would be in person and in short order. Her expectations were accurate and before long he stood at attention before her. She waved him at ease and to sit down with a single gesture, suspecting by his expression that he already had some idea why he was there.

"As you know, we're in an extremely critical situation," she stated. "I'm certainly aware of the efforts going on in the lab and don't want to distract from them or imply I don't have confidence in their outcome. However, as commander I'm responsible for everyone here and at this point safety is a serious concern."

"Yes, Ma'am," he said simply. "I certainly don't envy your position."

"Thank you. I want you to know that I have no choice but to put a contingency plan in place. I ordered Storm to initiate evac procedures based on our vehicle inventory. I'll be on the *Volition* as well as you, the Brightstars, and as many others as possible who were most likely to have been mindprinted."

His gaze shifted to an increasingly troubled and mystified look. "Where will we go?"

"I haven't decided. Once off-world we'll arrange multiple destinations, but the most important part is to get away from this location. I plan to return to my *naterra,* to resume my position as controlling chief exec of Woeyel Industries. I find their wars far more tolerable than these hopelessly one-sided battles. Anyone who'd care to join me would be most welcome."

He held her gaze in silence for several moments, as if digesting the information. "When will you tell the others?"

"Not yet," she replied and provided the same rationale she'd given Storm. "I just wanted to give you a heads-up in the event leaving turns out to be our only recourse."

"I appreciate your trust."

"And I, yours. Do you understand why I don't want them to know?"

"Yes. It would destroy what little hope remains."

She nodded, her throat constricting with the realization that hers had already fled.

Nothing she ever expected to see for the rest of her life would match the heights of exhilaration or depths of defeat she'd felt on Cyraria. Knowing her voice would fail her, she stood and offered the Miran grip, which she'd learned from Laren and his brother, Jen. Win returned it firmly, saluted, then left, Bryl quietly closing the door behind him, which she'd never done before.

She lowered slowly to the chair, relief mixing with losses greater than she'd ever imagined possible. Now that it was all but over, she allowed herself a moment to ponder how it could have been, but the indulgence ended quickly. For neither chief execs nor commanders were supposed to cry.

* * *

When nearly an hour had passed and her little brother still hadn't returned, Creena could tell her mother was deeply concerned, especially since Deven so seldom got angry.

"I'm sure he went to Cranium Cavern," 'Merama said with a maternal sigh. "I better check on him to make sure he's okay."

Once her mother was out of earshot, Creena sighed heavily, and fixed her eyes on the lab's ceiling. "He's right, you know," she said.

"It's pointless," Dirck grumbled. "We can't win, so why try?"

"Because," Creena replied, sighing as she cupped her face in her hands, elbows propped on the workdeck. "It's kind of cowardly to just sit here and wait to die."

"Yeah, right," he replied, folding his arms. "We should get busy doing something, no matter how futile. Then the time will go faster than if we mope around obsessing on how bad things are. No, thanks. I'm just going to sit here and enjoy what time I have left."

Creena's laugh echoed harshly from their stone surroundings. *"Enjoy?* Really? Somehow that doesn't quite seem like the right word." His lips tightened as he tried unsuccessfully to glare. "C'mon, Dirck," she went on. "Don't let your last breath be drawn as a snurk."

His eyes narrowed slightly, then a ghost of a smile crept into his expression as it switched from annoyance to discouragement. "So what should we do?"

"If we're going to just sit here, we ought to do what Deven said and think of something good."

"Such as?"

"Oh, I don't know. Maybe like when you and Win found me on Mira III. Or when the transport sank outside Dununda and we thought we were dead, then found out it was Enoch."

"Or when Win realized the transports were powered by fuel cells," he volunteered.

"Yeah! Or when we arrived in your quarters from the Caverns, when you thought we were dead."

Dirck's laugh was short and tinged with irony, but a laugh nonetheless. "I'd never been so shocked before in my life," he admitted, smile bitter-sweet, but there. "Or so happy. You know, you're right." He laughed. "Again, I admit it. We may as well spend our last day or so remembering the good stuff."

"Exactly. I wouldn't want to give them the satisfaction of thinking they made us miserable. I think we should get out of here and join Deven and 'Merama in Cranium Cavern. C'mon, let's go."

"You go ahead. I'll be along in a little while."

"How come?"

"I need some time to myself first. I'm just not ready to act all happy for 'Merama and Deven when I can't quite get past the fact we're doomed."

Her eyes softened with understanding and he answered with a firm, brotherly embrace. "Thanks, sis," he said softly. "I love you."

Her grip around him tightened. "I love you, too."

* * *

Igni sat at her console in *IP&S,* shuddering when a cold void rippled from the tips of her antennae to the barbed bottoms of her six feet. She knew intuitively what it meant. The *Volition* had broken orbit. A sigh escaped as she hung her giant head, devastated for causing false hopes. Straightening her antennae to their transmit position, she sent the cancel order, then awaited confirmation. None came. She queried the command queue; again, no response. Apparently the *ESM* had drawn attention to *Volition's* status and the HIO was retrieving it. Disappointment expanded to the grim realization she'd lost her ship plus the ability to evacuate a substantial group to safety.

The vessel had been part of her for so long that it had become a companion of sorts, perhaps even a friend, its abrupt absence as painful as when she'd lost her crew or left the colony. But worst of all, she'd have to report that the plan had not only failed, but now the vehicle was no longer available. Causing harm to one's group was a capital offense on Arcturus, regardless of circumstances. In a way, she wished such were the case here because it would end her pain.

Maybe, considering the pending attack, it would be better if she didn't say anything. Maybe that tiny bit of hope, albeit false, was better than no hope at all. If they were all going to die, it probably didn't matter much, one way or the other. Yet it wasn't in her to lie and she knew she'd be unable to sustain it for long. At the least she needed to tell Commander Woeyel the ship was no longer available for evacuation. Then it would be up to her to decide whether or not the others needed to know.

Karma

Bezarna Express

The lights came up on the *Bezarna Express* as abruptly as they'd extinguished, illuminating Rhodus' startled expression, which Laren was certain reflected his own. Sa'ata still had his face buried in his arms, rise and fall of his shoulders betraying the rapid breathing of a terrified man.

Having previously experienced a near-death experience, Laren was fully aware that he was still alive, though Rhodus apparently wasn't so sure, judging by his skeptical look as he repeatedly pinched his huge arm. He flinched multiple times, satisfied, and returned Laren's grin.

"What happened?" he asked. "I thought you said we were doomed. If you were kidding, Brightstar, that was a really, really sick joke, even for you."

The guard slowly lowered his hands, amber eyes so wide they were rimmed with white, giving him a ghoulish look.

"I don't know," Laren replied, stifling a laugh as he riveted his gaze on the guard to gauge whether favor or fury would follow. "As far as I could tell they were cutting the O_2 at sleepzone onset. But it felt as if the ship went through some sequence that interrupted the queue."

"Whats did you do?" Sa'ata snarled.

"Nothing. That command came from the ground. It certainly wasn't something I was capable of queueing up. Trust me on that one, Sa'ata."

"Yeah, but it's you messin' with stuff that coulda killed us all! And even if air's not cut, return may be cancelled, thanking to you!"

"Shut down, Sa'ata," he snapped. "I can't think with your whining. Rhodus, put him back in the wrings."

"No, please, don't!" the Pyxisite begged. "I shutted. Not be trouble. No wrings. Please."

"One move, Sa'ata, you hear me? One move or one word, and it's the airlock. Is that clear?"

"Yeah, man," he replied, hands raised. "No trouble. No talk."

"Okay," Laren continued, glaring at the guard for interrupting his train of thought. "We're still alive so let me see if I can figure this out."

"What do you think happened?" Rhodus asked.

"I don't know. There are a couple possibilities. There's a remote, but viable chance, it has something to do with the Clique or maybe even my family. Neither seem to know when to give up." He smiled, besieged by warm thoughts of both. "The odds of that are slightly better than raw, uncontained luck. But you never know. In either case, believe me, I want to know what's going on as much as you do."

He removed his c-com from his pocket, wondering again why it had suddenly shut down.

I'm not dead. I'm sleeping.

A chill ran down his spine, eyes widening at the strange impression.

"What?" Rhodus prompted, watching with a questioning look.

Laren waved him to silence, mind settling to a more normal rhythm now that fear had fled. Closing his eyes, he took a deep breath, pushing his mind to rationality as opposed to adrenaline-fed acceleration.

His freed thoughts wandered back to Esheron, to when he and Jen had been issued the devices, gradually recalling they'd done far more than accept them graciously and drop them in their pockets for future use. After the acquisition process, which had been one of the most exhilarating experiences of his life, they'd participated in some kind of ceremony. It included a charging procedure, which had created a seamless interface between the c-com and his mind. Prompted by memory, he held the device to his forehead and felt an immediate connection. A deep sense of satisfaction followed as he then held it to his chest and felt another jolt.

So are you awake now, my little friend? he psaid.

Affirmative, Commander Brightstar. Once again we are one.

He smiled at Rhodus while nodding at the device, his companion's grin indicating he understood.

Device, can you tell me why you shut down? If he knew that, perhaps he could prevent it from happening again.

Of course, Commander. There was an attempt to access you through an unauthorized psi channel.

He frowned, wondering at the source and whether it was friendly or otherwise.

It was not friendly, Commander. It hailed from the research facility at Integrator Central.

A cold shiver coursed through him, wondering what might have occurred without c-com intervention.

It was part of an experiment attempting to access those for whom they have mindprints. The source is now blocked.

Not surprised but shaken nonetheless, his growing fascination regarding what else the device might reveal yielded to more immediate concerns. *Device, I appreciate that information. Can you provide the current status of the ship's system?*

Much to his surprise, he had the impression that the c-com sighed, as if he'd hurt its feelings, which made no sense whatsoever, intelligent as it may be.

Don't you think I deserve a name, Commander? it responded.

"You've got to be kidding," he replied aloud, again motioning Rhodus to silence as he started to speak.

Certainly not, Commander. Is it that imposing of a request? Won't you feel more comfortable conversing with a named intelligence, perhaps even another part of yourself, as opposed to a mere device?

He tried not to roll his eyes, unable to believe he was having this conversation with a, uh, whatever it really was, sitting in his hand.

All right. You have a point. I need some time to think about it. There are some rather pressing circumstances transpiring right now that aren't exactly conducive to coming up with a suitable name, he psaid, marginally defensive. *My bondling always did the honors of naming our children, so I'm not exactly experienced at this.*

That is a fair request, Commander. I would like to think you would not execute such an important task casually. You are aware, of course, that a name has vibrational energy which combines with that to which it is applied.

I will give it my most careful consideration, he promised. *So what's the ship's command status?*

The ship's command sequence was purged as the result of an emergency failsafe procedure known only to the original RA-681 engineering designers and HIO vehicle captains. The intent of the ESM is to send the three nearest fleet vehicles to assist in the event the crew is disabled or encounters some other threat. It was originally programmed into unarmed HIO vessels as a means of protection.

Laren pondered that a moment, surprised, yet acknowledged it made sense.

Okay, he responded. *I can buy that. So where are we headed? Back to Cyraria?*

Negative. The vehicle is in standby awaiting your command.

Say again?

The vehicle is in standby awaiting your command.

How can that be?

The ESM has been disabled and the originating vessel is heading for its home port on Mira III under remote command.

Who originated the ESM? he asked, braced for the answer, which would undoubtedly provide a wealth of information.

The captain of the Volition. Formicidae/Ignatius.

Laren's face gathered into a pensive frown. Igni. That made sense, but why his ship was now headed for Mira III didn't. He wondered if Igni was still on Cyraria or had resumed his HIO mission. If so, how would he have known that such an action would save him? Of course! Because the prison ship was also an RA-681. How did they know that? A lucky guess? Either way, it had to be deliberate. And if the vehicle was returning via remote order, the Arcturian probably wasn't onboard.

Can you bring up the original schematics and hard system code for the RA-681?

No, Commander. They are secured beyond your clearance level.

But I can resume control of this vessel through you, as I did previously?

Affirmative, Commander.

He sighed amid what had become a storm of general confusion as the implications settled. Finally he smiled and met the expectant looks of the other two passengers.

"Looks like we've gone full-circle back to our original plan," he said, smile quickly evolving to a grin.

"What?" Rhodus asked, puzzled. "Why? Which plan?"

He momentarily returned the man's mystified look, confused at his lack of understanding until it dawned on him the entire conversation had been silent to the others.

"Okay, here's what's going on," he replied, shook his head as if to dispel his own disbelief, then relayed the story. When he'd finished, Rhodus looked entirely dumbfounded.

"You certainly live a charmed life, Brightstar," he commented, shaking his head.

"Maybe's it's just good karma," Laren replied, chuckling with the realization that he'd just found the name he was looking for. In confirmation he felt a nudge of approval from his shirt pocket.

Okay, Karma, he psaid to his newly named device. *Open navigation input channel....*

REFRACTIONS

D irck sat in the lab after Creena left, arms still folded, pondering that first time 'Merapa had explained choices. At the time, how they propagated into a complex network of multiple eventualities was incomprehensible. Now he understood only too well.

In spite of the fact Bryl was their commander, he somehow knew if anything was to be done about their sorry situation it was up to him. Why didn't matter; it just was. It was a responsibility he felt with every fiber of his being. He scoured his mind for ideas, yet found nothing. Humbled by the magnitude of the task and his inherent inability to execute it, he secured the door then sat on the floor, back against stone with his knees elevated. He'd been in a similar situation before, when the heat exchanger blew up back at their ballome. Meditating had worked then; maybe it would again. A heartfelt request to the *Benefics* certainly wouldn't hurt, either.

He buried his face in his hands, not in defeat so much as contemplation, then dropped his arms to his sides as he blanked his mind and dove into a meditative state. Ever so gradually fear and pain dissipated, freeing his mind's eye to drift amongst the stuff of creation. Superimposed within were countless ethereal threads, entangled in infinite interactions, origins attached to their creator, ends driven by choices.

Their character and strength differed, properties also, all dependent on what they were and where they'd been. Some were hopelessly twisted with indecision, others taut with resistance, or knotted with deceit. Others were resilient and alive, ebbing and flowing in response to well-established links that traced back to their origins. Still others, rare but outstanding, emanated a persistent glow that not only reflected their source, but contained an essence he felt he should understand, yet didn't. He sought his own, wondering, but found it not.

Neither did it matter. There was one choice above all others, one that could reconnect with the source of all life and goodness. Where he'd been before didn't matter, only where he could go. A place he didn't want to go alone. Nor did he have to.

With that, he returned to the present with a soul-wrenching sigh, then got up to join the others. Comforted but not quite optimistic, he slowly wound his way through the now-familiar climbs and descents to Cranium Cavern, still clueless what he needed to do. When he arrived, he found not only Creena, 'Merama and Deven, but Win as well, all sitting with their backs against Deven's cyllmat, each far more animated than he'd expected. The lumapoles were all on, giving the chamber a stark and somewhat sterile appearance.

"Hi!" Deven greeted him cheerily. "We've just been talking about all the neat stuff that's happened since we came to Cyraria."

He almost rolled his eyes, then remembered Creena's admonition. No matter how he felt, he had no right to impose misery on the others.

"I miss the Caverns," 'Merama said wistfully. "They were so beautiful."

"Remember the first time we saw them, with Enoch?" Deven asked his brother.

"I sure do," Dirck replied, smiling as he joined them on the floor. "It was like finding ourselves on a different planet, compared to Peak Opps."

"Or Dead Drop Winter," Creena added.

"This really is a pretty miserable planet," Win commented.

"You're kidding. Ya think?" Dirck replied sarcastically. "I wonder what it would have been like if 'Merapa would have had a chance to terralogize it? You can only do so much with seasons like this."

"After seeing to the immediate economic needs by finding plants and animals to raise commercially, he said that his first step would have been to bring as much water as possible to the surface, at least during Opposition," 'Merama said.

"Why?" Deven asked.

"To add water vapor to the atmosphere," she answered. "Zeta and Zinni's light wouldn't be as harsh, plus clouds would form, which would not only shade the surface, but eventually release moisture. That would make it possible to raise crops, and the more vegetation, the more favorable the weather would become."

"But it would still be dark during Dead Drop Winter," Deven commented. "And all the water would freeze."

"The water would be returned to the underground aquifers," 'Merama explained. "Subterranean and domed communities would have always been necessary for the extremes. But the planet could have been self-sustaining."

"'Merapa could have done it, too," Creena sighed.

"No wonder the INTEGRATOR wanted him so badly," Win mused.

Everyone sat in silence for several long moments, then continued reminiscing, trying to steer away from melancholy memories as much as possible. Sometime later, the conversation lulled as everyone became absorbed in their own thoughts, having at least generated a warm glow that partially eased the pain of dismal expectations.

* * *

Everyone jumped when Deven bolted to his feet and trotted over to the nearest lumapole. One by one he turned them off, but the chamber wasn't dark. Rather than the sparkles they'd seen earlier, the walls displayed a definite glow with wispy fingers of light dancing across the surface, similar to the prism-like emanations from the Think Tank, except rather than prism-like, these were mostly confined to the violet range.

"Whoa!" Win exclaimed. "Will you look at *that!*"

"Holy holocubes!" Dirck said with a gasp. "How did that happen?"

Deven was laughing so hard he was dancing and prancing all around, afraid he'd pee his pants, while Creena and 'Merama put in similar expressions of utter astonishment. Finally he controlled himself enough to explain his earlier experience, when the sparkles had temporarily disappeared.

"So I just figured it was reacting to what I felt, like the other Caverns did to my thoughts," he explained. "I decided to try an experiment and see if all of us being happy would stir it up even more. And it did!"

"We need to get a wall sample to Major Zee right away," Win stated. "If it's what I think it is, we might have a better defense than we realized."

"Why?" 'Merama asked. "What's happening?

"Apparently it's reflecting and possibly amplifying positive thought energy, similar to the Think Tank," Win replied. "Which implies that even if they have our mindprints, each of us should be able to defend ourselves from the attack with enough collective positive psi energy."

"Right," Dirck agreed. "It makes sense for everyone to defend themselves, yet band together. Anyone who has negative thoughts needs to either change their attitude or leave. The sooner the better."

Creena giggled in spite of herself. "A week ago it seems to me—"

"Yeah, well that was before," Dirck protested. "Before I understood what was going on."

"And that purple cast suggests there may be some devenite there, too," Creena noted. "Maybe it's a gigantic psitenna that can hold hundreds of people. As long as everyone has nothing but positive thoughts it just might work! Best case it'll not only repel the attack, but maybe even bring 'Merapa back, if Igni's plan doesn't work. Devenite seems to connect with what your heart needs most, so why not? We'd all be a lot happier with him here."

Deven grinned and could hardly stand still with excitement. Everyone was congratulating him and hugging him and smiling, the fingers of energy tickling the walls lengthening and increasing even more.

Win turned the lumapoles back on, then joined Dirck and Creena looking for a place to extract a sample, leaving a moment later to retrieve a suitable tool to remove it.

Deven took his mother's hand and smiled, more excited than he'd been in a long time. She smiled back, but she wasn't as happy as he thought she would be. Her eyes were sad and it almost looked as if she was going to cry. Sometimes adults cried when they were happy, like she did when 'Merapa and Dirck got home from looking for Creena. Maybe that was it. He gave her a hug and she squeezed back, but he could tell she really was sad, but couldn't figure out why.

* * *

After dropping off the sample with Major Zee, Win started back to Cranium Cavern to help remove the sleep experiment equipment. There were far more urgent matters before them now than generating a veridical dream. Facilitating the chamber's transition to a Think Tank or psitenna was far more important.

Halfway back to where he was meeting Dirck, he stopped mid-stride as a soul-wrenching impression seized his mind. He blinked and held his temples, seeing if it would go away; it didn't. Its logic eluded him, but he'd learned long ago not to ignore such promptings. He resumed his trek in the same direction, but when he found Dirck at their rendezvous point, he made some excuse about needing to check something first, then headed for Sharra's quarters.

As expected she was there, sitting on her cyll with her eyes fixed in a distant focus that barely wavered as he entered and sat down beside her.

"Hey," he said quietly. "Are you okay?"

She looked at him slowly, her green Miran eyes not quite meeting his. "I don't know," she answered.

"What's wrong?"

She sighed and hung her head, blond hair obstructing her face. "I don't think I can do this."

"Sharra! What are you talking about? Why not? I thought we finally were getting this all together."

When she looked up her expression spoke volumes, and while he never could have guessed what was wrong, somehow he knew.

"Are you still worried about that ECL stuff?" he asked, not surprised when her eyes filled with tears.

"Our Miran bonding isn't recognized here," she said, brushing the moisture away as if annoyed by its betrayal. "So if he somehow makes it back, it's not even a matter of giving permission. Esherson is their *naterra,* so she can claim him outright. I've lost him, either way."

"Bryl told you that?"

"No, but I know how it works."

On a world where women outnumbered men by eight to one, it was no wonder that Esheronian women of influence could claim whomever they wanted, with men free to take on as many consenting women as they could handle. Since the female persuasion ran the planet's economic structure, providing for them was rarely an issue. It worked well on Esheron—the human species had survived. Yet how such a practice could affect someone from a perfectly ordered, monogamous society like Mira III was only too clear.

And, unfortunately, her assumptions were valid. He put a sympathetic arm around her shoulders, trying to think of what he could say to make her feel better. Certainly Sharra hadn't lost her bondling, anyway; at worst she'd only have to share him. In her eyes however, they were undoubtedly the same.

"Laren would never forsake you," he said. "And this isn't Esheron. I'm sure he'll find a way around it."

She dried her eyes and shook her head. "I guess deep inside I know that. We're really more than bonded. He made *Promises* to me and the children that I know he takes very seriously."

"Promises? What kind of promises?"

"To watch over us, take care of us, that kind of thing. He made them when we first were bonded, then again before we left Mira III. It was some kind of Esheronian ritual. This last time, something to do with the Order. It was more than ordinary promises. I could feel it, and the difference it made in our relationship."

"The only Esheronian ritual like that I know of is a lot more binding than Miran civil law. It sounds like you were bonded by the Ledorian Order, which is recognized galaxywide. Miran or not, that gives you all the right to claim him you could ever want, even beyond the ECL. Which means you don't have anything to worry about, Sharra."

While hope returned to her eyes, relief didn't.

"But that's only part of it. The real problem is how I feel toward her," she explained. "I hate her, Win. There's no way I'll be able to have the positive attitude necessary for this to work."

Win sighed. Sharra wasn't simply worried about losing her bondling. Certainly she knew now she'd won that battle. Instead, the scars of resentment from the past could keep her from approaching the task before them with the right emotional backing.

"You have to forgive her, Sharra," he said softly. "That's just the way things are on Esheron, the way it's done. You have nothing to worry about and need to let it go."

"I know. But I can't."

"You have to."

"But I *can't!*"

"What about your children? How will they feel if you're not there?"

The tears started again, an endless, bitter stream. "I know! And I don't know what to do. I've tried, I really have, but I can't. Laren was everything to me, Win.   More than life itself. And she wants to take him away."

Win looked away and stifled a sigh, wondering if something as fundamental as human resentment, no matter how justified, would bring everything to naught. Then he realized the answer was essentially the same as the integrity of her marital bonds.

"All right, Sharra," he said, looking her straight in the eye. "There's something I can do to help you. But you also have to do something yourself."

"You can help me?"

"Through the Order, I can get you some extra help dealing with this."

"You're in the Order, too?"

"Yes. For a long time, probably since I was a little older than Deven. So I can help, but you're going to have to do your part, too."

"What?"

"Believe. Can you do that?"

"I guess."

He suspected from her expression that, while she'd thought she'd done so before, perhaps the all-important visualization component may have been missing.

"Do you know how?" he asked gently.

"Yes," she said, nodding her head. "Laren told me about seeing it in my mind as well as feeling it in my heart. I just haven't, in a long time."

"How long?"

She looked away evasively. "Probably since he told us to let him go. Maybe a little before."

He waited for her to look his way again. "Do you believe it will work?"

"Do you?" she countered.

"Absolutely."

"All right, then," she said with conviction. "If you do, I can, too. But how can the Order help?"

He gestured toward the chair by the comcon and she obediently got up and sat down, questions in her eyes. "Close your eyes," he said. When she complied, he placed his hands firmly on her head. The Universe responded to his request, the channeled pronouncement longer and deeper than he'd ever intended, inspired words flowing as if they'd originated from some outside source.

When it was over, he rested his hands on her shoulders for a moment, remembering the time he'd given his mother similar help, a time that seemed so long ago now. He uttered a quiet farewell and headed back to Cranium Cavern, wondering. Shortly after that first experience with the *Order,* his mother had left mortality. The second time, he'd brought someone back. Funny, how each time it had been a matter of life or death.

Of course, the real question was which way it would go this time.

Before he reached his destination, his pager went off, the tone Bryl's. As always, he reported in person, wondering what new development had arisen to summon him back so soon.

"Yes, ma'am," he said, stepping into her office and assuming by her expression that whatever it was wasn't good.

"More bad news," she said simply. "The *Volition*'s gone."

"*Gone?* Oh, no." His throat tightened with emotion at the implications. He swallowed hard and blinked against the moisture which had so rudely gathered in his eyes.

"Apparently the swarm attempt was unsuccessful and it broke orbit to return to Mira III."

"Can't Igni call it back?" he replied.

"Apparently not. Once it's homed in on the HIO they assume control, another safety measure in case they're dealing with a hijacking, piracy or other contingency where the captain may not be in control."

Win sighed heavily and closed his eyes, wondering what else could go wrong. "I guess that impacts the evacuation plans, too. How many can get out on the transports?"

Indecision lined her face, which had aged significantly in the past day. "I don't know. I need to talk to Storm and find out. Meanwhile, I'd appreciate it if you'd keep this conversation as well as our previous one to yourself."

"Right," he agreed. "It's probably better they don't know. Sometimes false hope is better than none."

"My thoughts exactly." She smiled weakly, caring in her eyes which matched his own.

"Okay," he sighed, then turned slowly to resume his trek, knowing the hardest part would be masking his disappointment.

They'd been through so much together that the Brightstars had become like his own family. The prison break had been the clincher, bonding them to his heart forever, making the loss deeply personal as well. It had been a long and trying day, riding one emotional sine wave after the other. Come what may, he was ready for it to end, one way or the other.

Benefics, where are you? he asked silently, glancing upward. *We could really use some help down here.*

Results

I t felt like a dream, but Bryl knew it was more, much more. It was memory, as vivid as the occurrence itself, yet she was seeing it through different eyes. After all, she'd been only six.

The rolling hills of Esheron were green with billowing summer grasses teased by the everpresent breeze. Her mother and two older siblings, a sister and brother, labored in the garden, harvesting the first of the season's vegetables, while a short distance away she picked a bouquet of wildflowers for her mother. She was the first to see its approach, a shiny disk rising silently from the distant horizon, glinting in the warming light of the rising sun.

Visitors were rare and usually welcome, breaking the monotony of long days of toil for a family lacking conveniences most took for granted. There were few others in the region, the craft's destination obviously their home as its altitude lowered, yet lacked lateral movement due to its head-on trajectory. She paused in her task and stood to watch as it grew larger, stopped and lowered to the ground. Even before she heard her mother's cry of despair she knew. It was the *callers*. Such visits were common and everyone, even children, knew what they meant. In war torn Esheron it meant someone, usually their father, would not be coming home.

Mouth agape, she watched as a man she knew as their Guardian and two women, all dressed in white, exited the craft and walked to the knot of individuals clinging to one another in the garden, too frozen with shock and fear herself to run the ten meters between them to join their collective grief.

After the craft's departure, they'd immediately begun preparations for their new life. With their father gone, so was their home. Her mother had domestic skills only, none sufficient to support them, which meant they'd join thousands of other widowed families in the *kolkhoz*, or farm community outside the city. There the local government sustained life, but not life style, providing food, shelter and education in the most rudimentary way while everyone participated in running the farm. Children could attain sufficient education to eventually leave and become self-supporting, at least the girls, the boys destined for military service with no exceptions.

Esheronian law allowed men to have multiple bondlings, given the ratio between them and women was high. However, back then, upon their bondling's death, women weren't allowed to remarry, having had their chance to have a man in their lives. How could it be fair to those who'd never had a mate if those who'd once enjoyed the benefits were to do so again and thus deprive others of progeny?

Unfortunately, often widows like her mother were not able to support themselves and had no choice but to join the *kolkhoz*. A situation she later remedied through authoring the Esheronian Contingency Law or ECL, which allowed a woman and her children to join another family unit, usually headed by her husband's brother or perhaps a sister's husband. Whether or not the bonding was consummated was up to those involved, but it at least provided another option which preserved family ties.

Yet the part she remembered when they'd gathered in the house afterward failed to materialize in the dream. Instead, Bryl joined the *callers*, an invisible stowaway in the craft's cramped passenger compartment. In the whirl of vector disks it lifted high above the ground, soared over the abandoned garden and small box of a house as it banked in a different direction than that from which it came.

Why am I here? Bryl thought. *Where are they taking me?*

Moments later and but a few kilometers away, the craft lowered again. The house was similar in size, its occupants inside. The fair, blond-haired, green-eyed woman who answered the door bid them enter, questions rather than knowing in her expression. Two boys, a few years older than herself, were in the galley, preparing food for the midday mealzone. The furnishings were humble but adequate, holos of family gatherings arranged carefully on a shelf beside the media array.

A small commotion ensued when the woman screamed and fainted, but Bryl was too distracted to pay attention. Why did these strangers have a picture of her father in such a prominent place?

Their efforts to revive the woman were joined by her two sons, eyes wide with questions as their mother regained consciousness. They helped her to a chair, the younger boy fetching a tumbler of water from the galley, as the *callers* explained the available options: join the *kolkhoz* or return to her *naterra*, Mira III.

"Do I have to decide now?" she asked, soft features already etched with a widow's grief.

"Yes, Madam Brightstar," the taller one explained. "We must know so we can arrange transportation, either to the *kolkhoz* or spaceport. You must vacate these premises by this time the morrow."

The name, of course, was different, women on Esheron retaining their birth names and passing them on to their children rather than assuming their bondling's surname as practiced on other worlds, including Mira III.

"I will return to my *naterra*," the woman replied decisively, rising once more with control and dignity.

"Very well. We will arrange passage. Be ready to depart before the sun culminates on the morrow."

The *callers* left and the fair-haired one embraced her two boys, heads bowed together as they continued to absorb the devastating news.

Bryl awoke with a start, implications of what she'd seen far beyond her craziest imaginings. She sat up in her cyll, mouth agape in horrified denial.

What had she just witnessed? Could it be? No! Her father had another bondling? Why had her mother never mentioned it? Could she have taken such knowledge to her grave? While older than she was at the time, the boys in the other household were about the same age or slightly younger than her older siblings. Was it possible that neither knew of the other?

A military officer, her father had some dealings with the HIO, headquartered on Mira III. Was it possible he returned from one of his excursions with a Miran bride? Perhaps her mother's permission wasn't required for offworld bonding. Yet Esheronian women grew up with plural marriage as the norm, objections unheard of.

But with a Miran?

Why would a woman whose *naterra* was populated by numerous members of the opposite gender to choose, from bond with someone from Esheron? She groaned as her answer surfaced from memory. Miran pairings were arranged by government decree. She shuddered at the thought. Of course.

But such ponderings were nothing compared to the echo of the woman's name combined with her knowledge of Laren's mixed heritage.

She didn't know whether to laugh, cry or scream, past aspirations and choices mocking her ignorance of something she couldn't possibly have known. Undecided, she indulged in all three emotions within a span of a minute, wondering if she should tell them and if they'd ever believe her if she did.

Eyes fixed straight ahead, she wondered herself if it had been real or imagined, yet the intensity was such it implied it had meaning. Had it been one of those veridical dreams that Dirck and Creena had mentioned? Like the one that prompted them to perform Laren's daring rescue from prison? No wonder they'd wanted to see if they could induce such a revelation. But why this, why now?

It was one of the most powerful experiences of her life, at least one that involved another realm of existence, and she marveled still why that revelation held such importance to be delivered in that way and at this time. She'd long ago given up her plan to claim Laren through the ECL, as she'd explained to him back in the Territorial Tower. What she hadn't told him was that she'd already started the process, but cancelled it, after he made it clear how much he loved Sharra. If she'd persisted, the request would have been denied, anyway, when their birth records indicated shared paternity. Apparently all choices lead to the same destiny, a concept that gave her considerable pause.

Nonetheless, there were numerous other implications if Laren was her brother. Esheronians took care of their own, which meant his family was also hers. She stiffened with resolve, realizing she couldn't leave Apoca Canyon alone. It was her responsibility to either take them along or otherwise make sure they were safe.

* * *

Sharra had never been there, but she'd heard the story so many times she knew exactly when and where she was. It was precisely as he'd described, including his mother's reaction to the *caller's* message and decision to return to her *naterra*. Her heart ached for this woman, so much like herself, suddenly plunged into widowhood with children not yet raised. But at least Laren's mother had the option of returning to a place where she could live in security and peace.

The change of scene mystified her, wondering why it didn't end where his telling always did. She watched as the *callers* gathered in a garden with an olive-skinned woman with exotic features and two children, a third standing a short distance away.   The woman's tears were profuse, yet her expression showed she was wise in the ways of Esheronian protocol. They called her by name and delivered their unfortunate information, but all Sharra heard was the name.

Like her nemesis, she laughed and cried, but stifled the scream which was horrifically un-Miran, even though she had certainly done so the first time commandos had taken her bondling away back at the ballome. Understanding saturated her in a transformational blast of forgiveness, compassion, and a sudden unexpected bond embracing her on the other side of the swell.

"'Merama? What's wrong?" Deven asked sleepily from his cyll a few meters away.

"Nothing, sweetness," she whispered, wiping her eyes with shaking hands. "Don't worry. I have to do something, but don't worry, I'll be right back."

"Okay, 'Merama," he replied, breathing quickly returning to the rhythm of sleep.

Sharra grabbed the standard issue cloak from the foot of her cyll and carefully made her way down the pathway, as if she knew where she was going and why. Within a few meters she saw a similar figure, staring back with as much surprise and uncertainty as she knew resided in her own expression. Both women beheld each other and then fell into each others' arms as Sharra's feelings toward the woman she'd seen as her nemesis found peaceful resolution.

Eventually both dried their eyes, laughing quietly so as not to cause a mid-sleepzone disturbance which could set off alarms, then held the other's hands as if they'd been lifelong friends.

The conversation that followed in the messhall took the remainder of their sleepzones, but it sealed the results, the only question remaining how to tell the others.

* * *

Later that morning, Bryl sat quietly in her office, still overcome by the dream's implications. For one thing, now she needed to tell Sharra about the *Volition*. The failure of their attempt to bring Laren back now made her responsible for the family's safety as much as his brother, Jen. As her mind wandered amongst unhappy options, she felt the gentle nudge of her c-com.

Bernie.

She retrieved the device from its usual niche, hoping there wasn't a problem. Of course it would figure if there was, since she'd probably be there herself to deal with it, sooner than later.

Bernie, she psaid. *Is everything okay?*

Better than you can possibly imagine, her chief ops officer replied cheerfully. *They're back! They're all back!*

Who? she replied, totally lost and having a hard time connecting with the source of the woman's joy.

The research teams! Both of them! Everyone is back on-world, safe and sound.

Speechless, her mind raced. Had she heard correctly? Or was she still in that accelerated dream state?

Bryl? Are you there?

Yes. But I'm in shock. How is that possible? What happened?

I guess you could say it involved a little help from our friends on the hill. Remember Friar Johann?

Of course. So tell me about the research teams. How'd you get them back?

Same technology with a few minor adjustments. The technical term is automorphic operations, which involves returning to the start after a certain number of steps have been completed. Since they were all in the c-com network, we still had quantum entanglement connections with them, even when they commanded their devices to reset to universal time. Teleporting was simply a matter of scale and proportion.

Bryl gasped as the implications settled. Teleporting through the c-com network? What if...?

Hold it right there, Bernie. I need to get someone else in on this conversation. In fact, a couple people. Three, actually. Stand by. I'll get back with you shortly and tie you in via audio because their devices are on a different network.

Bryl allowed herself a victorious shout of hope before comming Win, Creena and Dirck.

"Get down here right away," she told them simultaneously. "You're not going to believe what's happened."

They arrived a few moments later only seconds apart, each wearing a puzzled yet expectant expression. She told them what she knew so far, then quickly coded her c-com through her comcon's audio system so they could hear Bernie when they reconnected.

"Bernie? Can you hear me?" she asked, testing the connection.

"Loud and clear," the woman replied.

"Same here. Okay, I've got three people here who have a keen interest in this teleportation process and the technical savvy, I assume, to understand how it works. So go ahead."

Bernie repeated what she'd said earlier regarding automorphic operations and the quantum entanglement connections.

"So having a higher proportion of cristobalite allows thought energy to prevail and thus maintain control as opposed to the emotional element of e-waves," Creena mused aloud, Dirck and Win nodding agreement.

"Correct, except they have to work together," Bernie stated. "Without the emotional element, there isn't sufficient energy to cross from the local to universal time stream."

"But the Think Tank had teleportation capability and, as far as we know, it was all cristobalite," Win stated.

"Yes, but there was a devenite deposit close enough to interfere and make the shift," Creena added.

"The Think Tank only operated on this planet," Dirck stated. "Obviously c-coms don't have that limitation. Why not?"

"Good question," Bernie replied. "This is where pure and simple technology comes into play. Cristobalite is linked only to local time, what you call devenite to universal. C-coms calculate these time differentials so that arrival on the other side of the universal stream is correct."

"Like a Time Adjustment Station or TAS?" Dirck asked.

"Yes. But there's a problem if the person is in an area outside both local and universal time, such as a warp run. C-coms can't deal with that any more than a TAS could. The time adjustment capabilities of space vehicles themselves can only operate when they're at subluminal velocity or preferably within an inertial reference frame."

Win let fly with an expletive, everyone in agreement, but nonetheless wearing a variety of expressions ranging from embarrassment to surprise.

"Excuse me?" Bernie said, sniggering.

"Sorry," Win apologized.

"Yeah, real sorry," Dirck stated glumly. "My father's on an RA-681 traveling at warp five or six."

"Can I assume he's the one you wanted to apply this technology to?" Bernie asked.

"Unfortunately, yes," he replied.

Bernie echoed Win's crude remark, again reflecting everyone's opinion of the disappointing news.

"Why do c-coms work for communications at warp speed but not teleportation?" Bryl asked.

"Nothing physical is involved, only psi packets," Bernie explained, "Once matter's involved, it gets complicated. You're familiar with the equation $E=mc^2$, correct?"

"Yes," Dirck said with a sigh. "That makes sense, due to the energy conversion at the speed of light. But what about the interaction of negative and positive psi energy? What can you tell us about that?"

Bryl quickly filled her in on their situation with the INTEGRATOR as well as their current plans to combat it.

"Since c-coms can protect their owner from specific mindprint invasion, you should be able to withstand it, unless the influx becomes too excessive to neutralize, which would skip the c-com to universal time."

"Not everyone here has one, though," Bryl stated. "We do seem to have some natural capability, however, that we're checking on. There are large deposits of cristobalite and devenite at our location, with one cavern in apparently particular rich in those substances, which we hope to charge up."

"That definitely has possibilities, provided you can get everyone within the chamber."

Bryl winced. "Probably not. But we thought the ones who haven't been mindprinted might be safe."

"Maybe, maybe not," Bernie replied. "Depends on the overall amplitude and frequency of the incoming beam. If you can deflect it with equal force, well, in that case some interesting effects could result."

"Like what?" Win asked.

"Theoretically, it could deflect back to the original source or, conversely, the annihilation process could create a new universe. Worst case, if the amplitude of your defense is inadequate, you're gone. Unless you have the exact specifications of the frequency range and amplitude of the incoming energy as well as that of your countermeasures, there's no way to tell."

This time Bryl was the one who cussed.

Plans

"Well, looks like we're on our own after all," Dirck stated once they were out of earshot of Bryl's office and heading back to the lab.

"Right," Win agreed with a sigh. "We need to think this through. If they're harnessing the negative energy we saw surrounding the planet, maybe Aggie can calculate how much is there."

"What good will that do?" Dirck responded. "Knowing the specifics doesn't help produce countermeasures, which we can't quantify, anyway. We mainly need to know what to expect and what, if anything, we can do about it."

The trio arrived at the lab and assumed their usual places, as discouraged as before.

"Dirck's right," Creena agreed. "But something tells me what we just saw happen in Cranium Cavern can help. Maybe we can neutralize or deflect it."

"Good point," Win said. "First we need to figure out what might happen when positive and negative psi energy collide. For starters we know that $E=mc^2$ doesn't apply because psi is massless."

"True," Dirck replied. "That formula collapses with zero mass, plus psi arrives instantly, so its velocity is infinite. That means the usual energy equations based on mass and velocity, even at the speed of light, break down. We're dealing with an entirely different dimension."

"Aggie might know," Creena suggested. "She seemed to understand 'Merapa's work investigating cristobalite which she said had a collapsed time tensor."

Dirck shrugged and entered the 'troid's code. "Sure, why not? Can't hurt."

Aggie arrived in short order, assessing each of them with green-tinged photoreceptors.

"By the looks of your auras, you've already decided you're dead. Do you want me to confirm or deny that?" the 'troid stated.

Dirck and Creena exchanged sorry looks that acknowledged Aggie's accusation with an unspoken "Guilty as charged."

"We didn't invite you here to editorialize," Win responded tersely. "Yeah, we're bummed out, but we're trying to find a solution. We'd appreciate it if you'd listen to our ideas and tell us if we're on the right track. And ditch the sarcasm. Okay?"

Aggie shifted her torso ring indifferently. "Sure. Fire away."

"Nice choice of words," Win muttered.

"Okay, here's what we have," Dirck went on, ignoring Win's comment. "The latest TBA suggests they're going to blast us with negative psi tuned to match our natural psi frequencies. Our c-coms may help some, but there are too many individuals here without them, plus we're not sure they'd block it, anyway, since the devices are based on controlling incoming messages that don't exceed the usual amplitude of telepathic psi, nothing more. So. Let's start with the basics. What happens when psi negative meets equal amounts of psi positive?"

Aggie's photoreceptors blinked while she processed the input.

"Quadratic equations often has two solutions, one negative and one positive. This matrix is similar. There are two possibilities," she responded.

"Well? What are they?" Win prompted.

Aggie gave him one of her haughtiest looks, but refrained from a retort. "One possibility is simple annihilation," she continued. "If of equal force, the opposing waves neutralize each other, somewhat like destructive interference. However, psi, like energy, is never lost. If its amplitude achieves the psi equivalent of critical mass, it could collapse into a psingularity and instantaneously be assimilated by the zero-point field."

"That doesn't sound good," Creena stated, dark eyes wide. "In that case, what would happen to us?"

"You'd be thrown into the universal time flow," Aggie responded matter-of-factly.

"Which is essentially nowhere," Creena responded, brow crinkled with increased concern. "That's where we were before we arrived from the Caverns. Would we be stuck there forever?"

"Possibly," Aggie replied. "Depends on the net energy level. It could last for seconds, maybe millennia, maybe forever, who knows? Time is undefined in that dimension. However, unless it's confined within a psingularity, anything thrown into universal time eventually precipitates out as it's attracted by mental activity in local time, based on the polarity of the thought involved."

"What's the other solution?" Dirck asked, not liking the sound of that at all.

"No net change. In other words, nothing happens. The psi equivalent of an elastic collision. Both remain, same as before."

"What if one's stronger than the other?" Win asked. "Then what?"

"Then what's left of the stronger component remains after the other's annihilation," the robot explained. "Those on the predominant side would exit the universal time flow to a world that reflects the excess energy of whichever polarity prevailed. The losers remain in universal time *ad infinitum*. Or until they precipitate out, like I said before."

"It looks as if we can charge up Cranium Cavern so it's similar to the Think Tank," Creena stated. "What effect will that have?"

Aggie paused briefly, photoreceptors flashing yellow. "If the chamber is cristobalite, it would reflect or perhaps refract the incoming energy, depending on the angle of incidence. If it can store energy, it would at least increase your chances of being the stronger component."

"Would it prevent the annihilation phase?" Creena asked, expression hopeful.

"For a perfect reaction, yes. In that case, annihilation wouldn't occur so a psingularity would be by-passed. Nothing would enter the zero-point field because the incoming energy would be returned to its source."

"Then what?" Win prompted.

"If it reflects, they get back what they sent and nothing changes. If it refracts into the positive range, then it neutralizes the source with the same result as if you prevailed with a higher quantity of positive energy. It could also result in a combination which involves some level of annihilation."

"That implies we have a chance," Dirck commented. "But what's important is to figure out what we have to do to make that happen, even if we don't understand the physics. The more we know about what to expect and how to deal with it the more likely we are to succeed." He shifted his gaze to the door as his mother and Deven quietly joined them, closing his eyes briefly to thank the *Benefics* that their discussion had taken a more positive turn prior to their arrival.

"Exactly," said Creena. "If thoughts become things, that implies psi is a creative force. But not necessarily positive. We need to remember psi's creative potential, like we experienced with the psitenna. Especially since it looks like Cranium Cavern contains devenite, based on the purple aura it emitted during Deven's experiment."

She took a deep breath, then slowly let it out as she made eye contract individually with each person in the room. "My impression is that, more than anything else, we need to put our hearts into it. We need to not only know exactly what we want to happen, but feel it as well. We need a shared vision we all agree upon, and then use that to instruct the psi energy what to do."

"It will work, I know it will," Deven said.

"Not if you don't learn a little humility," Dirck replied, teasing his brother with a feigned punch in an attempt to further lighten the mood, for his sake as well as everyone else.

"I've known it all along," Deven commented, "I don't know what's taken you people so long." He dodged Dirck's playful swat, giggling.

"We need to decide exactly what we're going to do, fast, since we only have a day and a half," Win reminded everyone. "I think Aggie has provided all we need to know, at least for now, and would do well to resume work back in *Intel* scanning for updates on when the assault will occur."

"Good idea," Dirck agreed. "Aggie, you're dismissed. And thanks."

"You're welcome," the 'troid responded, then rolled out of the lab, rolopeds humming against the stone floor.

"The first thing we need to do is charge up Cranium Cavern," Creena stated.

"Which isn't a simple operation," Dirck replied. "Bryl needs to know and approve what we've found out and decided." He turned to the comcon and moments later their commander's image hovered above the workdeck. He summarized their findings and she endorsed their progress and plan.

"I'll notify everyone to assemble at their muster stations at oh-eight-hundred for further instructions," she replied. "If everyone converged on Cranium Cavern at once, it would be chaotic. I'll work with Storm to develop an orderly plan to get as many there as possible, probably using a shift rotation scheme. Keep me posted on any further developments."

"Yes, ma'am," Dirck replied, then turned back to the others when the connection faded. "Whether it will retain the charge is the question," he continued, solemnity returning. "Remember what happened at the Caverns."

"But that was because of all the negative energy," Deven said.

"Exactly!" Dirck said. "And that's what's going to be coming in with a whole lot more force than a few bad thoughts. So it's a matter of whether we can charge it up enough to repel it. Otherwise, we could all wind up in the universal time flow."

"Which is where those veridical dreams came from," Creena added.

"Right," Dirck agreed. "We somehow accessed universal time where we caught a glimpse of the future, which provided information we could use to avoid upcoming catastrophic events. At least when we understood the message correctly. Devenite apparently controls the process by factoring in the heart's deepest desire and bends time accordingly. So they work together."

"Speaking of veridical dreams," Sharra said. "I had one last night. But it drew from the past."

"Really?" Creena said, mouth agape. "What about? Did anyone else share it?" She glanced around the room for clues, but everyone else appeared as taken aback as she was

"Actually, yes," her mother answered with the hint of a smile. "The other person was Bryl."

Win nearly choked, then coughed as he tried unsuccessfully to suppress a grin.

"Do you want to tell us about it?" Dirck asked, as startled by Win's reaction as his mother's confession.

"Of course," Sharra replied. "It concerns all of us. A lot. Especially your father."

Win straightened, the intensity underlying his expression suggesting he knew something the others didn't. Dirck gave him a look, deciding to ask him about it later, then stared at his mother expectantly, waiting.

"The dream was about Esheron, and what happened after Laren's father was killed," she explained. "It turns out his death had a major impact on Bryl's family, too." She laughed softly and shook her head. "This is so incredible," she said. "I can hardly believe it myself."

"How?" Creena prompted. "Why did it have anything to do with Bryl?"

Sharra laughed again, tears glazing her eyes. "Because," she said shakily. "Laren's father was her father, too."

"Holy holocubes!" Dirck exclaimed, first to recover. "So Bryl's 'Merapa's half-sister?" His mother nodded, wiping her eyes.

Creena was speechless, mouth hanging open again at the unexpected news.

"Whoa," Win muttered, half under his breath. "Who would've guessed? That certainly puts us all on the same team."

Dirck exhaled sharply. "Wow. I'll say. That's incredible. Plus it proves veridical dreams access universal time."

"All right, I think some things are coming together here," Win stated. "Having that dream either indicates these caverns aren't any different from the others, or not involved at all. Back when we were planning your father's prison break, the bnolar implied the Tank could only be used for positive outcomes. Nothing dishonest or immoral. So the real trick is generating enough positive psi to do the job. Which we probably can't do alone."

"Even if we load up Cranium Cavern with as many people as possible?" Sharra asked.

"Possibly not."

Dirck stopped, bewildered. "Why?"

"Based on all the negative energy we saw surrounding the Cyrarian system when we came in, which has undoubtedly gotten worse, we may not be able to generate enough, even with the help of Cranium Cavern, to defend ourselves against it."

"Great," Dirck muttered. "If that's the case, we're dead."

"Here's what I think," Deven said, rolling his eyes at his brother. "If we get as many people as possible into Cranium

Cavern, all thinking the same, exact good thing, then it'll be a lot stronger."

"Deven's right. There's no telling what we might be able to do when devenite's involved," Creena stated. "Especially if all of us focus on the same thing. All we can do is hope."

"That makes sense, Dev," Dirck admitted. "If it's focused it would resonate."

"Like a psi-laser," Creena added.

"Yes!" Deven agreed. "You saw what we were able to do with only us. Just think if we get hundreds or even a thousand people in there!"

"I agree," Win responded. "Besides, if we do our part we can ask for help. The Universe has shown it's on our side by providing these dreams, if nothing else. If we do everything we can, those same positive powers should pick up the slack."

"Thoughts become things," Creena mused. "It works both ways, for good thoughts or bad, but cristobalite and devenite seem to be more responsive to good and may actually store it as energy."

"Exactly. We have two things going for us right now," Win went on. "A scientific knowledge of the basic principles involved and the intuitive knowledge that the Universe, in other words the *Benefics*, is aware of our situation. We also have the advantage of the *Order*. Through that, we can ask for things others can't and be heard, as long as it's done for the right reason."

"You're right," Dirck agreed. "Fear, uncertainty and doubt are negative energy which need to be eliminated. The real key is that we need to do our part, but not try to control the results. The Universe has shown us that it's a lot smarter than we are. At this point I think we need to do what we can to generate as much positive psi energy as possible and let the *Benefics* do the rest."

"Right," Win stated. "Let's get back with Bryl and get it set up.

* * *

The Bezarna Express

Laren lay in his cyll, arms propped behind his head, waiting for sleepzone to end; the one that was supposed to kill them.

Ha, he thought. *Fail!*

His companions were apparently still asleep, lucky to be alive, though he was probably the only one wondering how long it would stay that way. Rhodus, maybe, had such a thought, but Sa'ata probably assumed he was safe. Not necessarily a valid assumption, given his sole task was to assure that no prisoners returned. Another fail. What a bunch of incompetent morons.

So far the trip back to Cyraria had been uneventful, but he suspected that would change. If anyone was monitoring the ship's course, which he doubted, its change of direction probably only implied that its occupants had been properly dispatched and the vehicle was returning as planned. How soon they would catch on when it didn't return to its usual berth, much less what they'd do in response, was another story. One that wouldn't be simple to deal with, especially with an unarmed spacecraft other than the lasomag they'd absconded from Sa'ata, which lay beside him in his cyll. He rested his hand on it pensively, not necessarily wanting to use it, but comforted by the fact they had it, nonetheless.

He knew they needed a plan, but was at a loss where to start. Under the usual circumstances, the guard would probably egress upon arrival, report in and be done with it. Since they'd tried to kill them all, however, they would possibly be waiting with body bags. Nice. But not necessarily as soon as the ship berthed. The good news, if they were waiting, was that they had an element of surprise in their favor, which made him chuckle inspite of the seriousness of the situation.

Aren't you forgetting something?

He smiled as the gentle admonition tickled his thoughts.

Greetings, Karma. Can I safely assume that you can help with this situation?

Most certainly, Commander. What would you like to know?

Let's start with what to expect when we arrive at our destination.

Certainly. It would be best for you to guide the ship to its usual docking location at the Cyrarian Space Facility above Cira City rather than attract undue attention by hijacking it to the Apoca Clique Base. They have troubles of their own presently, which you would do well to avoid.

He sat up sharply, swinging his legs over the side with his heart racing as his thoughts shifted to his family, who were holed up in that location. *What kind of trouble?*

An attack is imminent.

They're well fortified beneath the ground and have plenty of defensive measures. How can that be?

Intelligence sources indicate that INTEGRATOR *forces have developed a psi-based energy weapon.*

He groaned at his naivety, assuming they'd be safe, while at the same time knowing there was little point to his return if everyone he cared about was dead. *Do they know?* he asked, holding his head, which had started to pound.

Yes. They are preparing countermeasures. But there is nothing you can do in that regard. Let's talk about your situation, which is equally grave.

PREPARATIONS

T he news of the impending attack had carved an icy pit in Laren's gut, banishing his appetite and instituting an adrenaline rush, both of which he was trying to ignore. All he could do at this point was do everything possible to save himself and Rhodus, but the thought of his family in mortal danger threatened to rip his heart out. Trying to put it out of his mind, he pondered what he needed to do when they got to the CSF, hoping to have a preliminary plan before the other two excylled.

Karma hadn't told him what to do, only how she could help. It was up to him to figure it out from there. She'd explained that as his cerebral companion, the function from which the term c-com had derived, her artificial intelligence programming forbade her from providing any information which exceeded what he, as its human host, specifically requested or at least implied. Based on the concept that whatever a person could conceive they could achieve, the device was not allowed to provide any more than the recipient could comprehend; to do so could literally blow their cellmate's mind or ultimately take over their consciousness, given the right circumstances.

Fortunately, he could conceive a lot, and thus came up with plenty of questions which were dutifully answered. One question the device couldn't answer, however, was what to expect from Sa'ata. Instinct told him he couldn't be trusted and thus he planned accordingly; Rhodus he could count on.

Knowing that communications were marginal from the upper echelons of any organization to those at the bottom, it was a reasonably valid assumption that those at the CSF had no reason to suspect the vehicle was returning under anything other than nominal circumstances, which Karma had confirmed through command logs. With INTEGRATION Security expecting Sa'ata to simply egress the vehicle as he would for any such mission, there would probably not be anyone expecting trouble; of course there wouldn't be if they were dead, either. If this was the case, as he'd previously thought, it was possible that no one would enter the vehicle, perhaps for a long time, unless they had actually received orders to remove their supposedly dead bodies.

Hmmmph. Surprise! he thought, smiling as he felt Karma giggle.

So far so good, except anyone who saw three people egress instead of one would immediately know something was amiss. According to Rhodus, security in the area was tight, though Laren had no firsthand knowledge, one way or the other, having embarked at Nifeir rather than from the CSF with the others. Security undoubtedly focused on loading prisoners, however, which implied a returning vehicle received little if any attention, especially if one were being loaded at the time.

Arriving exactly at that moment when guards were thus occupied was tricky to say the least; departures depended on when they had enough detainees to warrant a trip as opposed to any actual schedule. The average number onboard was five and Karma had determined they currently had four lined up for exile. The fifth could come at any time, and as Laren knew only too well, there was typically no delay once the final one was identified and secured onboard.

His heart dove briefly at the memory of his arrest, nearly taking his breath away, as it sunk in how close he'd come to dying. He took a deep breath, grateful for the ability to do so, and resumed pondering a plan.

Ideally, if their arrival coincided with another departure, they could save them as well as themselves, but that was probably asking too much. There was always the possibility that some, or even all of them, deserved it, though he suspected in most cases they would be political prisoners like himself. With a single service grade lasomag between them, thinking he and Rhodus could carry out such a rescue was little more than fantasy.

Another thought struck, which had interesting implications as well. If the INTEGRATOR had acquired psi-based energy weapons, there was really no further reason to exile prisoners. It would undoubtedly be quicker and require fewer resources to dispatch them on the spot. Simply executing dissenters had less psychological value than exile, however. As the airlock had proven, death was often preferred to an unknown fate. There was no way of knowing how many had it forced upon them in violation of numerous HIO treaties. Having your brain melted, however, fit a similar scenario. Not knowing whether your consciousness would be trapped in an unresponsive body was at least as frightening as a oneway ticket to Bezarna. He shivered, realizing again how narrowly he'd defied death.

Will there be any further trips like this one? he queried.

I thought you'd never ask. Negative.

He cringed, wondering who the four on the list might be, Karma claiming they were from other territories and no one he knew. At least it wasn't Dirck, Win, Storm and Bryl.

So I really have to ask? You won't volunteer information you know I need, even under these conditions?

Sorry, Commander. I can't. Artificial intelligence restrictions and all that.

Okay. It's time we had a little chat, then, don't you think? Why don't you start by telling me about some of your other capabilities, Karma?

Such as?

Defense?

Affirmative.

Lethal?

Can be.

Who decides?

You.

He smiled, intrigued more than ever by what other secrets she was guarding. *Okay. How about teleportation?*

Departure point and destination?

CSF to Apoca Canyon.

Affirmative. Simple with CSF geostationary.

Okay. What about cloaking?

Personal or vehicle?

He smiled, more than pleased with the response. It just kept getting better and better. *Both,* he replied.

Some limitations for vehicles, but usually effective.

He grinned, plans slamming into place even while he recognized that everything she'd promised sounded too good to be true; hopefully it wasn't.

Motion in the other cylls caught his attention as the other two stretched and eventually excylled. Rhodus stopped dead on his way to the sanicube upon noting Laren's satisfied expression.

"That good?" Rhodus asked, sarcasm evident.

"Yeah," Laren replied. "Actually it is. Here's the plan..."

* * *

Early the next morning, the first group gathered to begin the charging process. Creena heart swelled with excitement as she watched a large and diverse crowd file into Cranium Cavern for the charging process. Humans, Erebusites, jendaks, Pyxisites, Zinaanians, and various other humanoids slowly gathered inside, each clothed in the Clique's maroon uniform, establishing unity that far exceeded race, heritage or planetary origins. The gathering would also serve as a rehearsal for the actual attack, which current intelligence sources indicated could come as soon as the following day.

While those for whom the INTEGRATOR had mindprints were most vulnerable, it was apparent that the majority of such individuals refused to leave, despite the evacuation option Bryl had announced earlier. The show of support and comradery from those at less risk was strong as well, all showing so much confidence in the countermeasures that it bolstered that of its designers as well.   Word had gone out that the price of attendance was high. Negativity was not only unwelcome, but could cause catastrophic results when the final assault came, not only for the affected individual, but the others as well. A few took note and quietly failed to appear, most evacuating on the first scheduled transport, which had already departed.

Cranium Cavern was typically quite warm, temperature and anticipation rising with the increasing density of lifeforms. Participants talked quietly as the time approached. The projectron's image up near the entrance quivered into focus, the final countdown in progress. The crowd moved closer, forming concentric circles, the configuration decided upon for maximum refractive return. Fortunately, the high ceiling and spectral lighting within kept claustrophobic feelings at bay, at least for most, heat definitely reaching the uncomfortable range.

The inner-most circle comprised Dirck, Creena, Sharra, Deven, Igni, Storm, Bryl and Win with Thyron in the center. Aggie hadn't left the *IP&S* lab since the day before, and continued to monitor any late-breaking activity. Gradually, the murmur of voices faded and each circle joined hands.

Creena looked at each member of her family and tried to smile reassuringly. The only one who returned it was Deven. He was excited and could hardly wait, whereas she could tell that everyone else was still battling residual shades of doubt, especially with so many counting on its success. Creena returned the squeeze when her mother tightened her grip, smiling as her eyes met Bryl's, then Win's across the circle.

* * *

Win returned Creena's smile, then allowed his gaze to linger on Sharra until she looked his way and smiled back. How much his intervention had assured her presence, possibly even summoning that dream she'd shared with Bryl, he'd probably never know, yet seeing her now he couldn't imagine that a short time ago she'd planned not to attend.

The countdown ended, the projectron flashing zero for several seconds before commencing an upward count. As previously instructed, everyone began to recall their most cherished, loving memories, whereas for the actual attack, they'd focus on a common thought, *i.e.,* the good of the planet as opposed to individual desires. At first it was no more than a feeling, neither audible nor visible. Gradually, a low frequency hum began, felt then eventually heard.

It reminded Win of an overloaded transformer, a comparison that was far from comforting, as he pondered what was supposed to happen versus what could. In spite of the numerous operations of varying success in which he'd participated lately, the finality of this one was undeniable.

The heaviness which had befallen his heart when he'd learned about the *Volition* persisted, and he hoped that it didn't constitute a negative feeling. Since it was the result of caring, he assumed not, even though it felt far from what he would classify as good. Nonetheless, it was an expression of love, the ultimate positive emotion, which would hopefully not be a problem.

He looked around the circle and those that lay beyond, noting their different expressions. Several had their eyes closed, others not, some smiling, often accompanied by tears. The emptiness in his chest receded and momentarily he felt better. He realized he should be thinking about his own pleasant memories, but few matched what he felt now. He glanced up at the surrounding walls, feelings of happiness expanding even more as he saw their iridescence increasing as if controlled by a giant rheostat. The underlying glow remained the deepest shade of violet, yet thickening wisps of energy caressing the surface retained the full spectrum of prismatic hues. So far it was working as planned. What would they have done without Deven's inspired directive?

The initial plan was for the charging process to last for fifteen minutes, minimum. However, when the projectron reached that time no one moved or ceased their thoughts. No wonder, he thought. Who would want to stop when it felt better than anything he could recall for as long as memory served? If, indeed, there was some afterlife, this was hopefully what it would feel like, at least for those deserving of a reward. Thoughts of those who deserved otherwise were currently verboten, their fate appropriately left to the *Benefics*.

Gradually, tendrils of light skirting the walls reached the outer circle, then filled the entire chamber, the feeling so intense Win wondered if it possibly could be fatal. Eventually everyone broke into a spontaneous cheer at their collective success, breaking their grips in their respective circles to greet and embrace everyone else. Win joined in, laughing and back-slapping as much as anyone, thinking if it failed, at least they'd die happy.

The crowd gradually filed out amid a subdued hum of conversation, their exit taking a substantial amount of time due to the narrow tunnel and the fact roughly a thousand people had participated. The line wrapped around the walls and wound like a serpent far beyond the main chamber to where the cavern sloped into the mouth of another tunnel. It, likewise, glowed, illuminated as never before.

There were approximately eight thousand housed at Apoca Canyon, far beyond the chamber's capacity. Thus, other charging sessions were planned, allowing everyone to participate who wanted to do so. Those scheduled for later assembled in various other areas of the base, watching the initial proceedings via vidcon with some gathering in similar circles, their participation distributing optimism throughout the base.

He exchanged hopeful looks with the others, then Bryl gestured toward the tunnel where there was less noise and some measure of privacy.

"Well, what do you think?" their Commander asked.

"Looks pretty good to me," Creena replied, setting Thryon down beside her. "This is far more than I expected."

"I agree," Dirck stated. "This is at least as strong, maybe more so, than the Tank was, back when we used it for teleporting."

Win frowned pensively as once again he scanned the energized walls. "That's true. I wonder if we could."

"But where would we go?" Sharra asked.

"Good question, 'Merama. And if there's devenite involved, we also don't know when we might wind up," Creena stated. "Other than a time and place of emotional safety."

"Not a bad idea, actually," Bryl noted, a pensive look on her face.

"There's a rather large chance we'd all wind up in different places and times, however," Win said. "Is that really what we want?"

"Could be worse," Dirck replied. "Presumably it would be a safe one, based on Universal wisdom. Otherwise, we could all wind up dead."

Igni's translator crackled at the diversity of speculations, clearly not sensing consensus. "We should unite," he said. "*Victoro de Unitus.* Is not about own life, but those of many. INTEGRATOR must be stopped. Who but us can do?"

"You're right," Bryl agreed. "It would be cowardly, selfish and contrary to our mission not to proceed as planned. We all need to stay right here."

Everyone nodded agreement, exchanging the Miran Grip all around before joining the last of the scragglers and returning to quarters to watch subsequent sessions via vidcon, then await notice for when to reconvene the following day.

The chamber's energy increased with each group's efforts, further fueling their optimism as they viewed the proceedings from Bryl's office. Intelligence sources eventually picked up a time window for the attack, which turned out to be sooner than expected, scheduled for the midday mealzone. Fortunately, they'd completed charging the chamber, the information broadcasted base-wide for all participants to return in their assigned locations at least a half-hour prior to the expected assault.

Well before it was time to assemble, Win joined Bryl, Igni, Thryon and the Brightstars in the lab to report to their destination early enough to secure their position in the center before arrival of the others. Few words were spoken along the way, everyone's demeanor far more serious than that morning. This was not a drill. Would they survive? And even if they did, what about Laren?

When they arrived at Cranium Cavern, its energy level was nearly blinding, yet not visually uncomfortable, but far beyond what it had appeared via vidcon.

"Wow! Look at that!" Deven said, grinning.

The boy's optimism was contagious and it didn't take long for everyone to smile, though Win could detect a touch of worry in the others' eyes which probably matched his own.

Prismatic wisps of energy flowed throughout, so dense it was impossible to see the other side of the chamber from the entrance. While similar to the Think Tank, it radiated at an entirely different frequency, one that had an emotional component the other chamber lacked. Win had to admit that it felt good, really good, and could only hope it stayed that way.

They weren't alone for long, others starting to arrive with reserved yet hopeful expressions. He helped direct the crowd into the same configuration as before, while Bryl reminded everyone to focus on the good of the planet this time as opposed to their own memories.

Then they waited.

* * *

Integrator Central
Strategic Weapons Laboratory

Bareuth Argo eyed the gathering crowd in the lab with thoughts that ranged from disdain to pride. Hosting so many high ranking visitors was the last thing they needed at a time like this, the glass-enclosed viewing area overlooking the control room crammed full to overflowing with Regional and Territorial officials.

Only members of the Quadrumvirate and their deputies were allowed in the control room, although the covey of scientists tasked with assuring that this weapons demonstration succeeded found their presence, however supportive, unsettling. For one thing, such men couldn't be trusted not to touch critical controls at the wrong time, throwing everything out of synch. Being attuned primarily to lasomags, they didn't appreciate the complexity much less theoretical nature of what the science and engineering team was attempting to do.

The only one with whom Bareuth felt comfortable was Augustus Troy, who'd not only become his greatest proponent, but had sufficient background to understand and appreciate the process. Conversely, his cousin, Eulon, was usually too worried about failures, which could make the Quadrumvirate member look bad, given too many believed Bareuth only had his post due to political connections. This, of course, was entirely false, since he'd held the post long before Eulon had ascended to his current rank. But such it was, and at this point didn't matter a quantum fluctuation one way or the other.

While it had been established that cristobalite's birefringent properties split psi into positive and negative components, it was the augmentation process using systemic negative energy that was unstable. Drawing additional negativity from INTEGRATION'S global network as well as the environment, both on and offworld, complicated the process significantly. Furthermore, according to his calculations, if their target had any form of defense, matter itself could annihilate, perhaps destroying the entire planet rather than only the individuals for whom they had mindprints. When he'd pointed this out, however, the consensus had been it was worth the risk. Nonetheless, he'd noticed that a few officials had heeded his warning and fabricated excuses to be off-world, albeit with apologies for missing such a significant event.

Thus, there were two ways today's demonstration could turn out, neither of which was cause to worry. If it succeeded he'd be a hero; if he didn't they'd all be dead.

The countdown continued, Troy making his way across the room between consoles and equipment with a victorious smile that Bareuth hoped wasn't premature. When the TG reached him he gave his hand a hearty shake, then pulled up a stool next to the master control panel.

"Our deal's still on, right?" the TG asked, more statement than question.

"Of course, General," he replied. "I'm a man of my word, if nothing else."

Bareuth smiled, the man's enthusiasm contagious. He'd promised Troy the honor of completing the circuit the previous day when they'd enjoyed several rounds of celebratory drinks in Troy's chambers. The TG had also talked him into increasing the gain enough to attain maximum sideband influence to assure as many individuals as possible would be affected. Personally, he didn't think that was a particularly good idea since it could conceivably include some of them as well, but in his besotted state hadn't refused.

While he understood anyone who made it to Quadrumvirate level had to be ruthless, he'd never seen it to the degree present in Troy. Wars weren't usually driven by actual hatred so much as ideological differences, but clearly Troy possessed an unprecedented lust for power in addition to being involved at a personal level. He chuckled to himself, realizing that the negative psi Troy generated alone was probably sufficient for the augmentation process without accessing any from the other INTEGRATED centers such as the Tower in Cira City much less the celestial void.

A hush rippled through the control room like a frigid wave as the countdown neared completion, Troy's hand hovering above the panel which would initiate the process. At zero, Troy set his jaw and dropped his hand into place. An ominous rumble from deep within the planet's bowels increased in amplitude until it became an ear-splitting whine. Whether or not they had sufficient power to sustain the blast Bareuth didn't know, but moments later when his vision blurred, then failed completely, he knew how it was going to end.

FROZEN TIME

The assault came several minutes earlier than expected, but fortunately they were ready. A deep chill permeated the cavern in spite of the usual heat combined with the press of people, temperature plunging far below normal, its cause unquestionable. Win's first thought was that they should have known this would happen and suited up accordingly, then realized that psi knew no boundaries, making suits useless; otherwise the wall of stone around them would have provided sufficient protection. Hopefully the others wouldn't be distracted beyond participation. If too many succumbed, the chance of failure would increase significantly.

Memories surged and he wondered if he'd ever understand this strange propensity he had for impossible deeds or the tremendous bond that accompanied them. Perhaps it was no more than the brotherhood of the *Order,* precarious experiences part and parcel of his longing for family denied so long.

As the influx continued, Bryl's admonition to focus on the planet took hold and his thoughts skimmed Cyraria's surface, then entered the domain of time and space where he lingered, looking down upon their troubled world. Had it always been so malefic towards its inhabitants? In reply he felt a deep sense of betrayal and sadness emanating from the planet's core, which somehow conveyed how injured it had been by its domineering and dark-hearted inhabitants.

I'm sorry, he thought, as if to apologize for his fellow humans, even while marveling that Cyraria itself had been affected by what had transpired on its surface.

Was the planet itself alive? Could it possibly be healed? If so, how?

No matter the reason, neither the means, only the necessity to reverse the effects, he thought, purposely diverting his mind from the still plummeting temperature by recalling the heat of Opposition.

From there his thoughts wandered once more to the Brightstar family which had become his own, who had suffered so much in the time he'd known them. Their pain had been his as well and his last coherent thought questioned whether or not he could stand it if they'd never attain their hope to be together again.

* * *

Humidity condensed, first as wisps of swirling fog, next in tearlike droplets that glistened as nubby tracks on misshapen walls, finally dribbling downward to the gathering below. The chamber's energy waves dulled with the increasing chill, yielding to moisture laden clouds.

Creena wrinkled her nose as one hit her face, but didn't dare release Dirck or 'Merama's hand to wipe it away. She shivered as it grew colder, wondering how frigid it would get. Liquid water no longer fell, now frozen midcourse, ice encasing surrounding stone. Gradually, what little moisture remained precipitated to tiny flakes that floated amongst them, dusting the maroon-clad occupants with a mantle of white. She remembered the snow-capped mountains on Terra and wished Cyraria to be as beautiful.

The flakes covered Igni's shell, not melting as they did on humans and humanoids who maintained specific body temperatures. The pitch of his antennae confirmed consensus and she tightened her grip on Dirck's hand. He responded in kind, then, like the substance of a dream, everything began to fade as darkness thickened, leaving nothing behind.

Complete absence of light was only possible underground and Creena thought she knew what darkness was. Yet, as energy collapsed around her, she sensed a darkness that went far beyond. It was cold and still and empty, smothering each and every hope until all that remained was utter futility.

Her muscles quivered uncontrollably in a vain attempt to keep warm in the sharpening cold. Despair and pain struck simultaneously, her cries swallowed by the encroaching nothingness. Whether the cavern was merging with the vacuum of space or becoming a pocket of planet-bound cryogenics was impossible to tell. Not a sound escaped, the last sensation to fail that of Dirck's hand on one side and 'Merama's on the other.

Just when she was about to give up as something more powerful than she'd ever imagined consumed her, her thoughts skipped back to her brief encounter with the INTEGRATOR on Earth and a tiny voice inside arose in protest. With all her might, she willed her hands to tighten their grip, even though all feeling in them had ceased, and she concentrated even harder on a planet filled with love instead of hate.

Cold and darkness pressed persistently against her, feeding on itself. Her senses long dulled, even the memory of Dirck's or 'Merama's hands fled. Next the breath was drawn from within her, as if her entire body was about to implode.

* * *

Dirck knew they were going to die. While he tried to picture a peaceful and temperate planet, he had no further reference to cling to other than one that wasn't too hot or too cold. Beyond that, the thought crept in that the possibility of surviving the INTEGRATOR'S ultimate weapon had been no more than folly from the start. His senses were dulling, evaporating to an awareness of nothing but cold, cruel emptiness. He could barely feel Creena's hand and couldn't feel Win's at all. Desperation increasing, he pleaded with the *Benefics* for deliverance, for peace, for courage, even if it had to end, once and for all.

And then he knew. Knew like he'd never known anything before in his life. Lives were at stake, not just his own, and principles as well. If the Clique was destroyed, Cyraria would fall. Something had to be done, something beyond what he could do himself. Win had been right, absolutely right, as always. There wasn't the slightest doubt.

His plea changed in tone from a wimpy, frantic petition centered in his mind to a powerful command emanating from his heart. Commitment swelled inside him, gathering momentum until he knew exactly what was supposed to happen. Focusing everything he had on the task at hand, he willed it thus, never doubting that the forces around him would respond. The emptiness shifted from submission to power and strength. His thoughts were wordless but concise, willing the necessary conditions to transform psi-negative to psi-positive.

And even as he knew what he had to do, he also knew that it would be done, that nothing in the Universe could resist such a direct order.

* * *

Storm had felt humility before but never like this. While he didn't exactly feel out of place, he was acutely aware that bonds existed around him that he couldn't understand. All that had happened of late defied anything he'd ever experienced. If there could be a perfect planet it would contain such as this, those united in a common cause. Humans had always had an element of mystery about them, but those before him now transcended mere conscious thought to a realm he'd never before imagined. Fascination alone had steadied his concentration, inborn and trained instincts alike poised for the unexpected.

The chill darkness closing in was not a good sign and he braced against the cold, throwing his will into the battle for an outcome which would favor those whose intent was good and bring a long-awaited peace to a planet that was miserable enough without being further marred by INTEGRATED influences.

* * *

With what little strength remained, Creena's heart reached out one final time, determined that if she was going to die, it would be loving, not hating. Her ears rang with silence and her knees weakened beneath her, the floor seeming to lose its hold as substance evaporated. She sent love to those around her, willing it as never before. The emotion's momentum grew as she concentrated on expanding her affection to everyone in the room, then everyone on the planet, then the planet itself.

The slightest hint of purple emerged in front of her and she wondered if it was an illusion, no more than optic nerves confused by the negative energy flux, or if she'd once again stepped into universal time. She stared harder, watching what had been the hint of a shadow elongate from a tiny orb to a pillar, then gradually brighten as it oscillated between electric blue and vibrant pink.

Its intensity kept rising, finally stretching into a concentrated column in the blackness ahead, its presence building momentum as it refracted from the walls then back up through the ceiling. Then ever so slowly it began to expand. Creena stared at it, mesmerized, wondering if it would bring death or life.

It was only centimeters away, yet strangely unthreatening. She closed her eyes, waiting. Contact came with a torrid wave that spread across her skin as if at long last Zeta or Zinni, Cyraria's dual suns, had returned. Warmth swept through her, front to back, its touch soft but consuming, its affect more than heat for this felt like love.

She opened her eyes, surprised when she could see Storm with the violet wall beyond. Its retreat continued, the next circle of participants now visible as the light expanded to the slippery stone walls. It lingered, confused, swimming outward again for the tiniest moment, then flashed from purple to a shattered prism of white that filled every niche and wrinkle around them.

Sound returned, expressions of awe and wonder bursting into a multitude of conversations. The light stablized, energy wave gone, the chamber again illuminated by the walls themselves. Light rippled across shimmering stone, eddies swirling where it buckled with bulges.

"We did it!" Deven exclaimed. "Now its name *really* fits. And, hey! Look at our clothes!"

The cavern was so alive with light that Creena hadn't noticed, but he was right—everyone's clothing had become purest white, all color removed by the passing wave.

Dirck had sunk to the floor cross-legged, face as colorless as the surrounding stone. She crouched down in front of him, hands on his shoulders. "Dirck? Are you all right?" she asked.

He looked surprised to see her, then blinked a few times and hefted to his feet. "Yeah," he said quietly. "Where's Win?"

"I don't know. I'm sure he's here somewhere."

As the drone of conversation continued to rise, Storm called everyone to attention to conduct a numerical sound off. When it was over, eight were missing without a trace. One of them was Win, another Igni.

"Did you see either of them after the light came back?" Dirck asked.

Creena scowled, trying to remember. "I don't think so. Don't you remember holding Win's hand?"

"At first. After a while I couldn't tell if he was there or not."

"He's here somewhere," Deven said confidently.

"Did you see him?" Dirck asked, tone anxious.

"No. But he's okay."

"Where is he?"

"I don't know."

"Then how do you know he's okay?" Dirck insisted.

"I don't know." His little brother shrugged. "I can just tell."

Dirck sighed heavily. "I hope you're right."

Deven smiled his most winning smile, but resisted the words.

"Let's check *IP&S* and see what we can pick up," Dirck said, fears brewing in spite of Deven's optimism. "Maybe he's there."

Creena looked around the crowded chamber one more time and realized with a sinking heart that Thyron was gone as well.

* * *

Integrator Central
Strategic Weapons Laboratory

Silence prevailed, within and without, its magnitude only possible in the void beyond the reaches of time and space.

FINALE

The *Bezarna Express* shuddered as it settled into its docking collar, its three occupants eyeing one another with varying degrees of wary anticipation.

"All right, you know the plan," Laren said.

Sa'ata nodded, staring nervously at what had once been his weapon now pointed in his direction by Rhodus' steady hand.

"Any false moves or indication you're betraying us and you're dead," the man stated. "There's no reason all three of us can't get out of here and resume our lives, unless you decide losing yours is included in your pay grade."

The fear in the failed guard's eyes gave every indication he'd cooperate. If he didn't, chances were high they'd all be dead before the ship's systems had finished shutting down.

"Ready?" Laren asked. The others nodded and he released the hatch, which hissed with the pressure difference as the exit ramp lowered into position. Beyond lay an empty concourse, devoid of any lifeform whatsoever.

"All right," Rhodus said. "Walk out of here exactly the way you have every other trip. Slow and easy."

In reply, the Pyxisite gave him a final look saturated with a lethal mixture of hatred and fear, then treaded slowly down the ramp.

The waffled metal floor was the same reddish brown as the darkened planet below, the surrounding walls transparent metal which allowed an eerie view of the emptiness beyond. Trusses creaked as thrusters fired to maintain the CSF's orientation while other vehicles docked and departed.

Rhodus watched as their former guard walked the length of the concourse while Laren crouched low in the hatchway, locating security cameras. As he'd hoped, they were sparse and panned, allowing a few covert seconds between. Should they run to avoid detection or exit casually to avoid attention? As far as they could tell the place was empty, making the second option more attractive.

"Well, what do you think?" Rhodus asked.

"I think slow and easy, a few minutes apart, is our best chance. The last thing we want is attention or a fire fight. We didn't come this far to get killed."

"Think he'll blow it for us?"

"Hard to say. Could be a big reward in it on one hand or execution on the other, for not fulfilling what should have been a simple assignment. Coward that he is, I don't think he'll take the gamble."

"Hope you're right."

"Yeah. Me, too."

Rhodus sighed and lowered the lasomag as Sa'ata reached the end of the gangway and turned left down the main concourse where he eventually disappeared in distant perspective.

"Think we'll have any trouble at immigration?" he mused.

"You might with that thing," Laren noted, nodding toward the weapon. "But nothing's impossible, so let's see what we can do." He smiled and removed Karma from her usual place.

Karma, fix up Rhodus' records so when he palms in they'll think he's a CSF mechanic coming off shift. No, scratch that. Make that CSF security, so they don't question the weapon.

Will do, Commander. Anything else?

Only getting me to my final destination.

Of course, Commander.

"You should be good to go," he stated, engaging Rhodus in the Miran Grip. "Good luck resuming your work on Pi."

"Yeah, thanks. I'll need it."

"If you ever decide to join us at the base, let me know."

"Will do, Brightstar. Or should I say Commander? It's been more than a pleasure."

"Likewise."

With that, Rhodus gave him a firm and sincere salute then turned and stepped slowly down the ramp toward the concourse.

All right, Karma. Get me out of here.

The sensation was the same as when he'd used the Think Tank to come home from the Tower what seemed eons before. A breathless sense of nothingness followed by a flash of instantaneous pain as he materialized in what had briefly been his office at Apoca Canyon. It took a moment to catch his breath and get his bearings; then he listened.

Something was wrong. It was too quiet. Nothing. Not a single sound. As he recalled, even during sleepzone, many of which he'd spent in that very spot, a buzz of activity prevailed, even if no more than footsteps echoing through stone passages in repetitive random rhythm. But now, nothing. Only chill and eerie quiet.

His initial elation evaporated as the possibility that everyone was gone, possibly dead, settled on his mind. Had the psi-based weapon already been deployed? Had their countermeasures failed? So far it didn't look very promising. His heart beat slow, heavy beats, mind racing through a multitude of dismal paths as he prepared himself for what could be the greatest disappointment of his life.

He lowered into the chair, familiar fit triggering memories of when he'd brought the Clique from random pockets of resistance into a cohesive force, feeling as if he'd deserted willfully and caused its demise. He leaned back, nanobots confused by the unfamiliar occupant failing to relieve the tension as he leaned his head back and stared at the ceiling amid encroaching despair. Eventually, he covered his face with his hands, still trying to resist what the pervasive silence was telling him.

His breath caught in his throat when at last he heard the murmur of voices, then footsteps. He looked up, further appalled when individuals of all races, human, jendak, Zinaanian and Erebusite alike, stepped past the door in a steady stream, all clad in—white?

His memory flashed to Esheron, specifically to when white-clad *callers* had brought word of his father's death. Were they dead? Or was he?

Karma's reassurance rippled through him and he knew she could tell him. Still, he didn't dare ask, grateful she required his query to respond because he really wasn't sure whether he wanted to know.

* * *

Creena took Deven's hand and followed Dirck through the press toward the tunnel back to the lab, 'Merama right behind her, not knowing what worried her more, Win's fate, Igni's or Thyron's.

"Everything's fine," her little brother stated confidently. "So quit worrying."

She studied his face, trying not to frown. "How do you know?"

His expression reminded her a lot of the *snurk* look she used to give Dirck. "I just *know*," he insisted. "Just like I knew this whole thing would work."

Her frown materialized nonetheless, but it was more pensive than annoyed. As they proceeded toward the lab, it was apparent the changes wrought in Cranium Cavern weren't as localized as expected. While all of Apoca Canyon hadn't been transformed, the chamber's entranceway had, and the effects continued all the way into the residential area, its character changed from the dull appearance of a military base to the fresh sparkle of a new building. It even smelled better, the damp, dank smell of ancient moisture replaced by crisp, clean air. The cleansing and lightening of the walls reflected the emergency lighting to optimum brilliance, radiating as if reaching for infinity.

The equipment in *IP&S* was powered but still, only an occasional flicker of light signaling the arrival of data. A quick glance told them they were alone and again Creena exchanged a worried look with Dirck. No Win, no Aggie. 'Merama sat down slowly behind one of the comcons and called up an activity report. None of the monitored INTEGRATOR sites showed any action, including INTEGRATOR Central.

Dirck stepped to where they always did real-time audio monitoring during strategic ops. In the past, they'd always been able to pick up something, if only loop chatter. He inserted the ear piece, complete puzzlement overtaking his expression a moment later.

"What?" Creena asked anxiously.

He handed it over wordlessly and when she held it to her ear, her jaw dropped. The commline that had formerly held death and destruction was broadcasting symphonic swells such as she'd only heard once before on a faraway planet. Grafix, the artificial sounds that substituted for music on Mira III, were often used to identify frequencies that were off the air, but this was like she'd heard on Terra. While Creena listened in awe, Dirck called up one of the other centers several hundred kilometers away and put it on the squawk box.

"Hey, Wingless," he directed to another section lead via the secure line. "What are you picking up over there?"

"Not sure, Detailer," came the reply. "Things are pretty quiet. Too quiet. There was a lot of heavy activity the past few days that culminated about an hour ago, then everything started dropping off, sometimes replaced with—you're not going to believe this..."

"Try me."

"Uh, well it kinda sounds like music."

"Ditto," Dirck replied. "Got it here, too."

"Think they reworked their network or something? Some new kind of propaganda?"

"It would have been pretty tough to pull off simultaneously like that."

"I know. What do you think it is?"

"I've got a few ideas. I'll get back to you, Wingless, once confirmed."

"Roger, that. Hope it's good."

"Should be. Later, Wingless. Detailer out."

The familiar hum of Aggie's rolopeds arose from the data room, the 'troid's photoreceptors flashing a confused spectrum of rotating color.

"Whoa. That was certainly a trip," she commented, a quick status check indicating she was otherwise unharmed.

Next they went to the section where S3 data were received, sorted and filtered for surface activity. Even with the worst of Deep Winter still raging, some movement had resumed, and sensors were beginning to pick up signals again. Dirck zeroed in on known INTEGRATOR outposts with the finest resolutions and quickly found—nothing. A few blips emerged, tiny individual lifeforms, moving in totally divergent and independent paths.

"What about 'Merapa?" Creena asked. "Shall we try reaching him again?"

Dirck scowled with thought, then agreed. "If Igni's swarm worked, he should be on his way back by now. Hopefully he remembered how to recharge his c-com. Let's go back and find Bryl so we can give it a try."

"Yes!" Deven agreed with a huge grin.

Dirck started back to Cranium Cavern, stopping when 'Merama didn't move from her chair.

"C'mon, 'Merama," Dirck coaxed. "You should be the first to talk to him." When she still hesitated, Deven took her hand and led her along.

When they got back to Cranium Cavern, it was still dancing with light and energy as what remained of the crowd grew silent, their collective eyes fixed upon them as they approached Bryl in the center of the vast chamber. A warm smile brightened her countenance as she saw them and she stepped forward to give each of them a warm hug.

"We thought we should try to reach 'Merapa with your c-com again," Dirck stated. "If swarming worked, maybe by now he's figured out how to recharge his."

Bryl's expression immediately fell, sadness overtaking her formerly happy demeanor. She looked at each of them as if lost for words.

"Let's go somewhere else, okay?" 'Merama requested quietly, apparently sensing whatever she had to say wasn't good.

"Yes, good idea, Sharra. Let's go to my office," Bryl replied, and quickly headed up the rocky slope which had recently become a well-worn path back to the base. Maybe it was her imagination, but Creena got the impression that Bryl was avoiding eye contact as she led the way, 'Merama directly behind her, then Dirck followed by Deven with her at the end.

She could tell that 'Merama, like herself, hardly dared hope, that if the news was bad, it would almost be better not to know. After the emotional sine wave they'd ridden in the past, acceptance of the worst had settled into a dull ache of grief. Disturbing that with hope, only to be disappointed again, would not only aggravate the partially healed wound, but activate new and deeper scars.

Deven kept turning around, grinning, which was starting to get on her nerves. She wanted to tell him to stop, but didn't want to make a fuss, either, since 'Merama didn't seem to notice. The next time he did it she gave him a stern look, which he returned with an even broader smile. She sighed and ran her hand against the tunnel's cool wall, likewise lightened with transformation, knowing she couldn't stop clinging to hope, no matter how vain it might be. For all the other good things which had happened, would it even be worth it without 'Merapa's return? She'd secretly hoped he'd appear in Cranium Cavern if their efforts were successful. Instead, more of those she loved were gone as well.

As her thoughts wandered back to the chamber, her thoughts turned to Win. As hard as he'd worked and as much as he'd done, it didn't seem right with him gone. Somehow he'd always managed to be her friend and Dirck's, too, even when she and her brother had been at total odds. Igni, too. It just wasn't fair that they were missing out on their victory at surviving the INTEGRATOR'S attack. Where could they have gone? Or Thryon and all the others unaccounted for?

After they'd all scrambled down the last section of the path back to the wider main passage Deven came up beside her and nudged her with his elbow. She looked down into his still-grinning face, wondering how he could possibly be so confident everything was fine. She took a deep, impatient breath and decided when they got to Bryl's office that she'd keep him outside for a moment and tell him to shut down, once and for all. It was great they'd survived the attack but at what price?

When they reached their destination, Bryl stopped dead before the open door, staring inside with her mouth hanging open. Seconds later 'Merama covered hers with both hands and started to cry. Dirck glanced back from her to Deven with a puzzled look, then stepped to the doorway where his jaw dropped along with the others. Deven laughed out loud, pushing his way past everyone to run inside, Creena coming up slowly, hands over her wildly beating heart when she, too, saw who was sitting in Bryl's office, looking as startled as they were.

"There you are, 'Merapa!" Deven cried with glee, climbing into his father's lap and throwing his arms around his neck. "I knew you were here somewhere!"

Meanwhile, everyone else, including 'Merapa, simply stared at each other in silence as if moving or talking would shatter time itself and separate them again forever. When it was apparent that it wasn't an illusion, 'Merapa stood up, Deven still clinging to his neck as he moved around the workdeck and at long last gathered his family into his arms.

When the wild explosion of hugs had dissipated 'Merapa asked, "Why are you all wearing white? I was beginning to think you were dead and had come to get me."

Everyone laughed, hard, having forgotten their strange appearance.

Bryl was the first to gain enough composure to speak. "We just had quite a remarkable experience we'll tell you about in due course," she said, then smiling at 'Merama added, "As well as a few other things. For now, let me officially welcome you back, Commander. Then she turned to the others with a puzzled look. "What I was going to tell you was that Igni didn't think it worked. The *Volition* broke orbit and headed back to Mira III a day or so ago and he wasn't able to retrieve it. Of course we thought that meant swarming didn't work. We just didn't know how to tell you with everything else that was going on."

Creena's first thought was that they'd somehow brought him back through Cranium Cavern until her father explained what had occurred onboard the ship, which indicated that some part of the swarming process had worked somehow, after all.

"Hey."

Startled by the familiar voice, everyone turned to see Win standing in the doorway.

"Where've you been?" Dirck demanded, half angry, half relieved. "Do you have any idea how worried we've been?"

"Nowhere," he replied with a shrug. "Literally. When everything came back to normal, I was the only one there. Everyone else was gone."

"That's weird," Creena said. "It reminds me of when we first came here and were lost somewhere in universal time, even though it seemed instantaneous."

"Exactly," Win replied. "All I know is I didn't want to be the one to tell you swarming didn't work. But apparently it or something else did."

After Dirck explained how his father got there, 'Merama let go of her bondling and beckoned Bryl to join them. Bryl smiled as she came over and stood with her eyes locked on Creena's father who wore a guarded, rather uncomfortable expression.

"Laren, there's something we need to tell you," 'Merama said, taking his hand in hers as she looked into his eyes. "While you were gone, I figured out a few things I didn't know or understand before. It turns out there are several very good reasons for us all to be one family."

Creena bit back a laugh as her father's jaw dropped and the color drained from his face.

"What are you talking about?" he asked, caution evident in his eyes.

"We're a family and have been all along. And now that includes Bryl as well."

"What? What exactly are you saying, Sharra?"

"I'm saying we discovered something amazing while you were gone. Laren, you not only have your brother, Jen. You didn't know it before, maybe your mother didn't, either, but you also have a sister. And it turns out you've already met. Her name is Bryl."

'Merapa's response as Bryl and 'Merama took turns spilling out their tale was a monumental sigh of relief, followed by enfolding his newly found sibling in an affectionate hug. A moment later, he released Bryl and pointed at his bondling with a scowl while she tried unsuccessfully to suppress a grin.

"That wasn't funny, Sharra!" he said with the deep, no-nonsense voice that Creena knew only too well.

'Merama put on her most innocent look and replied, "No, Laren, to the contrary, indeed it was. As I recall, back on Mira III you used to have fun teasing me about the ECL. Given the circumstances, it was an opportunity I simply couldn't pass up."

He rolled his eyes in defeat and pulled both women into another hug. Then he took his bondling's hands into his own and gazed into her eyes. "It's so good to see you smiling again," he said, then gave her a long, sloppy kiss that left her blushing amid the sounds of various cheers and whistles, the loudest of which came from Bryl.

Creena found the fact that at long last they were all together felt oddly familiar, as if time which had passed so slowly before had compressed into an insignificant slice. Heartfelt longing had accomplished their desire, bringing them together in a timeless reunion that would forever endure as the most joyful experience of their collective lives. Brimming with exuberance, she clung to each in turn, particularly 'Merapa, collecting every sensory witness that they were indeed a family united once again.

As reality continued to settle, emotions shifted from excitement to gratitude. Her parents were holding each other again as if they'd never let go and she stole a look at Dirck, wondering if their parents' open displays of affection still bothered him like they did on Mira III. He caught her eye and smiled, then rested his arm around her shoulder.

"Thanks for never giving up," he said, giving her another hug which he released long enough to smack Win for making a snide remark about how long it took the two of them to get along.

"By the way, you were right," Dirck directed at Win.

"About what?"

Dirck smiled. "Knowing."

"Knowing what?"

"You know—when to use the *Order*."

Win's face lit up with understanding. "Oh. That. I could definitely tell when you kicked in. Good job."

"And we're all together again," Creena said.

"Of course we are," Deven said, hands on his hips. "Why wouldn't anyone believe me? It's a wonder all your doubts didn't mess it up!"

"So what exactly happened?" Creena asked, wondering how the psi-negative had interacted with Cranium Cavern's positive energies to perform such an incredible transformation. Whatever Dirck had done had apparently been a part of it, too, somehow assembling each person's unique contribution together until they all merged with the most magnificent power in the universe, its memory as familiar as going home.

"We've each been entrusted with amazing power," 'Merapa explained. "There's virtually nothing that can't be done, as long as it doesn't violate the principle of free will."

"Which is what I've been trying to tell everyone all along!" Deven declared.

In response, a familiar bouquet entered Creena's mind, its essence oddly content, followed as expected by a vegemal editorial.

> [While you're in mortality,
> ups and downs are sure to be.
> Peaks and valleys together flow
> So joy and sorrow both you'll know.]

She smiled, convinced of its truth. But even more amazing, that to feel as good as she did now was somehow dependent on all they'd all be through to get there.

"Thyron!" she replied. "I've been so worried. Where are you?"

> [Through the grace of time and space
> I at last have found my place
> While I care for you and yours
> Caverns left me limp and sore.
> Darkness isn't good for me
> It creates much misery
> Light I need to live and learn
> Thus to Sapphira I returned.]

"We'll miss you, but certainly understand. I wonder where Igni is," Creena mused. "Do you know, Thyron? He needs to know swarming succeeded after all."

> [It seems each of us has gained
> That which loss had yielded pain.
> Igni, too has gone like me
> To rejoin her colony.]

"As has everyone here as well," she replied, smiling at her family, together at last. "*Benefics* be with you, Thyron. Hey, wait a minute! What do you mean *her*?"

His reply was an enigmatic photosynthetic smile.

Epilogue

It wasn't long before S3 data indicated that the entire planet had undergone considerable transformation. Some speculated that they'd gone back in time to when Cyraria had been in stable orbit around Zeta and Zinni, its axis of rotation gently assuming an orientation within a few degrees of vertical, providing a stable length of days and nights as well as milder seasons. Opposition disappeared, since the planet no longer made the precarious passage between the two stars.

As if no longer hiding from the elements, the planet's complex system of cryptofluvial aquifers worked their way to the surface, nourishing the planet with vast lakes and rivers which further changed the climate. When rains eventually fell, the ruddy sky previously afflicted by dust became a backdrop of cobalt blue decorated with a variety of fluffy clouds which sometimes darkened and returned moisture to the ground, refreshing the atmosphere and allowing a variety of floral species to thrive.

All buildings which housed INTEGRATION-related personnel mysteriously disappeared along with any evidence of military outposts. The negative psi energy refracted by the collective effort at Apoca Canyon had shifted polarity and returned to its source, annihilating those who would do them harm. Cira City remained, but the Territorial Tower which housed the Quadrumvirate was no more. The park over which it loomed spontaneously spread to its vacated footprint, overhead dome no longer required for protection except when it rained. Excavating to provide shelter to withstand the weather was no longer necessary, so the population grew and a variety of structures spread across the land as immigrants from other planets discovered its favorable climate and the opportunities it presented.

With the threat of INTEGRATION eliminated, prosperity reigned. Thoughts had indeed become things, Laren Brightstar's original vision for the planet suddenly before his and everyone else's wondering eyes.

And thus it would remain for a thousand cycles, until leaks occurred in universal time as selfish and oppressive thoughts once again invaded the minds of the people. At which time the battle would begin all over again.

The End
or
New Beginning?

Acknowledgements

I want to thank the many individuals who have contributed to this story in one way or another. It would be impossible to name all those who have provided support and inspiration throughout the years of writing the Star Trails Tetralogy. I'm grateful for my friends, family, readers, fans, reviewers and fellow authors too numerous to name who have made this effort so rewarding. I am particularly grateful to Maria Lenartowicz who was gracious enough to read and provide numerous insightful comments on this manuscript, which I implemented in their entirety, improving the story, plot and character motivation in the process. Thank you, Maria, for your time, talent and friendship.

I'm also grateful to scientist and researcher, Dean Radin, PhD, for his dedication to psi research. While he doesn't know me from Adam, two of his nonfiction books, *The Conscious Universe* and *Entangled Minds,* provided considerable inspiration. I also would like to thank Marie D. Jones, author of *PSIence,* who doesn't know me, either, for compiling a wealth of additional information regarding psi phenomena, which contributed to the development of this story as well as its series predecessor, *A Psilent Place Below.*

Thanks to individuals like these, modern man will eventually learn to accept the existence of psychic abilities, a God-given talent which can enrich our lives if we simply accept the part of ourselves that can communicate through and with a higher realm.

ABOUT THE AUTHOR

Marcha Fox is a science fiction fan and writer who has always been fascinated by space and time. She's an old-time *Star Wars* nut whose favorite movies also include *Back to the Future* and *Déjà-vu*. Her life-long love of astronomy eventually drove her to obtain a Bachelor of Science Degree in physics from Utah State University, followed by a career of over 21 years at NASA's Johnson Space Center in Houston, Texas, where she held a variety of positions including technical writer, engineer, and eventually manager. Needless to say, during that time she got to see all sorts of very cool NASA stuff in locations that included Florida, California, Alabama, and Maryland as well as the European Space Agency in The Netherlands.

Her physics training allowed her to "do the math" regarding various elements in her books, especially Cyraria's starsystem, orbital dynamics, and resulting seasons in *A Dark of Endless Days*, to assure reasonable accuracy along with hoping to instill an interest in science and engineering to her fans by showing its relevance in an entertaining way. More detailed information as well as a discussion guide for parents and educators are included in *The Star Trails Compendium"* and on her website, **StarTrailsSaga.com**.

She's the mother of six grown children, seventeen grandchildren, and so far four great-grandchildren, though she denies being old enough to have such a huge progeny.

Connect via Social Media

Series Website: http://www.StarTrailsSaga.com
Facebook: https://www.facebook.com/marchafoxauthor
Website: http://www.StarTrailsSaga.com
Twitter: https://twitter.com/startrailsIV
Blog: http://marcha2014.wordpress.com/

Amazon Author Page:

http://www.amazon.com/Marcha-Fox/e/B0074RV16O/

Goodreads:

https://www.goodreads.com/author/show/6481953.Marcha_A_Fox
Author Facebook: https://www.facebook.com/marchafoxauthor